I0764495

APPRENTICE

BRIAN FENCE

MOON RABBIT PUBLISHING, LLC
Apprentice
Brian Fence

ISBN: 0989366340
ISBN-13: 978-0-9893663-4-2

This one is for my brother Bill, who, with his enviable height, stands tall for me in the most hellish of times.

By Brian Fence

Lenna's Arc

Librarian
Apprentice
Freewoman

CONTENTS

ACKNOWLEDGMENTS

My slightly abused editor James Aldous deserves the largest pint of beer in the universe for poking holes all throughout *Apprentice* while navigating the difficult waters of being a physicist; he even allowed me to live with him for a summer and survived mostly unscathed! Jim, you've saved my life so often, you're only two times away from unlocking an achievement.

Marissa Morris, my eternal partner-in-crime, has once again gifted me such beautiful cover art and I am blessed to have her in my life. Margaret Musselwhite, my copyeditor, as always did a bang-up job of tidying up the text (and she taught me a thing or two about ellipses). I am both grateful and indebted to the people who provided early feedback: Roger Fence, Daniel Niebler, Timothy Sebastian Robinson, and Laura Sauls.

And I simply couldn't have completed this darn thing without the support of a family — my parents, my brother, and my Aunt B — that somehow manages to love me no matter how much I screw up. I also have had over the past few years the joy of becoming close to people (not already mentioned) whose counsel and love keep me sane, mirthful, and more importantly, inspired. Special thanks to Maureen Castor, Teresa Cioffi, the Honorable John Michael Dempsey, Megan Dragony, Henry Hargrove, Mary Hibberd, Lori Kolb, John Manna, Tony "Pon" Maszeroski, JP Patterson, and Chris Pettican.

Dear Father,

I hope this letter finds you well; it has been nearly a month since the tumultuous events involving Gilbert showing up at the library door occurred. Are you eating properly? Did you finish work on that custom order for Mistress Hallan's shop? This is the third letter I have sent with no response, Father, and while I know you loathe written correspondence, do please take a few minutes to send me a brief response!

My stay here at Granemere Settlement, with Mother's people, has certainly been a learning experience. I know that as a child I was quite stubborn and resisted Mother's attempts at training me in the ways of the Freewomen of Laur, but really, Father, you could have at least prepared me by telling me I was some sort of Freewoman nobility! Besides being stared at for lugging around this accursed, glow-in-the-dark stone, everyone treats me with a politeness I simply do not deserve considering my ignorance of their culture. I am improving my knife skills, however.

Speaking of the jewel, Sebastien has written yet again, insisting I journey to Gallas, not only to learn more about how to control my magic, but because he feels that the Freewomen cannot provide "adequate protection." How one man thinks he can keep me safe if an entire settlement of trained warriors cannot amazes me to no end; then again, Sebastien is a former member of the Blue Crescent Brotherhood, so I suppose it comes as no surprise that he would be brainwashed to feel that women are inferior.

I have not heard much concerning Raif, the Ilyan airship pilot I mentioned in my first letter, and find myself worrying on his behalf. He insists on tracking down Luc, Gilbert's cohort, and retrieving his lost family heirloom, but I have heard that skirmishes between Ilya and the Krevlum Empire have, since last month's events transpired, taken a turn for the worse and an all-out war is inevitable. If that is true, Raif will almost certainly be required as an airship captain to join the ranks of his nation's military.

Please send word back as soon as you can, though it would not surprise me if Jeffer is intercepting all correspondence between us as some form of petty revenge for abandoning my position. I miss both you and my beloved Port Hollish terribly, but as long I have this burden to bear, I dare not return home, lest I drag Fallowfields into war with the Empire as well. Know that I am safe, relatively comfortable, and am being treated with great kindness.

Your loving daughter,

Lenna

PS — Pim has been nagging me almost nonstop; she is apparently dying for a timepiece like the one you made me. I have offered to make her something of her own, but lack the necessary equipment.

CHAPTER ONE

Lenna dropped a clattering of coins into the courier's hand, annoyed at the fee required to post a letter from a Freewoman settlement. She was not suffering for funds; she had saved most of what her father had sent her off with a month ago and had been rather forced by an Ilyan rogue and a dandy mage to take some money "just in case." In case of what, Lenna had no idea; after all, hanging around her neck and bound by silver chain was a small, globular gem that shone with the purest of azure light and hummed softly against her chest. It had been bequeathed to her by her dying friend and apparently had the power to alter reality and time and amplify magic.

It had also linked itself to Lenna, making her a target of a certain misogynistic order of powerful magicians, a technologically superior empire, a grief-stricken young mage possessing his own stone, and an influential merchant family seeking to acquire the world's greatest treasures. If Raif and Sebastien's "just in case" scenarios ever did occur, Lenna wholeheartedly doubted some extra coin was going to change the outcome. She, and the blue bauble of wonder vibrating against her breast, would have to.

"Sparkle ponies," she said to herself, and sighed.

The courier quirked an eyebrow but said nothing, and scampered off to his next delivery somewhere else in Granemere

Settlement, a tidy town of exquisite, if a bit spartan, construction. Neatly thatched homes were provided for everyone — Lenna, for the moment, was staying with her friend and traveling companion, Pim — and the town was almost entirely self-sufficient, complete with its own schools, craftsmen, and forge. Although she had not visited other Freewoman settlements, Lenna was certain that there she would find herself wandering the same orderly paths, surrounded by craftsmanship of the highest quality.

Brilliantly the sun sparkled and cast delicious reflections off the clumps of snow in the high trees of the forest surrounding the settlement; winter had come early this year — a bit too early, Lenna thought — and during this season, the Freewomen of Laur focused on education and research, though physical training was still an essential part of daily life. Lenna winced at that thought, suddenly remembering she was due for another private knife-training session with her teacher, Freewoman Werthe Dalm. The Freewomen were, by definition, a nation built on the theory that everyone — especially women — would learn to defend themselves, so that the slavery and rape that haunted their ancestors could never happen again.

Lenna shivered in the brisk winter air and, huffing steam in the cold, she swiveled around and marched in the opposite direction, past the residences and toward a large training facility at the edge of the settlement. Nestled neatly up against the sturdy wooden barricade and surrounded by towering, firm oaks, the facility looked like it belonged to the forest as much as the settlement, as though it had sprouted from an acorn.

The younger children had done a good job of clearing most of the snow from the main pathways throughout town, but as this particular training facility was rarely used until spring, when the year's official training regimen began, Lenna found herself once more trudging through the snow, an act she had acquired quite the knack for, given recent experiences. Thankfully, she had been gifted a pair of fine, fur-lined boots that shielded her from the cold and icy slush.

Taking a peek at her timepiece, Lenna noted that she was actually almost on time, not even three minutes late. The sturdy oak door, a massive thing that required most people to use two hands to yank it forward, swung open as if it sensed the would-be warrior's presence, and Lenna fell backward into a pile of snow. Framed by the doorway stood a hardy woman, barely five feet tall, with grey hair pulled back into a taut knot that sat neatly on the top of her head like a dome. Though considerably shorter than Lenna, Freewoman Dalm somehow always managed to glare down at her.

"You are late, Freewoman Faircloth," Dalm said in one long, even tone. Her speech was always so flat and mechanical that it constantly reminded Lenna of the automata with which her father constantly tinkered. Lenna scrambled to her feet, straightened her posture, and apologized as best she could, even though she hardly thought being three minutes late warranted such a scolding and so said as much.

"It was only three minutes, Freewoman Dalm."

"Outside," continued Dalm, "you may have claim to Council and thus command my respect, but here, in this facility, I am master, and you are my pupil. Be on time. Now, quickly: since you were 'only' three minutes late, you will only have three minutes to shed your garments, stretch, and be in place before the lesson begins."

Lenna mentally cursed herself. The "lesson" beginning without Lenna being properly prepared meant Dalm would launch straight into an attack, and if still clad in her bulky winter garments, the pupil would be dreadfully overwhelmed. With no choice but to comply, Lenna quickly stripped off her heavy, hooded cloak and shook her wavy hair about, a few of the curlier sections framing her face in what she thought was a pleasing manner. Her hair still had a few months before it would be at the length it was when she left Port Hollish, but at least it was growing out somewhat.

In under a minute, Lenna managed to kick off both her boots and shed the dark grey woolen sweater; though her teacher would prefer tidiness, Lenna decided she would rather have a pile of messy clothes than a bruising from being unprepared. Within moments, she had peeled away her layers of protection against winter's chill — which was still unpleasantly present within the facility — and stood in a simple long-sleeved muslin shirt and training trousers. From where they were stacked neatly against the wall, Lenna snatched a pair of lined training slippers, a Freewoman invention that provided an excellent grip on most surfaces while being exceptionally light and flexible.

Lenna reached the center of the training facility — a large, square mat padded with cotton and lined with worn-down leather — panting slightly, but ready. She pushed the frame of her spectacles up the bridge of her nose and, gulping a little, assumed a proper, straight posture. The knife strapped to her thigh, a beautifully honed length of steel crowned with a pommel of mother-of-pearl, was a gift from Lenna's late mother. Had Lenna actually taken instruction from her mother when she was a child, she would not have to be standing here with Granemere Settlement's matron of physical abuse.

"Impressive," Dalm said. "Did your time in Ilya teach you how to take off your clothes so quickly? Next time, arrive earlier; you will suffer tomorrow because you did not have time to properly stretch, as I have told you numerous times these past few weeks."

"Yes, Freewoman Dalm," Lenna replied forlornly. She was already well aware of the agony she would wake up to in the morning; her muscles would be screaming a reminder to arrive at training earlier. Resigned, Lenna peered at the solid, short staff Dalm had chosen to wield against her today. Come tonight, Lenna would be lucky if any part of her *wasn't* bruised.

Pointing the stick straight at the center of Lenna's chest, Dalm bumped the noticeable impression the Godjewel was making underneath her pupil's muslin shirt. "This will get in the way. You will have to find other means to wear it."

Lenna frowned. "Around my neck and tucked into my shirt seems the best way; I don't have any pockets and you won't allow me anything else to wear but this."

"It is impractical. I have allowed it up to now because I am aware of its importance, and that it must be always on your person. But your homework is to find a means to wear it better."

"I suppose I could glue it to my bosom?"

In a flash, Dalm butted Lenna in the left shoulder with her short staff, catching her by surprise. Lenna, unbalanced, began to plummet backward, but her teacher was faster than gravity: Dalm sped forward with a grace that belied her age and with her free hand grabbed the arm of her pupil, spinning her around into a tightly locked grip. The short staff pressed up against Lenna's throat and Dalm calmly proceeded to choke her with a bundle of silver cord she had extracted from under the collar of Lenna's shirt.

"Gack," Lenna spat.

Immediately, her teacher released her and helped her balance herself. "You could be choked or, worse yet, it could fall out from your shirt in battle, dangling, and be snatched away by your opponent. This treasure of yours must be protected."

"I thought that's why I came to this settlement in the first place: for protection," Lenna said bitterly. "I've never wanted to be a warrior."

"If you cannot be bothered to protect yourself, how will you be able to protect your loved ones? And how can you expect anyone to give their life protecting you? I demand a better means of securing the gem by tomorrow's lesson. Now, show me your first form."

Sighing, Lenna shifted into the proper stance once more and slid her mother's blade from its sheath, already longing for a bath. *Freewoman Dalm,* she thought, *whatever you think this thing around my neck is, I can assure you it is definitely* not *a treasure.*

Lenna gritted her teeth as she gingerly lowered herself into the steaming water of the large bath, her muscles already feeling the dull ache from her intensive training session earlier in the day. There were numerous tender spots along her body that soon would be bruises in varying shades of blue and green, rewards for

Freewoman Dalm's thorough thrashing. Her teacher was right, however; Lenna prided herself on punctuality and had no excuse to be late.

Despite her lack of spectacles, Lenna could make out the face of her freckled comrade-in-arms, Pim, across the way. The humidity from the baths made her cap of tight curls even kinkier. Flushed, the eighteen-year-old Freewoman looked as though she had already been in the baths for some time before Lenna arrived. Communal bathing was something new to Lenna, and she had felt quite shy at first, but after a few days the girl from Port Hollish had come to appreciate the strong bonds it formed between family and friends, as though here in the baths one's soul, not just one's skin, was bared.

"My goodness," Pim said. "You look worse than a sheep after a shearing! I guess that explains why I didn't see you at dinner."

Lenna grimaced, sliding down until she was submerged to her ears, her legs spreading out across the bottom of the pool. The tremendously hot water — which had taken Lenna an equal amount of time to grow accustomed to — was already starting to loosen some of the knotted muscles in her back. "I am not cut out to be warrior," she bubbled.

"No one said you had to be a warrior. But it's a good idea to learn how to use that knife of yours." Pim scooted closer to Lenna. "I don't think you should just rely on magic and that stone alone."

Lenna scooped up the small blue gem by its silver chain, pulling it from the water as her head rose, and watched as beads of moisture dripped from its glowing surface. The steam rising from the bath danced around it, but never quite brushed the flawless sphere as it twirled in midair. "I'd rather not have to rely on either at all," Lenna admitted.

"Then why don't we just throw that damn thing into the sea and be done with it?"

There was a satisfying splash as Lenna dropped the gemstone back into the large tub, where it rose up, floating and bumping against her breasts. "I think if getting rid of the Godjewels were as simple as that, Gilbert would have done it on his way to Port

Hollish. But it's tempting." Gilbert, her childhood friend, had died to get this stone to safe hands, and his last request had been that Lenna see his mission through.

"I guess it *is* pretty buoyant," Pim added, eyeing Lenna's chest.

"Hey!" Lenna blushed and splashed a bit of water at Pim; apparently she wasn't as comfortable with communal bathing as she thought she was. Laughing, Pim acquiesced and paddled back to the other side of the pool. She stretched out both arms on the sides of the bathtub and gazed up at the stars.

"I wonder what's gonna happen," Pim mused. "The Krevlum Empire, the Blue Crescent Brotherhood, a powerful Ilyan merchant family, and a crazy rogue mage with another Godjewel – they're not just going to sit around and ignore you for long."

"I know," Lenna said. She turned around and rested her head on her folded arms, enjoying the cool air blowing into the roofless bathhouse. "And even though I can't seem to control this gem fully, from what I've been told, the Emperor of Krevlum has mastered his. It won't be long before all eyes turn to this settlement. There are only so many places I could hide." With remorse, Lenna thought of the grieving Luc, the runaway apprentice from the Brotherhood, where he might be, and of his betrayal. He had committed such treachery – culminating in the theft of the green Godjewel from Raif Vandever's family – all because desperation had convinced him that acquiring the Godjewels and their power would somehow change things, maybe even bring Gilbert back from the dead.

Pim said, "Our wards seem to be doing just fine for now, but have you ever thought about what that Sebastien guy suggested? Y'know, let him teach you how to properly use the magic of the stone, far to the south in Gallas? It'd be a lot safer."

The cocky magician had strongly argued his case, and the logical portion of Lenna agreed that it would be ideal if she could learn to better control the Godjewel, but she simply could not fathom abandoning her life in Fallowfields and becoming the apprentice of an excommunicated member of the Blue Crescent Brotherhood. Still, if war was coming to the lands and the three legendary magic artifacts dubbed "Godjewels" were to become key factors in deciding a victor, maybe Lenna should, in fact, consider getting this object as far away from her loved ones as possible.

"Maybe you're right, Pim." She turned to face her friend. "If it were up to me, I *would* drop it in the ocean, but the farther I get from it, the worse it's going to leak magic all over the place. It'll be discovered in no time." Somehow, the Godjewel around her neck had formed a distinct bond with her; unless it was about her person, it became a blazing beacon to anyone even remotely sensitive to magic as it searched for its mate.

Pim was still staring up at the clear night sky. The Freewomen of Laur, not having as much access to steampower or other technologies as other societies, had unlimited illumination during the evening, rewarding stargazers with an unparalleled view of the heavens. "Say, Lenna?" she asked.

"Hmm?"

"Ever wonder why we're all so… spread out? Not just the Freewomen of Laur; 'course I know why we're scattered across the Continent. But when I go out on hunts or trading, there's just not much out there. Some villages, homesteads… but mostly nothing, 'cept for the main cities. Where'd everything go?"

Lenna awkwardly sloshed closer to her friend. "I don't know much more than what history's taught us, except what Jaice — or rather, Aunt Jaice, I should say — has filled in with some of the oral history passed down among Freewomen, but even that's fragmented. Seb gives me snippets here and there in his letters, but I think he's deliberately holding out to encourage me to apprentice with him."

"And?"

"Well," said Lenna as she joined Pim in her view of the sky. She held up the blue stone, its innate shimmer taking on a more pronounced effect from the brilliance of the stars. "No one really knows where the Godjewels came from or how they were made. Just that they're tremendously powerful. You know about the God War, right?"

Pim nodded. "A ton of centuries ago, a bunch of countries and city-states that don't exist anymore went to war over some religion."

"The truth is that it wasn't really a religion so much. Ytra, a king of the old nation of Zeist — I think that's pretty much where the Krevlum Empire is now — somehow united all three of the Godjewels. He became so powerful that people were forced to worship him like a god, hence the gems' name. We — humans, that is — knew much more magic then, and an army was raised to fight Ytra."

"So boom, the God War," said Pim.

"Ytra used the jewels to smite his enemies and caused such massive destruction that, in the resulting battle, civilization as they knew it back then was destroyed. That was when the Brotherhood was formed: a few remaining magicians took whatever knowledge and texts of magic they had and fled to an isolated island."

"But what about the rest of the people? They won, didn't they?"

"Most people died. Some went across the sea, Jaice says." The mayor, after Lenna had chosen to return to Granemere Settlement, not only had been visibly relieved that an object of power as strong as the Godjewel would be protected by the wards of her people but also relaxed considerably in Lenna's company, acknowledging the kinship between herself and Lenna's deceased mother.

"Go across the sea, huh?" Pim said dreamily. "I'd like to do that. You'd think more people would. Don't any of the boats in Port Hollish set out for the great unknown?"

Lenna chuckled and let the stone plop back into the hot water of the bath. "Port Hollish's fleet just circumnavigates the Continent, visiting all the important trade locations. Pim, you sound like such a romantic! You should have gone with Raif on his airship in search of Luc and that gemstone." The young Freewoman warrior, eager to prove herself, would be an amusing sidekick for the dashing Ilyan pilot. A strange, lurching sensation gripped her stomach, and Lenna felt ill for a moment.

"Nah. Someone's gotta stick around and make sure you're safe. You're about as useful in a brawl as a horse with no hooves!"

"Well, thanks." Lenna poked Pim in the shoulder. "I'll remember that the next time you need me to magic something up for you."

The two splashed about a bit, giggling and drawing some stares from the older Freewomen in other tubs in close proximity. Normally reserved and well-mannered, Lenna blushed and coughed, quieting down. Pim, true to form, went right back to prattling.

"Still, I wonder why nobody crosses the sea anymore."

Lenna pondered for a moment and realized that Pim was asking a very good question. She wondered why people didn't explore, or spread out and repopulate the vast, empty expanses that covered most of the Continent. After the War of Unification, when the old country of Laur fell as its slaves revolted and four new nations were formed, people should have begun to flourish. Steampower had been discovered; there were trains and motorcars and countless other machines that made life so much easier. Populations should be thriving, expanding, exploring. But they weren't, and somehow, no one ever seemed to talk about it.

After a moment of consideration, Lenna responded, "Pim, that is perhaps the most interesting and unique question I've heard anyone ask in a very long time."

Unaccustomed to praise in general, let alone praise for her intellect, Pim, already red from the almost painfully hot bath, turned such a shade of crimson that Lenna was instantly reminded of her previous supervisor at the Port Hollish library, Jeffer. He was prone to fits of rage so splendid he could stay a flaming scarlet for hours. Lenna laughed heartedly.

"What's so funny?" Pim asked, her face puzzled.

Lenna wiped a tear from her eye and sighed, half content and half achy. One month ago, if someone had told Lenna she would be leaving her comfortable home and organized life behind to find kinship with her mother's people, she probably would have snorted with derision. Yet here she was, sharing a bath with a young huntress, bearing the magical equivalent of a king's burden, and suffering the pains of an extensive walloping in training. And then Lenna groaned, suddenly remembering.

"What now?" asked Pim.

"I've got to go," Lenna announced, standing up and reaching for a towel. "I've homework to do."

"What? Homework?"

"You'll see," she said in resignation.

"You bet I will! I'm coming too." Pim scrambled out of the bath after Lenna and quickly began toweling herself dry.

Lenna wondered, not for the first time, if Pim was well in the head.

Three hours and several bottles of wine later, a less-reserved Lenna beamed at her final product. Pim, sadly not the drinker her roommate was, had lost consciousness shortly after the second bottle's cork was drawn. Flushed with wine and pride, Lenna looked down at the solution to her teacher's sudden homework assignment. Out of a basic leather gauntlet and some other random parts she and Pim had collected around the settlement, Lenna had created a new method of carrying the Godjewel.

Applying the skills she acquired at an early age by watching her father, a first-rate mechanist and clockmaker, Lenna simply fitted the gauntlet with a sturdy — yet not constricting — mechanism around the hand that led to a small bowl-shaped crevice fashioned from one of Pim's extra blunderbuss powder trays. Now, it was merely a matter of placing the Godjewel into the slot and locking the mechanism, thereby securing the stone to Lenna's hand.

She slipped the supple leather up her forearm, eager to wear the finished product. After securing the bindings, albeit awkwardly (which she blamed on the wine), Lenna whipped the Godjewel from around her neck and tentatively rolled the blue gem into its position in the bowl. Applying pressure with her right hand, she grinned with satisfaction when the smart click of the locking mechanism reverberated off the cottage walls.

It felt a little unwieldy at first, but Lenna was confident that the lock was secure, and after she threaded the length of silver chain through the leather of the gauntlet, she could easily ball her hand into a fist to protect the jewel further. The size of a large marble, it had a subtle warmth and vibration that were still tangible through the oiled leather, and when she closed her eyes, it felt to Lenna like someone was holding her hand. Rising from her seat and having double-checked that Pim was out cold, she struck an affected pose, lunging with her right hand as though it held her knife and then thrusting the gauntleted hand forward, as if firing a burst of magic at an invisible opponent.

This has potential, she thought, and admired her work in her reflection in the window, cast by firelight. Having the jewel strapped to her person in this fashion might prove restrictive if she were to take up needlepoint or dance, but at first glance the gauntlet, if Lenna refrained from waving her hands about, would attract no particular attention. However, if she were to wear it out in her current state — damp, wavy hair piled atop her head, spectacles that glowed eerily in the firelight, ill-fitting pajamas, and a ruddy glow, courtesy of wine — she would certainly cause a stir. Mortified, Lenna backed away from the window before she was spotted posing in her nightclothes by the settlement watch.

Pim was exceedingly difficult to rouse. The girl was only eighteen, but, despite her colorful turns of phrase and unrestrained zest for action, Lenna had taken on a kind of sisterly affection toward the girl. Pim's own parents had passed away during a dreadful outbreak of influenza that had spread through Fallowfields when Lenna was but a girl; Pim was then raised as a collaborative effort of the Freewomen of Laur in Granemere Settlement. She looked so scrawny that it seemed a miracle that baby Pim had lived through the epidemic at all, so perhaps, Lenna fancied, she had spent her alcohol allowance surviving the illness.

Lenna glanced at her watch and noted the time. Being awake this far into the night meant tomorrow morning would be painful, but she was of the mind that once she started a project, she would see it through to the end. She was immensely pleased with her design of the gauntlet, and if she was a little sluggish and a touch hungover tomorrow morning, at least, considering her circumstances and the scarce availability of proper parts, Lenna had a masterwork piece of craft for her efforts.

The tipsy woman nudged Pim a few times, encouraging her to move to a more comfortable location, such as a bed, but the diminutive, curly-haired warrior merely grumbled and resumed snoring. Smiling, Lenna fell into her own bed, wincing as she let her body stretch out. She'd feel more than just the wine come morning, she reckoned, but there was not much to be done about that now. A bit foggy, Lenna would not remember falling asleep with her mouth wide open, spectacles dangling off her ear, and gauntlet still strapped to her arm.

CHAPTER TWO

Dripping with sweat, Lenna realized for the first time in her life that physical exertion was an excellent cure for a hangover; the adrenaline quelled the aches and insistent throbbing in the back of her skull. Freewoman Dalm was working her hard, indubitably as retribution for Lenna's tardiness yesterday, and Lenna was making mistakes she knew she should be avoiding. Twice her feints had been uncommitted, and Dalm was quick to drop the humbled young woman to the mat with the slightest of efforts.

"You are distracted," Dalm said, helping Lenna up from the ground. "At first I thought it was the jewel, bouncing around your bust, that kept you from paying attention. Now I see that the real problem is inside you."

Lenna colored. Was she not trying her best? True, she had ignored her mother's efforts to teach her as a child, but Lenna had chosen to return to the Freewoman settlement of her own volition. And learning some knife skills, although the mayor had been insistent, seemed like the logical decision, Freewoman customs aside. Still, Lenna hadn't come here to be berated by an old woman with a stick who had probably never even read *A Guide to Gallas Culture and Etiquette*. She wiped the perspiration from her brow.

"You think because you can make fancy trinkets," continued Dalm, "and because you read and come from a cultured town, that you are better than us." The grey-haired weapon master tapped Lenna's custom-made gauntlet with the end of her short staff. "But there are many types of knowledge, Lenna Faircloth, and one does not necessarily hold more worth than another. What good do your books do you when my staff comes your way?"

Lenna's fists clenched until they whitened: she knew a challenge when she heard one. The intellectual side of her recognized that Dalm was provoking her, trying to infuriate her, but some deep part of her felt anger rising up against her will. The grip on her knife unconsciously tightened, and the tiny blonde hairs on her arm stood on end, as though Lenna had been tickled.

Freewoman Dalm's strike came quickly, an overhead swing expertly executed as the older woman slid her hand along the length of her staff, propelling it downward toward Lenna. Anger had set her on edge, though, and somehow Lenna's instincts sensed the blow before it fell: the former librarian dove forward to the left of Dalm instead of jumping back. She rolled hard over one shoulder, not as nimbly as she had been trained, but somehow Lenna had succeeded in ducking out of the blow's way and creating a few paces of distance between teacher and pupil.

Distance, however, was not a great boon in Lenna's case: Dalm's staff, a sturdy cudgel cut from oak, had a solid three-foot reach on Lenna, and all she had was a knife; unless she had become a knife thrower with amazing accuracy overnight, Dalm would not need to move within range of Lenna's blade in order to dispatch her. Until now, Lenna had always played — played, she realized, never actually taking this training seriously — and assumed defensive positions during lessons, but there was no way she could defend against a seasoned warrior with greater reach. She needed an advantage.

Her glasses were foggy with sweat and rising humidity, but a newly awakened sense in Lenna discerned Dalm inching closer, gauging her actions. A follow-up strike was imminent, and Lenna, snarling, launched herself toward her teacher, holding the knife blade down in her right hand. Her target was Freewoman Dalm's throat.

Surprise registered for the briefest instant in Dalm's eyes, but the Freewoman was far too accomplished in battle to be caught off guard by a novice, out-of-shape librarian. In a movement almost too quick for an untrained eye to see, Dalm raised the short staff in a wide-handed, diagonal pose, such that Lenna's knife forcefully struck the thick wooden shaft. Lenna, neither strong nor particularly coordinated, fell backward from the force of collision, landing roughly on her buttocks. Her knife clattered off to the side, out of reach.

Normally collected, Freewoman Dalm smirked at the display of her student's bravado before raising her staff in a grand, sweeping motion. Time seemed to slow for Lenna and all her senses felt suddenly heightened by some unknown power; she could instantly predict the exact trajectory of her instructor's blow. Supporting herself with her right hand, her knife hand, Lenna raised her gauntleted arm in front of her face. A lavender-scented explosion beset the training room as Dalm's staff connected with a magical barrier, the air shimmering at the point of contact. The magical aftershock traveled up through the staff and shook Freewoman Dalm's body to its core, and she stumbled backward despite her years of training.

Drawing on both her own innate power and the gem in her new gauntlet, Lenna cut an arc through the air with her left hand, and a swath of pure energy, a concentrated burst of anger, cracked against the dead center of Freewoman Dalm's short staff, splintering it in half. Dalm's sure grip betrayed her: as the staff was sundered by Lenna's magic, the older woman's balance crumbled as well. She faltered and, much as her pupil had earlier, stumbled ungracefully to the padding of the mat.

Blue fire flickered across the irises of Lenna's eyes, mimicking the soft glow emitting from her clenched fist. She rose seamlessly to her feet and in one swift motion she raised her left hand, pulling energy from the great vault of power centered in her body, supplementing and shaping it through the lens of her gem. Through her connection to the Godjewel, time drew to a halt once more: Lenna could feel her own hair curling tighter up against her head and heard Dalm's excited heartbeat slow to a calmer rhythm.

Lenna released the energy in a short, controlled blast that pummeled into her teacher, striking her directly in the chest. The wave of force propelled Freewoman Dalm clear off the pad and a few yards toward the wall of the training hut, where she crumbled into a heap on the floor. Panting, Lenna's shoulders slumped, her curls lank and a curious blend of lavender and ozone stuck in her nose. Her resolve faded: it was no longer angry and blazing, nor cold and steeled. The icy blue glow in her eyes and in the Godjewel dulled into nothingness.

Across the room, Freewoman Dalm lay jerking about and groaning, trying to get to her feet with great effort. Lenna shook her head, calm despite the sudden violence, and proceeded across the space that separated them, stopping to collect, clean, and sheathe her knife along the way. When she reached her teacher, the older woman looked up at her not with anger or fear, but with satisfaction.

"There are many types of knowledge, Freewoman Faircloth," Dalm said quietly. "And one does not necessarily hold more worth than another. Now, help an old woman up. I believe I will be the one needing the soaking tonight."

Lenna blinked, but extended her hand and helped Freewoman Dalm to her feet. She blushed and snatched up the two large pieces of her teacher's staff and a few of the salvageable splinters. "I'm sorry about the staff," she said.

"You should be," Dalm replied, putting one arm around Lenna and leaning on the taller woman for support. "It was one of my favorites. I'm glad that if any of my pupils had to finally conquer it, at least it was my brightest one."

"Huh," said Lenna.

"See me to the baths, will you?"

Lenna nodded, her body tingling from the recent use of magic, and her mind grew numb and detached, as though the actions of the past few minutes had not been her own. She wasn't sure whether it was her hangover returning or the steady hum of the gem pressed to her palm, but Lenna was overcome with disquiet and a slight nausea as she led her proud teacher to the settlement's baths.

Even though such was the way of things, Lenna was agape by how quickly news traveled throughout the settlement. In addition to being nobility, bearer of a strange magical artifact, and involved in an immensely intricate political situation, Lenna was now the quickest student in Freewoman Dalm's teaching history to have toppled her. The source of the gossip, it appeared, was none other than Freewoman Dalm herself, who, over a bottle of wine in the baths, boasted proudly of Lenna's usage of her skills, and not just the knife.

"I want all my students to use the gifts they have," she had evidently said. "She'll be all right, that one; she'll be all right."

Pim, already in the cups, was busy boasting about Lenna over slabs of roast lamb and crispy-skinned potatoes. Reticent by nature, Lenna tried to shrink back in her chair, wishing she could be swallowed up into a corner and avoid attention. It was anger and frustration that had motivated her to strike, not tactics or some improvised battle stratagem. Being praised for qualities Lenna didn't feel were especially good ones left her feeling duplicitous.

Though the Freewomen often ate in their homes like families in Port Hollish, they also made a tradition of holding common meals at least once per week, so long as the weather permitted, and now Lenna was obliged not only to attend but to be the weekly focus of the town's scrutiny. Light but durable wooden tables had been hefted from the town hall to the spacious courtyard before the building. Despite the snow blanketing the ground, which in Lenna's opinion did not mean "weather permitting," the Freewomen had dragged out mismatched chairs and benches, and various cooks from their various kitchens had produced a hodgepodge of dishes. Roast meats, vegetable stews, and savory breads festooned the tables, and the liquor flowed as steadily as the forest's stream. Being the topic of some conversation, Lenna was plied with glass after glass of wine from Freewomen and their husbands and wives alike.

"So you used magic to trounce her, eh?" said a sandy-haired man to her left.

"We don't have many battlemages in the Freewomen anymore," commented an old woman somewhere down the long table. By this time, Lenna's vision was already somewhat blurry. At least, she deduced with some relief, the last traces of her hangover had been successfully replaced with a new sense of drunkenness.

Across from Pim sat Jaice Northen, mayor of this Freewoman settlement. When she and Lenna had first met, the mayor had been reserved and calculated, her greying brown hair pulled back almost as tightly as her pursed face and lips. When her lover Bahl – scarred but healed to full recovery – had returned from Ilya with Lenna, the mayor had practically embraced Lenna as her own daughter. Some years ago Lenna's mother had saved Jaice's life and the two became sisters by Freewoman law, technically making Lenna the mayor's niece. Still, it wasn't until Lenna had decided after the incidents in Ilya to return to the Freewoman settlement that Jaice had truly become warm and protective of Lenna.

Jaice raised her glass, brimming with hearty red Freewoman wine, toward her kinsman. Judging by the hazardous swaying of the liquid in its vessel, it was clear that it wasn't Jaice's first beverage of the evening. "To my niece Lenna," she said mightily. "We'll make a warrior of her yet."

The other Freewomen raised their glasses or, if they were empty, found a quick excuse to fill them, and gave a heartfelt toast in Lenna's honor. She tried to smile but felt more penitent than accomplished, as walloping old women was a feat she had been brought up to think one didn't laud at dinner. Still, in the spirit of camaraderie (and as an excuse to drink more wine), Lenna gulped down the currant-flavored panacea; hangover and aches, thankfully, were soon awash in a sea of blushful drink.

Once the burst of jabbering in the aftermath of the initial toast petered out, the revelry's quiet chatter resumed and Jaice, allowing herself to relax and enjoy the more jocund effects of inebriation, leaned over the table, her bosom alarmingly close to a bowl of apple preserves. Lenna was surprised by the cut of the mayor's blouse; it was unbuttoned to a level that would make even the unshakable Thane Faircloth blush, though Bahl, grinning lecherously, didn't seem to share Lenna's sentiments.

"Alanna would be proud, Lenna," Jaice said with a thick tongue. "Every Freewoman must be comfortable with at least one weapon."

"I wouldn't say I'm comfortable with my knife yet," replied Lenna cautiously, "but Freewoman Dalm is an excellent teacher."

"Don't be shy, you pickle!" Pim, goblet refreshed, jabbed Lenna in the shoulder with her finger. "You've got *two* weapons: the knife and your Godjewel."

Lenna, wineglass in her right hand, unclenched her left fist to reveal the sparkling blue crystal clamped down against the leather of her gauntlet. Though she had used it in battle, until this point she had tried to think of the Godjewel as anything but a weapon; her best friend, Gilbert, had died so that this very stone would be hidden safely away, out of reach of those who would abuse its power. By harnessing its wild energies for herself, wasn't Lenna going against everything Gilbert and his former teacher, Sebastien, had striven for?

A coarse but gentle pair of hands cupped Lenna's own and pressed her fingers closed around the jewel. Jaice eyed her niece thoughtfully. "I don't think you need to worry about relying on the Godjewel as a weapon, Lenna. As long as you use its power sparingly and for matters of great importance, it won't corrupt you. And for now, the wards around our home keep it from being detected."

It was true that the Freewomen of Laur were protected by age-old magic, wards that repelled malevolent workings and blinded outsiders from scrying. If Lenna were to use the Godjewel outside of the trees' safety, the subsequent release of energy would be noticed not only by the other bearers of the remaining two gems — Luc, Gilbert's former lover, and the Emperor of Krevlum himself — but by anyone even sparsely trained in the magical arts. After her involvement in an incident in Tranum that resulted in the death of a high-ranking Imperial officer, Lenna chose sanctuary with her mother's people, despite Sebastien's insistence that they take the jewel south to Gallas. Raif, the rakish Ilyan airship pilot who set off in search of Luc, had wanted to use Lenna's connection to the Godjewel — and, more importantly, its vast magical reserves — to light a path directly to his purloined family heirloom, now in Luc's hands.

Ultimately, the stone needed addressing; Lenna could not imagine keeping it forever, even if the blasted rock had formed some sort of arcane bond with her. Based on its actions in Tranum, the Krevlum Empire was bound to engage in war with Ilya in the east, banking on its superior military and magical technology, and it had already assaulted her homeland of Fallowfields by destroying the village of Junction. Lenna was shrewdly aware, perhaps because of her bond with the Godjewel, that the Emperor would be using the power of the gem to strengthen his attacks. Despite Ilya's impressive fleet of airships, Lenna was not sure victory was possible without a Godjewel of its own. If she were to head back to Port Hollish, her hometown on the coast of Fallowfields, and use the magic of the stone, the presence of her Godjewel would be noticed by interested parties, and she was afraid she would bring the war back with her.

"You made the right choice," Jaice echoed Lenna's thoughts. "The only places in the four nations that the gem's magical signature can be successfully masked are Freewoman settlements. Even in Gallas, far away from the Krevlum Empire, you'd be instantly traceable by the holders of the other two Godjewels or any nearby mage the instant you used any of the stone's magic."

Pim, not known for her subtlety in social circumstances, blurted out, "Well, does she get to stay here forever, then?"

A silence fell on the feast as Pim asked the one question no one dared ask. Lenna had been indulging in far too much wine these past few weeks in order to delay thinking about the consequences of being a jewel-bearer. Even should the Krevlum Empire fail in its war against Ilya, that didn't guarantee that people would actively stop pursuing the Godjewel, and therefore Lenna. At the very least, the Blue Crescent Brotherhood, the powerful order of male mages who considered themselves the Continent's foremost authority on all things arcane, would seek her out, and they would not be pleased with her involvement with Gilbert and Sebastien and her claiming the jewel.

After a moment's pause, Jaice responded, her words measured. "By right, and by our own attachment, Lenna Faircloth is welcome to stay in Granemere Settlement as long as she desires. Unfortunately," she continued, "we cannot guarantee our ability to hide her or the gem once she leaves the safety of our enclave. The enchantments placed on our settlements and outposts were crafted with a level of skill we no longer possess."

"What if," Lenna asked, "I just left the gem here? In the care of the Freewomen?"

A line of worry creased Jaice's brow, and all of her previous mirth seemed to vanish. "The bond between you and the jewel has grown too strong for even our wards to mask its power if you were separated. The stone would reek of magic to call out to you — so strongly, I believe, that it would overcome the wards and become obvious to anyone with even a touch of magecraft, let alone those actively hunting it."

Lenna sighed, though the answer was not an unexpected one. For now, she would just bide her time with her Freewoman kin, hoping that the war between the Krevlum Empire and Ilya would result in the loss of the Empire's Godjewel. While that still left the problem of Luc Tural, the runaway mage in possession of a third gem, one frightened young man was easier to deal with than an entire nation. Lenna still clung to the secret hope that she could reach Luc and convince him that no amount of power — not even all three Godjewels themselves — would be able to bring back his dead lover, Gilbert. The Continent's future left a bitter taste on Lenna's tongue.

Lenna's wineglass was topped off by Jaice herself, who had somehow coaxed her expression back into a smile. "You're too young to hold the weight of the world on your shoulders," she said. "For tonight, at least, relax: you are with family."

The concept of so large a family was novel to Lenna, but she nodded and silently drank the robust wine, barely noticing its taste. She had not heard from her father; though she knew he was terrible at correspondence, considering the recent events and her inability to return home, Lenna expected at least a cursory response to her numerous letters. Jaice had, after all, established a regular messenger specifically so that Lenna might post and receive mail.

When she inquired of the mayor if there was any news from her father or even of Port Hollish, Jaice had simply shaken her head, saying that as far as her sources informed her Port Hollish was still safely nestled up against the sea, going about business as usual. Of Thane Faircloth, however, Mayor Northen had no information. Shaking her head, Lenna realized naught was to be gained by brooding the night away, and instead, she gave her aunt a hug.

Jaice reciprocated without hesitation and settled back down in her chair, next to Bahl. "Do you know your mother's name before she took the mantle of 'Faircloth'?"

Lenna leaned forward and crooked her head to the side. "She never mentioned it, and I guess I never cared enough to ask."

"Ameary. She always hated the alliteration: Alanna Ameary. When we traveled together, she used to joke that she would marry just to change her name. I never thought she was serious." The mayor paused and took a deep drink from her glass. "As a Freewoman yourself, Lenna, you're entitled to take her family name if you wish."

"Freewoman Lenna Ameary, huh?" Lenna let it roll on her tongue. "I think I prefer Faircloth."

Grinning, Bahl chimed in with a voice like a bassoon, startling everyone around him. "Your mom preferred Faircloth too, it seems."

Normally very guarded, Jaice Northen playfully struck the veteran warrior on his scarred noggin with a wooden spoon, and the two bantered like a young couple. Watching them, Lenna wondered if she would ever feel comfortable enough around a person, especially a man, to so flagrantly flirt in public, though now and then she found her mind rebelliously wandering to thoughts of proper, powerful Sebastien and the caddish Raif.

"Disgusting, isn't it?" Pim slurred in Lenna's ear.

"Yes, yes; definitely," Lenna hurriedly agreed, welcoming the interruption. "I think the wine is going to everyone's heads quickly tonight."

The eager Freewoman pulled Lenna closer, conspiratorially. "It's because we don't have many Freewoman inductions anymore. Shh." Pim's voice was at best a dramatic stage whisper.

"Why not?"

Jaice, from across the table, said, "Because there just aren't as many people anymore. Haven't you noticed, Lenna, the great stretches of fields and valleys, and fewer farms and towns? Most people have flocked to a great city in each nation, and no one leaves."

Lenna considered Jaice's statement. As a small child, she had frequently journeyed outside Port Hollish to the outlying farmsteads and villages, but after Alanna Faircloth's death Lenna, on the cusp of womanhood, retreated within both herself and Port Hollish's sturdy walls, preferring the company of books, her father, and her imagination. It was one of the many reasons she had never sought out her heritage, despite Granemere Settlement being so close to her hometown.

"And now war looms on the horizon," Pim intoned.

"Why is the Krevlum Empire so interested in dominating the Continent, anyway?" asked Chait, a fellow Freewoman warrior and one of Lenna's good acquaintances in the settlement.

"Because it's ruled by a man," said Jaice, and Bahl harrumphed. The mayor hit him with her spoon again.

Lenna thought about the Empire and its ambitions. The Continent wasn't so large that ruling it all would change things much, except the size of one's ego, especially considering all four nations had shared a solid peace for several centuries. What would the Emperor gain except more military clout and coin in his coffers? No one went too far into the sea, so it was not as though the Krevlum Empire was preparing to become a force against some great, mysterious enemy a world away.

"War comes to all Freewomen," Pim said cheerfully. "Simple as that!"

"You may be right, Pim," Jaice said, abruptly reverting to the usual stony determination of her role as mayor. "It appears we'll be entertaining another guest at our table tonight."

During their discussion, two of the scouts that wandered Granemere Forest in the evening had entered the town square. Between them they escorted a thin, tall figure whose hands were bound in sturdy rope and whose eyes were masked by a canvas sack. Since the harmlessly lost were escorted out of the forest and sent on their way, Lenna knew this person was definitely considered a trespasser, not just some unlucky farmer.

"Pardon our interruption, Mayor Northen," the scout to the right of the prisoner said. Lenna recognized her slightly portly frame as belonging to Freewoman Kryll. "But we found this one stumbling through the underbrush along the eastern edge of the forest."

Jaice rose from her seat. "Bring the trespasser forward, please, and I think it's safe enough to remove the bag now."

The two guards nudged the prisoner forward until he or she stood in the middle of the clearing, before the grand table at which the more prominent figures of Granemere Settlement's society sat; tonight, that number happened to include Lenna and Pim as her guest. Kryll, shorter than the captive by at least a foot, reached up and tugged the rough sack off in one quick pull. Although his angular face lacked a carefree grin, Lenna recognized his features even as a light-blonde ponytail tumbled down and fell along his back.

"Raif!" she exclaimed and leaped to her feet.

"Lenna!" Raif hurried forward, only to find his way barred by his two wardens. He grimaced. "Get them to lighten up a bit, would you?"

Lenna looked expectantly at her aunt, who, after a moment, nodded. Kryll and her fellow scout lowered the spears they wielded and untied Raif's bonds. He rushed forward and scooped Lenna up in an embrace, pressing her head against his chest. She squirmed a bit in protest and from the crowds around her detected a few snickers. Lenna hastily scrambled to pull away.

"Raif, what are you doing here?"

"Looking for you," he said. "Though I daresay I'm not the only one. Tranum has fallen: the Empire is coming."

The feasting crowd, more or less the entirety of Granemere Settlement, let out a collective gasp and then settled into startled silence. Tranum was the greatest city in Ilya and arguably the most important on the Continent. It was the epicenter of trade and commerce, connecting the four nations — the Krevlum Empire, Fallowfields, Gallas, and Ilya — via the steamtrain and the largest airship port in the known world. For it to fall to the Krevlum Empire, and so quickly, was a mighty blow indeed. It would mean all-out war, much sooner than anyone had expected.

"I have had no news of this," Jaice said quietly.

"You wouldn't, not yet," replied Raif. His voice, flowing in perfect Continental despite his Ilyan heritage, lacked its innate gaiety. "It fell but a few hours ago."

"How did you come here so quickly then?" asked the mayor.

"I flew, of course. I happen to be the best airship captain in all of Tranum," he said, before adding gloomily, "or what was once Tranum."

"You *flew*?" exclaimed Jaice. "And where, pray tell, did you dock your ship?"

Raif shrugged. "I landed in the fields at the outskirts of your forest."

The mayor shook her head in disbelief. "Chait, choose three of your warriors and go back with Freewoman Kryll to where the scouts found this idiot. Verify his ship's location, see if there's any way to make it less obvious: disassemble it, blow it up… in any case, do what you can and come back with a report as to its status."

"Hey!" said Raif. "That ship is all I have left!"

Jaice turned to Raif and parted Lenna and him with a firm shove to his chest before stepping between the two. "Then you were stupid to bring it here. Do you not think this will draw the attention of the Krevlum Empire? They are looking for Lenna and the jewel. A rogue airship, piloted by the heir of the Vandever trading family — which until recently possessed a Godjewel of its own, I might add — who leaves his home in the throes of war for a Freewoman settlement in the middle of Fallowfields? What, you impetuous, foolish youth, did you wish to accomplish by coming here?"

The blonde man blanched, looking for all the world like a pale, abandoned puppy. "I came here to warn you," he said.

"Warn us?" Jaice said. "Of what?"

"Jaice, please listen to him," said Lenna. Her hand fell to her aunt's arm.

"I agree with Freewoman Faircloth," called Bahl from across the table. "The young man proved himself in Tranum and sacrificed a great deal to keep our kind safe. Hear him out." It was true, thought Lenna. In order to defend Lenna, Raif had taken his family's Godjewel as an extra measure of protection, a choice that sadly cost him the gem itself and his reputation within the Vandever clan.

The worry line on Jaice's brow lifted, but she nodded at Chait to continue her mission. The dark-skinned woman slipped away with Kryll, gesturing at three women as she went. All five faded away into the darkness as they passed through the crowd and out into the settlement's outskirts. Lenna admired their stealth and presence of mind as they vanished. She turned back to find Jaice and Raif coolly regarding one another.

"Very well," Jaice sighed. "Young Master Vandever, what is it you wish to warn us of? I am Freewoman Jaice Northen, mayor of Granemere Settlement." She waved her hand in the direction of Chait's vacated chair. "Have a seat. Pim, fetch the lad something to drink."

Pim, squinting at Raif, began — as only the tipsy could —

sloppily pouring him a goblet of Freewoman wine. "I'm still not sure I trust that ponytail," she said.

Lenna let out a clipped chirp of laughter and sat down, her body sagging with relief that the tension, for the moment, had diffused. That Tranum had fallen was grave news, and whatever warning Raif bore could only mean ill for Lenna and the Godjewel, but having everyone warring among themselves would only make any calamity to come more difficult. Yet when she casually glanced at the palm of her gauntleted hand, Lenna was overcome with the realization that the false sense of security she had enjoyed for the past month was about to melt away.

After a long, labored pull, Raif placed the goblet on the table and wiped his chin with the sleeve of his fitted, if slightly mussed, frock. "The Krevlum Empire fell on us suddenly. Over the past few months everyone has been aware of their increased presence, but it was like their power doubled overnight. Their lightning-calling machines — their cracklers, as we've come to call them — suddenly appeared, not just on the border of Tranum, but in Landing itself. We were defenseless."

Pim whistled indelicately, though with good reason. It was no secret that the Empire had rented warehouse space in Landing, the vast courtyard built to house the airship port and facilitate Tranum's trade during the day; Lenna had witnessed one such warehouse herself. But for them to suddenly have the resources to launch an attack from within the city itself implied that the Krevlum infiltration of Tranum had been far more complete than even Raif's family had reckoned.

"The cracklers took out two of our fitted airships within minutes. Hundreds of citizens fell to the lightning. There were no battlemages, no prominent Imperial officers I recognized — just the cracklers and foot soldiers. Still," Raif added bitterly, "it was enough. We were so unprepared."

"For Tranum to fall so easily is troubling enough," Jaice said after a moment's thought. "But for it to fall without the Empire having sent any of its prominent generals or an envoy to claim the city? That is highly contrary to the intelligence we get from the

Freewoman settlements established within Krevlum's borders."

"Tranum isn't the real target," Lenna whispered, and all eyes turned to her. "It's me."

Raif, Jaice, and Bahl simultaneously scowled, but did not refute Lenna's statement. From her previous encounter with an Imperial general, one Khareen Valant, Lenna knew that the Krevlum Emperor, Alderic Sonnet, sought to acquire all three of the legendary Godjewels. The blitz on Tranum, she imagined, was to look for her or the missing Luc, who bore the Vandever clan's jewel on his person.

"We can't assume that," Jaice said. "And we are well protected, even against their lightning machines. The wards are strong."

"By now they know that Lenna isn't in Tranum," Raif said. "But I'm sure they know who she is and where she came from — that is, that she hails from Port Hollish, and her heritage lies with the Freewomen of Laur."

"She could just as likely have made her way to Gallas with the mage from the Blue Crescent Brotherhood," Jaice said. "There's no reason to think that they know Lenna is here in Granemere Settlement."

"Don't be daft, woman!" Bahl stood up in a rare burst of anger aimed at his partner. "Don't you see it doesn't matter *where* she went? Gallas is far to the south; they'll check there last. This settlement and Port Hollish are both in Fallowfields, and if, as the Emperor, you were to launch an assault on the entire Continent, Tranum, airship capital and steamtrain hub, the center of all bloody civilization, would be the best place to do it from. Port Hollish is the next city they'll go for, and this village is right in the middle."

Jaice glared at her partner, and Lenna shuddered at the thought of the tongue-lashing Bahl would receive much later, in private, from the mayor. Having the brass to publicly cross a mayor of the Freewomen of Laur was particularly dangerous, especially when you happened to be sharing her bed — though in Bahl's case, Lenna doubted there would be much bed to be shared this evening.

"Exactly," Raif said. "I was lucky that my ship was prepping for launch as the strike hit. I managed to take to the air and escape, to come here and warn you."

Jaice sat back in her chair, her eyes assessing the pilot. "I presume you're not alone in this escapade."

A warming sensation filled Lenna's stomach as she spotted Raif's casual smugness dimpling his face. Jaice sighed.

"What of the rogue mage, Luc? Have you found any information regarding him?"

"No," said Raif, serious again. "The trail went cold; he hasn't used the Godjewel recently, certainly nowhere near Tranum. For all I know, he could already be in the hands of the Emperor."

"He's still out there." Lenna's interruption cut through the yammering of the crowd. Her ears grew red as, once more, all attention fell on her. "I would know if the Godjewel he stole bonded with someone else. I would… feel it." She grimaced.

"Well," said Jaice after a moment's deliberation. "I suppose that's the best we can hope for at the moment." The mayor placed her wine on the table before her. "Lenna, what do you think?"

Even Pim seemed at a loss for words. It was unlike Mayor Northen to openly seek the counsel of one of the villagers, let alone someone who had only recently been inducted into Freewoman society. Lenna looked down at the gauntlet strapped to her arm and then up to the sky, searching the heavens for her favorite constellation. She couldn't find it, though she had gazed upon it so many times she knew the location intrinsically. Pim's conversation in the bath about the population of the Continent resounded in her head with a sobering clarity.

"Have any of us ever thought about why the Emperor wants the jewels?"

With the pride of a child who could spell a difficult word, Pim announced loudly, "To become as powerful as that Ytra curmudgeon from Zeist."

"But why?" asked Lenna. "The Continent isn't that large. There's no great advantage in controlling the entire thing when recent technology unites all four nations and we're at peace."

Bahl raised a bushy eyebrow. "So, you think his goal is something other than domination?"

Lenna looked down at her fist and into the blue depths of the Godjewel. "What's the point in ruling the world if you've no one to brag to?"

"You mean, you think the Emperor knows something about the world we don't?" asked Pim.

Maybe being in the constant company of the Godjewel was warping Lenna's perception of reality, but she found her mind wandering in directions in which it had never ventured. When the warm stone hummed against her flesh, it was like a great veil had been lifted from her eyes. Lenna could feel the Godjewel's message.

"I think this world is wrong, somehow," she said after a moment of communion.

"Right," said Jaice. The mayor stood up and cleared her throat. "Sorry, my friends," she announced to the revelers. "I'm afraid this conversation must be continued in more private areas. Lenna, Master Vandever, Bahl: with me, please." The mayor spun around with militaristic precision and began to walk toward the meeting hall, all effects of the wine seemingly gone.

"Hey! What about me?" Pim cried out.

Lenna genuinely agreed with the younger Freewoman and began to voice her opinion in the matter when she was interrupted by a terrific peal of thunder from the east. Raif, biting his lower lip, gripped Lenna's arm in what could have been fear or a desire to protect. Even the mayor looked stunned as she turned her head in the direction of the thunder.

"Cracklers," Raif said unnecessarily.

Before Jaice could speak, Chait came tearing down a lined path that led to the forest. Shaking her head, Lenna checked her timepiece and confirmed that it had only been a few moments since the warrior and her party had left in search of Raif's airship. Chait kept her pace until she reached the mayor and leaned forward, hands on her knees, breathing deeply until she could speak.

"A squad of the Krevlum Empire's lightning machines," she panted. Perspiration beaded her hair and glowed strangely in the torchlight. "They're tossing bolt after bolt at the eastern border, not far from the Ilyan ship."

"How many?" asked Bahl.

"Four cracklers," Chait replied. "And three soldiers for each."

"Are the wards holding?" Jaice inquired. Lenna wondered how the woman could remain so collected after that much wine and, she thought grimly, such gratuitous plot development.

"Yes, Mayor," Chait said. She paused a moment. "But I'm no expert in magic."

Jaice considered. "I'm the highest ranking magic user in the settlement. I will go."

"Jaice —" Bahl stood up, tight-lipped.

"Bahl, Master Vandever, Lenna, *and* Pim," Jaice continued, placing one hand on her partner's chest. "Two minutes. Be ready."

Bahl, visibly relieved, ran back to the town hall, followed by Jaice at a more deliberate pace. Pim grinned with a childish glee and, tugging Lenna along by the hand, swept them back toward her residence, no doubt to grab her blunderbuss. Raif, already as prepared as he could be, stood resolutely in the center of the town square as Freewomen scurried about, disassembling the feast. His gaze was fixated on the east, and his lips were pursed; he barely flinched when the next cry of thunder tore through the wintry night air.

CHAPTER THREE

Despite the events of the past month, Lenna still found herself awestruck at Pim's ability to quickly prepare and steel herself for any situation, even with a fair quantity of wine swishing about in her belly. Within moments — and Lenna was timing — the young warrior had her gun, Old Burt, and a satchel of ammunition slung over her shoulder. She had also strapped a long, curved knife to her belt. "Pointy things hurt just as much as bullets," she said.

Lenna, for her part, was already as prepared as she could be. Her knife was still strapped to her thigh, and the Godjewel securely rested in the palm of her leather gauntlet. The fastenings had held during her spar with Freewoman Dalm; Lenna hoped she wouldn't be placed in a situation anytime soon in which she would have to test if it would survive a real battle. Pim, ruffling through a pile of clothing near her bed, pitched Lenna a wolfskin cloak that smelled distinctly of onions.

Distracted, Lenna barely managed to catch the frayed garment. She grunted at the stench. "Pim, this hasn't been cleaned in a month."

"Better than being cold, right?" Pim swung another heavy cloak around her own shoulders.

Muttering something about the availability of cleaning facilities in Freewoman settlements, Lenna followed suit and donned the mantle. Both Freewomen headed back outdoors — the preparations had taken only forty-five seconds — and strode toward the town square. In the distance, the roar of thunder interspersed with another rattling sound cried out an omen fouler than Pim's stinky cloak.

"Gunfire?" Lenna asked.

"The scouts have probably engaged the Imperial soldiers," Pim said. "Let's hurry before Jaice heads out without us."

When Lenna and Pim arrived in the square, the Freewomen had nearly finished their hurried tidying up of the interrupted feast. Jaice, leaning on an elm staff and with a long, wrapped bundle under the crook of her arm, was exchanging abrupt words with Chait and Bahl. Suddenly in possession of a short sword, Raif stood off to the side, his expression lightening when his eyes locked on Lenna.

"I know you're not going to like this," he said with a tinge of hesitation. "But couldn't you hang back? Tranum aside, you're not much of a fighter."

"Lenna packs way more of a punch than you do, airpants," Pim quipped. "Unlike somebody, she's still got her Godjewel, remember?"

The Ilyan snarled in displeasure and for a short moment Lenna wondered if he was going to clobber Pim, though she doubted the young girl would go down without a fight. But it was a brash comment, bordering on harsh, for Pim to have made, especially taking into account Raif's indulgence and consideration of Lenna and the Freewomen. Rather than irritate him further — although wrestling with a picayune desire to kick him in the groin to prove just how much of a fighter she could be — Lenna exhaled deeply and stated, "Would I rather be in the baths, tipping back a bottle of wine? Yes. But life hasn't afforded me much liberty in making many decisions based on my whims lately."

Raif's murderous expression melted into a frown of abashed acquiescence, and Jaice, her voice popping out of the ether, interposed in his defense. "Pim Hartnell, for once, hold your tongue. This man, though uninvited, has done us Freewomen a great service by coming here to warn us and seeking to protect one of our own. He is a guest of mine and of all of Granemere Settlement; you will apologize for such un-Freewomanly conduct."

Lenna, Raif, and Pim stared at the mayor, uncertain how to react, though Chait let out a snicker. Bahl, meanwhile, allowed himself a hearty chuckle, his previous indiscretion toward Jaice apparently forgotten in the quarrel between Pim and Raif and the impending attack on the wards of Granemere Settlement. The mayor was no-nonsense, but not one to hold a grudge — so long as one repented.

"Sorry, Raif," Pim murmured. Her cheeks were scarlet. "It's just you haven't seen how much Lenna's grown since I've met her."

Lenna blushed, having expected more cheek from her friend, not praise. But both Chait and Bahl nodded, validating Pim's response. Raif's expression was still one of concern, but yielding. It was at this moment that Jaice tossed her staff to Bahl and stepped forward, standing before Lenna with the curious, elongated bundle in her arms.

"Albeit lacking the discretion a mayor comes to expect of her villagers," the mayor said, "Pim is right. Freewoman Faircloth has proven herself more than capable this past month and has exercised prudent judgment regarding numerous matters. I have brought you this, as it is yours by right." She held out the bundle toward Lenna. "Though," she added quietly, "I pray that you have no need of it tonight."

Lenna took the package, curious. The parcel was not excessively heavy, but its contents felt sturdy enough. Quickly undoing the bindings around the cloth, she gasped as the cover fell away to reveal a gleaming sword. It was the long, delicately curved blade once wielded by General Khareen Valant, a high-ranking representative of the Krevlum Empire who had perished at the hands of Lenna and Pim. The sword was not of Krevlum origin, though: Valant had won the blade at the cost of a Freewoman's life — and her own ear.

"You want me to take this?" Lenna asked.

"It's yours or Pim's to take. Your position would dictate it go to you, and Pim has willingly forfeited any claim to it."

"Take it, silly," Pim said. "The only difference between that and your dagger is that it makes you a cock instead of a hen. Why peck something with a knife when you can slash it with a sword?"

Pim's bumpkin-like speech aside, Lenna considered the sword as her hand wrapped around its grip. The metal from which it was forged was thin and well-tempered, making it a much lighter weapon to wield than its size, practically three feet long by her measure, suggested. Intricate leaf carvings etched along the blade and hilt resembled trees like those of Granemere Settlement, and though she did not want to use it in violence, Lenna Faircloth was glad that an item so beautiful and delicately crafted was in the hands of the Freewomen and not the bloodthirsty, calculating Khareen Valant. The blade shimmered silver in the moonlight and the glow of the town square's torches.

"I've no sheath for it," Lenna stuttered.

Chait, grinning cheekily, stepped forward and revealed an item she had been concealing behind her back. In her chiseled hands, the hands of a warrior, Chait was holding a deep red scabbard, fit to be belted to Lenna's waist. It was the shape of Valant's — no, Lenna's — sword, and bore in gold leaf a pattern similar to that on the blade. Lenna gasped in appreciation at its ornamentation; this was elegant craftsmanship worthy of her father.

"It's been a secret project of mine," Chait admitted, still beaming. "I've just finished a few days ago and was waiting for the right time to give it to you."

"It's beautiful," Lenna said honestly. "I'm not worthy of this."

"You are one of us," Jaice said. More gunfire drummed off in the distance, and another clap of thunder echoed throughout the night. "We must go. Today, my niece has earned her rightful position in the Freewomen of Laur. Let us gird her, and be off."

Lenna had absolutely no idea what girding her entailed, but from the brief conversation that ensued she determined that it meant someone had to strap the scabbard to her belt. Pim vociferously pronounced her desire to be the one to do it. Chait stood back, her eyes eager but understanding. Jaice had deliberately moved aside; Lenna presumed it would not befit the mayor to equip someone beneath her rank. Since no one else in the party moved, the choice, it would appear, was Lenna's to make.

"Raif," she said, ignoring Pim's outcry. "Would you mind helping me with this?"

Much to Lenna's surprise, he blushed. Apparently the intimacy of the gesture was not lost on the Ilyan captain. "Are you sure?" he asked.

"Please."

Raif delicately took the scabbard from Chait, who nodded with approval, and he knelt down before Lenna and fastened the scabbard to her waist. His hands fumbled a bit, but only she noticed. As he finished the second clasp, he said, "May this be a shield to protect rather than an instrument to oppress."

The group was stunned silent. No one had expected an Ilyan nobleman to be so knowledgeable of Freewoman ways. Jaice put one hand on Raif's shoulder and urged him to rise. "You do us a kindness," she said. "Your choice to come to us instead of staying in Tranum must trouble you greatly. Know that you are in our debt."

Raif's face was still quite red, but he said nothing.

Pim helped a struggling and embarrassed Lenna sheathe the sword properly and then danced about, almost merrily, on the balls of her feet. "Right! Let's go help our friends."

"To the border," Chait said.

"To the border," Lenna repeated, and the group headed off down the path before her. Only Raif lingered behind. He grabbed the newly initiated Freewoman's hand.

"To the border," he said.

Lenna sensed some sort of hidden meaning or urgency in Raif's statement but couldn't quite puzzle it out. Shrugging it off, she nodded once and, freeing herself of Raif's grip, quickly pursued her friends, leaving him to follow a few paces behind.

***

Chait, in addition to being an exquisite craftsman, was even more of an expert guide. The Freewomen kept Granemere Settlement organized enough for Lenna to navigate it without fault, but once beyond the fence that barricaded the village from the forest she was lost without a leader. Brambles poked out of the darkness, and snow-laden branches trembled overhead. With each pelting of lightning against the Freewoman warding, Lenna flinched, expecting a pile of snow to land on her head.

Raif kept up a solid pace behind Lenna, who in turn followed a hushed Pim, whose seamless metamorphose from a drunken chatterbox to a battle-hardened warrior on a moment's notice was almost as disconcerting as the magics the Blue Crescent Brotherhood evoked to cloak themselves. Lenna frowned, pushing away the unwanted emotions that came bubbling up to the surface of her mind at the thought of the Brotherhood. Though weeks had passed, the image of her childhood friend, Gilbert, lying dead in the snow only a few miles from her present location haunted Lenna daily.

As for the mayor and her partner, they followed Chait's guidance with resolute grace. It was obvious to Lenna that Jaice was no slouch; her aunt had probably engraved every inch of the forest onto her memory. Even the reach of her long staff seemed to mystically elude protruding branches and obstacles along the dark road through the forest, yet Lenna somehow managed to trip over or bump into them all. Luckily, every time she stumbled, Raif's swift reflexes propped her up and helped to propel her feet forward.

Though the he kept mute, Lenna could sense magic pulsating urgently outward from him: whatever mixture of emotions Raif was experiencing, it was inhibiting his ability to mask the clean, fresh scent of his power. It came out in gentle waves, and Lenna eventually realized that the steady rhythm of the Godjewel had begun to match Raif's. Was the Godjewel becoming used to Raif, or was it just reflecting her own subconscious desires? Jaice shot Lenna a glance over her shoulder, and Lenna wondered if she was just as noticeable.

Chait signaled the group to a halt, and they all — most awkwardly, Lenna — knelt in a small circle. The battle was audibly closer, so Lenna knew they must be near the border of the forest and the vast plains that lay beyond it. It was the closest she had been to the outside world, away from the protective wards of Granemere Settlement, since she had departed Tranum as a determined bearer of the Godjewel. A queer sensation was flittering about in her stomach: Lenna was nervous.

Their guide, her eyes starkly bright against her dark skin, made a few motions that Lenna didn't recognize. Jaice nodded and Bahl frowned a bit. Pim leaned over and whispered to Lenna and Raif, "Chait wants the mayor to send out a magical warning shot."

Raif cocked his head to one side. "Is that a good idea, announcing our presence like that?"

"My scouting party had no magic users and only one gunner with us," Chait said quietly. "Their lightning machines are devastating; we need to give them a reason to not enter the forest. Though the wards protect against malevolent magics, they won't keep the Imperial soldiers from entering the forest itself. I'm not certain if the wards will stop the cracklers either, as they appear to be mechanical."

"Then I'll do it," Raif said, ready to leap up from his haunches. "Something big and flashy, right?"

"No." Jaice's voice was solid, channeling the stalwartness of the towering trees surrounding them.

Lenna stared as Raif sank back to his squatting position, expecting an argument from the headstrong captain. But something in Jaice's tone must have conveyed a powerful sense of finality, because before Raif had even finished dropping back down to a crouch, Jaice had already stood up, propped against her staff. Bahl remained silent, but from the dark scowl he bore there was no mistaking his displeasure in Chait's choice of tactics.

Decision made, Jaice shrank into the shadow of the trees, the natural terrain and some kind of magic — Lenna could sense it — making her almost invisible. The mayor's footsteps were barely audible against the crunch of dead undergrowth mixed with pebbles and snow. Chait, Pim, and Bahl gathered to form a barricade in front of Lenna and Raif, who exchanged looks of uncertainty.

Another crackle of lightning and its subsequent fizzling sound accompanied a brief flash of light not far from their position, though it was filtered by the network of branches and trunks of the forest. Lenna gasped at the memories the lightning evoked: Gilbert, Luc, and herself desperately scrambling through the snowy fields, perverse dark bolts of energy raining down upon their magical shielding. She recalled the acrid scent of ozone and, for the thousandth time, saw her precious friend Gilbert drop to the ground after having being struck by a blast of magic originally intended for her.

"Jaice," she breathed into the night. "No." The Godjewel throbbed intently, and Lenna stood up despite the muffled protests of her companions.

A feeling of dread washed over Lenna so forcefully that it rendered the cries of the group indecipherable as she scrambled after her aunt. Twigs cracked beneath her steps and an errant branch drew a line of red as it scraped against her cheek, though Lenna barely registered any pain. Her mind was cluttered with images of Jaice lying prone on the ground, burned and marred by the Empire's lightning-calling machines. The Godjewel pulsed steadily: *go,* it said.

Jaice hadn't had much time to get far, and considering her deliberate pace, it was not long before Lenna came upon her aunt standing at the very edge of the trees, using a sturdy pine for cover. She hissed with displeasure as Lenna drew near, her arrival announced in advance by the steady trampling of Granemere Forest's undergrowth. Heart pounding, Lenna hastened up to the tree and leaned against it, beside her aunt.

"What are you doing here?" Jaice said angrily.

Lenna was too busy panting to articulate a tactful response. "Worried," she gasped.

Jaice's expression was unreadable, but her tone lightened. "You have good cause to be," she said. "Look."

Pushing her spectacles up the bridge of her nose, Lenna edged her head out around the broad tree trunk and took in the snowy plains beyond the forest line. The night sky glowed with electric intensity above four machines and numerous soldiers standing barely fifty meters away. The machines resembled Krevlum's motorcars that had recently come into fashion with the more wealthy inhabitants of the Continent, except that where the carriage for passengers would normally sit, there was an awkward-looking contraption.

Shaped like a large box and made of some kind of metal, the crackler was mostly comprised of wires, levers, and dials; atop this main unit was what looked to Lenna like some kind of forked antenna, glowing unnaturally. Arcane energy and fizzling currents of electricity slid about the length of it like wriggling, mystical worms. All four machines, in unison, hummed with a vibration that reminded Lenna of the Godjewel, setting her heart racing in sudden distress. This was a power not meant to be in the control of soldiers.

One of the men shouted something in Krevlum, a language for which Lenna had no aptitude, and the troops organized around each of the cracklers and began to manipulate the controls. The humming of the machines increased to such magnitude that Lenna began to feel the vibrations rising up through the forest floor and resonating within the trees themselves. Tiny hairs on her arm began to rise as the cracklers charged for another strike against the Freewomen's magical barrier.

"Shut your eyes," Jaice commanded, and Lenna sealed her lids shut. A tremendous clap of thunder split the air and four brilliant flashes of light reflected off the snowy ground in such a dazzling whiteness that Lenna registered them even through closed eyes. Only meters in front of the pair, the sound of a million hornets erupted with each of the four strikes, and Lenna could tangibly discern the threads of the forest's wards quivering against the power of the lightning.

"They'll have to recharge; it takes a few moments," said Jaice, and Lenna cautiously opened her eyes and looked out to see the troops moving about the curious cracklers at the bark of their commanding officer's orders. Jaice nodded off toward the distance, and Lenna turned her head to acknowledge the party of Freewoman scouts, sheltered behind more of the forest. The gunner, a girl whom Lenna didn't recognize, began taking potshots at the Imperial soldiers, but either she was terribly inexperienced with a gun or something was preventing her from striking any of her targets.

"It's a siege," Jaice said quietly. "They're testing the strength of our wards and our resolution."

"The Emperor is trying to draw me out, isn't he?" asked Lenna. The Godjewel was still throbbing insistently within her clenched fist, telling her the answer before her aunt could respond.

"Yes," said Jaice. "Sonnet must have dispatched this unit weeks ago. I wouldn't be surprised if they have a similar force at Port Hollish as well."

Lenna gasped. Her precious city on the ocean, where she had grown up and to which she longed to return, was not prepared for war with the Krevlum Empire and had none of the magical wards the Freewoman settlements boasted. Under the constant assault of these lightning-calling cracklers, the walls of Port Hollish would fall in hours, and that would mean Fallowfields, one of the four nations of the Continent, would fall as well. Lenna's right hand fell to the pommel of her newly acquired sword and thoughts of her father, Thane, unknowingly tinkering with the mechanisms of a clock as death slowly wheeled toward his doorstep, hovered in the back of her mind.

"What if we just… stayed back? Let them fire away; the wards will hold." Another gunshot pierced the air, and Lenna heard the Krevlum troops call back something mocking.

Her aunt frowned and shook her head. "This technology might utilize magic, but I don't believe the device itself is magical."

"So while the wards can shield us from the lightning attacks…" Lenna began, her brain making an exceedingly unpleasant realization.

"I see no reason why they could not just power down the cracklers and drive them across our borders," Jaice finished.

Lenna was adrift in thought. Even now, the machines had begun to rattle again, meaning another strike from the cracklers was imminent. This was merely a ploy by the Emperor, forcing Lenna to make a choice: if the soldiers needed to, they could simply cross the wards and set the entire forest ablaze with their lightning. Granemere Forest and the Freewoman settlement would be burned to the ground. But Alderic Sonnet, much like Lenna, knew the secret of the Godjewels. Once a stone bonded with an individual, it would not transfer to a new host lightly. He wanted — almost needed — her to give up her gem willingly.

Jaice noticed the grim expression on Lenna's face and was quick to place a hand on her shoulder. "No, Lenna," she said. "I know what you're thinking, but I will not allow you to sacrifice yourself."

"War comes to all Freewoman," Lenna murmured. "I can't run forever. I can't *hide* forever, Jaice." She unclenched her fist and looked at the source of her troubles, the spherical blue stone glowing with the light of a sun against the clouds.

"War might come to all Freewoman," Jaice said, "but when it threatens one of us, it threatens us all." Her aunt pulled Lenna close to her in an embrace that shielded her eyes from the burningly bright strikes of the cracklers. The matronly gesture made Lenna recall her own mother, and she realized that Jaice Northen was the closest link she would ever again have to Alanna Faircloth. After the attack halted, Lenna was slow to withdraw from her aunt's arms.

Jaice smiled and Lenna glimpsed for an instant what she thought was a tear in the corner of her aunt's eye. She knew the mayor was not one to display such affection, so she was taken completely by surprise when Jaice placed one hand to Lenna's chest. Jaice, her eyes shut, exhaled a mournful sigh and in one rough motion pushed her niece with such force that Lenna fell back into the forest undergrowth behind her.

"Stay here," Jaice commanded, gripping her carved staff with both hands and turning around. She sprinted past the forest line and onto the white expanse of the plains, beyond the reach of Granemere Forest's magical protections.

Winded and dumbfounded, Lenna could summon no words to call after her aunt. Jaice ran directly toward the four cracklers, staff at the ready, issuing a guttural battle cry into the night. The soldiers, nearly as taken aback as Lenna, paused in their preparations of the cracklers and gaped at the Freewoman rushing toward them. Several meters in front of the two middle lightning machines, the ground erupted in an explosion of white, powdery snow and rock. The soldiers cried out in dismay before a harsh voice began issuing orders.

She cannot be, Lenna thought. *She cannot be taking on four cracklers and twelve Imperial soldiers by herself.* Images of Gilbert's death and her mother's coffin being nailed shut, ready for its eternal journey into the unexplored territories of the great sea, ravaged Lenna's mind, and a darkness in her heart that she had long feared and struggled against threatened to pull her down and swallow her. She was drowning in herself.

Suddenly a pair of strong arms was shaking Lenna roughly by the shoulders. She tilted up her gaze and found herself focusing on the concerned face of Raif, his deep eyes searching for recognition in Lenna's own. She blinked rapidly before she regained a sort of detached self-awareness; she was on the ground, her long blade and wolfskin cloak entangled in the brambles of the forest floor.

"Lenna, are you all right?" Raif's voice was almost shrill.

"Jaice, she's —" Lenna began. The sound of another explosion and shouting, followed by a gunshot, made its way to Lenna's ears.

"Yes," Raif replied direly. "Her cry alerted us. Pim and Bahl and Chait, the scouts — they're all out there, but they only have moments before the cracklers are ready to fire again."

Lenna could sense the vibrations of the machines again. Raif was right, more strikes would be coming soon and Jaice and the others stood no chance once the cracklers were operational again. She struggled to get to her feet, damning the scabbard and cloak and all things under the sun. Thankfully, Raif disentangled Lenna and helped her into a standing position without much effort.

"Now's our chance," Raif spoke urgently. "We have to make it to my ship."

"Why are they attacking?" Lenna asked, unable to contain the quavering anger in her voice. "This is asinine!" That searing fury was beginning to build up inside her again, corrupting her senses. She detected the smell of ozone and found that it was coming from herself.

"Lenna, listen..." Raif's words were cut short as a terrific burst from the cracklers cut through all the noise of battle, and one solid, white explosion glared against the snow, blinding Lenna and Raif. Between the deafening boom and stark brightness, both stumbled, a slight ringing in their ears.

When Lenna's vision finally cleared and the buzzing in her head stopped, the plains beyond the forest borders were quiet, save for a few guttural groans. One of the cracklers was now a smoldering heap, and in the immediate vicinity before the remaining three the ground was charred and jutting up in unnatural shards of rock. There lingered on the air a scent of burning, and Lenna and Raif both paled as they stared out into the plains at the prone bodies of at least a dozen people around the war machines.

"No," whispered Lenna, her eyes darting back and forth. The only bodies rising to their feet were easily identified by their white military uniforms as Imperial soldiers.

Raif swore in Ilyan with a level of heat that rivaled his nation's spices. He soon switched back to the Continental tongue, but Lenna heard nothing.

"No," she repeated. All that remained in her now was that fiery anger, a rage that craved release. Pim. Jaice. Bahl. Chait. Their names dropped into the bubbling cauldron of Lenna's wrath as she once again relived the pain of loved ones putting themselves before her. Dying for her.

Let go, said an insistent thump from her tightly clenched left fist. *Release.*

Lenna shouldered Raif aside and advanced to the pine tree behind which Jaice and she had hidden just a few minutes earlier.

"Release," she repeated to herself. Her voice was distant and strained.

Before Raif could intervene, Lenna raised her gauntleted hand into the air and shredded the night with a scythe of pure light, a mesmerizing blue explosion of fury.

CHAPTER FOUR

A curious sensation, as though her body were being pulled in eight directions at once, gripped Lenna. She lurched, jamming her eyes shut against the oppressive light flooding her vision. From all around her, high-pitched whispers seemed to nag at her being, and an acute wave of nausea threatened an appearance from the potent Freewoman wine.

With a jolt, reality came sharply back into focus and the burning blue light, summoned by the jewel fastened to Lenna's gauntlet, vanished in such a tight instant that it might have never sullied the sky with its tremendous presence. Lenna fell to the ground, hard, like when Jaice had pushed her and she found herself on her buttocks in the crunchy mix of undergrowth just within the border of Granemere Forest.

"Lenna, what the hell did you just do?" a female voice called.

Lenna opened one eye to look up at the person standing before her: tall and slender, but her frame was lined with a firm layer of muscle. Her hair was pulled back, and her brow was deeply furrowed. The woman held out one hand before her, as though she had just shoved someone.

"Jaice," Lenna stammered.

Thrashing and curses announced the arrival of others, obviously in too much of a hurry to be concerned about raising any alarm caused by the trampling of the verge. Lenna turned her head, both eyes now open wide in a mixture of confusion and unbridled elation. Bursting through the thicket with such enthusiasm that they were practically stumbling over each other — as opposed to the errant branches — were Raif, Pim, Bahl, and Chait. Their questions, all asked in unison, became one muddled expression of incredulity.

A humming noise in the distance and an exacting order of silence from Jaice cut through the gibbering crowd. All eyes fell to the mayor. "The cracklers; the next strike will come soon." Jaice paused. "Wait. Something's wrong."

Lenna felt it too, though at first she could not quite place the sensation. She felt more vulnerable somehow, exposed and bare to the winter's cold. Then she came to a realization and clapped a hand over her mouth.

"The wards," Jaice said grimly, "they're gone."

The silence was quickly interrupted by a series of gunshots and howling, meters outside the forest. Whooping, the original scouting party ran from the cover of the forest toward the Imperial unit and its complement of lightning-calling machines. Chait, without comment or question, sprinted past the mayor and out into the wide fields from which Lenna's nation had acquired its name.

"Jaice, what's going on?" Bahl asked, striding forward and hoisting Lenna up from the twigs and stones and onto her feet with coarse hands.

Lenna rubbed her arm, too addlepated to comment on Bahl's roughness. Though her anger had subsided, her thoughts were still muddied with confusion and a hopeful happiness at the sight of her friends.

Jaice's expression was cloudy and dismal. "I do not know how it could possibly happen, but the shielding that for centuries has protected this forest has, in an instant, fallen."

No one responded. Lenna noticed that Raif had shuffled up to stand behind her. His clean scent was reassuring and grounded Lenna's thoughts in the immediacy of the situation. Bahl, now beside his partner, regarded Lenna dispassionately, and Pim, looking between all parties, was quite visibly twitching as she tried to compensate for keeping her tongue still.

"Lenna," Raif began, his voice trailing off. "You unleashed a huge blast of power from the Godjewel. It was unlike anything I've ever felt before. What did you do?"

"I don't know," she answered. The experience reminded her of another occasion, when she and Luc, after Gilbert had been killed, had been desperately trying to escape freezing to death during a magical snowstorm. The Godjewel had reacted violently and, almost of its own accord, unleashed a terrific gout of magical energy. When they awoke, they had traveled several hundred meters and, now that Lenna riffled through her memories, it had been a different time of day.

Lenna uncurled her fist and revealed that same blue stone, its persistent thrumming calmer than normal. She frowned as her brain made connections that, despite her recent cavalier attitude, her reticence had helped her to ignore most diligently. The strength of the Godjewel, though no one had really any accurate measure of it — the last known time any of the gems had been used, all three were together and created a veritable god — was something that over the past month Lenna had come to understand better with each passing day.

Quietly, she said, "I reversed time."

Bahl and Pim stared at her with unreadable visages, while Raif and Jaice blanched. "Lenna," Raif said, "that's impossible. And the repercussions would be unimaginable."

Jaice glanced over her shoulder, presumably to observe what her scouting unit was attempting. "The cracklers aren't functioning," she stated. "And the soldiers were taken by surprise." The mayor waved her hand about, frowning. "Master Vandever, could you conjure up some magelight for us?"

"Magelight? Of course, Mayor Northen, but I don't see the need…" Raif began.

"Please, just try."

Raif shrugged and extended his hand. Lenna expected there to appear an incandescent ball of energy bobbing in the air above his open palm, neither warm nor cool and completely insubstantial, which could be brightened or dimmed at will. It was one of the simpler spells magicians on the Continent learned when studying magecraft; even Lenna was capable of it.

But nothing happened. Raif scowled and then looked up at Jaice, obviously annoyed and embarrassed. "Sorry, Mayor, but it appears I can't."

"Don't worry, Master Vandever," Jaice replied. "Neither can I. Lenna, can you explain what you meant when you said you 'reversed time'?"

Lenna kicked at the snowy grit on the forest floor. "When I… used the gem," she began, "it was after witnessing what should have happened moments ago." She grimaced, but, knowing there was no way to avoid divulging the horrifying scene replaying itself over and over in her mind, Lenna found herself expounding on how Jaice had pushed Lenna back and rushed the cracklers.

"And we were all just lying there? Dead?" Pim said, her voice rising an octave as she spoke. "Why, Old Burt and I could take on a platoon of those…"

"Be silent, Freewoman Hartnell," Jaice commanded. "Lenna, when you witnessed what you believed to be our deaths, how did you feel?"

Despite having achieving what she believed to be a fair amount of personal growth (for a reclusive librarian) in the past month, Lenna's stomach dropped and her tongue became limp when it came to expressing her emotions to others. "It reminded me of when Gilbert died to protect me. All of you, out there, just *dying* to protect me. And," she said as she waved her gauntleted fist, "all because of this damn stone."

Raif gently placed a hand on her shoulder and Lenna flinched at the sudden gesture. He said, "But what did you *feel*, Lenna?"

Rubbing one eye with her knuckle, Lenna tried to recall the emotion. It wasn't just anger; it was an anger filled with desperation that threatened all of her being and and everything that was the existence known as "Lenna Faircloth." It was powerful and old, lying deep within her for many years. She inhaled deeply and said, "Rage. Such violent rage. I wanted to erase what I was seeing. I didn't care what the outcome was; I just focused on that wrath and… unleashed the power of the Godjewel."

There was an awkward shift in the atmosphere, a tenseness in Raif's fingers on her shoulder. Even Pim shambled about as though she was ill at ease. Suddenly Lenna was surrounded by a group of people who were afraid of her. *So,* she thought, *this is the real power of the Godjewels. The power to make a person alone.*

Jaice, however, carried on unfazed. "I had no idea the bond between you and the gem was that strong, Lenna. That was my mistake." She stepped forward and embraced her, and Lenna, the shredder of time, quite unexpectedly began to cry. Raif pulled away, stumbling somewhat, like he was unsure what to do with his lanky limbs.

"I'm sorry," Lenna muttered through her sniffles. "I couldn't control myself. I couldn't see any more death."

For all her sturdy exterior, Jaice held Lenna with a mother's touch. Battle-hardened hands, armored in calluses from constant practice with her weapon, combed through Lenna's wavy mass of dirty blonde hair. She smelled of chamomile. "You can be as stubborn as your mother. Fate's placed an unfair burden in your hands, and you finally shed a tear — for saving our lives."

Lenna coughed and laughed through her crying, a strange, sputtering sound. Jaice was right; rather than grieve Gilbert's death, or even her mother's, Lenna had always kept herself occupied or lived for someone else. Somewhere along the way her grief had multiplied, turning gradually into unchecked wrath. These tears she shed — however embarrassed she was in front of her friends and especially Raif — represented one of the purest, most cathartic moments Lenna had felt in a long, long time.

"Sorry to interrupt," Raif interjected. "But the reason Lenna is here in Granemere Settlement is because your wards were supposed to shield the Godjewel's power. They prevent workings being cast through the borders. They also prevent workings being cast out from within it. Lenna shouldn't have been able to affect any of you or the soldiers out in the plains."

The mayor gave a weak smile, breaking her embrace with Lenna and stepping back. "Lenna, can you still draw on the power of the Godjewel?"

Wiping away some of her tears with a clean handkerchief provided, surprisingly, by Pim, Lenna's face contorted as she stared at Jaice. "After what just happened? And on that note, I'm not entirely certain what just happened anyway..."

"Indulge your aunt," Bahl said firmly. It was no longer a mere request.

All right, then. Lenna nodded and consciously tapped into the blue orb in her left hand, feeling a ripple in its vast pool of power. She funneled a trickle of energy from the Godjewel's core out into the air, forming one perfectly round, glowing globe of magelight. It floated lightly up and down over her hand like a balloon on a string.

"It's what I thought," Jaice said. "Lenna's connection to the gem has grown so strong that it unconsciously reacts to severe bursts of emotion from her."

"What does that mean?" asked Pim.

Raif stroked his chin, frowning at no one in particular. "Lenna made a wish, Pim. It might not have been a conscious decision on her part, but the anger she felt was so strong and the gem is so closely tied to her will that it... well, it made her wish come true."

Lenna thought on this. "I wanted to erase what I saw, for things to be reset. The only way the Godjewel could do that was by bringing the world back to the point where things could change. But the barrier from the settlement prevents magic going through it either way, so..."

"Yes," intoned Jaice. "The Godjewel destroyed the barrier. No; it *neutralized* it, and all of the magic around here. It was the only way it could grant Lenna's wish." She turned and pointed out into the plains, where the scouting party was quickly tying up the confounded Krevlum soldiers. "The cracklers, however they're made, generate magic. They won't work now, so we're safe. As to whether Raif and I will be able to use our magic again, I suppose that depends on the nature of the Godjewel's spell. Are we just in a magic-free zone? Are we permanently cut off from accessing our power?"

The group grew silent again, each member no doubt lost in his or her own thoughts. Lenna's brain was once more aflutter with conflicting emotions and conundrums. The Godjewel had magicked both Luc and herself through the barrier once before without erasing it; how had it worked then, yet destroy the wards now? Had the power of her pain been that much stronger? That her bond with the gem had been growing stronger daily Lenna had known, though she chose to keep it from her friends. But for it to somehow respond to her will and take measures that seemed so calculated made the stone seem almost intelligent or sentient… that was a thought by which its wielder was more than disturbed.

"Then," asked Lenna, "shouldn't I be unable to use the Godjewel? It should be neutralized too."

Raif shook his head. "I don't think so, Lenna, not from what I've seen. And Mayor Northen, I think this is just a local phenomenon. I'm not sure that one Godjewel alone could destroy all magic everywhere. Not with two other Godjewels still out there, freely operating. And the fact that the Godjewel works at all within this area means that its magic is still stronger than the spell it used to wipe out the wards."

"But that also means that when Lenna uses the Godjewel around here, the other Godjewels and mages and whatnot will sense her," Pim said, her face lighting up with comprehension.

"That is precisely what it means, Pim," Jaice said. "Even if the wards' destruction is only temporary, Lenna is no longer safe in Granemere Settlement. And," she added with a trace of melancholy, "Granemere Settlement is no longer safe with her here."

Pim, Raif, Bahl, and even the quiet Chait at once erupted in a furious verbal assault against Jaice. Lenna was touched by their defense of her courage and gladdened at their eagerness to have her stay just because, even slightly, they had come to think of her as a member of their family. It must have wounded Jaice terribly to imply that Lenna should go, but she was a leader and a

Freewoman, and all of the residents of Granemere Settlement — including the men, women, and children who hadn't formally chosen the life of a fighter — would be caught in the war between Lenna and the Empire. Lenna would be a danger now, and she couldn't bear to see her aunt suffer with a difficult choice.

Eyes red from her recent cry, Lenna turned and looked to her Ilyan airship captain. His eyes brimmed with curiosity. "What is it, Lenna?"

"Raif, I need to ask a favor."

"Name it."

"I'd like a ride on your airship."

The puzzled expression on Raif's face shifted to one of sheer mischief, and Lenna was gratified to see that annoyingly smug smirk of his.

Jaice appeared visibly relieved at Lenna's selfless request to leave the confines of the Freewoman settlement, but as she scampered about the village making her preparations, Lenna every so often spied the glistening of a tear in the corner of her aunt's eye as the morning sun crested the treetops. She knew that the mayor was losing not just a member of her community but her niece as well. Lenna sighed: there was nothing she could do, not now that the magical wards protecting the forest had fallen at her hand.

For what felt like the eight hundredth time, Pim whined about Lenna's departure, irritatingly loitering by her side. "Why can't I go?" she moaned. "I was plenty helpful last time!"

Last time, Lenna thought, *I didn't have an uncontrollable godlike power at my unconscious disposal.* "With the barriers down and the Empire presumably aware that I've been staying here, Mayor Northen is going to need all able-bodied Freewoman warriors here to help protect the village. We don't know how soon we can expect reinforcements from other settlements."

The mayor had indeed sent out several riders at haste following the previous night's events, but the individual Freewoman settlements were scattered across the Continent; it could take a week or longer for a sizable force — one large enough to at least protect Granemere Forest — to be mounted. With Tranum under Imperial control, all of Ilya would be in disarray, and Lenna doubted that the Krevlum Empire would have launched an attack here without taking precautions concerning her hometown of Port Hollish. The best strategy, then, was for Lenna to leave, and to leave quickly.

Pim frowned, plopping herself down on her bed and beginning what was another link in a long chain of sulking. "But I want to ride on the airship too."

Despite the gravity of the situation, Lenna gurgled with laughter. "Is that it? You're not worried about the future of civilization or your people or even me; you just want to ride on an airship?"

"That isn't what I meant at all!" Pim cried, and launched a pillow at her friend.

The ensuing pillow fight left both Lenna and Pim breathless and their curly hair in even worse disarray than normal. As the girls collapsed on their respective beds, panting, the door to Pim's cottage opened quietly and the tall figure of Raif stepped in. He shut the door behind him as he took in the scene before him, a hint of amusement creasing his lips.

"Looks like I've missed the fun," he said dryly.

Lenna bolted upright, adjusting her spectacles. "Raif! I was just finishing getting ready." The statement was mostly true; Lenna had stuffed her few personal belongings, one of them Gilbert's old cloth rucksack and another a browned, leather-bound book about the history of the Freewomen of Laur, into the sturdy leather backpack Jaice had provided her. Her knife, once her mother's, was strapped to her right thigh. Unlike her previous adventures, Lenna had this time more sensibly decided to wear leather pants with high boots, a belted long muslin shirt, and the deep purple jacket Raif's family had gifted her before she left Tranum. More experienced than a month before, Lenna imagined she'd be far more mobile in trousers than a skirt.

"Remember to take a heavy cloak," Raif reminded her. "The air above will be much, much colder than it is on land, so you'll need the extra warmth."

"I know, I know," she retorted. Actually, she hadn't thought about that, but Lenna had spent most of last night and every waking moment this morning being told by someone what to do. She wanted to feel like she was in control of something despite the chaos around her. She hastily grabbed the onion-scented garment.

"Right," said Raif. "If you're ready, we'll head off to my ship. Pim…" Raif turned to face the short, scowling girl on the other side of the room. "Take care of this village. Lenna needs a home to return to."

After a moment of stuttering, her freckles stingingly poignant on her flushed face, Pim replied, "Of course! And I'll be here, waiting for her!"

Raif beamed and Lenna looked fondly across the room toward her cohort; she was going to miss her amusing outbursts and strange colloquialisms. Through Pim, Lenna had for the first time experienced what she could only describe as the bonds of sisterhood. She stood up, gripped her sheathed sword and tossed it through the air toward Pim, who, despite the emotions clouding her face, dropped the pillow onto the bed and caught the scabbard effortlessly.

"Pim, would you do me the honor?"

"Me? Really?" Pim asked, flabbergasted. After last night's ceremony, it was unnecessary, but Lenna wanted Pim to know she cared for her, and secretly — perhaps selfishly — she hoped that by having her firecracker of a friend gird her, Lenna might receive some of the bold gallantry Pim radiated.

The young warrior's hands were quick and deft, much better than Raif's or Lenna's own. When Pim was done, she embraced Lenna tightly, and Lenna in turn squeezed back with unfamiliar strength and, for the second time in twelve hours, felt her eyes beginning to well with tears. Both women pulled away before either had a chance to start to cry.

"Don't let that prat boss you around too much," Pim announced loudly, "or I'll ride down there and whack him over the head with Old Burt faster than you can say 'chicken-and-feather; pickle-the-weather'!"

Lenna was not sure she would ever say such a thing, but she assured Pim she wouldn't allow herself to be bossed around by anyone. She nodded to Raif, who opened the door to Pim's cabin, and bid her friend a brief farewell: Lenna loathed long goodbyes. Shutting the door behind her, Lenna led Raif toward the meeting hall, next to which was Jaice's cottage, from where they would formally be escorted back to Raif's airship.

"You've changed in the month since I've seen you," Raif commented.

"How so?"

"The Lenna I remember was pretty feisty, but I never picked you as one for roughing it with the Freewomen," he replied.

"It's no Tranum or Port Hollish," Lenna agreed, "but over the past few weeks, this place has started to feel more and more like a home." Lenna mused over her thoughts for a moment. "I wonder if I can ever go back to just being a simple librarian, content with a good book, a warm meal, and a bottle of wine."

"Hmm." Raif's eyes were on the sky; no doubt he was thinking of the voyage ahead. "We'll see. You've changed, but there's still something very 'Lenna' about you. I don't think you'll ever be quite the same, but that's how people grow."

"Grow, huh?" Had time just been standing still for her up until a month ago, when Gilbert appeared on the doorstep of her library?

"One thing's for certain, though," Raif added.

"What's that?"

"You'll always be content when there's a bottle of wine around."

Lenna jabbed him in the ribs with her elbow and hurried on ahead to the gathering hall. She didn't want Raif to hear the clinking of a bottle of Pim's beloved breakfast wine she had secretly stashed in her backpack.

Parting ways with Jaice was welcomely concise; before her people, Mayor Northen would do her best never to show weakness, and indeed quite the crowd had turned up in the town square. Dalm and Chait made more of a fuss over Lenna than her aunt did, and Lenna was inwardly thankful for Jaice's stoicism. She wasn't prepared for any more tearful departures.

"I've sent word ahead, as you requested," Jaice said matter-of-factly. "Though I daresay in Master Vandever's airship, you'll arrive far sooner than my message."

"I've learned it's best to be thorough," Lenna said. "Crossing borders without permission can prove troublesome at times."

Jaice smiled and handed Lenna a writ bearing Jaice's signature and Lenna's name. Lenna folded it and carefully stored it in the inner breast pocket of her coat. "At least," she said coyly, "I'll be traveling as a woman this time." Soft laughter echoed throughout the crowd. The last time Mayor Northen had given Lenna papers for customs officials, Lenna had pretended to be a boy, a ruse that her voice — and bosom — had found extremely problematic.

"I presume, Master Vandever, you have your own documents?" Jaice asked the trader.

"Indeed I do!" He grinned. "Airships bearing valuable goods are always welcome in most places."

Both Jaice and Lenna eyed him dubiously, wondering if he was referring to the Godjewel or to Lenna herself. "Well, with that matter settled," the mayor continued, "I believe you're ready to be on your way, Freewoman Faircloth."

"Thank you for your hospitality, Mayor Northen," Raif said.

"Thanks for everything," Lenna said, rather informally. She clasped arms with Jaice and was surprised by an interrupting embrace from Bahl, which earned him another warning glance from his partner. Lenna and Raif then slowly made their way down the groomed path that led from the settlement out through the forest, toward his airship. Chait was their guide.

"And this flying machine of yours," she remarked to Raif like an overprotective mother, "are you certain it's safe?"

"About as safe as staying in the company of the Freewomen of Laur," he responded cheerfully.

Lenna thanked her lucky stars, the ones she could remember to thank, anyway, that Chait wasn't as prone to violent outbursts as some of her other acquaintances (or even herself, lately) were. The tall Freewoman simply shrugged and led them through the densest of the trees on a practically indiscernible route toward the border. While the scouting parties of the Freewomen might be accustomed to skirting through the overgrowth, Lenna was not; despite her more practical attire she found her large sword whacking trees, Chait, and Raif more often than not. At least, she thought with some peevishness, Chait and the trees didn't swear back at her.

When the trio finally breached the border and stepped out into the plains of Fallowfields, where the rising sun cast a spectacular glare against the snowy ground, Lenna caught her first up-close glimpse of Raif's airship, the *Trilyala*. For a young woman who was fascinated by the schematics of the steamtrain, an airship was a mechanical marvel, and the Vandever family, being of a certain prominence that guaranteed them the finest things the Continent had to offer, had acquired what Lenna regarded as the most beautiful of airships to date.

Of newer construction, the *Trilyala* was sleek and shone silver in the sunlight, its body constructed of a lighter metal alloy as opposed to the wooden airships of earlier generations. It was about the size of one of the larger trading vessels Lenna used to watch docking at Port Hollish, though it required no sails. Indeed, unlike earlier models, the *Trilyala* did not even require the bolstering envelopes filled with gas to rise: a series of rotating propellers mounted at critical points would help the craft achieve the power of flight, and smaller, similar sets at the stern would help control the ship's direction.

Raif jostled his new passenger with his elbow. "Impressive, huh? I knew you'd like it."

Lenna choked on a mouthful of air as she realized Chait and Raif had been staring at her for nigh on a minute. She coughed, making an attempt to regain her composure. "It's very impressive. Elegantly built." Lenna coughed again.

"All right, you two," Chait said. "Let's keep the flirting to a minimum. I'm sure you're eager to be on your way."

Raif clapped Chait on the shoulder, and the steadfast warrior knuckled him back with enough force to make him stumble a few feet. He rubbed his aggrieved bicep and headed off toward the ladder that led to the main deck of the *Trilyala,* muttering something faintly audible about "warrior women" under his breath. Chait took the moment of privacy to turn to Lenna and fix on her a pair of deep chestnut eyes.

"Lenna," she said, "are you certain this is the right choice? We all know Jaice would let you stay… and we would all fight to protect you."

Lenna smiled, unusually touched. "I'm not sure it's the right choice. Who's to say he'll even want me around after the disaster I caused here? But it's the only place I can go now, if I expect to gain any control over this." She waved her gauntleted hand in the air.

Chait frowned. "It's a long journey, but my family hails from there. The people are kind, so you will be safe for some time. But you do know the Empire won't stop, right?"

"Yes. That's why I have to be better prepared the next time they come — so last night doesn't happen again."

Nodding in acceptance, Chait clasped Lenna's arm with her hand. "Be safe. Send word as soon as you can. I'll be waiting. All the Freewomen in Granemere will be waiting."

Lenna promised, and took a deep breath. "All right, Chait. Off I go to Gallas; let's hope Sebastien is ready for his new apprentice."

With that, Lenna spun about on her heel and marched determinedly after Raif toward the *Trilyala*. She was desperately scared of heights but, as she told herself repeatedly, that's why she brought wine.

CHAPTER FIVE

The airship glided smoothly through the clear blue skies of the early winter morning, and the expansive plains of Fallowfields and snow-covered trees of Granemere Forest shrank before Lenna's eyes. Off to the side of the ship, she caught a glimpse of Port Hollish, set solidly against the blue waters of Bonebreaker Bay. Despite the fact that it could be at this very moment under siege by the Krevlum Empire, had she a pen handy, Lenna might have been moved to jot down a poem to try to capture the beauty of her world, miniaturized.

Or so Lenna would later convince herself of her first experience with flight. In reality, it was only when the ship breached a wispy layer of clouds and reached a cruising speed that Lenna, hands white-knuckled against a sturdy railing, finally pried her eyes open. She then saw the diminishing features of the landscape and immediately felt dizzy. Heights were not her specialty. With countless assurances from Raif, who was piloting the ship from inside a glass dome toward the stern, Lenna was convinced to stay on deck (against her will) to get the "full experience" of an airship takeoff. With the cold, wind, and noise from the propellers, all coupled with her fear of heights, Lenna Faircloth's "full experience" was one filled with terror.

On unsteady feet Lenna turned back toward Raif, who cheekily waved at her from beyond the ship's controls. *Bastard,* she cursed inwardly. As if he had heard her thoughts, Raif mimed whistling and did something that made the *Trilyala* cut hard to the right, and Lenna felt her stomach lurch with it. This was the moment they discovered that she suffered from acute airsickness, and Raif's maneuver rewarded him with a deck splattered with Lenna's breakfast.

Shortly thereafter Lenna had been safely installed in a corner of the bridge, encapsulated by its glass dome. Any remaining food in her stomach had long since gone over the side of the ship, and in her moments of lucidity Lenna wondered about the poor farmers or travelers who might have been the victims of an unpleasant shower. She groaned and snuggled into her heavy cloak, ashen and wishing for death.

"Here." Raif's tenor rang out somewhere above her head. He was fawning over the semi-comatose Lenna, looking guilty. He pressed something leafy into her hand.

"What is it?" Lenna replied mournfully.

"*Ghran*," said Raif. "It's a plant we've used for generations to combat nausea, even when we were still caravan traders. It's called saving-grace in Continental."

Lenna was familiar with the herb: her job at the library afforded her the opportunity to acquire more than her fair share of useful, if varied, knowledge. Saving-grace had long been used by the sailors and fishermen in Port Hollish; the lore behind the name suggested that its efficacy at combating seasickness made the men safe from their wives' wrath should they not provide a stable livelihood in a port town. Lenna also recalled under the plant's entry in the encyclopedia of plants a line about saving-grace's effectiveness as an abortifacient, and she wondered if its name had a connection to that use as well.

Barring any divine intervention on behalf of the Godjewel, Lenna's body currently wasn't hosting anything other than airsickness and a few grudges, so she figured eating the herb couldn't make her feel any worse. She took the leaf and stuffed it into her mouth. Once she began to chew, a strangely astringent taste coated her palate: she recalled a bitter concoction a homely innkeeper named Joranne had prepared a very hungover Lenna about a month ago. *So this was the strange flavor in that remedy,* Lenna recalled as she chewed dutifully. The plant was fibrous, and with each gnash of her teeth its gummy extract trickled down Lenna's throat. After a few minutes of tenacious jaw work, the nausea subsided enough for Lenna to stand.

"Back with me, then?" a cheery Raif asked. "*Ghran* fixes even the worst of us."

Lenna, not having to worry about Freewoman gossip for the first time in several weeks, leaned against the lanky pilot at the wheel, trying to look directly forward so that the passing clouds did not summon another bout of nausea; she was uncertain how long this *ghran* would be effective. Unused to so intimate an action from Lenna, Raif coughed, shifted his stance a little, and began to prate on about the mechanisms and controls for the airship.

"This can be used to adjust the altitude," he said nonchalantly, indicating some kind of lever.

Lenna was barely paying attention, half her mind focused on keeping her stomach under control and the other half juggling various questions. "Raif," she inquired, "why were you the only airship able to escape Tranum?"

Her friend ceased his commentary and went back to steering, and Lenna finally established a sense of equilibrium against the rocking of the floor. "Well," he responded, "the *Trilyala* is designed for speed and to operate with a skeleton crew. Even with one pilot and an engineer, it's possible to launch in minutes."

"And because it's so light and agile, it's probably one of the fastest craft in the air?"

"I'd bet my life on it."

"And it stays so fast because of its construction and because it doesn't carry much in terms of crew or, I suspect, weapons."

Raif frowned. "None of the airships in Ilya are armed at the moment, Lenna. We use them for trade and transportation. With the *Trilyala*'s speed, we'll be in Eran Point in a few hours."

"Don't you think it's funny that the Krevlum Empire would attack other airships, hurl lightning at buildings, but let Ilya's prized flagship… just take off?"

"What are you suggesting, Lenna?" Raif tugged on his ponytail in what Lenna had come to recognize as a gesture of irritation. "That this is all a meticulously orchestrated trap?"

Lenna took a glance at her timepiece, lovingly crafted by her father, Thane. Though she took pride in keeping it in excellent condition, a small crack had appeared on the watch's faceplate. Miffed, Lenna said, "I'm not sure, but as of late I've learned that serendipitous encounters are seldom as serendipitous as they seem." She rubbed idly at the scratch in the glass, but it was etched too deeply to be buffed out. The plate would need to be replaced.

One hand still on the wheel, Raif slid another lever and Lenna felt a surge of speed. She buckled under the increased momentum and thanked saving-grace for its stomach-steadying properties. Raif braced Lenna against the speed of the *Trilyala*. "I'll get you to Gallas safely, Lenna," he promised. His expression was dark and grim, and Lenna suspected Raif knew more than he let on.

"Oddly enough, I'm fairly certain you'll do just that." She glanced once more at her cracked timepiece. *I'm not so certain I'll get you safely there.*

Raif looked at her curiously. "Are you feeling all right?"

Lenna shrugged. "Resigned, I suppose. May I see the engines?"

The pilot pointed a long finger toward a door at the back of the bridge. "Through the door and down the ladder; Lazarz is our engineer. He's a bit of a unique character, which is why I left him behind on the ship. Thank goodness Jaice didn't blow it up."

"Your concern for your comrades is remarkable," Lenna replied flatly and headed in the indicated direction, but not before catching a glimpse of the deep, worried frown cockling Raif's face.

If Lenna's stomach had a say in the decision, it would have chosen to remain behind on the bridge. On the lower deck, among the stuttering and rocking of the *Trilyala*'s engines, airsickness swiftly resumed its advance and the saving-grace was proving less efficacious by the minute. Still, Lenna was curious about the workings of an airship, and she could not, considering recent events, presume to think she'd have an opportunity to witness them firsthand again. Determined to ignore her raging insides, Lenna hopped off the ladder, boots emitting a satisfying clack as she landed on the metal deck.

Immediately, as if responding to a war cry, a head sprung up from behind a long, plated length of piping, about waist high. This head was coated in an explosion of white-blonde hair, frizzy as though it had been the victim of a lightning strike, or at least in the immediate vicinity of one. A pale Ilyan man hopped up and over the piping, dressed in overalls and greasy gloves, and scurried up to a bemused Lenna. He barely reached her chin, a rarity for her, since she was accustomed to being shorter than most Ilyans.

"You must be Vanny's new girlfriend!" the man exclaimed and grasped both of Lenna's hands, shaking them with sticky gusto.

"Vanny?" Lenna asked, a little shaken. She broke free and wiped her hands on her leather trousers, hoping to shed some of the grease.

"Master Vandever, of course." The short man grinned. "The crew calls him 'Vanny.'" He paused for a few seconds. "Though I'm the only crew at the moment."

"You must be... Lazarz?" Lenna guessed. She was uncertain as to whether or not the man was right in the head.

"The one and only! The best airship engineer in all of Ilya!"

"And so, the best airship engineer in all the world."

Beaming like a schoolboy praised by his headmaster, Lazarz once again took Lenna's hand in one greasy mitt and pulled her toward the engines. "Vanny said you're something of a bookworm and would want a proper tour once you stopped spewing up your guts," he explained.

As tactfully as possible, Lenna removed her hand once more from the puzzling engineer's grasp, stepping besides rows of piping-hot, steam-pumping vents and various other mechanical contraptions that seemed alive with a loud, deep humming that reminded her of the Godjewel. Her father would love to witness all of these parts working in motion, each finely tuned to make the impossibility of flight something obtainable to man. Lenna was fascinated, despite Lazarz's insane chittering.

"My name is Lenna, by the way," she added. "And I'm not 'Vanny's' new girlfriend."

"Sure, sure," said Lazarz. He was adjusting a valve with a wrench that looked far too big for him to handle. "Turn that knob on the thermoregulator all the way to the right, please."

Lenna adjusted her spectacles and surveyed a wide panel of buttons and dials in front of what she assumed was the device in question. She'd read enough about airships to be somewhat acquainted with their operation, but that didn't mean Lenna was anywhere near proficient enough to start adjusting settings on them. She turned her gaze expectantly toward the little mechanic, who had stopped his work to regard her.

"Well?" he asked.

"I don't know which knob you mean."

"You're something of a mechanist, right? Use your intuition."

Frowning, Lenna took a second glance at the panel before her. Many of the triggers and switches were labeled clearly in Ilyan, but they were words Lenna was unfamiliar with, probably technical terms. Her left hand reached for a knob toward the middle of the panel that Lenna supposed could possibly control whatever a thermoregulator was. She turned the knob all the way to the right and hoped she hadn't just plotted them on a course straight to the ground.

"Ha!" whooped Lazarz.

Startled, Lenna hopped back a few paces and raised her hand to her face, waiting for something to explode. After a moment or two she lowered her arm, looking between a giggling engineer and the panel she had just fiddled with. Red with humiliation, Lenna had a strong desire to spit her wad of saving-grace straight into Lazarz's wild hair. The spritely man, still bubbling with glee, scuttered up to the panel and tapped it with his wrench.

"Silly Fallowfieldian girl!" he said. "This isn't the thermoregulator."

"How should I know what one is?" Lenna responded, exasperated and indignant. "And more to the point, why would you have someone who has *no* idea what she's doing handle such a delicate object?"

Lazarz pointed his wrench at Lenna's gauntlet. "Isn't that what you're already doing?"

Lenna uncurled her fist and looked into the depths of the Godjewel in her palm. She had no idea how much information Lazarz possessed regarding her situation, but Lenna still felt like she was being chastised. What indeed was she doing but playing around with powers beyond her comprehension? Throw in the dashing airship pilot, and she was practically a walking work of trashy fiction. And even with plenty of people willing to help, she still felt like this burden was uniquely hers to bear, and the more involved her friends became, the more she wanted to keep it to herself, solve the problem by herself. Lenna shook her head.

"Trust Vanny," Lazarz said. "He really is the best airship pilot in the world, and an especially nice guy to boot. I mean, who else would give a job to a crazy little man like me?"

Lenna laughed in spite of herself. "I suppose you're right; I should trust him more. Thank you, Lazarz, for the tour of the engine room." Perhaps it was time for Lenna to confide more to Raif and, hopefully, ascertain some answers to the queries budding in her mind.

Nodding his head so that the wispy strands of his hair became a great blonde cloud, Lazarz ushered Lenna off using his wrench as a cattle prod, back toward the ladder leading to the bridge. All the while, he muttered about being overworked and underpaid for all he was meant to do on this needy airship of Vanny's.

Lenna placed her right foot on the first rung of the ladder and paused. Turning back to consider the engineer, whose eyes didn't seem quite so delirious as before, she asked, "Lazarz, what did that knob do?"

"It dumped the contents of the latrine," he replied in a grave tone.

"Where's the thermoregulator, then?"

"How should I know? I don't think they exist. Maybe they do. Sounds like they'd come in handy; Vanny's hell-bent on flying at full speed for you!"

Nodding, Lenna climbed back up to the bridge, perversely conjecturing how many people today had been on the receiving end of an unpleasant jettisoning at her hand.

"You have an interesting crewman there, Vanny," Lenna commented as she reentered the bridge. Raif was staring forward, watching the clouds pass by.

"I told you Lazarz is unique," he replied offhandedly, "but he's quite the mechanical genius. We all have our quirks."

"Raif." Lenna approached the steering console. "Did you know about the impending attack on Tranum?"

The pilot crooked his head to face Lenna, his glassy eyes assessing the woman to his side. He sighed. "Yes. I had received word that it was to happen. I took care to make sure my family was protected and had Lazarz prep the ship to launch a few hours before the attack began."

"Then you weren't there when it happened," Lenna said. "How do you know it truly fell?"

Raif didn't reply at first, but adjusted the same lever that Lenna deduced manually monitored the speed of the craft. Then he said, "I have reliable information."

Lenna felt annoyance creep up on what was, she thought, a proactive mood. After all, she was the one hauling around a stone worth the whole of the Continent to a certain power-hungry emperor. "Who, Raif?"

"That stuffy snob from the Brotherhood I'm taking you to."

"Sebastien? *You've* been in touch with Sebastien?" She pushed the frames of her spectacles up the bridge of her nose, ready for an argument. "So while I've been off, ignorant in my forest, you two have been planning all sorts of schemes…"

Raif activated a clamp to keep the steering mechanism in place and spun to face Lenna directly. "What would you have had me do? It's not like I could just stick a letter in the post and send it off to Granemere Settlement to discuss battle strategies with you." His face and lips were pale with frustration.

Good, Lenna thought, feeling a bout of righteous anger welling up in her chest. "That's one of the reasons I specifically had Jaice arrange for a courier! You could have said something, sent some kind of word!"

The pilot twiddled with his ponytail. "You don't think that Jaice has direct control over what letters leave — and arrive in — her village?"

Surely he wasn't suggesting that the mayor, Lenna's aunt, was manipulating her personal communications with the outside world. That Jaice Northen wanted to keep the Godjewel protected safely behind the wards of the village — the ones Lenna and the bloody stone had managed to shatter in an instant — was no secret, but Raif and Sebastien were on Lenna's side, and they all shared the same goal: to keep the Godjewel away from the Krevlum Empire and the Blue Crescent Brotherhood. Her aunt would surely allow them counsel with her.

Raif sighed. "I don't know what your aunt's motives are; the Freewomen of Laur are as secretive as the Brotherhood. Sebastien was certain his messages were being screened; how he knew, I'm not sure. I imagine it was some kind of magical tracking." He shrugged. "So he contacted me and I responded. He seemed to think a need might arise to get you out of Granemere quickly, though why he'd want me to stop searching for that little bastard Luc is beyond me, especially with you tucked safely away. But it looks like his information was right. I received word of the impending attack and followed the plan we'd discussed to extract you, although a bit sooner than expected."

Lenna's brain fired up an unpleasant thought. All those letters she had sent to her father in Port Hollish, yet not a single response. Had Jaice been deliberately withholding messages Thane had been sending to Lenna? She could feel her anger surge and the leather straps of her gauntlet grow taut as she squeezed her hand over the Godjewel. An oppressive cloud of lavender invaded the covered bridge and Lenna began to feel her heart beating with anxiety, her control starting to slip.

Suddenly the lavender smell in the air dissipated and was replaced with the fragrance of freshly washed linen. Raif placed one hand on Lenna's shoulder and let his magic coax the blue, angry tide of the Godjewel back into calmer seas. Lenna found her breaths slowly synchronizing with his and, after a moment, her anger — and the raw power behind it — vanished. She sighed.

Raif removed his hand from Lenna and said, "That's better; thank goodness my magic returned as soon as we left the borders of the forest. We don't want a repeat of last night."

"I don't understand it, Raif," Lenna said, her voice shaky. "It's like the Godjewel almost *encourages* me to get angry, to use its power..."

"The stronger your connection to the gem grows," Raif replied, "the more easily it will respond to sudden changes in your emotions. It's a huge amount of power for you to constantly be damming, which is why we're going to Sebastien, to see if he can teach you better control."

"But that isn't the only reason."

"No," Raif said grimly.

"Will you tell me, or do I have to attempt to explode the bridge again?"

"Neither Sebastien nor I know any reason why, but there's been some indication that there has been communication between Granemere Settlement and the Embassy of the Blue Crescent Brotherhood in Port Hollish."

Lenna sucked air in through her teeth, momentarily gobsmacked. "Jaice would never conspire with the Brotherhood; she *hates* them."

"I agree with you in that regard," the pilot remarked and disengaged the clamp on the wheel. "But it looks like some Brotherhood forces are gathering in the waters outside of Port Hollish, and the Empire already has established a presence in Fallowfields."

"Leaving Granemere Settlement — and the Godjewel — right between them."

"So Sebastien and I thought it best to extract you before it was too late. I was hoping my coming directly would be enough to convince you, but unfortunately the Empire decided to make an appearance as well."

The inside of Lenna's head buzzed with conflicting thoughts. Large parties were operating based on motivations not entirely disclosed, tossing Lenna about like some tiny rowboat caught in the wake of wide ships. She had fled to Granemere Settlement for refuge; now she was fleeing it much as she had fled her hometown of Port Hollish a month ago. Were all these different factions manipulating events so that Lenna ended up right where they wanted her, or was the will of the Godjewel influencing the threads of fate around her for some unknown reason?

"Raif," she said, "I need some air. I'll be outside on the deck."

"I pity any travelers below," he replied, and Lenna slammed the door shut behind her, stepping out into a snapping wind that tousled her wavy hair.

The nation of Gallas sped past Lenna, the mountainous region dotted by verdant valleys and cut by numerous snaking rivers. Where the valleys fell, so did settlements and towns, some thriving on orchards of the exotic fruits Lenna would get from the markets in Port Hollish; others probably dedicated to producing the rich fabrics and silks for which Gallas was famous. Unlike other nations, where the populations mostly gathered in a prominent city and its immediate environs, Gallas's population was still spread out. Though the terrain was harsh in some areas, Gallasian people loved their land and chose not to flock to the city of Eran Point, the site of the harbor and airship port, the administration, and the University that, years ago, Lenna had dreamed of attending.

But Lenna could not enjoy the view from the airship. Her heavy brooding was noticeably stronger than both her fear of heights and her airsickness, and so she leaned, heart and head heavy, on folded arms up against the rail of the deck. As they traveled further south toward Eran Point, the temperature gradually warmed as well, the winter winds not having found their way to Gallas yet. Lenna, in a moment of gratuitous self-indulgence, considered tossing the Godjewel over the side of the ship. *Let someone else deal with this rock,* she thought bitterly.

What connection was there between Jaice and her band of Freewomen, the Blue Crescent Brotherhood, and even Lenna's father? Despite the fact that Jaice had been upset when Lenna's mother, Alanna, had chosen to leave Granemere Settlement and marry Thane Faircloth, Lenna could discern no clear reason why her aunt would deliberately withhold letters from him. Matters she thought she had resolved, or at least come to understand, grew much foggier with each cloud the *Trilyala* passed. Lenna remembered Pim and her innocent questions about the Continent and the world beyond; Lenna dreamed of stars whose names she could recall but whose locations she could not find in the night sky.

And magic. Magic returning to the Continent, to people who should have lost the ability before the transition into adulthood. Lenna had been fortunate enough to have Gilbert to teach her the basics of control, but people like Mistress Meeks, an old family friend who maintained an apple orchard outside Port Hollish, who had no such access to help, would be driven insane and ultimately die as their inability to process the power within them ate away at their souls.

Once again, Lenna opened her palm and regarded the Godjewel. With its power, she had leveled an ancient magical barrier and reversed time itself. The gem created a zone that nullified magic in people. Could she, then, use it to help people like Mistress Meeks? She shook out her hair in the breeze — Raif was right, it actually was a pleasant feeling — and sighed. If one jewel had this much power, it was no wonder various parties were after all three.

Stretching, she held the gauntlet to the sky. A hint of sunlight struck the orb at just the right angle and sent out a bright blue flash from the stone, across the horizon in an arc. Whether due to the pure blueness of the light, stark even against the sky, or the surprise of its glare, Lenna shut her eyes in pain, feeling as though they had been scorched by the sun's rays. The agony receded almost as quickly as it began, and after a moment she warily opened her eyes to find the world before her a blurry mess of shapes.

Lenna took off her spectacles to clean them, wondering if a wisp of cloud had fogged up the lenses, and gasped in surprise when her vision cleared. Without her glasses she could suddenly see with a piercing clarity, so sharp and focused that she could make out features on humans down below in the valleys of Gallas. Lenna shook her head and once more hooked her spectacles around her ears. Her vision blurred again.

She removed the glasses and scowled at them. Why on earth was her vision suddenly better without the spectacles? It was high time that the Godjewel got a firm talking-to about acting without Lenna's permission, but first she wanted Raif's opinion as to the nature of whatever had just happened. As she drew her gaze back up to the horizon, she spotted a black object she hadn't noticed before. It was massive and bulky, wobbling about like a drunken crow trying to fly. It was steadily approaching, and Lenna had no doubt that it was another airship, but as far as her knowledge went, it wasn't of Ilyan design.

Lenna ran to the aft of the deck, almost hanging over its side. She squinted, urging her amplified vision to make out more details of the approaching craft. There was some movement, yes, and discernible propellers and a gas-filled envelope, probably both required to hoist the behemoth into the air. Then her vision focused on little turrets spiking out of the sides of the ship.

Cannons. The airship was armed, and it was headed straight for the *Trilyala*. With unusual grace, Lenna sprinted straight toward the bridge, waving her arms like a madwoman as she ran.

CHAPTER SIX

Raif pulled a mouthpiece cabled to the console to his lips and, in Ilyan, ushered brisk commands to Lazarz down below in the engine room. Lips pursed, Lenna stared out the glass of the bridge's dome at the hulking black airship. At the *Trilyala*'s current speed and course, assuming Lenna's newly enhanced vision and concept of physics were accurate, the two ships would engage each other within ten minutes or so. Lenna said as much to Raif and inquired what he intended to do.

"There's no way that thing can outrun us," Raif said. "But now that we've been spotted, I doubt we'll be able to shake them off and land without repercussions." He leaned on the steering console, glowering. "Cannons, Lenna. There have been rumors, of course, that the Empire was preparing its own fleet, but nothing concrete." He waved one hand in irritation. "And the sheer size alone! They would have had to dispatch that thing days ago."

Lenna toyed with the sword buckled to her belt, her right hand suddenly itching to draw it. "Are you certain that airship is of Krevlum origin?"

"Well, what else could it be? Gallas wouldn't build something like that monster."

Considering the circumstances, Raif was probably right; Lenna couldn't imagine a peaceful nation such as Gallas constructing a massive warship. No, this had to be the Empire's doing, and it served to prove to Lenna that Emperor Sonnet and his minions were more than aware of her movements and plans. Ironically, she thought to herself while Raif went back to conversing with Lazarz, this made her options clearer. Why should she hesitate if the enemy appeared to already know her entire plan? What if she did something less librarian-like?

"Raif," Lenna began, "they expect us to run, right?"

He craned his neck to one side and answered, "We certainly can't succeed in a firefight against them, so our only course of action is to flee and hide as best we can."

"And that ship isn't likely to be able to maneuver as well as this one, you'd say?"

Raif nodded.

"Then let's be aggressive. Do the unexpected," Lenna said, feeling a bit brave, which itself was something like an unsettling surge of anxiety and eagerness.

The look on Raif's face was, to Lenna, priceless. Not that she could blame him — for the scant time the two had known each other, Lenna had not exactly been one to lead a party to battle — but Lenna so rarely caught the Ilyan at a loss for words that the sight of his jaw dropping made her want to giggle.

"Don't look so smug," Raif said, poking her in the shoulder. "All right. What do you have in mind?"

Lenna placed her hand on the pane of glass separating her from the wind and the enemy airship it carried. "Let's act like the heroes in one of those silly action stories. Go at them, full speed."

"Are you insane? Has the Godjewel scrambled your brain that badly? They'll just shoot us out of the sky."

Casting a glance back over her shoulder, Lenna responded, "Not if the best pilot in Ilya — and the world — outmaneuvered them."

To her surprise, Raif flushed. "Look, Lenna — I'm good, but I'm not sure anyone is that good. One sure shot from any of those cannons could ground us. But…" Raif's mouth puckered as though he were trying to assess the characteristics of a fine wine. "You're right that they wouldn't expect us to charge. If we got up enough speed…" He muttered to himself, his fingers tracing flight paths in the air.

"Raif," Lenna interrupted.

"Hm? Oh, sorry. Right." His smile returned. "So say I get us close. What then?"

"I'm going to use the Godjewel to ignite the gas in their air sack."

As if Raif's expression before hadn't amused Lenna enough, his current countenance would have had her on the floor, clutching her stomach in laughter, were she not in better command of her faculties. His slightly slanted eyes widened to two huge white pools and he coughed so vehemently he may as well have been choking on some kind of noxious gas. After the fit subsided, he blinked thrice and stared at his friend with the most serious expression Lenna had seen since he had lost his family's Godjewel.

"Lenna, Empire or not, there are people on that ship. Are you really prepared to kill them?"

Looking down at the Godjewel and remembering last night, Lenna believed she knew what she was capable of. Raif might not realize it, but by unleashing that horrible deluge of power and resetting time itself, she had effectively erased — killed — the Raif that had been present with her in the aftermath of the massacre of her friends. This Raif might act the same, look the same, but in the back of her mind he was somehow different from the Raif who had existed beside her up until the moment she unleashed her magic. With the power behind that stone, Lenna had changed countless lives already; her course was set the moment Gilbert bequeathed her the Godjewel.

"I'm prepared to live," she answered.

Raif nodded, picked up the speaking device, and began issuing a hurried explanation to Lazarz.

Minutes later, Lenna found herself at the bow of the *Trilyala*, tapping her fingers against the hilt of the curved blade sheathed at her waist. *War comes to all Freewomen,* she thought grimly, recalling the words scribed in the leather-bound text she had "liberated" from her library and Pim's usage of the phrase. But was she truly a Freewoman? A month roughing it and some slapdash training didn't exactly transform a dormouse into a warrior. And, considering what Raif had said about Jaice and her possible treachery, did Lenna even want to be a Freewoman at all?

The black airship drew closer, its presence an unwelcome blemish against the sun. It would be in range within minutes, and Lenna's decision was beginning to become yet another unwelcome burden. Still, she was at a crossroads; Lenna would either have to stand and fight or run forever (or at least until she was killed). She groaned. Though she was no expert at airship engineering, in her stone-heavy heart she harbored a secret hope that the destruction of the air sack would cripple, not destroy, the ship and its pilot would somehow orchestrate a safe crash landing.

"Second thoughts, partner?" a manic voice behind her twittered. Lenna jumped and spun around, shifting her line of sight downward into the glistening eyes of the *Trilyala*'s engineer. He grinned so intently it bordered on a leer.

"Lazarz!" exclaimed Lenna. "What are you doing up here? Shouldn't you be down below, maintaining the engines?"

The short man stood on tiptoe and peered over the rail of the bow. "We've got a few minutes yet. How're your eyes?"

Lenna blinked. Barely any time had passed since she had announced her plan, and she didn't think Raif would bother to disclose the very brief details Lenna had shared with him even if he had had the opportunity — especially since neither she nor Raif understood what had caused Lenna's sudden optical advantage anyway. "They're fine, thank you."

"Your glasses," Lazarz explained, "they're hanging from your jacket."

Of course, thought Lenna. In her haste and for lack of a better place to store her spectacles, she had hooked the frames to the collar of her long coat. The Godjewel's powers were anything but predictable: how long this boon, if she could call it one, would last was indeterminable. Lenna wanted to be able to see should her eyesight suddenly return to being that of a ninety-year-old woman.

Lazarz cupped his hands over Lenna's gauntlet. "You know, you don't *have* to do this. It'd be a waste of good technology and parts and people and people-parts."

She considered the queer little man. "What would you suggest we do instead?"

He grinned and began shaking her hand with mad fervor. "Teleportation! The lost magic of transference! A miracle of science!"

Aghast, Lenna stepped back from the engineer, breaking his grasp. She didn't think even Raif knew that much about the gem's power to move people through space as well as time, and even if he did, Lenna strongly doubted he would tell a member of his crew. Lazarz continued to smile benignly in Lenna's direction, sight trained on her left hand. His eyes were watery and maniacal, almost ravenous.

"Who are you?" she asked.

"Lazarz," the engineer answered calmly. He took a single, deliberate step toward Lenna, and she responded by placing her right hand on the hilt of her new blade.

"A sword? What good will it be against *that*?" Lazarz pointed one of his fingers toward the approaching airship. "It might be slow compared to the *Trilyala*, but it's got four cannons and a crew complement of twenty-two at the moment. And they aren't your friends! Stay true; stick with me and Vanny!" He skipped about on his feet, a sprite dancing in a fairy circle. "Team Laz-Len! Len-Laz? Team L?" He broke off into indecipherable mumbling.

"How do you know so much about that ship?" Lenna asked, doing her damnedest to keep her voice flat and unemotional. Both she and, Lenna feared, the Godjewel were growing very suspicious of the odd mechanist; Lenna did not want to risk another incident like the one last night, fueled by uncontrolled feelings.

"It is called the *Talonstrike*," he expounded grandly, arms wide.

"A silly name at best. It's one of the Empire's secret weapons. It's even equipped with some experimental technology, like the giant crackler in its hull."

"A crackler?" Little goosebumps prickled the flesh on Lenna's arm. An airship that could rain lightning down on villages and cities would be an almost invincible enemy. Lenna cringed as she imagined her library being obliterated by one mighty strike from the flying death machine. Only Freewoman settlements with wards and possibly the mages back on Crescent Island would be able to either withstand or counter such an assault. Lenna felt her resolve harden.

Over the roar of wind and the airship's propellers, a muffled voice called out. "Lazarz!" Raif yelled. "Back in here! Time to punch it!"

"You got it, Vanny!" the mechanist called back, offensively cheerful. He began to skip back to the bridge.

"Lazarz, wait!" Lenna grabbed the engineer's arm. "Tell me why you know so much about that ship."

He spun about, shaking off Lenna's grip in the process, and clicked his tongue at her. "For a member of Team L, you're remarkably uninformed," he said seriously. "Of *course* I know about the *Talonstrike*. I'm the one who designed it!"

Lenna gaped as her determination melted away in a sickly sense of violation. Why the hell was the designer of an Imperial airship — a machine to kill — acting as an engineer on Raif's *Trilyala*? More importantly, did Raif know? Was he, too, keeping things from her? She could only watch in dismay as the small man flitted down the length of the deck and entered the bridge, briefly chatting with the pilot before heading back down into the engine room.

She shook her head; it appeared, Lenna thought jadedly, that she was due for another one of those weeks, the kind that start with angry geese and lecherous Ilyan men. She supposed one might substitute Lazarz's strange actions for a goose (he was very bizarre and inclined, it seemed, to shocking acts of randomness), and it was probably more than fair to write Raif off as lecherous.

All right, Lenna, she told herself firmly, *you should be used to this sort of thing by now. Let's start making good on promises.* She thought of Gilbert and, as the warship drew closer, she knew it was time to leap into action.

A smart salute from Lenna signaled to Raif that she was ready. He nodded and Lenna, with her improved vision, studied the unreadable blank surface of his face. It reminded her of the time when Pim, normally crackling with enthusiasm, had shifted handily into warrior mode to confront a trio of thugs pillaging the countryside of Fallowfields.

The *Trilyala* sped up: the roar of the engines crescendoed and Raif leveled the bow with the advancing metal heap that was the *Talonstrike.* Holding her breath, Lenna braced herself against the port side of the hull. Built into the framework of the ship, under the rail, was a series of belts and restraints made from some flexible material.

Lenna looped a section of the fabric around her waist and slipped up the metallic buckle from the rail to secure it around herself. Experimenting, she leaned forward to test the tension on the line; as Lenna moved away from the hull, the belt tightened and pulled her back up to a standing position. The buckle should prevent any more of the fabric from loosening, at least as far as Lenna could be a judge of such things. Hopefully, the restraint would keep her safe, but considering she was about to engage a flying war machine with a magical artifact she could hardly control, her concern regarding the harness only extended so far. She raised her left hand, indicating her preparations were complete.

Whatever magic had imbued Lenna's eyes with enhanced sight had bolstered her body's other defenses as well. When Raif aggressively dipped the *Trilyala,* the expected revolt from her stomach never came: the Godjewel — or maybe Lenna's own adrenaline — was blocking any airsickness. Her balance was steady and confident, and she braced herself on the hull with her right hand. Palm open, she held her other hand before her, exposing the blue stone. *Here we go.*

As she squinted, Lenna's vision narrowed and fantastically sharpened its focus. Raif coaxed the *Trilyala* into a disconcertingly fast route directly toward the meaty bulk of the *Talonstrike* and Lenna could begin to distinguish individuals on its main deck. Dressed in the typical white uniforms of the Krevlum Empire, a combination of men and women bustled about, some appearing to ready the cannons Lenna had spied minutes ago. Raif, as per Lenna's instructions, was taking them straight toward the firing lines, presumably on a crash course. Noticing the *Trilyala*'s sudden plunge, several of the crew began shouting in the direction of what appeared to be the *Talonstrike*'s bridge.

The *Trilyala* bolted forward, and despite the Godjewel's magical buffering Lenna's stomach plummeted with the tilting of the deck and the tightening of the restraint around her waist. Her hair, still not fully grown out from its uninspired trim last month, tumbled back behind her as the cool breeze became a harsh, constant gale. With the increased speed, Lenna would have only seconds to make her move before Raif would have to maneuver the smaller airship out of the *Talonstrike*'s way. Searching deep within herself, as her friend Gilbert had taught her, Lenna found the secret tome that was her magic.

She shut her eyes and it unfurled its pages before Lenna, and everything around her — the rushing of the wind, the scampering crew on the *Talonstrike* — seemed to halt. Lenna floated in the dark recesses of her unconscious, and before her a flaming sphere of power pulsed in rhythm with her heartbeat. Manipulating the energy with an invisible hand, she coaxed a tendril of essence away from her core and fed it with motherly gentleness to the awesome pervasiveness of the Godjewel.

The gem responded in kind. It accepted Lenna's magic readily and she tingled throughout her body, limb to limb. A bubble of power encapsulated her thoughts and pushed Lenna's consciousness away from the smooth surface of the *Trilyala*'s deck and down, deep into an unconscious network of interwoven threads. Along the threads appeared rapidly blinking pulses of light, spiraling downward in a mind-warping phantasmagoria.

Lenna had been here once before, this dark, psychic realm, and had almost lost her soul in its limitlessness. She had not intended to come back again.

You, a voice echoed across the plane. It was a tight and controlled voice, like the chinking of ice against a crystal tumbler.

Who's there? Lenna's own voice came across far more confidently than she intended. What was this strange presence? A shadowy concept brushed against the borders of Lenna's mind, a consciousness that was slick and oily. She felt sullied.

So this is the site of our third and final battle, the voice harped at her. It was taking on a decidedly female pitch, and Lenna shrank away from its infringing blackness. She had heard this voice somewhere before, and its grave severity threatened to pull her down into the deepest recesses of her mind, so far away that she might never return.

Lenna reached out for the one person she felt certain would hear her call, as he had before. *Seb,* she implored with her mind, seeking that one pinpoint of light among thousands that represented the mage who had offered to train her in the ways of the Godjewel. Would she find him again?

The other consciousness must have sensed her pleas, because from the corners of Lenna's mind's eye she could almost see a jittering movement, something chortling with amusement. It mocked her, made her feel that her efforts at reaching out into the darkness for a source of friendship were nothing more than the actions of a helpless child. *You cannot be saved,* it said.

But the voice didn't know Lenna as well as it seemed to think, for if it had truly understood the headstrong librarian, it would realize the one surefire way to motivate Lenna was to tell her what she *couldn't* do. *Sebastien Branford!* Her mental shout echoed throughout the void, and Lenna could feel the slimy existence of her enemy shrink back at the might of her psychic emanation.

A rush of wind battered Lenna, both physically on the deck of the airship and magically in the unconscious realm. On the sudden gust she could sense her own magic, a strong, floral scent of lavender, but it was mixed with another fragrance. She easily recognized the aroma of clove and citrus — Sebastien — but there was an undercurrent of something delicate, a flower Lenna knew well: a lily.

No, her enemy called.

Open your eyes, Lenna, said Sebastien's voice. She could feel his presence now: it was open, direct, and highly sensual. Lenna let the warmth of his consciousness embrace her, and she could almost feel the reassuring strength of his arms wrapped around her body. *Go,* Sebastien commanded, and he pushed.

No! The slimy clutches of darkness that had been slowly invading Lenna's mind were ripped away and Lenna felt her will rise upward, out of the spiraling collection of souls, up through the layers of her mind. A spurt of light flashed from the Godjewel and Lenna was once again fully present on the deck of the *Trilyala,* strapped to the bulkhead by the bands of strange material. The *Talonstrike* loomed precariously close to their position, and Lenna thought she could hear Raif shouting in the distance, his cries barely carrying over the bellowing engines and propellers.

Her connection with the Godjewel was firm, and Lenna's physical senses sharpened to the point where the creaking of the *Trilyaya*'s plating reverberated in her bones. As her heartbeat accelerated in excitement, the gem pulsed in a perfectly syncopated rhythm. Squinting against the light of the sun, Lenna pulled on more of the Godjewel's power, focusing it on the thronged deck of the Krevlum airship. Toward the rear of the *Talonstrike*'s bridge Lenna, with her augmented vision, could now make out the officer to whom the soldiers were calling. She let out a gasp as she put a face to the cold telepathic voice. Garbed in a military dress uniform so starched that it barely moved despite the wind, with long straight hair flying, was a person that simply should not have existed. A demonic smirk of desire decorated the woman's ivory face.

"General Khareen Valant," Lenna Faircloth shouted, her voice amplified by the magic of the Godjewel. "To our final encounter indeed!"

Lenna was filled with smug satisfaction at the look of genuine surprise from the general, one that quickly shifted into a grimace. Valant should be dead; Lenna had seen for herself the exploded body soiling a warehouse floor in Tranum. As she returned Lenna's piercing glare, the general tucked her hair back with both hands, revealing two perfect ears, when Lenna knew by rights there should only be one.

Furor rose to the forefront of Lenna's thoughts. The bulbous bag of gas providing the main support for the *Talonstrike*'s flight welled before her, reminding Lenna of the oppressive clouds that chased her, Gilbert, and Luc across the snowy plains of Fallowfields. She let the rage course through her veins, and unknowingly she found the hilt of her curved, long blade in her right hand, drawn and at the ready.

She focused, letting her gauntleted hand curl around the pommel as well. Energy flowed freely into the weapon, and its silver-sure blade flashed blue, reflecting Lenna's fury. "I hope you've enjoyed the new ear, witch," she said, and swung the sword aloft in one great, sweeping arc.

Lenna awoke with her head on something pillowy and wondered if she had either had too much wine or been slammed up against a heavy cement wall — again. Her head throbbed and her vision was blurry, and when she attempted to move a queasiness even worse than airsickness overtook her body. "Glug," she said.

"Steady now," said the familiar voice of Raif. "You're pretty weak at the moment."

"I can't see," Lenna said.

With fingers more delicate that Lenna would have imagined from such a scamp, Raif slipped her spectacles back onto the bridge of her nose and the world sharply snapped into focus. Apparently, whatever magical enhancement the Godjewel had provided to her vision had worn off. Sight restored, Lenna realized she was lying face up, looking at the concerned face of a certain ponytailed Ilyan and the deep blue Gallas sky. "It really is going to be another one of those days," she deadpanned. "What did I do this time?"

"It was all very elegant, considering your normal method of operations," Raif responded. He rose from his squatting position beside her and offered a hand. "Get up slowly."

Accepting Raif's firm grip, Lenna allowed herself to be pulled to her feet, even though the world around her, a rolling meadow blanketed in lush green grass and heather, was still a touch rattletrap. If Lenna was not being tracked by numerous enemies at the moment, or at least not suffering from a magical hangover, she would have found the countryside quite enchanting. It reminded her of the idyllic Fallowfields of her youth, before gems and generals and death had found their ways into her life.

Across the meadow rested Raif's *Trilyala,* cozied up in a quaint dimple between two small hills and looking no worse for wear at having just dodged a collision with an Imperial warship. Its polished, metallic frame glittered in the sunlight like a bit of silver among the silt of a riverbank. It looked tremendously outlandish against the backdrop of Gallas's natural beauty, but, considering the insanity of Lenna's day thus far, she found herself strangely comfortable with its presence. *Welcome to Gallas,* she told herself.

Raif coughed with purpose and Lenna drew her attention back to him. He looked eager to explain the outcome of their plan, though Lenna's curiosity was far from genuine; anger, blue fire, and subsequent unconsciousness on her part usually meant that she had just done something she would most likely not be proud of. She huffed and nodded at Raif as if to tell him to get on with it.

"You're really something," Raif said. "You used that new sword of yours to direct a strong bolt of force straight toward the *Talonstrike.*"

Lenna twirled a bit of curl around one of her fingers, scowling. She recalled furiously raising the sword at the sight of Khareen Valant, the bloodthirsty general of the Krevlum Empire who had attempted to take not just the Godjewel but Lenna's and her friends' lives as well. But Valant should be dead: Lenna had used her magic to set the general's clothing ablaze (and a good portion of Lenna's own hair, as well) and Pim, bless her, had dispatched Valant rather messily with a blast from Old Burt, her blunderbuss.

"And then what?" asked Lenna.

"I know you were aiming for the air sack, but I'm glad you didn't hit it. There would have been some massive damage done to that ship, and I would hate for you to have to live with that much death on your hands." Raif was wringing his hands, and Lenna wondered if his flight from Tranum — leaving so many of his fellow Ilyans behind — weighed more heavily on his shoulders than he let on.

"Raif," she said, "just tell me what I did."

"That attack of yours went straight toward the deck and cut through that massive blimp's hull like a... well, like that sword of yours would go through a loaf of bread. It severed a good quarter of the ship right off, the aft section. The soldiers had, as luck would have it, scrambled away, though."

After Lenna's devastating burst of magic sliced off a chunk of the *Talonstrike,* Raif explained further, its crew panicked as the warship became dreadfully unbalanced. Being an expert in all things flying, Raif took the opportunity to navigate the *Trilyala* away from the buckling zeppelin at full speed as it slowly began to descend to the Gallasian countryside. He had managed to put miles between the two vessels before he landed here in this field.

"I don't remember any of that," Lenna said.

Raif scratched at a bit of blonde stubble on his chin, but there was a hint of merriment peeping out from behind his eyes. "You just stood there, really. You didn't move much at all, thanks to the harness. After we were out of harm's way, I came to check on you, and you fainted into my arms."

"Ugh!" Lenna said with warranted disgust. Not only was she suffering from memory loss, but now she was swooning into the embrace of an airship captain. Perhaps she should wear a sash or something similar that displayed how ineffectual she was at being an epic adventurer. "Least Qualified Hero" sounded appropriate.

Raif chuckled. "Don't worry about it. At the very least, you held onto your sword." He jerked his head toward a spot on the grass where the blade lay glistening in the sun. "Had to pry it out of your fingers; you've got quite the grip."

Lenna walked over to the longsword and looked at it in fascination. She had instinctively used it as a focus for her magic, but how had she known how to do that? Keeping her back to Raif, Lenna attempted to sheathe the Freewoman blade as deftly as possible, but as with most things martial it took several attempts to guide it back to safety without any loss of fingers. The cool silver steel slid into Chait's scabbard with a pleasant metallic ringing.

"So what now?" she asked. "How far are we from Eran Point?"

Raif's simpering drooped into something between a pout and a frown. "Not near enough to walk, I'd say. Even if that were a quick option, there's a regrettably banged up *Talonstrike* that will be sending out its crew in pursuit, I imagine."

"Can we fly?"

The pilot shook his head. "I made some pretty nice maneuvers, but I had to push the *Trilyala* hard to get so much speed out of her. The engines will be out of commission for a few hours; Lazarz is doing his best, though."

Lazarz. He knew about the Godjewel and Lenna, and, even more bewilderingly, he had apparently designed the schematics upon which the *Talonstrike* was based. How much of that knowledge, if any, did Raif possess? Lazarz's fascination with the "science" of magic and his inherent understanding of and involvement in the matters concerning the Godjewel immediately set Lenna at edge.

"Raif," she began, "how much do you know about Lazarz?"

"Lazarz? I've known him for years, since before I was even a captain. He's always been closely associated with the Vandever family and is one of the best engineers I've ever met. A lot of the technology in the *Trilyala* is based on his designs."

"He knows about the Godjewel, Raif," Lenna said bluntly. "About what it can do, and he wanted me to try to perform teleportation magic."

If the eldest child of one of the wealthiest families in all the four nations had ever the opportunity to look surprised, this was the moment. Her words were like a slap to him, and Raif rubbed his cheek as though to alleviate the sting. Perhaps Lenna could have been a bit more subtle in her exposition, but in truth she really hadn't benefited much lately from trying to be subtle.

"I've never told him anything, Lenna," Raif assured her. "I swear it."

Lenna nodded, idly fiddling with the straps of her gauntlet. "It's not just that, though. Lazarz says that he's the one who designed the *Talonstrike*."

The silence between the pair was so complete that Lenna fancied she could hear the buzzing of a honeybee forty paces away. Raif regarded her with a face that incorporated every emotion from surprise and indignation to complete disbelief. Perhaps tact wasn't so unnecessary after all. If Lenna could shock Raif, she wondered what effect her words could have on someone with more delicate sensibilities. Then she remembered the cruel words she had spoken to Luc on the night that everything changed, and felt sick with distaste.

Raif opened his mouth to speak, but before he uttered a single syllable, a loud call echoed across the clearing. Lenna and Raif both turned to look in the direction of the *Trilyala,* from which a tiny man was currently scurrying with ant-like purpose. Lenna considered his timing convenient.

"Vanny! Vanny!" Lazarz called. "We've got a visitor requesting permission to board!"

"A visitor?" Raif asked, still stammering from Lenna's claims. A taller figure followed Lazarz, coming up from the crook of the hill at a deliberate, confident pace. The man wore pressed linen trousers and a stylish blouse that hugged his frame with impeccable tailoring. Every now and then, bobbing with his soldierly gait, a blue jewel in his ear flashed blindingly as it caught a sunbeam, reminding Lenna of her own Godjewel.

"In the name of all things natural," Lenna remarked, "what on earth is going on?"

"Hello to you, too, Lenna," Sebastien replied. "Nice magic back there, but a little flashy, don't you think?"

Lenna desperately wished for something — or someone — to punch.

CHAPTER SEVEN

"Shouldn't you be at your estate outside Eran Point?" Lenna and Raif asked more or less simultaneously, though Lenna noted that Raif's tone contained considerably more spleen than hers had.

The mage regarded Lenna and Raif with a blank expression; to him, his actions obviously warranted no explanation. "Shouldn't you be off roughing it with your warrior woman family?" Lenna noticed that Sebastien pointedly didn't mention their very recent psychic contact. Seb swiveled his shoulders and focused on Raif. "And shouldn't you be trying to wrestle your capital city back from the Krevlum Empire?"

Was Sebastien trying to pick a fight? Stepping between the two men as nimbly as possible – she was still not quite accustomed to being girded with such an awkward weapon and did not want to damage anyone's manhood – Lenna placed one hand on each of their chests. She already had her thoughts on the nature of the relationship between Seb and Raif, and Lenna decided it was in her personal best interest to stop any row before it happened.

"Seb, what are you doing here?" she asked. "How could you have known where we landed?" Lazarz bounced off to the side, pensively glancing between Sebastien and Lenna with each shifting of his feet. Lenna made it a point not to show her irritation.

Eyeing the bopping mechanist, Sebastien sighed with pronounced effort and made a show of fixing his already perfectly parted hair. "I happened to be in the area," he said loftily. "And that spectacle in the sky was hard to miss; it's not every day one witnesses an airship battle, let alone one that ends in fireworks."

"If you've been spying on our movements…" Raif began, his face growing red.

"I wouldn't say 'spying,'" came Seb's nonchalant response. "And as I mentioned in our correspondence, I do keep track of Lenna — and the Godjewel — as best I can. That shouldn't come as much of a surprise, considering it was my plan to steal it in the first place. And," he added, "a little appreciation for my continued diligence wouldn't hurt either, in light of recent Krevlum activity."

As much as it made Lenna cringe to consider how many people were actively monitoring her comings and goings, she still felt somewhat relieved Sebastien was aware of the general state of affairs — even if it came loaded with biting comments aimed at Raif. Since it was he who organized the original theft of the Godjewel from the Blue Crescent Brotherhood, it was logical that he was maintaining a vested interest in its whereabouts and its owner. And of all the parties Lenna had consulted, Sebastien had proven the most knowledgeable about the origins of the cursed stone and how to properly use it. She didn't feel quite so alone knowing Sebastien was, for whatever motive, watching out for her.

The grass crunched pleasingly under her feet as Lenna backed away. With any luck — not that this month had been a very lucky one for her thus far — the Ilyan and the Gallasian would refrain from killing each other. Lenna sniffed, with some displeasure, at the petty male rivalry that hung heavy and musky in the air, as it had on the train platform the day she left Ilya, and she felt a pressing need to fill the quietude with some form of distracting chatter, something that would disperse the tension and allow her to ignore the nagging questions at the back of her mind.

"Fine," Raif said after a moment. "So you've been monitoring Lenna. How did you get here so quickly? We've been on the ground all of fifteen minutes. There's no way you could have traveled from your estate to this location in that amount of time."

Lenna frowned at Seb; Raif had a point. By what means could he have arrived at their location so swiftly, even with prior knowledge of events? It wasn't exactly as if Lenna and Raif had planned to confront an Imperial warship and have an emergency landing in the middle of a field. The former Blue Crescent mage was definitely concealing something from her. Suddenly, a lightning bolt of an idea struck Lenna, and she turned to the hyperactive little man at her side.

"Lazarz," she said, catching him in mid-skip. "Do you know how Sebastien arrived here so quickly?"

Blonde hair still in its terrific state of disarray, Lazarz nodded up and down so emphatically Lenna worried he might injure his brain. "Of course I do!" he said adamantly.

"Might it have anything to do with a certain 'lost' miracle of science?"

The mechanist's jittering stopped. Lenna grew convinced the connections she was making were correct; the stony, distant faces of both Lazarz and Seb further proved her assumption. Raif, face blank with confusion, turned his head from Lazarz to Lenna. This confirmed at least that Raif was oblivious to the extent of Lazarz's knowledge about the Godjewels.

"Lenna," Raif began, "what are you talking about?"

Brusquely, Lenna repeated Lazarz's earlier comment, a comment casually made to her on the bridge of *Trilyala*. "A great miracle of 'science,' the 'lost art of transference' — in other words, teleportation." She strode up to face Sebastien, who, to her surprise, looked almost guilty. "You arrived so quickly because you teleported here."

After what felt an eternity, so slow and still that Lenna thought she could feel the green shards of grass beneath her feet growing, Sebastien exhaled and shook his head in her general direction. "At least your brain still appears to be functioning, despite your penchant for putting it in absurdly unhealthy situations. Yes, Lenna, I teleported here. And I am going to teach you how to do it too."

***

Lenna realized, with some relief, that Raif wasn't aware of the means by which she had sought out Sebastien; the strangely easy psychic link they shared had allowed her to find Sebastien yet again during a time of great need, and it was something she treasured. She wasn't completely sure why she kept this topic to herself, but Lenna knew that it was something very private and transcended any words she knew. Her mind also didn't want to confront a fact it was acutely aware of: Raif would be wildly jealous of Sebastien and Lenna's magical bond.

Even though he hadn't outright stated it, Lenna surmised that Sebastien had known her location not just because of the tremendous release of energy that occurred when she had used the Godjewel but because he had helped her fight against the deepening darkness in the chasms between minds. Just as before, Seb had rallied to her defense, protecting her from the miserable cruelty that was Khareen Valant — who had somehow been resurrected and was now hunting Lenna. She shuddered.

Raif briefed Sebastien on the order of events pithily, their conversation punctuated by a nod or two from Sebastien. For his part, Lazarz inserted his fluffy head into the exchange by asking about the methodology behind Sebastien's teleportation magic. Though Lenna was intrigued — and probably Raif too, for that matter — Sebastien brushed aside all questions as though he were politely declining sugar in his tea. Something about his nonchalant dismissal exasperated an already frustrated Lenna. Sebastien was obfuscating some of the facts, such as how he even knew Tranum was about to fall; if she thought she could physically shake those answers out of him, Lenna would be eager to try.

"Well," said Raif, "it's not entirely surprising that the Brotherhood has been keeping yet another magical secret from the rest of the Continent." The pilot shrugged.

Sebastien merely grinned in response. "We all have our secrets, don't we?"

"But how do you compensate for random changes in weather patterns and the various degrees of —" Lazarz began to pester the mage with another question, but Lenna quickly cut him off in the same tone she'd use against an adolescent mistreating one of the books in her library.

"What are we going to do about that rather large Imperial airship we've deposited somewhere in the middle of Gallas?"

All parties turned and stared at Lenna like she had uttered an inappropriate epitaph at a funeral. After a moment Raif turned his eyes skyward, but Sebastien continued to glower at Lenna, and Lazarz attempted to flatten his wild hair. Dealing with this group, Lenna thought, was going to require a persona a bit more forceful than the one she regularly exuded. It simply wouldn't do to faff about in the meadow all day when Khareen Valant was probably plotting the best way to use Lenna's skin as curtains for her barracks, and Lenna hankered to press on.

"Well," Sebastien said, "the Empire is about to find itself in a complicated situation. Gallas is a peaceful nation; more importantly, our commerce and connection to Port Hollish are among the biggest resources a military campaign can hope to have. Krevlum would do well to avoid dragging the conflict here so soon if it wants to make use of Gallasian trade with Fallowfields and the rest of the Continent."

"So a sudden invasion from an obviously militarized airship is not going to go over well with the Gallasian authorities," Lenna deduced.

"Exactly."

"What do we do about the *Trilyala*?"

"I presume that Master Vandever has the appropriate documentation for travel through Gallas's boundaries," said Sebastien, and Raif gave a stiff nod. "Then it's simple: you had an emergency landing. Between his reputation, his documentation, and my connections, this can be quickly explained away to the local authorities, who, if we contact them proactively, will more than likely cooperate with the necessary repairs and, moreover, provide us with a place to dock."

Raif's shoulders drooped; much like Lenna, it appeared Raif did not much care for other people telling him what to do. "That makes sense," he conceded after a moment's deliberation. "But what do we do in the meantime? I can't just let my airship sit here."

"I suggest you wait here with your mechanist until your craft is capable of getting to Eran Point. I want to get Lenna — and the rather obvious Godjewel — back to my estate, which is at least somewhat more reclusive and comfortable than a hillside."

"Now, wait one second…" Raif began, scowling.

"Raif." Lenna put a hand on her friend's arm. "Seb's right: with the Empire on the move and the huge amount of magic I've been using, half of the Continent could probably find me with their eyes closed. I need to move to a more discreet location, and the sooner, the better."

"I'll take care of Vanny," Lazarz offered.

"Joy of joys." Raif kicked the grass with his boot. "Very well, Sebastien: I'll be along once matters in Eran Point are sorted. Take care of her. Lazarz, you and I need to have a few words below deck."

Lazarz paled and gulped, looking like a guilty chipmunk caught pilfering nuts from a squirrel's horde. Lenna stifled a laugh and nodded at Raif as if to say, *it'll be all right*. At the very least, she decided it was best not to inform Raif that Khareen Valant was on the *Talonstrike;* let Raif pry such alarming information from the man who designed that war monstrosity. Lenna's priorities consisted of getting out of the exposed meadow, unravelling some of the mysteries behind Seb's claim of teleportation, and elucidating the reason why a previously headless general could now be commanding an airship in search of the blue Godjewel.

Lenna and Sebastien made a brief farewell to a lamentable Lazarz and a less-than-happy Raif before walking several meters off into the distance, barely an arm's width apart from each other. Though Lenna could feel Raif's burning glare on her back, there were certain things that needed saying that she thought were not fit for his ears, despite his aid in removing her from Granemere Settlement before the Empire descended upon her in full force.

Once they were a suitable distance from Raif and Lazarz and the former of the two stomped his way back to the *Trilyala,* Lenna dared to ask a question that had been on the tip of her tongue for several minutes.

"You couldn't have teleported here without the power of a Godjewel." She struggled to keep her tone sanguine.

"Theory would argue otherwise," Sebastien replied. His response, to Lenna, seemed lackluster at best; though her physical interactions with the older mage had been few and far between, something about the way his chin rose during that flippant statement signaled to her that Seb was hiding something.

Lenna ran her fingers through her hair. These silly games of politics and allegiances, particularly when she really wasn't sure where her own allegiance lay — except to her father and friends — exhausted her, and in the warming Gallas day she wished for nothing more than to strip off her dark coat and lie down in the grass with a new book to read and something sparkly to drink, preferably alcoholic in nature. Her stomach rumbled a bit; she could probably do with a sandwich as well, now that she thought about it. Most of her previous meals had been rained down across the countryside.

"Not that I'm an expert on such things," Lenna commented, "but I was under the impression from Gilbert that those kinds of ancient, powerful magics were lost a long time ago. If the Blue Crescent Brotherhood was capable of teleportation, I would think its members would have been using it to pursue me — and this damn stone — a bit more aggressively than they have been."

Sebastien, surprisingly, let out a weary sigh. "Gilbert's understanding of magic ran very deep for someone so young, but he wasn't privy to as much information as he thought he was. However," Sebastien continued, "he was certainly privy to more information than he shared."

"So you're saying that Gilbert wasn't entirely truthful with me?"

"Let's just set that conversation aside for now. But you're right, and Gilbert was right: most of that old magic has been lost or is simply… inaccessible to most mages."

"But not to you."

"Not at the moment."

"But I have a Godjewel, and I can't control how or when it decides to teleport me somewhere."

"I hope to teach you otherwise."

"So how did you accomplish the teleportation?"

Sebastien turned and looked down, considering, into Lenna's face. "Through dubious means that I doubt you'd approve of, Lenna Faircloth. Do you want to pry further and be even more disappointed in me, or shall we just agree that there are other matters of urgency that require addressing?"

Lenna didn't bother to hide the frown she could feel forming on her face, but she already knew from personal experience that Seb could be as stubborn as a constipated goat — thank you, Pim — when circumstances dictated the need. She supposed she would just have to play along for now, even though her brain was threatening to walk out on strike unless it received some answers. Pulling her timepiece from the inside of her long coat, Lenna grimaced when she saw that the crack on the glass frame had deepened. This rough-and-tumble lifestyle was taking a toll on her more delicate belongings, and it was still only just about midday; she still had half a day to go!

"All right," she said after a moment's deliberation. "So we're teleporting back to your estate then?"

Sebastien shook his head. "The method I used to get here is irreproducible from this location, and I don't want to have to rely on you using the Godjewel without rest and time for precautionary measures. No, I'll just raise a wind."

"Raise a wind?" Lenna regarded him inquisitively. "What is the merit in that?"

Seb grinned at Lenna with boyish glee, a rare sight. "This is Gallas; hills and valleys, rivers and wide berths. The wind loves it here. I can use it to speed our way back to my estate, but you'll have to stay very close to me, all right?"

Lenna inched closer, allowing her skepticism to color her tone. "You sound like the Freewomen."

"Their approach to magic is different, but that doesn't mean it's wrong. Now, stand close and enjoy the ride." Sebastien rather brazenly slipped his arm around Lenna's waist and pulled her up against his body, which was more muscular than she had imagined. The shock of the sudden, intimate action stunned Lenna, so much so that rather than engage in her normal response — a swift elbow to the side — she bundled up her hands, clasping them to her chest.

"Apprentices on Crescent Island are often scolded for these kinds of shenanigans," Sebastien said, "but we've all done it once or twice."

The scent of Sebastien's magic whirled up around Lenna and danced on the breeze. The grass around their feet bent forward and a surge of wind pressed up against them, catching the brocade of Lenna's coat and lifting it into the air. The pressure from the rising gusts increased to such a degree that Lenna was actually thankful for Sebastien's strong grip around her waist and, involuntarily, let her hands slip to his chest.

Sebastien coughed briefly, but smiled; it was a soft, subtle smile that poked about his lips, showing a side of the cocksure mage that Lenna had only ever experienced during their time together in that strange, subconscious realm. Though he wasn't, in Lenna's opinion, being entirely truthful about all of his actions, at this one moment she implicitly trusted the man, and her body relaxed into his like plaster into a mold. She nodded in his direction, signaling she was prepared.

"When I say 'jump,'" Seb said, "jump with abandon, and hold on to me."

Lenna nodded again and, at his command, they sprang from the grassy knoll and soared on the air, the rushing wind at their backs carrying them across the Gallasian countryside.

Sebastien's idea of summoning a wind was both elegant and exhilarating, though Lenna could easily understand how its application as a means of reliable transport was limited. In Gallas, with its countless hills, and on the cliffs of Crescent Island, the mages would have plenty of opportunity to call forth the great gusts of air that propelled them forward. The wind gathered up behind them in one solid blast, which Lenna suspected was somehow buffered by a moderate form of magical shielding to prevent any physical harm from the gale itself or to increase maneuverability. The air pushed them forward from one pass to the next, two great frogs leaping from lily pad to lily pad.

After being so firmly bonded on the subconscious level, it was surreal for Lenna to have her body pressed against Seb's, or for his arm to surround her waist in so gallant a fashion. Lenna found that she could still sense not just Sebastien's magic, as she could when others used their powers around her, but his strong psychic presence as well. It was hugely comforting, and with each great jump and surge of wind, Lenna felt the tension in her body fall away from her.

"This would never do in Fallowfields," Seb shouted over the wind in some attempt at explanation. "Too flat. The amount of magic needed to generate a gust strong enough to propel us from hillock to hillock would be impractical."

Lenna was only half listening, having deduced that much herself. Instead, she momentarily forgot her fear of heights and looked outward, taking in the scenery of the nation she had dreamed of visiting since she was a child. They were almost perfectly centered inland, but every so often, the wind carried the couple across a spectacular grassy ravine, dappled with flowers in shades of violet and crimson, and Lenna could glimpse, off in the distance, the twinkling of the sun's rays striking the waves. She wondered if any of Gallas's famed wild horses were running along the beaches.

After a few moments of silence from his partner, Sebastien ceased his tutorial on wind-making and fell into a quiet of his own, and from time to time, mid-jump, he glanced at Lenna with something of a reflective expression on his face. When he noticed Lenna returning his gaze he was quick to stare forward, coloring faintly. Her only response to this was to plant her feet and jump each time Sebastien commanded, "Leap!"

They traveled for some time in this manner, soaring over babbling rivers and curving roads cut into the landscape. Lenna supposed Seb was choosing to avoid being seen by any local villagers or, worse, officials who might recognize the widely known member of the Brotherhood and owner of a large Gallasian estate. She wondered how the officials would respond if they were enlightened to the fact that Sebastien was now a traitor to his order and hiding something of a political fugitive. Lenna's darkening meditations pushed her to wonder how the Gallasian government, a council of five elected officials, would respond if it knew one of the three legendary Godjewels was suddenly within its reach?

Minutes later the distance between the hills seemed to grow unpleasantly wide and a queer sensation in the back of Lenna's mind made her cling to Sebastien's frame as her fear of heights began to reassert itself. At the next bluff, the wind abruptly — and thankfully — died out and Sebastien executed an acrobatic miracle by walking Lenna to a somewhat respectable stop. Feet happily settled on the turf, Lenna took a gander at her surroundings. They appeared to be on a landing of some size, just on the outskirts of a well-cultivated orange grove. The trees' scent drifted toward her and Lenna drank it in as though she were a child on the docks of Port Hollish, biting into the tender flesh of the juicy fruit.

"Are these yours?" she asked, intoxicated on the tangy perfume.

"Yes, these are part of my estate." Sebastien shuffled his feet, stiff and uneasy. His haughtiness seemed to vanish the moment they set foot on his family's land. He hadn't even bothered to dust off the knees of his trousers or his boots; they were still smattered with grit from their rather fantastic means of transportation.

"They're lovely," Lenna said awkwardly.

"Thank you; I keep them thriving even in the cooler months with some specialized magic. Shall we?" He grabbed Lenna by the wrist and began trudging them off toward the line of trees and into the orchard's smartly manicured rows.

"What's wrong?" asked Lenna, obligingly keeping pace with Seb and allowing herself to be led. "This isn't like you at all."

Sebastien kept his eyes forward, aloof. "I'm always a bit hesitant about coming here," he said.

"Why?" Lenna was curious, but she was also trying to take in the beautiful examples of fruit as they waltzed by tree after tree. A single bushel of the fresh oranges would garner a handsome fee in Port Hollish; Lenna was forced to question exactly how wealthy Sebastien and his estate must be. It seemed to be her lot in life to end up in the company of excessively rich Continental families.

Sebastien replied, almost flippantly, "Bad memories. My father and I didn't exactly get on, which was one of the reasons I was thankful to leave my Gallasian life behind and join the Brotherhood."

Thrown, Lenna held her tongue for a moment. "I'm sorry to hear that," she said finally.

"It doesn't matter. He's been dead for some time."

"What about your mother?"

"She's been dead for much, much longer. I'm the master of Branford Estate now."

"Oh." Lenna wasn't sure what the proper response to such a cold and emotionless statement of fact would be, other than "mine's dead, too," and so she said nothing as they reached the line of orange trees and came upon the rest of the estate. It was a wide expanse, full of well-tended gardens and delightfully curving paths that skirted around bubbling fountains and spectacular floral arrangements. The paths all led to a large manor house of marvelous stone, several generations old by Lenna's guess.

She whistled in true appreciation. Sebastien's bad memories aside, Lenna selfishly wondered if, after experiencing luxury such as this, she would ever be able to return to her sensible bed, sensible two-story home, and sensible job as a junior librarian.

CHAPTER EIGHT

Half an hour later, Lenna found herself seated on the plush sofa of a sitting room decorated with such expensive exquisiteness that it made her hesitant to breathe, lest she disrupt the perfection. Across from her, Sebastien sat in a high-backed chair, flanked on either side by tables on which sat vases representing, in swirling blue designs against porcelain, the tropical fruit trees and hillsides of Gallas. The whole affair screamed of old money, and Lenna immediately began to question exactly how prominent and old the Branford family was. Whereas Raif's family, the Vandevers, were conspicuously wealthy and active in the matters of the Continent, Sebastien's wealth spoke of something much quieter and reserved.

Sebastien seemed content to sit rigid as a plank in his chair, not speaking. Lenna wasn't sure if she should initiate conversation or not, so she bided her time and looked around, taking in the flowery images that speckled the wallpaper. Her eyes fell upon a remarkable hanging clock on the eastern wall. It was carved from oak and Lenna recognized the handiwork in the intricate swirls and curls that framed the timepiece, which was in its own right a work of art, with a face of ivory and slender, golden needles. There was no mistaking the clock's origin.

"Yes, nosy," Sebastien said. "You needn't stare: it's a Faircloth clock, all right."

"It's beautiful," Lenna replied, startled. "Did my father make it?"

The master of the estate shook his head. "No, it must have been your grandfather's piece, or even your great-grandfather's; it's been in the family for some time. It's quite valuable; you really underestimate the reputation your family has."

The Faircloths had been well-known as some of the finest clockmakers in Fallowfields for several generations, but to think her family was providing pieces to such noble families — Lenna was at once impressed and humbled that she hadn't the skill her predecessors had had. She thought about the spreading crack in the glass of her own pocket watch and felt her spirits sink. The glass faceplate would have to be replaced, and soon, if it was to be salvaged.

Conversation lulled once more and, ears burning with irritation, Lenna wondered just what exactly she and Sebastien were waiting for. After a moment more, just as Lenna was about to open her mouth to speak again, the polished wood door of the drawing room swung open silently, and in rolled a tea cart of marble and wrought iron that rivaled the opulent decor. Wheeling it was a tall, broad-shouldered man with cropped dark hair and very pale skin, giving him an odd, waif-like look despite his muscled physique.

Along with the cart came the light scent of jasmine and another whiff of fresh orange; Lenna was, she inwardly acknowledged, thankful that here in Gallas she would be able to have a cup of tea instead of strongly brewed Ilyan coffee. And, now that she thought of it, just what kind of wine cellar would a place such as the Branford Estate harbor? Perhaps learning some control from Sebastien would have some additional benefits, after all.

The servant poured the tea, which was accompanied by flaky biscuits for which Lenna had a particular fondness. Conscious of proper etiquette (or her idea of it, anyway), she waited for Sebastien to begin nibbling before Lenna herself indulged. A voracious rumbling in her stomach reminded her that most of her sustenance had been lost along the way to Gallas, and that now, with no threat of air travel in the immediate future, Lenna was free to refill her belly. Apparently Seb felt similarly, as for the next several minutes the two maintained their silence, though this time accompanied by a rapidly decreasing stack of biscuits.

Lenna had brought the beautiful teacup — also porcelain — to her lips and was prepared to take a sip of the orange-sweetened drink when once more the room's wooden door opened and in glided a woman with an air of command that was disarming in comparison to the plodding servitude demonstrated by the tea courier. She wore an elaborate silk frock in red that bordered on theatrical; Gallas, known for its fabrics and even better tailoring, offered some of the best finery on the Continent, and this woman's attire was no exception. From satin high-heeled shoes to the delicate chiffon gathered at her neck, this figure represented wealth and power. Lenna hastily put down her teacup.

Sebastien rose to his feet in a clattering of cup and saucer; it was one of the quickest, clumsiest actions that Lenna had ever witnessed from him. Following suit, she stood to greet the newcomer, who was about the same height as Lenna but had volumes of enviable smooth jet hair, streaked with white and offsetting her deep caramel skin and brown eyes. Her entire bearing was the pinnacle of refinement, and Lenna wished — ironically, considering the merits for which she had chosen her current garb — for a dress to match the woman's fashion.

"Master Sebastien," the woman said, carillon-clear. "Welcome home."

"Mistress Juniam," Sebastien replied with a voice that contained a trace of something that Lenna couldn't distinguish. Awe? Fear? "I did not know you'd be at the estate this afternoon; I thought you would be in Eran Point, sorting out the household business."

Juniam smiled, revealing a row of perfectly white teeth. "When you left so hurriedly this morning, leaving certain…" She paused a moment, training a shrewd eye on Sebastien. "…Matters of the estate unsettled, of course I found it necessary to delay my trip into the city. I am also fortunate enough to now greet Miss Faircloth personally."

Word about Lenna's arrival must have spread around the estate faster than an outbreak of chickenpox. Sebastien, his confidence sagging like his shoulders, stood abashed and silent. Lenna wasn't certain what Gallas decorum dictated in this circumstance, especially since she had no idea who Mistress Juniam was or what she did. "Nice to meet you," Lenna said with some hesitation.

Mistress Juniam curtseyed just so, barely bending her knees. Her eyes were smart and quick, assessing Lenna, her character, and any faults therein during the scant seconds it took them to survey the length of Lenna's body. Lenna attempted to return the curtsey but, having left the long scabbard buckled to her belt, found it highly awkward to bow without disrupting the tea set. Inwardly sighing, she resigned herself to being, yet again, a disruptor of social conduct. Mercifully, if she was displeased by Lenna's lack of grace, Mistress Juniam tactfully declined to comment.

"I was told that Master Sebastien was hoping to take on yet another apprentice, and indeed we have been glad of his return from the Brotherhood to the Branford Estate," Mistress Juniam commented knowingly, "but I am surprised that the order would allow him to teach a female. Its views on our sex are... questionable, at best."

So Sebastien has been spinning the story to this woman, Lenna thought. Or was Mistress Juniam simply expecting Gilbert to have been the apprentice, as Seb and Gil had originally planned to flee back to his home in Gallas? Either way, Lenna knew she was once again embroiled in a delicate game of truths and half truths, and she wished some divine being would just hand her a reference book so she could catch up on the action. Providence failing in that, Lenna had no choice but to stand expectantly before the woman.

"Based on your original information, I had made arrangements for another gentleman in the house," Mistress Juniam went on. She cast Sebastien a look that caused him to drop his eyes to his feet. "I've already begun arrangements to have your quarters made more suitable to a lady's needs." She gave a terse nod before adding, "Master Sebastien, after you finish your tea, you'll find a small luncheon in the kitchen. I'm afraid Cook wasn't expecting guests for a proper afternoon meal. I will speak to you more, after your stomach is contented." Her look warned Sebastien that it would not be in his best interests to avoid that conversation. She swept imperiously out of the sitting room, the soft ruffling of silk taffeta trailing in her wake.

Lenna exhaled deeply; she had no idea what had just occurred, but being in the company of Mistress Juniam was like standing next to a pile of explosives at a spitting bonfire. Settling back on the balls of her feet, Lenna realized that she quite literally had been standing on tiptoe in some form of shock. She tilted her head in Seb's direction and was fascinated to see that his face was pasty and he still regarded his feet with a disquieting intensity.

"What was that all about, Seb?" Lenna asked. "Who is she?"

"She runs the Branford Estate for me while I'm away on Brotherhood business," Sebastien explained. "We have tenants and staff, in addition to duties to the council in Eran Point, so she acts as my official representative."

For a woman, and one not of Branford blood, to run the family's affairs meant that Mistress Juniam was no slouch indeed. Lenna would not like to find herself on the receiving end of the woman's wrath, not if she could competently handle Sebastien's personal affairs and quell his audacious character with nothing but a sharp look. It was hard to reconcile someone like Seb to compromising his lofty demeanor in front of anyone, let alone someone in his employ.

"For a servant," Lenna commented, "Mistress Juniam certainly seems to have quite the effect on you, Master Sebastien."

Seb looked Lenna woefully in the eyes, his mouth drawn into a grim frown. "She's not just a servant, Lenna," he bemoaned.

"Well, what on earth is she, then, to have you so flustered?"

Running his fingers through his hair and dislodging its carefully arranged part, Sebastien groaned. Lenna was alarmed: a disheveled Seb was like a silent Pim.

"She was my nanny and governess," he said quietly. "You'd be surprised how many spankings this backside has had at the hand of that woman."

Lenna chortled with sick glee at the image of a disgraced young Sebastien being smacked on the bottom; her cackling rattled the teacups in their saucers, and she couldn't stop giggling until Sebastien, growing purple in the face, threatened to blast her back to the hilltop with another gust of wind.

The "small luncheon" Mistress Juniam had had Cook prepare for Lenna and Seb consisted of a plate of cheddar and chutney sandwiches with some salad and a pickle, light fare for which Lenna was most grateful; her stomach was still a bit delicate from all the flying, and she had had perhaps one too many biscuits with her tea. The only thing the meal lacked was a pint of ale.

In between bites of sandwich, Sebastien explained a bit about the nature of his estate and the general politics of Gallas. "There were many noble families that chose to separate from the plethora of treaties and different bureaucratic kerfuffles that broke out during the establishment of the four nations. Gallas's remote location became an ideal place for families with fortunes still intact but little desire for governmental nonsense. As a country, we try to take a neutral stance, and we take pride in knowledge, our own personal growth, and the quality of our goods. Our policy of general noninterference facilitates easy dealings with the rest of the Continent and its numerous factions."

Lenna nodded; she had known as much from her reading, and of course the best place for study in the Continent was the University at Eran Point. As Seb said, because of its secluded location and desire to maintain neutrality, various peoples had, over the course of several generations after the Unification, migrated to Gallas to establish themselves in a calmer, more polite society than might be found in the bustling main cities of Port Hollish or Tranum, or in the striking and technologically affluent, albeit rather regimented, Krevlum Empire to the north.

"The Branfords are one of the older families, so we maintain certain ties to the government, and thus frequently have business in the city. My father," Seb said with a tart expression on his face, "was quite the bureaucrat. It never pleased him that my propensity toward the arcane arts and desire to leave his home were stronger than my desire to inherit." He pushed away his plate, having eaten only half his sandwich.

Lenna felt a surge of sudden kinship for Sebastien, and she placed one hand on his arm. He flinched, admiring her hand with a strange level of curiosity, but did not withdraw. "I know what it's like to have a parent who wants you to follow a certain direction, one you don't really want for yourself." Lenna recalled with a bittersweet fondness her mother's insistence that she learn and follow certain Freewoman ways and her own outright refusal. "The feelings that come later — after they're gone — are difficult. There's lots of anger, still, but there will always be that guilt that you should have done more to make them proud."

"Guilt?" Seb yanked his arm back. "My father was a cruel bastard. The way he treated my mother, the beatings… I was almost happy when she died. It was her only way of getting back at him. Enath Branford never forgave her 'selfishness' for leaving him, even if it was in death." He rose to his feet with such force that Lenna feared for an instant that the simple wooden chair would clatter to the floor. "Enough of this. I'm not one to talk about this sort of thing. Mistress Juniam should have your rooms sorted by now, if I know her, and I'm more eager to explain the details of your apprenticeship."

Wincing from the biting dismissal, Lenna acquiesced and, in a manner which would no doubt warrant a spanking from Mistress Juniam, stuffed the rest of her cheese sandwich into her mouth and choked it down. Brushing the crumbs from her hands — mostly back onto the plate, she noted with pride — she gathered herself and hurriedly pursued Sebastien, who had already exited the kitchen and headed down a wide, window-lined hallway decorated with exotic vines and flowers. Lenna scrambled to match Seb's pace, but he barred her advance with a stiff arm.

"No, Apprentice Faircloth," he said. "You must walk behind me. And at all times during our training, you are to refer to me as Master Branford — although, if I deem you worthy enough, we may become more familiar and you may refer to me as simply 'Master' or 'Master Sebastien.'"

Lenna stared. After all the two had been through, and taking into account that Seb was a rogue from the Brotherhood, she saw no reason to adhere to their strange, unyielding code of conduct now. Their priority should be *learning*, she reckoned, not protocol. Lenna said as much, causing Sebastien to whirl around on his feet and fix her with one of his sterner countenances.

"You also won't speak out of turn," he said. His expression lightened for a moment, considering. "I know the formality seems constricting and strange after everything that's happened, Lenna. But many of the teachings of the Brotherhood rely on form and function so that the greater, more powerful magicians can exercise control over the vast powers they have within them. Adhering to the rules will, I promise, make you a better mage. It will provide structure to your mostly untrained magical potential." He nodded, apparently pleased with his own response, and turned back and resumed walking. "It is how I was trained, and how I trained Gilbert," he added in a low voice.

Keeping a few paces behind her new teacher, Lenna struggled with her contradictory thoughts on the matter, but managed to vocalize, "I understand, Master Branford." The Godjewel must have been contented by this response as it began to pulse — almost eagerly — in Lenna's gauntleted hand.

Lenna received word from Raif via a hired courier that he would be in Eran Point for an evening or two, securing a safe place for the *Trilyala*. His message cryptically hinted that he would be questioning Lazarz regarding the details Lenna had managed to bring up before they were interrupted by the sudden appearance of Seb… no, *Master Branford*, Lenna reminded herself. Teacher and student had spent the rest of the day outlining various protocols that, however irksome they appeared, would be necessary for Lenna to receive the full benefit of Sebastien's tutelage. He encouraged her to take notes, but there was a limit to his student's supplication.

Over the course of some years following his father's death, the new head of the estate had gradually transformed what was once Enath Branford's study and library into his own magical emporium. Lenna nearly burst with elation as her eager eyes took in priceless first editions of books she had never seen in person, and there were some she had never even heard of. She imagined that Sebastien must have been even more influential in the Blue Crescent Brotherhood than he let on; either that or he had acquired the texts through more questionable means. As Lenna traced a finger lovingly along a row of books, all precisely arranged by subject and author, she would every so often exclaim in joy when she came across a compelling title. How many of these, she mooned, would Master Branford permit his apprentice to read?

According to Sebastien, his refurbished study was well-suited for his academic pursuits; in addition to the broad oaken bookcases and large main desk, which was so well organized and completely devoid of any clutter that Lenna felt an urge to dump a rubbish bin on it, there were a pair of smallish but practical-looking desks and matching chairs for students and a jet chalkboard affixed to one wall. Still, Sebastien further explicated, he had found that for any sort of practice involving larger workings, the study as his father left it — despite already being larger than Lenna's kitchen and her father's workshop combined — was substandard in his "professional opinion." His solution, thus, was simple: carpenters knocked down a portion of the wall separating his study and an adjoining ladies' waiting room, formerly his mother's, and Seb had the spacious (and once-luxurious) retreat transformed into something Lenna could, peeking through the open wooden doorframe, only describe as an arcane gymnasium.

Lenna laughed at the expression on Sebastien's face when she commented that it seemed a bit of a strange use for a room where women should be perfecting their needlepoint; indeed, some of the original wallpapering (a muted carnation pink) and a bit of fair-colored paneling betrayed the room's original purpose.

Sebastien hushed his apprentice and instead proudly pointed out some of the more mystical fixtures of the training room. A stack of mortar bricks occupied one corner; one of Seb's fascinations, Lenna learned, was discovering a means of melting them, as magicians of old were said to be able to cause the rocks themselves to dissolve. Gilbert had told her that this level of power was no longer within the capabilities of the Blue Crescent Brotherhood.

"Have you made any progress?" the student asked dubiously. "Er, Master Branford." Sebastien shot her a wilting glare that forbade further discussion on the subject.

Various other less-normal-appearing apparatuses, such as piles of crystals and curious humanoid statues missing limbs, were scattered in no particular order about the room or lined shelves built into the walls; one rack, in particular, was full of spears, swords, and staves and rekindled memories in Lenna of her time spent training with Freewoman Dalm in Granemere Settlement. So little time had passed since their last spar, and yet she felt out of shape, losing what little edge she had. In the center of the room was the most curious of features: a circle, chalked into the hardwood floor in deep carmine. It was wide enough for about two or three people to stand within it, though Lenna could suck in her belly enough to squeeze Pim in for a fourth, if necessary.

"Is there where you've been experimenting with teleportation?" Lenna inquired. "Master Branford."

Expecting a harsh rebuke, Lenna silently thanked every star in the sky when Sebastien responded, almost distracted. "Yes," he said. "It must seem rather archaic, but as the magic hasn't been attempted for some time, and due to the loss of a lot of information on the subject after the God War, I've had to rely on what little documentation I've been able to obtain."

Once more Lenna's mind was forced to question the means by which Sebastien was acquiring rare texts. "Actually," he added in an almost pouting tone, "the texts that were being sent to you in Port Hollish with Gilbert included some smuggled volumes with insights I was looking forward to making use of."

Thinking back, Lenna realized she had yet to have an opportunity to question the nature of the loaned texts sent to her library in Port Hollish. Her hurried departure, accompanied by Gilbert and Luc, had prevented her from having any time to examine them. Sebastien, like Lazarz, seemed focused on the concept of teleportation, something Lenna had thought possible only through an act of will subconsciously exercised upon a Godjewel. Could he be close to reviving a stable means of its execution? The power to transfer physical matter across great distances would drastically change life in the Continent, defying both steamtrain and airship alike. Thankful for the low level of lighting in the training room, Lenna didn't bother to hide the stupefied expression on her face. An image of Sebastien being heralded as the new face of transportation innovation made her both feel sick to her stomach and want to laugh.

"Master Branford." Lenna chose her words with caution. "If you don't mind me asking, what is the importance of teleportation? You're not trying to revolutionize the transportation industry, I imagine."

Apparently adrift in thought, Sebastien stopped trifling with the stone hanging from his ear and turned to look at Lenna, puzzled, as though she had just told him she'd murdered the governess and planned on serving her up as a raw starter at supper. On the stale air of the training room Lenna caught a whiff of citrus and clove: Sebastien's magic.

"Apprentice Faircloth, step into the circle with me."

Lenna stood, frozen in place by the wonder of the order. A demonstration was the least likely response she would have predicted from her strict teacher. Swallowing hard, she tiptoed meekly into the circle. Sebastien slipped up beside her, standing just as close as when he summoned the wind, still surveying his student. She could sense a gentle flickering within him, a budding energy steadfastly growing. Surely, the mage wasn't about to teleport the two of them somewhere?

"Haven't you noticed, Apprentice," Sebastien said quietly, "how strange the Continent has become? How barren the land is, how the sky is slowly becoming devoid of stars? You're smart, Lenna; you must have realized."

Lenna had not noticed, or if she had, she hadn't given it much thought until recently. Before Gilbert and the Godjewel had upended every part of the librarian's natural existence, Lenna had been aloof and withdrawn, not one to question her surroundings, let alone the lives of anyone not immediately around her. But now she was forced to confront issues the old Lenna would have preferred to ignore, and she recalled the conversation with Pim in the baths of Granemere Settlement. Names of stars floated around in her head though, whenever she looked upward, those stars no longer graced the night sky. Farmsteads like the Meekses' apple orchard had fallen to ruin, and Mistress Meeks herself had dwindled into a shadow of the woman she once was as untempered magic returned to her body and overwhelmed her mind.

And no one — save Pim — questioned these strange phenomena, or at least if they did, they kept such questions to themselves. Why did the boats that launched from the docks of Port Hollish never head out into the uncharted seas beyond the Continent, despite certain books of legends or the mildewy scrolls in the Back Room of the Port Hollish library indicating that there might be more to the world? All of these questions taxed Lenna's brain heavily, and as her mind wandered, her head and the Godjewel began to throb. Lenna closed her eyes and angled her head downwards.

"That's right." Sebastien's voice tickled her ear. "Things are vanishing; information is being lost. The world is changing or being rewritten."

"Magic," Lenna said simply. "Magic is returning when it shouldn't."

She felt Seb's thin but tightly muscled arm slip around her waist, and Lenna did not flinch. "Yes," he sighed. "And the Godjewels. We should not be able to teleport; such power shouldn't exist. The more it returns to the world, the more we lose."

"So," asked Lenna, "what was there before? When did this begin?"

"I don't know when it began," Sebastien stated, his free hand slipping over the wrist cradling the Godjewel. "But I can show you what was there before."

Sebastien's essence sidled up against Lenna's own ephemeral magical consciousness, almost playfully, as though he were tantalizing her power to come out for a romp. Normally hesitant, Lenna let the chaste hold on her feelings and mind slip away, and blithely Seb's magic began to mingle with the summery floral scent of Lenna's own power. The aromas intertwined, and instinctively Lenna pulled on the power of the Godjewel in her palm. With Seb's presence buffering hers, Lenna felt no fear as she wound them down the spiral of thought and into the massive network of the unconscious world.

There, in the infinitely vast void, Lenna and Seb were as one, each anchoring the other to a single point as the web of human minds slowly fanned out before them. Lenna mentally trembled at the sensual tightness of Sebastien's now completely naked embrace. Along the ebbing filaments of light that spread unending into the darkness, one by one points of brightness appeared: other minds, other beings. Lenna thought of the stars.

There are so many, she thought.

Yes, a voice echoed in Lenna's mind, unsettling her for a moment. Of course she could hear Seb as clearly as he heard her. Here, their minds were joined; they were one.

Then why are they disappearing from the world?

They are being corrupted, becoming inaccessible — their lights are bleeding together and being released as magic, pure information and energy.

Then — everyone and everything — is here, in some form? Lenna's thoughts rang out through the subconscious space.

Yes, Sebastien's mental voice, more tranquil than his spoken one, replied. *But not as they were. They're changing, leaking. But if we had enough power and the skill, we could bring them back. Pull them back. Help give them form.*

So everything and every soul Lenna had known or would know was spinning about in this great cosmic whirlpool. Things like the stars… somehow they had slipped away from her physical universe and been left drifting, losing their unique identities and pouring out into the world as raw power, as magic, rekindling childhood gifts in people such as Lenna and Mistress Meeks, gifts that should have long ago died completely. But with enough power, Lenna thought, one could reshape the leaked energy, and…

Yes, the mage emphatically thought toward Lenna. *Even those who are lost could probably return.*

Lenna's mind recalled the rushing of air against her face and the monstrous blob of the *Talonstrike* hanging in the sky; she still felt begrimed from that oily creature she had previously experienced in this realm. Back, whole, with another ear…

Yes, Seb's voice resounded throughout her being. *Emperor Sonnet used his Godjewel to call back Khareen Valant from the early death to which you and Miss Hartnell sent her.*

The power of a Godjewel can do all that? Lenna was overcome with possibilities, and was taken by surprise when Sebastien pulled her upward, back into her body. The sudden return was swift and jarring, and she stumbled as her eyes and limbs adjusted to the harsh pressure of the physical world. In the low light of the training room, the chalked crimson ring flared with residual energy.

"And that," Sebastien said, steadying Lenna, "is why I took the jewel from the Brotherhood: to deny them such power. The power to control life and death, to manipulate the nature of the universe itself."

Lenna looked up into her new teacher's eyes. "But — the power of teleportation, of moving consciousness or matter by force of will and having the physical form reappear elsewhere — you couldn't possibly have done it without the aid of a Godjewel, even with all of your magical training. I can feel it."

Nodding, Sebastien turned and led a slightly dazed Lenna out of the magic circle, toward the door to his study. Yellow light streamed out of the open doorway, silhouetting a male figure leaning against its frame as though in need of support. His shoulders were hunched, and at a cursory glance Lenna thought he might be panting for breath. Still, there was a sense of pride in his stance, a haughty strength in his tensed muscles. His hair cut a clean shadow on the training room floor, and emotions of all sorts – animosity, betrayal, despair, too many for her to name – savaged Lenna's mind as it recognized the man.

With a forceful push, so determined and unforeseen that it caught Sebastien off guard and sent him staggering backward, Lenna found herself with her mother's dagger to hand and visible, ozone-laden ribbons of fiery magic surrounding her left fist. One word would destroy the calm of the Branford Estate. Lenna stared ahead and uttered it with perfect clarity.

"Luc," she said.

CHAPTER NINE

The person who had betrayed her, betrayed the love her best friend Gilbert had freely given, stood before Lenna, bathed in the gentle light from Sebastien's study. Lenna felt molten, blue-hot anger rise from the pit of her stomach, and in response the Godjewel began to vibrate, threatening to tear free from its shackles. An overwhelming sense of Luc's presence, once a feathery, light consciousness perfumed with lily, now rolled off him in smothering waves. His power was so bright Lenna might as well have been staring straight into the lamp at the top of Port Hollish's lighthouse.

"Lenna, wait," Sebastien started, but Lenna's shove had left him winded, slow. She drew upon the power of her Godjewel, channeling its sky-blue currents and flooding the room with an aggressively strong floral scent. She might have grown two feet taller; she felt as though she could reach wide with both arms and gather the contents of the entire room into her embrace.

Luc, though his expression remained unchanged, took a step back from the training room and reentered Sebastien's study. *I have the upper hand,* Lenna thought. *Sparkle ponies be damned.* Gilbert had once tried to explain to her that anger was good for a quick strike, one solid blast of energy, but seldom could it be used for anything more focused or purposeful. Indeed, even as she seethed, Lenna could sense that both Sebastien and Luc sought to smother her blazing outrage with their own magical auras. And she knew they simply weren't strong enough.

Feeling them trying to stifle her, she lashed out with her ire and felt the Godjewel resonate in kind; both Sebastien and Luc grunted as Lenna shut down their attempts to seal in her magic. She had destroyed the wards around Granemere Settlement; she had altered time itself. Even with a Godjewel and proper Brotherhood training, Luc and Sebastien could not outshine her, not this time. Lenna flared, glowing divine, but, as Gilbert had told her, she funneled the blind wrath into something cooler, more calculated: deliberate revenge.

Pulling on the fibrous strands of energy flowing from the Godjewel's core, Lenna wove them one by one into a thick, sturdy plait. She repeated this for what seemed liked infinity in the depths of her mind, though she intrinsically knew only seconds were passing in the Branford Estate. With a flick of her wrist the apprentice cast her uncanny net over Sebastien and the back half of the training facility. It was a new type of working for her, but it felt potent: she was confident it would bind both Sebastien and his magic so long as she held the pattern in her mind. A gasp of shock from her master confirmed this.

Luc cautiously moved one foot forward onto the training ground. *Good,* thought Lenna. *This is where I want him.* He stared off into the distance, regarding neither Sebastien nor Lenna but some entity she couldn't detect. The lily scent of his magic reasserted itself, but now there was something sick and sweet about it, like the scent of too many funeral bouquets wilting in the summer heat. She wanted to recoil and gag, but Lenna, hardened from her recent battle with airsickness, held her ground.

Bits of probing magic prodded around the solid block Lenna had established in her mind. Luc, she realized, was still trying to find a crack in the resolute wall she had erected between herself and the other magicians. Sebastien shouted something in the background, but her arcane cage not only imprisoned his physical and magical capabilities, but muffled all noise between the barrier and the rest of the room. Luc was holding back his offense, and therein Lenna found Luc's flaw: he was still expecting her to be weaker, less trained. She grinned, a debauched feeling of superiority coursing through every tingling particle of her being.

Even through lidded eyes, Lenna could still see the burning presences of the other two mages. She spun a small tornado of power into a glowing, pulsating ball of pure kinetic energy buoyed between her hands. She knew both mages could not only sense the emanation but see its physical manifestation as a mass of wavering light that warped reality around it. All it needed now, Lenna the apprentice realized, was a push, and that traitorous existence known as Luc Tural could be gone from her life. Gilbert avenged; Raif's treasure — the purloined Vandever Godjewel — recovered.

Relaxing her shoulders, Lenna dropped her stance and felt her feet connect to the ground beneath the manor's foundation; her center of gravity balanced, she became a pillar that thrust through the earth itself in one great, perfect signature of energy. The rush of power left Lenna lightheaded but invincible, and she gathered the nerve to hurl the swirling vortex of Godjewel energy toward Luc, her betrayer.

But in that fleeting moment when Lenna prepared to strike, there was a voice, ephemeral, that bounded off the walls of the training room, unhampered by Lenna's magical barrier. She couldn't place it as male or female, but the voice said, firmly, *no*. It was not a cruel command or the begging of desperation; the being simply, with that one simple word, convinced Lenna to let go.

And so she did, letting both the churning missile of energy and the mystic shroud isolating Sebastien dissipate back into the ether. Suddenly overcome with fatigue, Lenna felt her feet slide out from under her, and with a hearty thump that raised a light cloud of dust, she fell to the floor. Every piece of her — hair, limbs, eyelids — felt lank and lifeless. Her mother's dagger clattered to the ground at her side.

Luc recovered swiftly and fell back into his languid position against the doorframe; Sebastien, unbeknownst to Lenna, had crept up behind her and placed his hand on her shoulder. The action startled her, but Lenna, lost in the murk of the training room, was in too much of a fog to move. There was no option but to yield to the pressure her master was placing on her shoulder.

"Lenna," Seb said softly, "you cannot let the Godjewel unleash its power like that. Your bond is too strong."

Weary, Lenna merely leaned forward, bundling up her knees and placing her chin on them as a child would. "Why is he here, Seb? Why?"

"He needed control, just as you do. He came to me."

"And it's through him — and the Godjewel he stole from Raif — that you managed to harness enough power to teleport."

Not one to mince words, Sebastien simply acknowledged the statement. Luc kept his own counsel. As Lenna brooded, the training room became a shrinking cage, the tangible wariness of the two people in close proximity to her disquieting and overwhelming. She yearned for her bed back home in Port Hollish, for her father, and even for the strange familiarity she had acquired with the Freewomen of Laur in Granemere Settlement. A faint moan passed her lips.

"For now, though it's highly, highly irregular," Seb continued, "I'll be taking on two apprentices."

Luc, his expression shifting from slight mania to barely contained wrath, glowered at Sebastien. "I do not approve of this," he spat. "I was not told of this!" He dashed through the study and out its entrance, the booming thud of mahogany reverberating all the way back into the training room as the door slammed shut behind him.

"He needs help, Lenna," Sebastien said. "And we can't have him running around with a Godjewel emotional, untrained, and unpredictable."

"Mmm," vocalized Lenna, keeping her thoughts her own. Emotional, untrained, and unpredictable. Sebastien might not be saying it outright, but Lenna saw his meaning clear as day. *Luc isn't the only who needs help*, she opined.

***

Thankfully, Lenna had no further encounters with Sebastien's unnerving governess that evening as, in her currently rumpled emotional state, she was not certain she had the strength to be subjected to Mistress Juniam's discerning eye. After being deposited in her rooms, a set of two apartments even more generous than the guest room she had occupied during her stay with the Vandever family in Tranum, Lenna threw her knackered body on top of the fluffy duvet and stared absently at the ceiling. In the span of twenty-four hours, she had gone from an apprentice Freewoman to an apprentice mage of a traitor from the Blue Crescent Brotherhood, and had gained a fellow pupil in a treacherous, mentally unstable young man, someone she considered her enemy.

Lenna had pinched a goblet of wine from the dinner table and brought it up with her, the delicate crystal of the glass casting crimson hues on the pale walls of her sleeping chamber. Contemplative, she brought the wine to her lips but could not drink. Too many thoughts were trying to be processed by her brain all at once, and it appeared that not even the sweet solace of drink could free her. With the growing aches in her bones, Lenna wondered if all the recent events had aged her body beyond its years. Maybe she had some kind of magical sciatica?

Raising her left hand to the ceiling, Lenna considered her makeshift gauntlet and the Godjewel socketed to its palm. The Empire was certain to find out that two of the three Godjewels were now at the Branford Estate, and Lenna was not fool enough to think that Emperor Sonnet — and, more precisely, his general, Khareen Valant — would not redouble all efforts to acquire both. Should, by some minor miracle, Lenna and Luc decide to work together…

She shook her head, unconcerned with any motes of dust that might escape her curls and sully the bed. Working with Luc was out of the question as far as she was concerned, and for the meantime it seemed she had few options other than to listen to Sebastien's suggestions and teachings as best she could. The almost conscious impulses of the Godjewel were beginning to trouble her, particularly when Lenna ruminated on the recurring instances of herself boiling over with rage or despair; it was during those moments that the Godjewel made her capable of what would normally be the most impossible of feats.

What would Pim say? That the Godjewel was just another tool and that by fearing it, Lenna was letting the stone's hold grow stronger and control her. Pim would tell Lenna to be wary of both Sebastien (the stuffed shirt) and Luc (the traitorous, sparkly-handed trickster), but to master the powers of the Godjewel before those powers mastered her through fear. When war came, as it always did to Freewomen, Lenna would have to be prepared, though she had the distinct impression that war had already found her — and that it found her lacking.

Glass of wine untouched, Lenna didn't even bother to crawl beneath the duvet. Sleep, when it found her, was fitful; when she did achieve actual moments of pure slumber, Lenna's dreams were loud and unforgiving, showing images of her mother's death and Gilbert's death, of the shattered head of Khareen Valant laughing at the new, healed version. Now and then a strangely nostalgic voice urged Lenna to move in a certain direction, though what direction it wanted — or how it expected her to proceed — remained a mystery to the dreaming apprentice.

The next morning Lenna awoke with a rancid taste on her tongue, as though she had gone to bed after far too much wine and without cleaning her teeth. She smacked her lips, frowning, and sat up. Her body complained loudly, probably because of a combination of the recent intensive training with Freewoman Dalm and the chill she seemed to have caught in the night. *Learn to use the duvet,* she chastised herself. Groaning, Lenna slipped out of the bed, joints creaking and knots popping in her back as she stretched.

Taking a peek at her cracked pocket watch, which she had placed rather haphazardly on the nightstand next to the bed, Lenna frowned as she realized its hands pointed out that she was up far, far too early. It appeared her body had become accustomed to a month following a strict Freewoman training regime.

Begrudging this altered internal clock, Lenna tossed back the contents of last night's wineglass with abandon and headed into the washroom.

The extent of Sebastien's wealth came to Lenna in the glorious revelation of the hot- and cold-running taps, which the Freewomen settlement lacked and which, to be honest, were treated as something of a luxury in Port Hollish. The Faircloth home had the taps installed in the kitchen, primarily to assist with the clock-making work, but Thane and Lenna, in their usual manner of procrastination, had yet to actually run the piping up to the second story, where Lenna lived. Or used to.

The steamy water opened her pores, and Lenna scrubbed her face vigorously with the lightly orange-scented soap Mistress Juniam had provided. Bits of the fruit's flesh were embedded within the bar, and when Lenna scrubbed she felt as though she were peeling away several layers of physical and emotional grit. The soap was such a simple comfort that Lenna found herself mentally thanking Mistress Juniam for the attention to detail; it restored some of the lost confidence she'd need to go to some sort of magical tutorial starring herself and someone who had made himself Lenna's mortal enemy. *Life*, she whined to herself.

By her reckoning and the very determined schedule of Sebastien's former governess, Lenna would be able to break her fast despite the early hour. Breakfast, in typical Gallasian fashion, was served as a sort of rolling admission meal wherein people could drop in, have a cup of tea and some toast, and pop out to start their day. If Lenna's current luck held, she'd no doubt be forced to share a slice of bread and a lukewarm beverage under the discerning glances of said matron, Sebastien, and her newfound classmate, Luc.

Determinedly she navigated her way down the guest corridors — and, in her opinion, she did a bang-up job of it — and arrived without mishap at the dining room, a long, narrow chamber heavily dominated by the lacquered wooden table and intricate place settings. It appeared that the Branford Estate were catering to twenty guests, not two. Lenna idly wondered if it was customary to set enough plates to fill a table, even though a lack of sufficient numbers of people — and conflicting schedules — ultimately meant that the places would never be seated fully.

Lenna plonked her stinging body into a chair and waited as the pale servitor from the day before served her a cup of freshly squeezed orange juice and some mild tea, brewed just strongly enough to give her a bit of courage — when combined with wine from before — for the day ahead. The toast was mealy, but a trickle of orange-flower honey turned it into a beggar's feast; Lenna was caught between sticky bites of it when Luc found his way to the breakfast table.

"I'd have imagined your curls would be in the tea by now," Luc said, settling into his chair and buttering his toast in such a serious manner that the bread, were it alive, would probably be rather alarmed.

Lenna arched an eyebrow and readied herself for battle. "And here I thought you'd be off berating scores of women in the University's central square by now, to be received by shouts of displeasure and a shower of overripe oranges."

"This will not a good scholarship make," Luc said cattily.

"I didn't plan on making it one," said Lenna and, having stuffed the rest of her glazed toast into her gob, swaggered out of the dining room.

Breakfast settled (however awkwardly), Lenna gave herself a light smack on the cheek in an attempt to mentally calm herself for what would be the first of multiple tutorials with her new teacher. Grimly she recalled that aside from Sebastien's own immaculate desk, there had indeed been two wooden desks among the other academic paraphernalia in the study. Two desks for two students. Lenna moped down the spit-shined corridor toward what she had already reconciled to being a miserable day.

The door to Sebastien's study was a sturdy, no-nonsense mahogany plank that seemed to say, "I know what lies beyond me and, frankly, you don't measure up." Recalling some of the firmer of Master Branford's instructions on the decorum between scholar and pupil, Lenna, rather than barging in as her currently grouchy mood left her inclined to do, dutifully rapped at the door, knowing that at the very least, she'd arrive before Luc and have her choice of seats. Her teacher's cool voice bade Lenna enter.

Exhaling, she turned the brass handle and opened the door. The study was as it was yesterday, though in addition to several gas lamps and candles, a rosy fire crackled away in a hearth Lenna hadn't noticed before. She would not go so far as to say the room was now cheery, but it was certainly not nearly as dreary as she recalled, despite the books. Lenna's teacher seemed to have frightened the dust mites and any gloom away, making the study at least a warmer — if not necessarily a more exciting — place.

"Apprentice Faircloth," Sebastien said from behind a stack of papers. "I appreciate your punctuality, and, in this case, earliness. I've heard of your proclivity for dillydallying and daydreaming."

The tutelage was off to a fine start, it seemed. Swallowing a sigh, Lenna stood before her new teacher's desk and looked down at him sagely through her spectacles. Sebastien ignored her. According to the numerous laws that composed Brotherhood protocol, as it was her first time before this tutor, Lenna technically needed to ask permission to take her place as a student in a formal classroom. The sigh she so desperately tried to squash did not go down without a fight.

"May I be seated, Master Branford?" she asked, irked at the entire situation.

"Very well," Sebastien replied. "I suppose we need a moment to talk before the other apprentice arrives, anyway."

Lenna peered dubiously in her teacher's direction, but thankfully he was still consumed with the sorting of numerous documents, no doubt detailing the intricate, lost, and more than likely forbidden "art" of teleportation. Knowing a free pass when she saw one, Lenna stuck out her tongue like a first-year student and settled down at the desk propped up against the wall, waiting for her lecture to begin.

After a moment or two of deliberation, Sebastien sorted and neatly stacked his pile of papers, sliding them off to a corner of his wide desk. He cleared his throat and rose to his feet, pacing around in circles, seemingly lost for words. Lenna watched out of the corner of her eye, waiting for him to bring up the subject about which she least desired to chat. The wait was almost as annoying as the topic, and Lenna was half-tempted to start the conversation herself.

"Apprentice Faircloth," Sebastien finally began after a few moments, "I understand that you might consider it a betrayal of your trust in me to have Apprentice Tural here at my estate, learning alongside you."

Lenna barely stifled an unladylike word. After a few seconds, during which she collected herself to the best of her ability, she formulated a slow and deliberate response. "I must admit — Master Branford — that his appearance was a bit... disconcerting." A lifted syllable at the end of her sentence made it more of a question, suggesting unintentionally — yet truthfully — that she might think her teacher was being a bit of a numpty.

The scholar sighed. "And I must admit that I didn't anticipate the turn events would take. I intended Gilbert to bring your Godjewel here. For two Godjewels to arrive, and both in the hands of untrained apprentices — well, it's frankly inconceivable." He scratched madly at the back of his head like a dog with fleas, giving Lenna pause. "Though he fled the city of Tranum half-crazed, I believe he's come to realize that he needs guidance. I'm sure you're already experiencing it, but the Godjewels possess a certain... will. They exercise influence over their host, and, considering the trauma inflicted on him by the loss of Gilbert, I can only imagine the distress he felt."

Lenna, despite her slapdash schooling in Brotherhood decorum yesterday, could no longer be bothered to hold her tongue; Sebastien was treading onto very dangerous ground now. "You do recall that he was an accomplice in trying to kill all of us and working with the Krevlum Empire's most decorated general, Khareen Valant, yes?"

Ignoring protocol, thankfully, Sebastien responded with candor. "Yes, and it is precisely because of those sins that I can never fully trust Luc Tural, but it's also the very reason he needs to be here, under my supervision." Sebastien strode forward and knelt beside Lenna's diminutive desk and looked almost pleadingly into her eyes. "I cannot trust him elsewhere. Were he to fall back into the hands of the Empire, the Continent would be damned."

"But he betrayed us... betrayed *Gilbert,*" Lenna cried. "This... this just isn't okay with me. Am I even allowed to feel that? Has anyone asked how I feel about things? Does anyone give a damn?" She waved her gauntleted fist in the air in front of Sebastien's face. "It's all about the jewel, not me." Immediately Lenna flushed, regretting her words. She felt like a spoiled young schoolgirl who wasn't getting her time with the toys or proper attention from the teacher.

Out of compassion or just good breeding, Sebastien ignored her outburst and let out a disgruntled moan. His gaze was distant, either not able or not wanting to meet Lenna's own. "It isn't quite fair, I know." Delicately, the teacher placed his hand on his reluctant pupil's shoulder.

Inwardly, Lenna fumed. She wasn't sure how long she'd be able to maintain her happy student act without clocking Sebastien in the face. Quite fair? Well, she supposed that was a tactful way of describing her situation; fleeing from her home, losing her best friend, and then having his lover — who subsequently went a bit crazy and tried to kill her — join her for lessons shook her concepts of healthy living out of her like a strong cup of coffee knocks out a hangover. And, she thought, said crazy boy is in possession of a jewel that had the potential to alter the fabric of the universe.

"Luc hasn't had the easiest of lives..." Sebastien continued.

Lenna dismissed this thick statement with a sweep of her hand. "If this is about his twin sister and her death, I already know. Gilbert made sure I was aware of Luc's tragic childhood." She half grunted; while she pitied the loss of Luc's sister due to his family's reluctance to train a female in the ways of the magical arts, Lenna still couldn't quite get past his deranged, murderous side.

"I'm sure Gilbert shared a great deal of Luc's life before the Brotherhood," Sebastien said carefully. "But what did he have to say of it after Apprentice Tural joined the order?"

Lenna shrugged. "All I was told was that Luc was extremely gifted and excelled in his studies." After all, Lenna wasn't sure that there was much more to be known or if she even cared. She did not put into words that she thought Luc was also something of an insufferable snob.

Shaking his head, Sebastien removed his hand and stood up. "Talented people like Luc are often the source of jealousy and subsequently scorn, particularly among their peers. I'm sure your own talents and control — or lack thereof — of the blue Godjewel in recent weeks may have garnered you a similar response?"

Turning her head to the wall, Lenna ignored her teacher's prod. The Freewomen had been kind but always somewhat wary of her possession of the Godjewel. By Jaice's own account, battlemages were a dying breed in Granemere Settlement, and to think of one armed with the power of a demigod... scorn, fear, resentment: Lenna deemed these all valid emotions. She had grown up being first in class in most of her studies, being different and detached; she was used to that kind of behavior. It was still no excuse to, for example, kill the best friend of your deceased lover. Lots of people are teased; it's how you grow beyond that that proves your mettle, at least in Lenna's mind.

"You really do wear your thoughts on your face," Sebastien commented drily. "We all know that you were no doubt the source of jabs in your youth and that you, in your adulthood, overcame them. That's not what I'm talking about."

Blushing, Lenna damned the Brotherhood from Port Hollish to the moon. "Well, get it out, then, Seb. What made his life so miserable that I should look more kindly on him?"

Her teacher initially frowned at the forward behavior, but then Lenna discerned a fascinating war between stoicism and frustration engaging his face. Was her teacher going to chastise her, or accept a little chastising himself? Lenna had had enough double entendres, subterfuge, and deliberate obscurities over the past month for a lifetime and, apprentice or not, as long as she was strutting about with the Godjewel, she was going to get an answer. She stared her mentor straight in the eyes, issuing a challenge.

With yet another definitive slam, the door of Sebastien's study collided against its frame and threatened the safety of the delicate wainscoting along the walls. Glancing toward the entrance, both mentor and pupil found themselves unable to hide similar looks of embarrassment as the topic of their conversation, Luc Tural, fumed in their direction. The anger in his eyes was cold and focused, and though Lenna sensed no rising of power from Luc, through the fabric of his simple tunic she could feel the consistent pulsing of his Godjewel dangling from his neck.

"Master Branford," Luc began, "I respect your wishes and teachings, but I do not believe it's appropriate for tutors to expose their students' pasts to other apprentices. Forgive my brashness." Delivering the line with an almost rehearsed precision, the young mage slid into the desk next to Lenna, ignoring her completely.

Taking his position in front of the grand desk, Master Branford was quick to school his surprise and resume an air of command. This was his study, his classroom, and Lenna imagined he would run it as tidily as he kept his hair. Despite the situation, a debased gratification bubbled in Lenna at seeing Seb so rebuked.

"Noted, Apprentice Tural," Sebastien said smoothly. "I suppose you're correct; it isn't my place to divulge your stories to one another. Perhaps, in time," he continued, "you'll share them with each other, willingly."

Lenna and Luc snorted.

"Then again, time is fleeting. I wonder..." Sebastien once more began somewhat theatrically, in Lenna's opinion, to pace circles around his desk. She disliked the affected melodrama and took off her spectacles to rub her eyes. Should she say something?

Luckily, it was Luc who spoke up first. "Master Branford, are we to begin our lessons?" There was a challenging edge to his voice.

Sebastien stopped as though something had grabbed him from

behind. He managed a quick recovery and, clearing his throat, stepped pointedly toward Luc's desk. "Apprentice Tural."

"Yes, Master Branford?"

"Do you believe you can effectively work with Apprentice Faircloth? Answer honestly."

Lenna sensed a shift in Sebastien's stance and a faint gathering of power. He was raising some kind of magic, though Lenna couldn't ascertain its purpose. Her neck rocked back and forth, looking between the two mages, interested in the answer and its repercussions.

Luc pursed his lips and Lenna was tempted to offer him a sugar cube to sweeten his sour disposition. He responded, "No, Master Branford. I don't believe I can."

The sense of magic emanating from Sebastien suddenly dissipated, fading away into the dry air of the study. His expression was blank for a moment, before he plastered on his most winning smile. "I expected such an answer," he said.

"Are lessons to be canceled then, Master Branford?" asked Lenna.

"Oh, certainly not, Apprentice Faircloth." Sebastien trained his beaming facade on her. "But how am I to teach two students who refuse to cooperate? It will never work, especially since much of the concentration will be on the two of you mastering usage of the Godjewels in tandem."

"In tandem?" Lenna and Luc each turned to regard the other, and Lenna supposed her face bore a scowl similar to his.

"Thus," Sebastien declared, sweeping his arm upward — more theatrics, to Lenna — "we will go back to the basics of Brotherhood initiation."

"Forming a parliament?" Luc's voice broke like that of a twelve-year-old boy. "For two people?"

"Not only that, Apprentice," Sebastien said. "To further strengthen the bond between the parliament members, I shall arrange for an outing."

"An outing? Now?"

"Yes," Sebastien said.

"What," Lenna interrupted, "is a parliament?"

"Protocol, Apprentice," said her mentor.

Lenna replaced her spectacles and steadied her temper. "Apologies, Master Branford. What is a parliament?"

"It's a group of apprentices, placed together in a social unit by age and skill," Luc said with evident disdain.

"And we're to go on an outing... now, of all times?" Did no one realize that beyond these walls were dangers like Khareen Valant and twenty-odd Imperial soldiers? That neither she nor Luc had proper control over the power at their disposal?

"What student doesn't like a field trip?" asked Sebastien gaily. "Perhaps seeing how proper students behave might encourage you and Apprentice Tural to get along."

"Proper students? You mean..."

"Yes, Faircloth. Gather your things: we're off to Eran Point, home of the Continent's finest academic institution."

CHAPTER TEN

Much to Lenna's chagrin, Master Sebastien Branford, or rather his estate, was in possession of a fine motorcar, painted a garish rose color that clashed violently with her outerwear. Not that fashion was of great concern to her; rather, Lenna's displeasure stemmed from the fact that, like air travel, this form of locomotion rendered her terribly nauseated. Matters were not made much better by the fact that she was forced to share the rear seat with a silently seething young man.

"Nothing better to get you acquainted than a drive into the city," Sebastien explained, or rather shouted, as he steered his vehicle at a highly unsafe — to Lenna, anyway — speed down country lanes that dipped around and up and over the hillocks of Gallas. Oh, why couldn't someone bring the steamtrain here? Lenna shut her eyes and gripped the side panel of the roofless motorcar, praying for a journey without stomach upheaval.

"You're perverse," she said under the veil of wind and the purr of the engine.

"What was that, Apprentice Faircloth?" called Sebastien.

"I feel ill! Master!"

Luc sniggered, but Lenna just pretended it was the engine suffering from some kind of mechanical hiccough. Sebastien continued, "You'll get used to it, Apprentice. And the drive isn't that long." If Lenna didn't know better, she'd think that Sebastien was getting some sort of sadistic pleasure out of torturing her. She tightened her grasp on the side and wished for some *ghran*. "Open your eyes," her master commanded.

Like a rolling ream of green silk, the rich foliage of Gallas billowed past the car, and despite her tumultuous tummy Lenna couldn't help but be awestruck. It was a different kind of beauty than Fallowfields; roads, estates, and small villages all seemed to organically spring up as a natural part of the Gallasian landscape, not unlike the buildings in Granemere Settlement. One moment the trio would be whizzing along a windy path through a dense patch of woodlands, where broad leaves and fluffy clouds of silkworm nests filtered the sunlight through an organic canopy; next, the motorcar would crest a hill and pass along the well-paved roads of a village.

Lenna hadn't known Sebastien could drive, not that he had had any need to disclose possessing either the skill or the car before now. Still, it dazzled Lenna how effortlessly driving came to him; with only one hand on the wheel, he and the motorcar exhibited a strange balance similar to that between the natural and cultivated landscapes of Gallas itself. She wondered a bit wistfully if, when this dreadful outing was over, Sebastien would give her lessons in operating the machine. If her stomach agreed, of course.

After about forty minutes of consistent speed, a speed that, while it didn't quite rival the steamtrain's, was entirely more perilous, Sebastien steered the motorcar around a bend, curving around one of the stouter of the hills, before their road joined a wider highway. Other motorcars, fine carriages, and riders clad in silk riding gear kept up a steady pace of traffic toward the bastion of Eran Point, the home of learning and enlightened culture in the Continent. The tallest point of it was the clock tower of the University, about fifteen stories in height; the neutral brown of the stone pillar was crowned by a large timepiece, a handsome face of alabaster engraved with gold numerals.

Thane Faircloth often spoke of this marvel, and in truth it had been one of the reasons Lenna, in her youth, had so longed to attend the University. She recalled thumbing through various paintings and sketches, some nothing more than pencil on crumbled notepaper, and telling herself she'd be there one day, not as a tourist but as a student. It seemed, Lenna thought, that she had come to see the clock tower after all, but as a student of a different sort. What would Thane Faircloth think of his daughter now?

Sebastien coasted the car up to a tidy, two-lane bridge, lined on either side by a wall of old-fashioned bricks. Several other vehicles had queued up for the pikeman; as the city government was concerned with keeping Eran Point free of pollution and excess traffic, preserving its tidy streets for patrons of the arts, citizens, and students, so did it require a hefty toll from all those traveling via motorcar. Lenna imagined that tariffs on airships and conventional seafaring vessels were just as steep. This, of course, gave entrance to Eran Point, and particularly the University itself, a certain exclusivity: they were so secluded that the most efficient means of transport were also the most expensive. Though, for the sake of academia, the University granted scholarships or waived fees entirely for promising pupils.

"Is it wise," Luc asked over the dull noise of the idling engine, "to be gallivanting about Eran Point when we know that there are Imperial forces looking for her?" He jerked his head in Lenna's direction, refusing to acknowledge her by name or even grace her with eye contact. While Lenna shared his sentiments — with the Godjewels on their persons, no less! — if this was the attitude Apprentice Tural intended to maintain, he'd have something far more unpleasant to worry about than a platoon of soldiers.

"I strongly doubt the Krevlum Empire will actively move against Gallas, not yet," Sebastien replied. "We're a bit more defensible than Tranum or Fallowfields."

"That's what the nation of Ilya thought," Lenna griped.

"Regardless," Sebastien continued, inching the motorcar a length forward, "I've matters to attend to in the city; Mistress Juniam is here as well, as is Master Vandever. As long as you don't go walking headlong into danger…" At this point, Sebastien glanced warily over his shoulder at his protégés. "A little tour of the University, together, might help the two of you to get on somewhat more cordially. I cannot instruct you together until I diffuse some of the tension, and I'd hate to use less enjoyable methods."

Lenna and Luc rolled their eyes and folded their arms in unison, sinking back into the leather upholstery of the motorcar. Smirking, Sebastien turned his attention back to the road and steered his red automobile up to the pikeman. Gallas was a blending of cultures, so seeing the gaunt, angular features of an Ilyan this far south did little to faze Lenna. The fee the pinched young man collected from Sebastien, however, made Lenna cringe: an amount like that could pay for a return trip from Port Hollish to Tranum via streamtrain!

Of course, to Sebastien Branford the toll was a pittance, a simple but necessary inconvenience associated with ingress to Eran Point. "You see," he called back to his students as he maneuvered the motorcar down High Street, which contained the more affluent boutiques and outfitters and culminated at the main gates of the University, "the city government, in fact the Gallasian government as a whole, has so many checkpoints into Eran Point that it would be highly noticeable if a group of Krevlum soldiers were to attempt to enter."

Lenna doubted that any city could be so protected; there would always be loopholes, less-protected gates. Her own experiences in fleeing Port Hollish and navigating the labyrinthine streets of Tranum had taught the sheltered librarian that much. Still, as the car puttered along — there were many pedestrians, and signs indicating strict speed limitations were posted at prominent street corners — Lenna was overcome with awe at the pristine nature of the buildings and the people. The entire town looked freshly scrubbed, right down to the cobblestones. Shop windows sparkled in the rising sun (Lenna's stomach told her she had a solid hour or so before she would require lunch and wine), and as she leaned over the frame of the car, she caught her own wide-eyed expression glancing back at her in the glass.

Perhaps a trip to Eran Point wasn't such a bad idea after all, Lenna thought. If it served to diffuse tension between Luc and her, then huzzah indeed, but at the very least Lenna could allow herself, after the rather draining events of the past month and especially the last few days, to unwind and take in some culture. Maybe she could even induce a fellow librarian to grant her access to one of the University's libraries if she was lucky.

Though the great monolith of time that stood as the symbol of the University rose over the buildings of Eran Point and was clearly visible from most of the city, High Street, Lenna realized, stretched for some length and the gates to the institution were still a fair distance away. As they approached the next corner, Sebastien signaled with his left hand that his motorcar was about to turn and guided the vehicle into a narrower street. It was still wider than most roads in Port Hollish, but despite groups of youths and serious-looking adults traversing the paths on either side, this side street was nowhere near as thriving as those of Tranum. Sebastien slowed the car down and drew to a halt a few meters from the intersection. He leaned over his seat and looked at his students expectantly.

"Well?" he said. "Off you go. I have a car to park and some bureaucratic affairs to attend to."

Lenna and Luc turned their heads and regarded each other, skepticism making Lenna's ears want to twitch. Both were strangers to the city; did their teacher really expect the two of them — who could barely converse without coming to the equivalent of a magical fistfight — to be able to explore the city on their own? After a moment, Lenna looked back at Seb and raised her index finger in question.

"Yes, Faircloth?" Sebastien asked, keeping his voice deliberately innocuous. Lenna curled her fist and stifled a grimace.

"Um, Master Branford. What would you have us do?"

"That's up to you, but get along and, for the sake of the Continent, avoid getting into trouble. Meet me back at this location in three hours' time."

"Three hours?" Both Luc and Lenna raised their voices in a simultaneous outcry of utter dismay.

"Three. No more, no less. Now, out with you both." Sebastien, seemingly eager to assert his authority as an instructor, jerked his head to one side and the door of the motorcar, which Lenna hadn't realized she'd been gripping with dread, was flung open by an unseen telekinetic force. Disembarkation, it would seem, was the only option.

Begrudgingly, Lenna scuttled out onto the path, feeling very much like a child being delivered to school by a parent, and Luc, ever the whiner, muttered something incoherent under his breath. The door swung closed with a dull click, demonstrating Sebastien's apt hand at delicate magic. The motorcar hummed back to life and proceeded down the lane at a speed significantly faster than the one posted on the sign under which Lenna stood.

"So, what now?" she asked Luc.

He looked at her with a scowl that could scorch a flowerbed. Lenna almost leaped back at its severity, and considered dismissing Luc entirely and heading toward the University. After all, High Street led directly to its gates; Lenna would be able to handle herself from there. Luc, apparently oblivious to Lenna's presence, stalked past her and back onto the wide road, turning left and heading south toward the very destination Lenna sought.

No avoiding him now, she thought grimly. *Of course he'd head to the University as well; it's not as though he'd stop somewhere for tea and scones.* And so it was that Lenna pursued Luc, forming a most unusual "Team L," and they were left to their own devices in the city of Lenna's childhood dreams. Wishing she had had the forethought to have downed her smuggled bottle of Freewoman breakfast wine, Lenna gulped and hurried after the ponderous youth a few meters ahead.

Luc exuded an aura that reeked of displeasure. It was so noticeable that people all along High Street paused, cast assessing glances, and promptly headed off in the opposite direction. Shaking her head, Lenna hurried to keep up with him, though she still tried to deliberately lag a few paces back. Displays in shop windows — an alluring stand in an antique bookstore in particular — threatened to waylay Lenna, but as of late her will was strong (except when it came to good wine) and she managed to keep up a healthy, if not completely undistracted, stride.

Considering Luc's pace, it was no surprise that only a few moments passed before Lenna arrived, in his wake, at the massive iron gates of the University, cast wide open to allow students and faculty alike to come and go as they pleased. As it was shortly before lunch, some of the pupils, in casual attire but wearing black scholarly robes and mortarboard caps, milled about near the wide fountain in the center of the paved courtyard. Numerous paths, snaking into further ivy-lined ways, stemmed from this hub, and each would eventually arrive at the various institutions representing the University's individual fields of study — or maybe a library or two.

Luc stomped up to a signpost chiseled out of stone indicating, in Common, directions to each institution. Lenna obediently followed, trying not to color as some of the dillydallying members of the University turned their heads and regarded, with evident interest, the peculiar young man and the skulking woman behind him. Moments passed, and Lenna was with each passing second becoming acutely aware of the growing number of eyes trained on her back.

"Luc? Where do you want to go?" She attempted to keep her voice as civil as possible.

"The astronomical facilities here are said to be second to none," Luc replied. "Or perhaps the botanical garden? The work done here on crossbreeding certain flower species is impressive."

Lenna gawped openly. She hadn't encountered much of this side of Luc, when his academic interests actually brought him out of his misery and contempt and made him less of a maniac and more of an automaton, which, Lenna thought, she preferred. And an interest in flowers? That was unexpected, to say the least, and now to learn that they shared an interest in astronomy…

She shook her head. Not being students, they probably wouldn't gain access to anything truly interesting, and even if through some miracle they stumbled across something provocative in the gardens, Lenna wasn't quite sure she had the stomach for mulling over unique varieties of roses for three hours. Speaking of stomachs, a dull rumbling in her belly was gurgling as a solid indication that lunch was in order. A purely hedonistic burst of satisfaction temporarily filled Lenna as, in scanning the signpost, she noticed that the Scholar's Cross — listed as a pub — was only a few hundred meters off a northeastern path. While she didn't want to spend the next few hours in a greenhouse, Lenna wouldn't mind talking shop about flowers over a hot lunch and cold pint.

"I've got an idea," Lenna said. "Follow me."

Stunned by her gusto, Luc hastened to keep pace as Lenna led him down her desired path. Once he realized the direction in which they were headed, though, he caustically gibed, "Of course; it's time for you to tie one on."

"Come off it, Luc," Lenna answered without any real heat. She expected that kind of remark. "We both need to eat." She glanced at him and noted his churlish expression. "And you could learn to relax a little. We're stuck with each other, remember?" She pointed at the small bulge in Luc's tunic, where he concealed his Godjewel. "These things aren't going away anytime soon."

He made a disgruntled noise, but put up no further resistance. "Do try not to embarrass me or the Brotherhood or Master Branford."

"That's the spirit," said Lenna, the pitch of her voice a little queer for her liking. Was this a good idea? The pair had barely functioned at breakfast, and Lenna, in a fit of rage, had attempted to destroy Luc yesterday. Then again, she considered as her boots walked in tidy steps along the cobblestone path, a bit of social lubrication over topics they both enjoyed might be just what their teacher had intended. And, Lenna rationalized, she *was* hungry.

Not ten minutes later, Lenna and Luc, dressed rather smartly in stark contrast to the students (who, though they wore robes, kept the clothes underneath in various states of disarray), were standing before the sticky wooden counter of the bar. Some of these aspiring academics, Lenna noted with interest, had likely been at this pub for some time, shirking their tutorials. And this could have been her! She sighed. Still, one of her dreams was technically being fulfilled: the Scholar's Cross was famous for being the only pub actually housed on the University's grounds, and many a famous architect and engineer, poet and playwright, had been known to take a pint here or discuss various thoughts that the freedom of Gallas allowed. Lenna might secretly long for some black, draping robes of her own, but for now a pint would have to do.

The Scholar's Cross was seedy compared to the cleanliness of the rest of the University's environs and smelled of stale beer. Pint glasses and mugs from last night's revelries huddled in corners of the bar and on a few of the tables toward the sides and back of the narrow pub, which was divided up into smaller segments, each the size of Lenna's kitchen back in Port Hollish. Despite its being midday, an alarming lack of windows and huge growths of ivy — another resemblance to Lenna's home — shrouding the few entrances kept the public house dimly lit, but not in a spooky fashion. In some crannies of the Scholar's Cross, students pored over academic journals and jotted notes from various texts into notepads, and Lenna even caught wind of what sounded like scholarly debate. She felt at home.

"Haven't seen you two here before," the barkeep remarked as he approached his new patrons. He was tall and instantly reminded Lenna of Bahl, Jaice's partner, with his grizzled bearing and rumbling voice. "Tourists?"

"Something like that," answered Lenna.

"What'll it be?"

"A pint of the house ale, and whatever the lunch special is."

"And you, young master?"

Luc started; he had been deep in conjecture or some other study of the bar's patrons. "Water," he said. "Just water."

The barkeep's smile was pinched, displeased, and he sauntered off to draw Lenna's pint. Taking advantage of the moment's peace, she turned to Luc and said, "I know you're not much of a drinker, but you should at least eat lunch."

Luc shrugged. "Eating is irrelevant. I'll take sustenance when I need it, and right now I just want this day to be over." His eyes had glazed over, and Lenna could tell he was drifting off into darker thoughts.

With an oaky thump that splashed beer on Lenna's hand, the barkeep plunked a chipped pint glass down on the bar. The ale was foamy and dark amber, a local brew that Lenna had heard of from her father, though she couldn't recall its name. If she was going to make a habit of absconding to different cities around the Continent, she thought idly, she might want to start keeping a journal of the interesting beverages she encountered.

"Your food will up be shortly; it's lamb stew today. Here's your water." The barkeep's disdain for Luc's lack of custom was evident and, though Lenna thought Luc should order *something*, the man's overt surliness piqued Lenna's already frayed nerves.

"Thanks," she said, shaping her voice into a terse, aristocratic pitch that was hopefully a spot-on mimicry of Luc. Lenna turned her glance away from the barkeep, affecting an air of a mistress dealing with a lowly servant, and regarded Luc as he sipped at his water in regulated intervals. Taking a sip from her glass of ale, Lenna enjoyed its bitter and hoppy character, though she'd only be able to have one or two pints if she expected to fit in lunch on top of the heavy beer.

"Do you miss him?" Luc asked suddenly. Lenna coughed, choking on her mouthful of the slightly warm brown beer. "Gilbert, I mean."

"Yes," the baffled Lenna responded, trying to think of how to properly express her feelings concerning such a raw topic for both of them. She hadn't talked about Gilbert's death much in the month that followed it; indeed, Lenna took great strides to avoid even recalling the affair. To find herself suddenly at a bar talking about it to Luc, someone who had almost gotten her killed and someone whom she had very much tried to kill yesterday, was a tad overwhelming. After a moment, Lenna was able to form a few more words. "I miss him, though in a very different way from yours, I think."

"Who knows," Luc said. "Gilbert saved me much as he saved you." Lenna wasn't sure where Luc was steering this conversation, but it had all the markings of leading both of them right off the edge of an emotional cliff. She was almost thankful when she heard a cough and something that could have been "pardon me" as two men — students, by their robes — swaggered up to her at the bar.

"Welcome to the Scholar's Cross," said the one to Lenna's right. He was shorter than her, and while at first glance he seemed stocky, Lenna decided it was muscle coating his frame, not excess ale. Lining his chin and jaw was the dark stubble of a young man trying desperately to coax a few hairs into a manly beard.

"Thank you," said Lenna. Ever since her "date" with the half-Ilyan coffee merchant back home a few years ago, Lenna was always hesitant about engaging strangers in bars, especially ones intent on making propositions. She shifted her stance to angle her body toward Luc, affecting a level of intimacy the two certainly didn't share. He recoiled, and Lenna hoped fervently she was the only one who noticed it.

"What are you two drinking?" said the other man, who, albeit taller than his pal, was scrawny and sallow. His speech was flecked with sluggish, slurred words that suggested he liked his beer a little too much and that he spent more time at the Scholar's Cross than he did in a classroom. *Sloppy*, Lenna thought.

The barkeep returned with Lenna's stew and placed it before her; it smelled of clove and mint and sweet, sweet lamb, but the unwanted arrival of the two students had stolen her appetite. "Beer," she said over her shoulder, and desperately wished that Luc would at least attempt to engage her in conversation or act like they were a couple, leaving her free to disregard the ruffians at her side.

But he did no such thing; he merely applied to his water like clockwork, taking small mouthfuls at regular intervals. The men next to Lenna began to laugh and comment on the nature of Luc's choice of beverage, questioning his masculinity with words that most people would probably have slapped them for.

Luc, however incensed and psychotic he had acted in the past month, swiveled tidily to face his fellow patrons. "I'm drinking water, gentlemen, to keep a clear head. So that I do not lose control." His eyes had been beset by an early frost.

"'Lose control?' 'Gentlemen?'" the shorter man snickered. "Listen to that uppity voice! Another noble here as a tourist! And that affectation! What, do you fancy yourself an Ilyan? Or do you just fancy Ilyan men?"

Lenna grimaced. Luc's manner of speech was always eloquent and elegant, suited for theater, she had thought, but she was repulsed by the nasty implication the beefy oaf beside her had just made, especially after all Luc had been through in losing Gilbert. She could feel an urgent, frothing power growing within Luc, oily and tainted like General Valant's. Would she be able to suppress his magic? Most of her power came from rage, not practice, and Lenna could already sense — and understand — that Luc's anger ran far, far deeper than hers did.

"What did you say?" Luc pushed Lenna aside with one hand and she just barely managed not to stumble. It was as if the Godjewel fed off Luc's outrage, for as he shoved her, tiny bubbles of anger compounded Lenna's dismay and rushed to her brain, feeling like a wall of fire burning behind her eyes.

"Don't you push a woman, you fairy. Act like a man. Or wait, are you the woman in your relations, and you just need this little bitch to pretend for you?" The short man butted his chest up against Luc, who surprisingly didn't falter, as the other man slammed his pint glass down on the countertop. The room grew redolent of ozone as Lenna felt a furor of indeterminable strength pour out of her soul and onto the Godjewel. The bonds between the two gems told Lenna that the green stone around Luc's neck was responding too, though in her rage she didn't care. As Luc's right fist connected with the man's eye, the bar exploded in light, force, and a gratuitous amount of beer and lamb stew.

A young officer with mud-colored hair and a well-intentioned smile led Lenna and Luc down a long hallway from their respective cells — cells that, prior to today, had probably never witnessed such rancorous verbal exchanges through their mortared walls, with Luc blaming and harassing Lenna for causing the entire situation — and through a side door into the main office of one of Eran Point's police stations. A few hours earlier, though by now it felt like days, she and Luc had been processed and registered and placed into custody. Lenna Faircloth had been arrested. For a bar fight. What would she ever tell her father? What would Jeffer Scalla, the persnickety older librarian in Port Hollish, say?

The square room, dimly lit in the approaching twilight, was neatly divided in half by a long counter of polished mahogany, with constables and convicts on one side and the free on the other. Apparently Lenna and Luc's escapades had drawn an impressive crowd. Sporting a bright, cheeky grin, Raif waved at Lenna and Luc as the junior officer lifted a portion of the counter, allowing the crestfallen pair of criminals to pass through into freedom. Lenna plodded up to Raif, head low, trying to will away the not-quite-subtle catcalls from the crowd. Another officer tried to wrangle some of the hubbub back out into the streets.

Raif leaned down and whispered into her ear. Was that pride in his voice? "Well, I suppose that's one way to settle a bar tab. Remind me never to allow you and young Tural there to frequent any of my family's establishments at the same time. I've paid your bail, no worries there, but I'd be careful about the trip back to Branford's place." He peeled away with an annoying adroitness and melted back into the ever-growing hodgepodge of students, faculty, and citizens just as Sebastien pushed his way through and stalked up to Lenna and Luc. Still flecked with bits of dried food, both waited, breath held, for their master's wrath. The constabulary's chambers were quickly starting to feel cramped.

"The Branford Estate will of course be covering the damages," he said, his mild tone unable to disguise an underlying chill. "Though I daresay I'll be receiving quite the earful from Mistress Juniam when it comes time to account for the monthly expenses. Come."

"Is that it?" Luc asked. "Are we not to be further held for this… this crude act of vandalism and destruction of private property?"

Lenna felt sorely tempted to kick Apprentice Tural; the bitterness in his voice made her wroth. Did Luc really feel as though he had no role in the events that had landed them in the clink? She mentally checked herself; did Lenna really just use the word "clink" in her inner monologue? Letting out a heavy sigh, she folded her arms and girded herself as best she could for the berating to come. *Clink indeed,* Lenna thought. *Three hours in a small jail and I'm already tossing about prison slang.*

Despite Sebastien's calm visage — he had to maintain face, after all — Lenna could not believe that the future would be especially peachy for his two apprentices. If Lenna and Luc were being treated as the responsibility of the Branford Estate, their inappropriate behavior no doubt reflected on his family's good name, and Sebastien had every right to be offended. They had, after all, acted like quarreling schoolyard children.

A polite cough ruptured the forced quiet that had blanketed the office. Sebastien, biting his lower lip, stared so pointedly at the young man before him that Lenna wondered, for a moment, if he would strike Luc for his comment. Instead, Sebastien shook his head in resignation. "The charges have been dropped. The authorities have been most understanding." Something in the rogue Brother's tone told Lenna that Master Branford had been a particularly active agent in securing her freedom, despite Raif paying the bail. *Well, at least I'm not a convict,* she thought with a minor sense of relief.

"My motorcar is outside," Sebastien added, the finality of his delivery making this more of an order than a statement of fact. "I'd offer Master Vandever a ride back to the manor as well, but there shan't be enough room for him and his engineer." *And Sebastien probably wants to scream at us privately,* Lenna surmised.

Eyes down, Lenna and Luc slogged their way to the door, keenly avoiding the stares and phrases like "children" and "raised in a barn" thrown at them from townsfolk. She was secretly relieved that Luc's face corresponded to her own as they settled into the rear passenger seat of Sebastien's automobile: both pupils matched the cherry-red paint perfectly.

"I hate men," Lenna opined.

Luc refrained from commenting.

"You aren't popular with the lads at the moment either, Faircloth," Sebastien said as he dropped into his seat.

"They started it," she offered.

"And you both finished it. With loads and loads of unchecked magic that resulted in scorching half of the Scholar's Cross bar and putting one student in serious need of healing."

The following morning, after another dour breakfast — a sulking Luc in the morning was worse than geese, Lenna reckoned — a weary Lenna found herself marching determinedly back to the study where Sebastien would be waiting for his two pupils. Luc, unfortunately, was close on her heels, and Lenna doggedly wished she could lose him somehow. Granted, her sense of direction in the manor wasn't so keen that "getting lost" would be far removed from the ordinary, but somehow her leather-clad feet found their way, with displeasure, to the door of her instructor.

"Enter," he called after Lenna's customary knock. Luc lagged back, leaning on the wall opposite the entrance. Discounting the searing glare she felt on her back, Lenna cast open the door and walked, head held as high as possible, into her makeshift classroom.

"Thank you for being punctual today." Sebastien was seated at his desk, flipping through a stack of papers. He didn't even bother to look up as Lenna and, shortly after, Luc entered and took their seats. *This doesn't bode well,* Lenna thought. After the tongue-lashing the two students had received on the aggressively driven ride back to the Branford Estate, she had hoped, perhaps naively, that her teacher would have moved past the incident at the pub.

Two and a half minutes passed without one utterance. Sebastien finally lifted his eyes away from the documents before him and directed them toward his pupils. It was a piercing look, and Lenna felt all color fade from her face as Master Branford regarded both her and Luc in turn. She was, admittedly, a bit curious as to how Luc was faring under such a terrifying stare, but the power behind Sebastien's eyes kept her own gaze locked in place.

"I did not rise so quickly through the ranks of the Blue Crescent Brotherhood because I am stupid or slow. Indeed, I've sometimes been commended on my ability to detach and almost clinically solve issues without emotional concern. However, I took a gamble that my two *sensitive* apprentices could behave themselves in public. Perhaps even learn from each other. It seems I was wrong to place such trust in you both and I should have been more aggressive from the onset. That was my mistake. In order for us to work together, it is imperative you learn to coexist. So, perhaps a bit of — how shall I describe it, indeed — forced candor from both of you would serve us well enough for you to better understand each other."

Luc scowled, placing his hands on the unadorned wooden desk at which he sat. "Master Branford, you can't be serious. I..."

"You what, Apprentice? You refuse?"

Luc sat back in his chair with a huff, his arms folded across his chest. "No, Master Branford."

Subtly, Lenna attempted to glance between teacher and student, trying to decipher what secret battle had just been determined. That Sebastien wished for his two apprentices to share their pasts Lenna could — at least on an intellectual level — appreciate. Despite her misgivings about working with Luc, the volatile nature of the Godjewels was unquestionable: perhaps if the two could understand each other better and come to terms with their roles in Gilbert's life and death, then maybe Lenna and Luc could unite and gain some control of the terrible forces they wielded. And avoid any more bar fights.

"Faircloth," her Master suddenly spoke in her direction. "Through the power of the Godjewel, you've been able to dive deep into the unconscious."

Did he expect an affirmation? Lenna studied Luc for a moment, then turned to her teacher. "Yes, Master Branford."

"Tural, you're aware of what I mean?"

Luc nodded stiffly, but something in the resolute way he held his shoulders made Lenna think he wasn't nearly as knowledgeable as he was pretending to be. Had someone — something — as intense and deranged as Luc access to that ethereal plane, Lenna was sure to have noticed it, much like she could detect the slimy essence of Khareen Valant. No, Luc could only have conjectural knowledge at best.

A furrow in his brow suggested Sebastien considered Luc's response as dubious as Lenna did. Nodding, Sebastien settled tailor-fashion atop his desk in a most unscholarly way and began massaging his temples with his thumb and forefinger. Lenna counted the seconds before he finally removed his hands and spoke.

"So that we better understand each other, and the Godjewels' purpose, I'm going to have you delve into that unconscious realm and learn about the other."

Lenna sharply sucked in a gulp of dusty air and began to cough. From her experiences with Sebastien, she was well aware of the strength such psychic bonds had and was not at all enamored with the idea of becoming so intimate with Luc. And if the lurid expression on his face was any indication, he felt the same. The Godjewel struck a beat, twice, as though indicating its approval. Lenna gave it a stern frown.

"What will this entail, Master Branford?" Luc asked.

"I'll guide you; Lenna is already familiar with the process." Despite herself, Lenna blushed. She could feel Luc's glare trying to bore a hole straight through her skull for possessing magical knowledge he didn't. Sebastien, taking no notice, continued. "If we're going to do large-scale workings with the Godjewels, strong enough to ward off the Krevlum Empire's advances and the Brotherhood's machinations, I'll need you two to understand each other. To work as one."

Not since Gilbert had died had Lenna Faircloth and Luc Tural released such unified voices of despair. Neither party had any desire for such a poignant, permanent union. Sebastien, however, was unmoved: with authority he corralled his students, like foot soldiers going off to war, into his arcane gymnasium and made them stand, side by side and hands held, in the chalked circle upon the floor.

"Lenna," said Sebastien. "You know how to enter the realm of the unconscious by using the power of your Godjewel. Open your mind, Luc, access the power of your gem, and let Lenna guide you down. I'll assist you with the rest." The master took a position directly before — but carefully outside of — the magic circle.

"Are you really sure about this?" Lenna asked. "Master Branford."

A steely look from her tutor resigned Lenna to whatever experience was to come. At his instruction, Lenna shut her eyes and searched inside herself for her core of magical energy, and then fed it into the thirsty blue Godjewel. Instantly the scent of lavender filled the otherwise dusty chamber, and after a moment, she felt Luc's hand tighten around hers and his own scent, lily, intertwine with hers. Slowly, Lenna submerged their psyches in the vast depths of their collective subconscious. One by one, in their minds' eyes, tiny twinkles — souls and stars and all of creation — winked into existence.

Luc's presence, similar to the one time they had worked together in an attempt to save Gilbert from death, was still cloud-soft, though there was a frantic, feral edge to it, a side of him that could recoil and raise its hackles like a caged beast. There was also, Lenna noted, an unexpected sensation: fear. *There are things hard for us to know,* the fear seemed to say.

Like a hedgehog, thought Lenna. The closer a person drew to another, the larger the chance of being hurt. It was that invisible barrier adults erected around their hearts that prevented them from drawing on their magic, because it left their souls so bare and vulnerable.

Yes, said the voice of Sebastien, resounding in Lenna's and Luc's minds. *To understand another is to know their pain.*

Lenna felt a magical nudge from Sebastien, and suddenly the swirling spiral that was the unconscious network straightened sharply into one single shaft of light. Lenna and Luc were plunged headfirst along that ray, and at its end pulsed a violent, miniature sun. They seemed to strike the globe from opposite directions, and in the queerest of ways felt their connection torn apart and pulled together again like the snapping of elastic in one lurching, psychic explosion that filled their minds with flashes of blue, green, and finally, white.

CHAPTER ELEVEN

The bucketful of water was cold and biting, and it lingered on Luc's pale cheeks and lips, briny like tears. His robes, soaked black by the sea, clung to his skinny frame, noticeably marking his rib cage and knobby, trembling knees. Backed up against the smooth stone wall, Luc was captive to a semicircle of boys his age and a few years his senior; one of them, the most malicious lout, Taryn, stood in the center, his apish hands grasping the wooden bucket, deliverer of Luc's punishment.

In the two years since having come to the Island, the dark-haired youth had known little but torment. Poor little rich boy; must be nice to have private tutors to teach you the ways of magic. When he excelled in his studies in the Brotherhood, he was praised by his tutors but pissed on by his peers; when Luc deliberately refrained from answering, the other boys accused him of being condescending. But he could handle that, and on some level had been prepared for it by his father, who had warned him that while many aristocrats' sons joined the Blue Crescent Brotherhood for training in the magical arts, seniority was master there, not wealth or influence.

That was all right; he had learned to shiver before the jeering crowd when he was twelve. He'd grown a thick skin in those two years, so that cascades of water were practically repelled by his haughty exterior and the bombs of refuse flung at him for his heritage no longer left long, rank stains on his heart. And after a few minutes of torment, the bullies would eventually give up on the unperturbed boy, and when darkness fell Luc would wash away their filth and secretly yearn for his sister, shedding the tears of the desperately lonely.

But today the reason for the teasing wasn't his family or his magical ability. For the past few weeks, the pranks had turned violent, more territorial, as though Luc were a beast usurping the hunting grounds of a pack leader. His voice had begun breaking a few months ago, a change he had been told to expect and indeed a malady from which even the brutishly large Taryn suffered. The water had found a new way to sting and the fists had increased their force again with the renewed onslaught of tormenting. And today was the worst yet.

Luc winced more from shame than the actual blows themselves. His parliament, as the groups of similarly aged boys were addressed, had been preparing for their daily physical exercise: in addition to being the foremost arcane training society in the world, the Brotherhood insisted their young mages be fit in body as well as mind. Once a day, they would climb the rocky bluffs of the island or run miles around the outer facilities of the academy. Luc had recently begun to dread the routine.

It was not a dislike of physical exertion that troubled him; it was the times surrounding their sport. His parliament, all fifteen of them, would gather in the narrow changing room that opened into the Brotherhood's arena, a gymnasium that was used primarily for the practice of magical combat but that, if the weather proved too inclement for the younger boys to scurry about outside, served as a substitute location during sports. Eager to shed the cumbersome blue robes that signified their apprenticeships, the boys unceremoniously stripped before shrugging into loose-fitting trousers and breezy white shirts.

It was not a dislike of physical exertion, no, not at all, thought Luc, and as he stared at the ring of young men around him, his teeth chattered, not from the stinging cold of the seawater thrust upon him moments before, but because he remembered in vivid detail glancing at Taryn, and Taryn noticing. Luc hadn't meant to look — well, not really look — but something in his adolescent brain made his yearning eyes turn toward the larger young man as he was changing. Though he quickly averted his eyes, Luc knew it was too late and that, more importantly, he'd never be able to hide the rising in the folds of his loose trousers.

When he was finally found by another novice, a blonde man a few years above him, Luc's left eye was swollen shut and the blood from his nose trickled down and mixed with the smears of fecal matter caking his neck and chest. Despite the dampness and stench of urine, the upperclassman gingerly lifted Luc and slung the tattered mage's arm around his shoulder. A salty, seaweed-like smell washed away some of the stench, and Luc, the world still fuzzy, realized the blonde man was using magic, which was forbidden for novices unless instructed.

"You'll be penalized," Luc said, spitting out a wad of blood on the cold stone of the dressing room floor.

The older boy grinned sheepishly. "Only if you tell my master," he said, and escorted Luc to his chambers, from which, thankfully, his roommate was absent. Novices, from age sixteen onward, were able to share small apartments, rather than the cramped dormitories assigned to individual parliaments.

Gilbert Hovey, in ways both emotionally and physically, had saved Luc's life that night, washing away the most immediate filth with delicate, steady compassion. The older mage made no comment as to how or why Luc might have fallen prey to such treatment, though he did grimace as he peeled away the urine-soaked trousers and promptly threw them into the fire. Turning away, Gilbert pointed to a washbasin on the plain wooden chest next to the entryway to his apartment, and he stepped off to the side to give Luc the privacy to wash on his own. Stunned by his kindness and ashamed at his own actions, Luc bumbled about until he managed some state of cleanliness.

"My fellow novice left the Brotherhood some time ago," Gilbert announced loudly to the wall. "And they have yet to find a replacement to force upon me. You're free to spend the night in his bed, as I bet you really don't want to head back to your parlie's dormitory."

Luc, dressed in a borrowed pair of bedclothes one size too large, nodded to Gilbert's back and scuttled over to the tidy, unoccupied bed against the far side of the room. He sank into it and pulled the covers up around his neck, weeping silent, hot tears that burned his swollen eye like a brand of iron. He would know no sleep tonight, lost in his pain and shame.

The light in the room dimmed, the senior apprentice having snuffed out the gas lamp. The flickering rosy embers from the fire cast strangely comfortable shadows against the wall, and Luc could imagine he was back in his many-towered home along the coast of the Krevlum Empire, straddling the northern border of Fallowfields. His sister, his twin, would be there, gabbing idly about the most nonsensical of matters, and Luc would simply dote on her every word, dreading the day he would turn twelve and be shipped off to the island of the Blue Crescent Brotherhood.

Luc started as a hand suddenly slid through his hair and pressed lightly against his skull. The seaweed smell returned as Gilbert worked healing magic on the fourteen-year-old apprentice, unknotting tense muscles and reducing the swelling in his eye until it was free of pain and returned to normal size, though still red and stinging from tears. After a moment, Luc heard his savior exhale, satisfied, and felt the hand retreat.

"You'll be punished," was all Luc could say.

"No more than you have been," the mage replied quietly. "I'm Gilbert, by the way. Gil."

"I'm Luc Tural."

"I know," Gilbert said. "Now get some rest, Apprentice Tural." And Luc's senior pulled away to the bed across the room as the fire crackled and popped steadily against the persistent ocean cold.

When Luc awoke the next morning, Gilbert had already left, the more advanced novices having to rise in the early dawn hours to spend extra time under the tutelage of their masters. "Good luck today!" was emblazoned in glowing runes on the oaken door of the apartment, unabashedly written by Gilbert in what Luc considered a misuse of magic and strictly against the rules of apprenticeship. He hastily dispelled them, thankful that the older mage had not tried to make them more bothersome to remove.

Luc would indeed need luck today, he thought. The members of his parlie would be expecting him, blackened and broken. Tentatively, he raised one hand to his cheek and eye, but there was no sign of swelling or trace of pain. Gilbert had been an effective healer indeed. Once Taryn and the others saw Luc's face, though, they'd know that he had either healed himself, which was grounds for further punishment from the masters, or gone to the medic, which would be telling tales, grounds for further punishment from his enemies.

Gilbert had somehow managed to retrieve a clean uniform for the younger apprentice, so there would be no reason for Luc to return to his parlie before his morning tutorials. He dressed with the grim resolve of a prisoner heading to his sentencing and painfully longed for his twin sister; she would know how to handle the bullies. But, being female, she had been denied the same access to the Brotherhood Luc was afforded, despite the affluence of his family, regardless of her own innate magical abilities.

The hallways outside Gilbert's apartment were empty of apprentices, leaving Luc alone with his thoughts as he tiptoed down the cool stone floors built into the natural rock formations of Crescent Island. Though they did provide the bonus of trapping warmth in the colder months and cool air in the summer, the serpentine passageways cut a confusing path through the numerous divisions and departments of the Brotherhood.

Luc silently blessed his innate sense of direction and found himself before the chamber of his first tutorial — Continental history — a few minutes early. Though the subject fascinated him, Luc knew he would have to keep a low profile if he wanted to survive the morning. Willing his hand to stop trembling, he reached for the solid handle on the wooden door, turning it and pushing the door open.

The misty morning light fell upon a mostly full classroom. Luc was puzzled. Taryn and his cronies normally flirted with tardiness, and to have them all present and eyeing the door hungrily could only mean that they had arranged their early attendance to witness Luc's state. Thankfully, Master Petrip, a mournful old wizard who hated teaching almost as much as he hated adolescents, had yet to sweep into the classroom in his usual self-important way. Luc gulped inaudibly and scurried toward his place in the middle, making certain to keep his head down.

Taryn's boot had "accidentally" found its way into the aisle as Luc passed, and the hurrying mage tripped and stumbled, though he somehow managed to regain his balance and make it to his seat. His parlie was small enough to afford him a desk not adjacent to any of the other savages in the class. Still, a few mere rows and seats couldn't deter Taryn from resorting to his usual catcalls.

"Hey, pervert, where were you last night?"

"Wallowing in your own tears and piss?" asked Driggs, Taryn's second-in-command.

"Silence, please," a voice said from the rear of the class, and Master Petrip made his way down the aisle to the lectern. "Where Apprentice Tural spent his evening last night is certainly a matter of curiosity for us all, but it is a matter that has very little to do with history." Petrip was dressed in the full regalia of an initiated member of the Blue Crescent Brotherhood, with intricately embroidered scalloped sleeves falling to his waist, bulging a bit at his burgeoning belly. Luc always pictured the completely bald Petrip as a giant, self-indulgent baby, but even his infantile appearance couldn't hamper the excitement that stirred in the apprentice when he thought that one day he, too, would be able to wear the robes of a Brother, to be in charge.

"Seems like yesterday is history enough to me to warrant a discussion," Taryn pronounced loudly.

"Enough, Apprentice," said Petrip. "Parliament, today we will be having a special... guest speaker." There was an edge in his voice that alerted Luc to the fact that Petrip wasn't particularly pleased about an unannounced addition to the tutorial.

The boys chatted among themselves for a moment as an older apprentice confidently breezed down the aisle to stand beside Master Petrip. His strides were almost too long for his legs; it was the walk of the man into which his body had not yet fully grown. When he turned to appraise the class, he nodded his shaggy blonde head and gave a large grin when he saw Luc and waved.

Blanching, Luc sank into his chair: it was Gilbert. There would be no hiding where he had spent the evening now; his parlie would either make the connection themselves or beat out the reason why an older mage was lowering himself to pay attention to a younger apprentice like Luc. The murmuring from Taryn and his gang stopped abruptly, and Luc was almost tempted to perform a glamour on himself to distract their attention, though he knew it was beyond his current ability and, even if possible, would be certain to cause more trouble.

"Apprentice Gilbert Hovey," Master Petrip announced with the acidity of someone who had just taken a bite out of a lemon. "A few years ago he presented a very compelling argument on the cyclical nature of our world's history, and under the guidance of his current tutor, Master Branford, he has, I am told, proposed some even more interesting ideas. It is at Master Branford's behest that Apprentice Hovey will be presenting some of his recent theories to this class. Apprentice Hovey."

Petrip stepped down from the podium, settling his plump frame into a rickety chair that looked as old as the school itself. Gilbert assumed the master's place and gripped both sides of lectern in his large hands, completely at ease despite being only a few years older than the members of the parliament. "All right, lads," he said cheerfully. "Let me tell you the secrets of the universe." He grinned again, and Luc gradually found himself enraptured — and, after a quick glance around the room, noticed that his classmates were as well — by the older apprentice's ideas on their world's history.

The lecture seemed to end as quickly as it began, thought Luc sadly, and he shuffled out of the classroom. Unsurprisingly, Taryn and his lot stood waiting off to the side of the corridor, huddled in conspiracy. When Luc's slight form caught their eyes, a hush immediately fell over the gang and they turned, Taryn in front. Luc stared at the ground, hoping that avoiding their gazes would somehow spare him from what would unfailingly follow.

The silence was dense and heavy. These boys meant to fight, and Luc's fists were balled so tightly beneath the folds of his robes that his nails dug into his flesh and drew blood. He daren't swing first: all he could do now was look at the floor and count his breaths before the assault began.

But it didn't. The instant Taryn opened his mouth, before the even most basic of syllables could escape his lips, Luc felt a heavy clap on his shoulder from behind. He jumped in surprise just as Taryn's mouth slammed shut. Looking up, Luc saw the glowing features of the young man who had risked much to protect him last night and now, as if conjured by the very magic they were on Crescent Island to study, appeared at his side: an older, stronger mage who didn't fear the wrath of Taryn and his mob.

"You lads seemed to enjoy the talk," Gilbert said jocularly. "It's a topic I happen to find particularly interesting; would any of you care to join me for further discussion in the junior library? I'm fairly certain your parliament has a few free hours before sport."

Taryn's group stood, stone-faced, and stared at their senior as though he had asked them to accompany him to the moon. It was highly unusual — in fact, almost an unspoken breach of decorum — for an upperclassman to fraternize with his inferiors so publicly. Even within the same year, parliaments seldom socialized with any novices outside their own immediate social circle.

"No," Taryn said. His attempt at keeping his voice flat did little to mask his anger.

"I'm sorry," Gilbert responded, sliding his hand from Luc's shoulder and stepping forward to bridge the gap between himself and the group of rallied youths. "Is that the way you address an upperclassman?" Any trace of joviality had disappeared from Gilbert's tone.

Frustration contorted Taryn's face, and Luc immediately regretted staying the night in Gilbert's chambers. Spending the evening battered and covered in excrement in his parliament dormitory would have been miserable, but probably preferable to the beating he'd receive because of the older novice's intervention. Inwardly groaning, Luc wondered how he would ever escape revenge for Gilbert's interference.

"My apologies, Apprentice Hovey," Taryn said through gritted teeth. "I meant no disrespect. Thank you for the invitation, but I think we'll go prepare for our upcoming examinations. Excuse us." He shot Luc a caustic look, then stamped off down a southern corridor with his thugs in tow. Their heavy footsteps echoed like small bursts of thunder against the stone walls.

Gilbert turned to face Luc. "And what about you, Luc? Do you want to join your parlie mates, or shall we go have a talk instead?"

Frowning, Luc took a step back. It would simply not do to continue provoking the wrath of his fellow novices. But then something in his mind shifted, changed, when he saw Gilbert's diffident but reassuring smile, and Luc realized that there might be some things in this world worth suffering for. Unintentionally, he felt his frown melt into something of an awkward smile, and Luc managed a nod.

Gilbert, pleased, grabbed his young companion by the hand and began tugging him down another corridor, not toward the library but toward his quarters.

Like the blur of quickly turning pages of a picture book, the next two months flew by. Gilbert, or a platoon of Gilbert doppelgängers, always seemed to be one step ahead of Taryn and his squad of bullies. When midday and evening meals came, rather than associate with novices of his own year, Gilbert secured a pair of seats at one of the small tables in the dining hall, and when Luc would enter, scampering in before or trailing after his parliament brethren, Gilbert would wave boldly and pat the table with his hand. Luc's face grew red each time the older students looked at him, but he shared the table with Gilbert even so.

Even the rumors among novices of his own rank never seemed to faze Gilbert, who laughed off their questions or concerns and flashed them a casual, if a bit lopsided, smile. The older mage, who excelled in his studies and was well-liked even by his superiors, carried himself with the ease of one who was comfortable just being himself — just being *Gilbert* — and would shrug and ruffle Luc's hair whenever anyone questioned his behavior. It didn't seem to matter to Gilbert that Luc was his junior, and for a time, Luc found a happiness and a sense of protection he hadn't known since he'd left his sister's company.

Letters from Luc's parents were rare. His father was too busy for idle correspondence, and his mother too occupied with matters of society, but silence on Clarie's part was unusual and disconcerting. Gilbert's carefree kindness and occasional embrace, however, wiped away Luc's concerns. Slowly, under the tutelage of the Brotherhood and extra lessons in Gil's quarters, Luc blossomed into the promising young mage Gilbert had assured him he would become. In his happiness Luc gradually became immune to the abhorrent glares from Taryn and his other parlie members as his skills progressed far more rapidly; he failed to feel the impending pressure, a tension in the air building like a storm rolling in across the sea.

One morning Luc awoke to a wide-eyed Taryn leering down at him. The moonlight softly illuminated the barrack-like dormitory of their parliament, and Taryn, dressed only in a pair of airy linen trousers, towered over him, his height seemingly doubled in the past few months. At first Luc was overcome with fear, the gripping, vise-like terror from being bullied, but through his association with Gilbert, a cocky confidence quickly overcame any paranoia.

"What?" Luc said in his normal voice, not caring if he woke the other boys. He squinted up at Taryn expectantly.

"Tomorrow," Taryn said. He walked off toward his own bunk, having delivered his message to his apparent satisfaction.

Tomorrow, thought Luc. What could Taryn be planning? Still, Luc had grown over the past two months as well, and the rigorous physical training that was mandatory for all apprentices in the Brotherhood had bestowed upon Luc's once-frail frame firm, lean muscle. He was no longer the last to arrive at the end of a race; no longer was he fearful of changing into his exercise uniform. His magic was stronger than his peers' and, most importantly, he had Gilbert. And though Taryn's warning, or threat, still echoed in the back of his mind, Luc found a few more hours of sleep before the Brotherhood's auditory cantrip roused the boys in the parlie from their slumber.

Taryn's strange moonlit message seemed barely more than a dream, and Luc chatted merrily over a plate of rubbery scrambled eggs and floppy toast. Gilbert, strangely, seemed withdrawn and lost in his own thoughts, only grunting in acknowledgement at appropriate moments during Luc's prattling. Prodding Gilbert's hand with his fork, Luc inquired if something was amiss. "You're not even touching your breakfast," he commented.

"Hm?" Gilbert said, taken aback. He had been idly poking about the overcooked eggs with his fork, but none of the food ventured anywhere near his lips. "Oh, it's nothing."

Luc stared at Gilbert with as commanding a countenance as he could muster. The urge to throw some toast may have entered his mind, but Luc was too well-bred for such crass behavior. "Gil, what is it? You know you can't keep secrets from me; I can tell something's on your mind."

Running a hand through his cowlicked hair, Gilbert attempted a reassuring smile, but it was feeble; his eyes were red and the corners of his mouth pinched. "I have a meeting with Master Petrip today," he said vaguely.

"A meeting? But he isn't even one of your tutors."

"I know, but my field of research has, apparently, attracted the attention of some of the Brothers, and Petrip wants to see me about another presentation."

That was odd; by all accounts of gossip and Luc's own personal experience in Master Petrip's tutorials, the older Brother hated any sort of collaboration, particularly when it involved his inferiors. That he would summon Gilbert, still a novice, was odd indeed, and Luc said as much (even though Luc had the utmost faith in the solidity of Gilbert's scholarly achievements).

"I agree it's a little out of the ordinary," Gilbert replied, stuffing some of the toast into his mouth. After a solid gulp, he continued, "But an order from a Brother is an order. I can't very well say no."

"When is the interview?"

"After your tutorial."

Luc paled. Every day for the past several months, Gilbert had been deliberately arranging his schedule to be waiting for Luc after Petrip's tutorial, so that Taryn and his henchmen could have no alone time with Luc following the lesson. And today Petrip had summoned Gilbert away; could Taryn have known? Could he know that today, for the first time in ages, Luc would be alone and vulnerable?

Suddenly Gilbert's hand was on Luc's shoulder, giving it a firm squeeze. "It will be fine. Petrip is a pompous arse, but he's not an idiot. If he were to deliberately endanger an apprentice, he'd be stripped of his robes."

Despite Gilbert's reassurances, one look at his concerned expression, thinly veiled by the guise of a cheerful countenance, and a sudden sense of dread filled Luc's belly. Something was terribly off, and those rubbery eggs did not feel nearly as settled as they did a moment ago. Taryn would be waiting.

The order's magical clarion sounded again, indicating the conclusion of breakfast, and despite Luc's desire to linger, as he normally did with Gilbert, the older mage quickly gathered up his tray and bussed it to the cleaning station. Crestfallen, Luc tidied up his own platter and followed suit, keeping his steps slow and deliberate. As he passed the tray to the apprentice on cleaning duty, the sleeves of Gilbert's robes brushed Luc's own, and in a fleeting gesture, the older mage's fingers slid across Luc's hand. The hair on his arms stood on end.

"See you later," Gilbert said, and quickly made his exit. A second ringing of the bell startled Luc, who realized with embarrassment that he had been holding up the line for almost a minute. Face scarlet, Luc hurried off to his tutorial, determined to focus on the matters at hand, and ignore Gilbert's apprehension and Taryn's warning.

CHAPTER TWELVE

The morning drew on strictly according to routine, though the knot of tension in Luc's stomach never diffused. It wasn't as though he was particularly concerned about Taryn; as he gathered up and replaced his notes and texts into his standard-issue apprentice satchel, Luc came to the conclusion that he wasn't even entirely sure what he was worried about. Something, he realized, was just *off*. Shaking his head, he prepared himself for Petrip's lesson, which was bound to be either boring or, perversely, dangerous: both results required him to steady his mind.

Surprisingly enough, Luc was the last to arrive; even Master Petrip was present as Luc cautiously stepped across the threshold and into the dusty classroom. Taryn and all of his fellow parliament members were already seated, books open, and Master Petrip's eyes traveled over Luc with a mixture of curiosity and… hunger? Mentally shrugging it off, Luc pushed forward, trying to avoid everyone's ogling, and settled in his usual spot. He could feel their stares, but he kept his own eyes forward, glazed over and avoiding everything but the impending lesson.

And everything proceeded without incident. Petrip taught, or rather spoke at, the class with his usual grandstanding, his own voice cracking at the height of his lecture. Luc, with elegant strokes of his pen, took down line after line of notation, though he was fairly certain most of the material was superfluous and would never appear again, either practically or in an examination. But Luc scribed and scribed, so as not to let Taryn find one drop of weakness or deficiency inside him. Even in his fastidiousness, though, that nagging feeling in his gut continued to grow.

Petrip finished his lecture a few minutes early, which was odd considering his propensity to be what Gilbert referred to as an "infinite source of hot air and noxious gas." Muttering something about an important meeting, the bulbous Brother and his long-sleeved robes swished out of the room, brushing against chairs and leaving clouds of dust motes trailing behind. Luc sighed; he knew from here on out, he was alone.

With their instructor's departure, a hush had fallen over the group of young men. Knowing Taryn and his tactics, Luc presumed the other boys in his parlie would wait until they knew Gilbert was not lurking about the corridor before transitioning into whatever aggressive formation they chose for today. Despite the curious, foreboding sensation Luc experienced, he still felt no fear toward the boys. Something might be wrong, but he was stronger now; he would not let Taryn abuse him any longer.

Deciding not to delay the inevitable and having finished storing his belongings, Luc slung his satchel over one shoulder and strode confidently out into the corridor, ready for whatever Taryn and his gang might have prepared for him. Petrip was aware of the situation; Luc was certain he had to be. It was no secret that a rising, powerful apprentice was watching out for one of his juniors — a particularly hated one at that.

Luc placed himself in the corner of the small foyer outside his classroom, the corridors — and only forms of egress — well out of reach should he be surrounded. Still, that was what he wanted; the foyer was only so large, and having the solid support of stone at his back made certain that the other boys couldn't catch him in a massive pincer attack and pummel him from both sides. And there he stood, braced against the coolness of the walls, waiting for attackers who never came.

Luc watched with amazement as, one by one, Taryn and the other members of his parliament walked out of the classroom and headed down the northern corridor. They completely ignored him, as though he had somehow managed the art of true invisibility. Within a moment the classroom had emptied, and the normally boisterous group of thugs had already disappeared into the distance. Though Luc was naturally inquisitive, he seldom pursued untoward, foreign situations. But something within told him he had to follow.

The soles of his simple apprentice boots made nary a sound as he crept along the northern corridor toward one of the quadrangles where apprentices tended to idle about during free time between or after tutorials. Taryn and his ilk were huddled around a large board positioned at the northwestern corner, where apprentices could post messages or Brothers announcements of extra tutorials or current news. It was also where the courier deposited all correspondence from outside Crescent Island.

Despite his attempt at stealth, all eyes turned to Luc as he entered. Any apprentices not affiliated with his parliament or Taryn's gang quickly departed, and suddenly the common room was mostly empty, and the wide expanse between Luc and Taryn an arena hungry for a kill. And still, Luc's curiosity propelled him forward. Taryn and his group turned to face the giddy young mage as he approached.

"Come to get your letters, Tural?" Taryn asked. "That's rare. I thought you didn't hear much from the rich family back home." The oaf was clutching a piece of paper, an opened letter, in his paw. Luc's eyes were immediately drawn to it, because there could only be one reason Taryn and his group would be lurking here, reading the post.

"Do I have a letter, Taryn?" Luc asked, drawing a few paces nearer.

"Yeah, go figure. You should check more often; it's been there since yesterday."

"Who is it from?"

Taryn shrugged, dropping the letter to the ground. "Your mother, maybe? Couldn't be bothered to get through all the pedantic courtesies you high-society lot are so fond of writing in your letters."

Luc dove for the sheet of parchment, falling to his knees onto the stone floor where it had landed in the space between Taryn and him. The bigger boy stepped forward, hovering over the letter. His scent was musky and dominating, an alpha male leading a pack of hungry dogs. Luc looked up pleadingly into his classmate's vacant eyes.

"Now, now, you precious little thing, you," said Taryn. "You know that you have to pay for the post, don't you? It isn't free, and knowing you, you should be able to pay handsomely." The taller lad began to tug at the strings of his hempen trousers. "Trust me, you want to know what's in the letter."

Revulsion welled up in the pit of Luc's stomach. A letter from his family was rare enough, but this sort of sickening behavior, after all the previous incidents of cruelty and his newfound strength from Gilbert, was enough to set him over the edge. He could feel the magic building inside him, but rather than unleash it upon Taryn, Luc howled an anguished cry and launched himself upward, pummeling the bigger mage in his midsection. The sheer surprise of Luc's ambush caught Taryn unawares, and the apprentice faltered, his balance shattered.

Luc got in one sweet, satisfying punch, his fist driving right into Taryn's fleshy cheek, before he was pulled off by the other members of his parliament. Enraged, Luc struggled and strained against the restraints of the older boys. Taryn stood up, stroking his jaw and appreciating the blow. His trousers still partially untied, he smiled at Luc and began to urinate on the fallen letter, smudging its ink and rendering it indecipherable mush on the stone floor of the quadrangle.

Watching in horror, Luc looked up at Taryn with what he could only imagine was a primal stare of desperation. "The letter. Taryn. The letter… what did it say?"

"Just some family news," Taryn replied coolly. He finished up and tied his trousers. "Your sister's dead. Magic went out of control." He spat on the ground.

There was a ringing in Luc's ears, a physical manifestation of the utter shock his mind was trying to buffer. He knew Clarie was magically gifted — maybe even stronger than Luc himself — but she couldn't have died. Could she? He couldn't believe it; he *wouldn't* believe it. If he was telling the truth about what was in the letter, then Taryn had known since last night. Gilbert had been called away. Luc was alone, Luc was threatened, and, like a caged animal expecting to be struck with a stick, he howled and thrashed against his captors.

The blows came one after another, mixed with slurs and gibes about Luc's heritage and his relationship with Gilbert. Luc was bounced around like a child's toy, from one parlie boy to the other, each member of Taryn's gang swinging, jabbing, and eventually, when Luc fell to the cold stone floor, kicking. The wetness all became one concoction of blood, urine — some of unknown origin and some Luc's — and eventually the salty tang of tears as he wept, not from the pain or the humiliation, not from the mockery, but from this tear in his heart, the vacant place where Clarie was, had been, would never be again.

"Clarie," he whimpered, his voice the barely audible and a line of blood-laden spittle dribbling to the floor.

"The magicking bitch-sister of yours is dead, you perverted little shit," hissed Taryn as he leaned forward and grabbed Luc by the hair, yanking his head up from the cold floor. "See where your depravity has gotten you? Your smugness?" Luc felt his body rise and trembled as Taryn, who with age had developed quite capable muscles, lifted the battered mage up by his hair.

Luc thought he heard a voice, and on the air there was a faint, floral scent that wasn't strong enough to fully permeate the thick wall of sick surrounding the gang. Somewhere in the depth of his mind a voice called. *Shield,* it said. Luc's addled brains could barely grasp the idea of producing a formulated magical effect, but he found that his diligence, his tutelage under many Brothers and his extra lessons with Gilbert gave him the subconscious control he needed. Delicate threads of power enveloped Luc, and a shield, albeit tenuous, was formed.

"Magic is forbidden, Apprentice," one of the boys sneered.

"Looks like this twisted fairy needs even more punishment," another piped.

"Clarie," Luc stuttered again, the tears freely streaming down his dirty, bloody face.

Taryn, grinning like a man possessed, easily tore through Luc's makeshift barrier with the simplest of gestures. "Punishment it is," he said, and brought his knee swiftly up between Luc's legs. A flash of light and an angry, surprised shout was all Luc registered before his head met the solid stone of the floor and oblivion came.

Lights were dim as Luc slowly returned to the world of the living. Though his head mildly ached, there wasn't much pain in his body. He tried wiggling his toes and fingers, but there was no response; despite a mild sense panic, whatever magics were restraining him appeared to calm him and try to force his eyelids shut. His memories were piecemeal at best. Rage, such rage, and despair. *Clarie.* He wanted to cry out but discovered he could not even open his mouth to utter her name.

It was then that he became attuned to the sounds around him. There were two voices, one at once recognizable as the high-pitched vocals of Master Petrip, speaking in heated bursts. The other, a voice that Luc couldn't place, replied every so often in quiet, moderate sentences, as though he wasn't really paying much attention to Petrip's incessant rant. Luc realized that both parties, though he could barely make out their shapes through his heavy-lidded eyes, were standing quite close to wherever he was lying.

"He needs more healing, a specialist," said the unknown voice. "Though the wards around him should keep him stable until I send for one."

"And why am I here?" Petrip whined. "I'm too busy with my research to be involved in petty squabbles between apprentices."

"Too busy interviewing *my* ward, Petrip?" There was a hint of a challenge in the second voice, and Luc struggled to focus. "You know such meetings need to be cleared through me, his mentor."

Petrip huffed audibly. "Nonsense — it was a harmless few minutes; I was just curious about his research. The apprentice is promising..."

The Brother's voice was abruptly swallowed by the slamming of a wooden door. Luc could make out heavy footsteps pounding against the stone floor toward their direction. Through stuffed nostrils Luc detected ozone, a sign that powerful magic had been recently used, mixed with the briny scent of the sea: Gilbert's magic. Although half-blind, Luc easily distinguished the form of his hero approaching Master Petrip.

"You bastard." Gilbert's voice rang out, bouncing echoes around the corners of the confined room. "You called me away because you knew they would be ready for him. With that letter."

"Know your place, Apprentice Hovey," Petrip snapped. "I won't stand for such language."

"I won't stand for you trying to have him killed," came Gilbert's reply. "That's a warning."

"You dare to threaten me? I could have you expelled for that alone." Luc could feel power rising from the mages, stifling pressure in the air around them.

"Enough," said the third voice, and with a blurry motion Luc couldn't make out clearly, he dispersed the urgent surge of magical energy. "Petrip, do not threaten *my* apprentice. I will reprimand him for his actions."

Both Gilbert and Petrip raised their voices in outcry, but Luc's head was still too muddled to make out what was being said. The third voice cut them off again. "I'm hereby granting an indefinite change of Apprentice Luc Tural's parliament and living arrangements. Gilbert, he'll be sharing your quarters and, though it's irregular, I trust you can keep him apprised of anything he might miss in Brother Petrip's... stimulating tutorials." A muffled noise of disgust came from Petrip's direction. "He'll receive private tutelage from Apprentice Gilbert Hovey until he is assigned a fitting Brother to become his official mentor. Judging by his magical aptitude, any number of Brothers will be eager to take on such a promising young student."

Gilbert's shoulders dropped in overt relief. "Thank you, Master. I won't let any harm come to him."

The figure nodded. "Off with you now, and prepare your quarters and arrange for the transport of Apprentice Tural's belongings."

"Yes, Master." Gilbert leaned over Luc's prone body, and Luc made certain to keep his eyes shut to maintain the pretense of being asleep. The older boy's hand swept over Luc's head, shifting a stray lock that had fallen to his forehead. "I'm sorry I wasn't there," he whispered, and walked quietly out of the room.

The chamber remained silent for a moment or two after Gilbert had shut the door behind him. Luc took it as an opportunity to sort out the jumble of thoughts sloshing about his addlepated brain. *He was going to live with Gilbert now, permanently. Gilbert would take care of him.* He clung to those words like a piece of flotsam in a stormy sea. *Clarie...*

"This is highly irregular," said Petrip, affronted. "Moving a younger apprentice into the quarters of an older apprentice, especially considering... the nature of their relationship."

The unknown voice shut down Petrip, mid-sentence. "While I am aware of your opinions regarding such relationships, it's none of your concern. It's not as if we can return him to his parliament, not now."

"There *is* no parliament left. What will you tell him?" Luc could feel Petrip's eyes travel along his body and hoped the elder magician didn't notice his consciousness.

Unconcerned, the unknown Brother responded, "I'll tell him the boys were expelled for their assault on him. It's more or less the truth."

"Hovey killed them, Brother," Petrip said. "In cold blood. He could have easily just overpowered them; his magic was stronger and more trained than that entire lot's combined."

The inner workings of Luc's brain ground to a halt, unable to comprehend the words Petrip was uttering. Gilbert was no murderer; he was only protecting Luc, as he always did. Petrip was twisting the situation because he loathed Luc, loathed Gilbert, and loathed their combined talent and their relationship. Sensation was beginning to return to his extremities, and Luc wiggled his toes in impatience.

"Hovey rescued a fellow apprentice from being brutally assaulted," said the stranger's voice. "And the apprentices at fault have already been shipped home on this evening's charter, as far as anyone is concerned."

"You expect me to lie?" Petrip's voice became shrill.

"I would never ask a Brother to lie." There was a brief pause and Luc thought he could hear the shuffling of feet. "Just like you'd never ask me to keep it quiet that you gave an apprentice's personal correspondence to his parliament, or more specifically, to a notably hostile, jealous pupil who wanted him dead. Or that you arranged for any protection to be conspicuously absent during the time Luc Tural was almost beaten to death."

Petrip's wrath was like a summer sun against Luc's skin, blistering and raw. His head was spinning, not just from the magics the other Brother had worked on him, but from the sheer implications of everything being discussed in front of the seemingly unconscious apprentice. A tallish figure walked toward the door and Petrip turned to follow.

"What are you scheming at, Sebastien?" Petrip said acerbically. "Hovey knows too much; don't tell me your interest in the artifact recovered from that traitorous ginger bastard Faircloth has spread to your pupil as well. Or wait — is it because Hovey is from Port Hollish? What are you hiding?"

The door squeaked on its hinges, but halted midway, partially open. The other mage spoke tersely. "I'm sure I have no idea what you're talking about, Brother Petrip. Thane Faircloth's 'treachery' to the Brotherhood was before I was even an apprentice; the acquisition of a supposed Godjewel from him later on was also something I was not involved in. And, much like your research, mine is my own. I'd advise you to apply yourself to yours; I'm summoning the healer now, and we'd hate for you to have to answer difficult questions." The door creaked shut behind the wizards.

Luc had no idea what a Godjewel was or who Thane Faircloth, supposed traitor to the Brotherhood, might be; for now, he was once again overcome with weariness. Whatever magics had kept him stable and unconscious seemed to be reasserting their hold on his body, lulling him back to sleep, so perhaps it wasn't a fluke that he was awake for those secret conversations, after all.

Faint sunlight filtered through a small window — barely an arrow slit — in Gilbert's chamber and cast shadows over the few pieces of furniture in the room. Luc awoke slowly, his brain foggy from the potent spells that had kept him asleep. The evening sea air flirted with the small fire in Gilbert's hearth, creating the perfect mixture of cool breeze and subtle warmth. As he roused from his slumber, Luc realized the warmth wasn't just from the fire: a pair of arms surrounded him from behind, embracing him.

Body aching, Luc rolled around and found himself looking into the deep eyes of Gilbert, whose back was pressed up against the wall, legs wrapped around Luc's own. The younger man was quick to blush and awkwardly shifted about, unsure of how to behave. He felt strange emotions and sensations in his body beginning to stir.

"Don't thrash about so," Gilbert said softly. "Even with all the healing, you're going to be sore for a few days."

Luc settled, but his limbs felt gangly, out of place. He still wasn't sure where to put them, or if he should even look Gilbert in the eyes. He felt ashamed, and he had so many questions. The close proximity and Gilbert's rich oceanic scent blanketed Luc, and he felt as though he could drift off to sleep again, forever, in Gilbert's steadfast arms.

"Is this all right?" Gilbert asked, and he once again brushed a stray lock from Luc's forehead.

Conflicting emotions in his head rendered Luc speechless, and all he could manage was a timid nod. Gilbert smiled in return.

"They won't hurt you, not anymore," said Gilbert.

"Did you… did you really kill them?"

Gilbert's expression went stony and distant. "They were going to kill you. Maybe today you would have survived. But as Master Petrip aptly demonstrated, there will be certain forces that try to tear us apart. I will protect you; I swear it."

Luc wished he could feel remorse or guilt at the loss of the members of his parliament, but secretly he was relieved. Gilbert had saved him again, and this time for good. There was such a sense of comfort, here entwined with Gilbert, that somehow, beyond the logic that fathomed the scope of his protector's actions, Luc could do naught but sink into Gilbert's body.

"My sister, Clarie," Luc began quietly, his head buried in Gilbert's shoulder. "Is it true?"

Luc heard a sigh, and Gilbert's hand was once more combing through his hair, stroking the back of his head. "Yes, Luc. She succumbed to the fate of those whose talent is so great that their bodies can no longer contain their own power."

It was not an unforeseen scenario. The Tural family was adamant in its tradition of adhering to the Brotherhood's tenets: only sons could be trained; daughters, if they possessed any magical gifts at all, would have no such option, and hopefully, like most children, their power to access magic would fade with time. But Clarie's hadn't, and now… and now…

Two lips pressed against Luc's eyelid, which he had already jammed shut to dam the outpouring of tears. His thoughts went to his twin sister, to images of her calling for him as she was slowly driven insane and her soul eaten away from inside. The hurt was such that Luc forgot the beating, the aching in his body. All he knew was a wall of insufferable grief that he would never be able to surmount. The tears did not stop until much later that evening, but when they finally did Luc found an exhausted sleep, cradled in the arms of his savior.

He only barely heard Gilbert whisper into his ear. "I will fix things," he said. "I will set things right. And make certain that no one suffers such pain again."

Gilbert adhered to his promise of protecting Luc, and for the next few years the two were inseparable, even after Luc had resumed normal lessons with another parliament. Word had spread around Crescent Island that the apprentice had potential, much like the soon-to-be-ordained Apprentice Hovey. Eventually, Luc came to know of the jewel, and how dangerous men like Petrip should never be in control of such an artifact. No one should, Gilbert had fervently explained. He and his former master, Sebastien, would take it away to keep it safe from those, like the bullies of Luc's former parlie, who could abuse its power.

Of course Luc would follow Gilbert. His love was pure and unsullied, and the very thought of waking up in their quarters to a sunlit day without Gilbert's smile in the bed next to him would be more devastating than losing his place in the Brotherhood. Though over the years Luc had hardened and excelled in his studies, and turned his bitterness toward his family for not giving his sister the proper education she needed for control into a rigid adherence to the tenets of the Brotherhood, in his heart his strongest allegiance was to Gilbert.

But then came that night. The night a clap of thunder struck his cheek in one swift, decisive moment. The force of Lenna's blow knocked the balance from Luc and stung him as deeply as the piercingly cold crystals of snow he fell into. He felt every blood vessel in his face rise up to the skin, a vilely purple bruise starting to flower. The twitch of an eyebrow, a shallowness of breath, a tightening in the stomach. Every memory of Taryn and his gang flooded Luc's mind, but still he was not prepared for the blow that was to follow. *Clarie. Gilbert. I couldn't help you, because…*

"You were never worthy of Gil's love," came the cutting words from the librarian's lips.

It all ended there; Luc was young again, alone and frail. Darkness and despair; that wall of sorrow crumbling down upon him, crushing all light and hope in his frail, battered heart.

Lenna's eyes shot open and she clapped her hand to her mouth, salty tears lining her cheeks. "Luc," she called, but the mage's back was already turned to her as he walked out of Sebastien's training room.

CHAPTER THIRTEEN

Lenna stood, statue-still, in her teacher's magic circle, her mind overflowing with a grotesque amalgamation of misery, enmity, and disgust. All of those feelings and impressions, once Luc's and Luc's only, were now part of her; the pain he had felt had merged with her own. She now comprehended Luc, knew him in a way that was raw and and permanent. Tears she couldn't stop burned Lenna's face, biting like the strike of her hand across Luc's face.

Off to the side of the makeshift training facility, Sebastien stood, his entire frame tense. An all-consuming fire filled Lenna as she cast Brotherhood decorum to the side and stormed toward her teacher. Curiously, the magic of the Godjewel did not flare up with Lenna's wrath; whether because of the emotionally intense experience she had just endured or the amount of magic such a working had required, she found no power at her call. Instead, she gripped the collar of Sebastien's starched linen shirt and, catching him by surprise, hurled the entire weight of her body against him. He let out a yelp of shock and pain as Lenna slammed him into the wall.

"You bastard," she growled. "How dare you violate him like that? You're no better than those bullies, no better than…"

"No better than you?" Sebastien said, his voice muffled.

Stunned, Lenna slouched and lightened her grip. Sebastien was quick to gently push away her hands and smooth out the creases

Lenna's grasp had left on his shirt. She stared into her teacher's eyes, and they were filled with the compassion Lenna had before only felt from Sebastien when they had embraced each other's minds in the deep realm of the subconscious. His eyes, too, were beginning to cloud with tears.

Spluttering, Lenna couldn't form a coherent syllable with her lips; she half-grunted, half-sobbed, and fell into the open arms of Sebastien. His embrace was unpracticed and unaccustomed to human contact, but Lenna welcomed its sanctuary. She buried her sodden face into his shoulder, hiding from her past, Luc's past, seeking asylum from her own self-aggrandizing behavior and conviction that her treatment of Luc had been warranted and justified. She wanted to hide from the fickle, capricious creature Lenna Faircloth had become over the past ten years.

After a moment, Sebastien said, "I'm sorry. But you had to know. You both had to know."

Lenna tore herself from Sebastien's shoulder and looked up into his face through blurry eyes. "What does Luc know?"

A single tear had streaked down Sebastien's delicate features, and in the soft lighting of his training room he looked patient and saintly, as beautiful as he was when Lenna first met him and he had been wrapped in an intoxicating glamour. "You," he said.

Of course, thought Lenna. It wasn't just that she had experienced Luc's memories — the process must have been the same in reverse. In the instant Lenna had lived the most painful moments of Luc's life, he had surely experienced hers. How she felt about Gilbert; her own disappointment and hesitance to *live*; the final days leading up to her mother's funeral. Sparkle ponies.

Seeing the understanding dawn on Lenna's face, Seb simply nodded and coaxed Lenna's head back onto his shoulder with one hand. There she wept, though she wasn't sure for whom. Lenna felt exposed; her heart had been placed on display as some sort of specimen in a museum. The tears did not stop quickly, and when she choked and coughed, Sebastien offered no words of comfort, but he stood there, tall and resolute, his hand slowly stroking her head and his fingers running through her curls.

After some time had passed, Lenna began to digest the vast amount of information she had just assimilated – not the grief, which was a protracted, malignant cancer, but the facts and memories of Luc's life. Spells she had never been taught she found had carved their names on her mind like a child might carve his name on a tree. Lenna suddenly possessed an intrinsic understanding of the Brotherhood's hierarchy. The knowledge, though, was fragmented and incomplete; for every new fact she gained it seemed like she was missing another.

Then arose a powerful query. She recalled when she — Luc, rather — had been lying in the small room on Crescent Island, pretending to be unconscious after the beating. Sebastien had been there, and the tutor, Petrip, and Luc had heard a name: Thane Faircloth. There was treachery and a Godjewel, taken from Thane Faircloth. Gasping with her newfound cognizance, Lenna recoiled from Sebastien as if she had been stung by a hornet. She glanced down at the blue stone resting in her hand and then back up at Sebastien, who wore an expression of genuine worry.

"What's the matter, Lenna?"

Did Sebastien not know what she — Luc — had seen and heard? Since Sebastien had been the one to stabilize Luc after the horrific torture, it was he who would have been responsible for keeping Luc unconscious during the aftermath. Surely, Sebastien had kept Luc awake to overhear that conversation, unless…

Lenna clapped a hand to her mouth in horror. Gilbert had found Luc, not Sebastien. Gilbert, as he had always done, would have violated the rules and started the healing process, placing Luc's body at rest to prevent further injury while they waited for a specialized healer. Sebastien might have maintained or reinforced whatever charms Gilbert had cast, but the initial protective magics had to have been Gil's. Gilbert, best friends with Lenna Faircloth, the daughter of Thane. Gilbert, who murdered a group of younger boys in cold blood to protect someone he cared for from ever being hurt again…

"Lenna, what is it?" Sebastien didn't draw any closer, but an unlikely warble of wariness spoiled his voice.

She steadied herself, both mentally and physically, before asking, "Seb, how is my father involved with the Brotherhood?"

Sebastien's eyes widened and he reached out a hand toward Lenna like he was trying to offer support or pull her close; from Lenna's perspective, however, Sebastien was the one who looked like he needed someone to brace him at the moment. He finally asked, "Lenna, what did you see in Luc's mind?"

"Answer my question, Seb." She did not want to get angry. She wanted to assume that her friend and teacher was not withholding information, hiding the events that she had witnessed in Luc's mind. Lenna wanted calm; she wanted answers. But the more Sebastien delayed, the more she felt a strain on the bond that had been forming between them.

He frowned. "I don't know what Gilbert told Luc..."

Like a petulant child, Lenna kicked the wall next to her teacher in an outburst of pure vexation. "Enough games, Sebastien! Why was my father considered a traitor to the Brotherhood, and what connection does he have to the Godjewels?"

Lenna had never seen Sebastien more shocked; he doubled over as if she had punched him in the gut. Between that and her previous violence against his person Sebastien was probably experiencing more surprise today than he ordinarily felt in a year's time. He ran his fingers through his hair, mussing the part, and, after a moment's deliberation, gave a disgruntled sigh.

"Lenna, I will tell you what I can, but there's a certain limit to my knowledge as well, and I need to know you're logical enough to understand that," he said with some hesitation.

Scowling, Lenna felt her urge to become physical steadily returning. "As long as I possess this damned stone, *Master* Sebastien, I am not going to tolerate any more deliberate obfuscations of the truth."

"As far as I've been told or discovered," Sebastien began, "Thane Faircloth was one of the most promising apprentices the Brotherhood had ever seen. His magical abilities dwarfed mine, Gilbert's, Luc's, yours... he was supposedly a prodigy. When he took up the robes and became a pledged Brother, the council at the time was convinced they'd have a strong, confident leader in him."

There was nothing in Lenna's mind but pure whiteness, a blizzard of nothingness. "My father... was a member of the Brotherhood?"

Sebastien leaned back against the wall, staring at the ceiling. "Not for very long. Much to the council's dismay, he broke the vow we make to the order and left the Brotherhood."

"What vow?"

The mage turned his head to Lenna and studied her rather dispassionately. "He fell in love and decided to marry. I deduce Alanna Ameary was quite the woman, not unlike her daughter."

That falling in love was considered treachery to the Brotherhood was not especially surprising to Lenna — she already knew it was considered a taboo, thanks to her newfound understanding of the Brotherhood's internal politics — but she couldn't help but let out one squeak of bitter, amused laughter. "So marrying my mother made him into a traitor? That's it?"

"That's it."

Lenna was expecting more. She wanted more, something more delectably complicated that, when put under the lens of her scrutiny, would unravel the various riddles knotting up Lenna's life. "And the Godjewels. How is my father connected to them?"

"Lenna, if he hasn't told you himself..."

"He hasn't."

"And you never made the connection?"

"No." Something inside Lenna was pricking at her consciousness, stuck inside her like a splinter.

Looking Lenna squarely in the eyes, Sebastien cleared his throat. "The Brotherhood, as I'm sure you've noticed, doesn't take treachery very lightly, whatever the form. Once you swear your fealty, you no longer have claim to your own life."

Lenna growled with impatience. "Get on with it."

Sebastien's mouth twitched with an equal amount of frustration as he struggled to choose his next words. "The Brotherhood was doubly angry because of how promising Thane

Faircloth was. Is. They hounded him, threatened him, but your family is old and well-liked in Port Hollish; Faircloth sought solace there, and the Brotherhood could only make inconspicuous movements against him."

"And?"

"He thwarted them. Every time. And then, one day, he marched into the Embassy in Port Hollish and asked to speak with the senior mage representative, and when he left later that afternoon, the council swore to never bother Faircloth again."

"Why would they do that?"

"You know why."

The world around Lenna was wavering like the hot pavement of Port Hollish's trading district in the summer. She knew the answer; she always knew the answer. There was just something in her mind that didn't allow her to think about it because of the implications it bore. All this time, she had convinced herself that all the events of her life, her misfortunes, were all because she was the victim of cruel circumstance. A fluke.

"Lenna?"

"I want to hear you say it; I want to know that you knew."

"Lenna..."

"Say it."

"So that the Blue Crescent Brotherhood would leave him and his daughter in peace for the rest of their lives, a decade ago Thane Faircloth surrendered the blue Godjewel, the one now in your possession, to my order."

Lenna punched the blue-hot pulsing gem resting in her left palm with such force that her chafed knuckles cracked open, spilling blood over her right hand. The Godjewel throbbed in response to her anger and disgust, seemingly picking up on the electrifying sensation as Lenna's synapses connected, making insinuations and recalling events her brain would rather shut out. Its power edged to an orgasmic precipice, craving realization. It quashed the nausea she felt, and Lenna considered succumbing to its luring call, but she knew it would serve no purpose. Rather than feed it her despair and react, Lenna heaved mightily against the building of the Godjewel's power with her will, squelching the unbidden force. *Not today.*

"Lenna?" Sebastien asked.

Wispily, Lenna raised her head slowly to meet Seb's puzzled gaze. "You knew," she said flatly. "Gilbert knew too."

"Yes."

"I see," she mustered before collecting her wits and heading toward the door. She didn't look back, even though Sebastien called her name several times. His voice was tinny in the training room, its summons falling on ears that had chosen to stay deaf.

Sebastien didn't pursue Lenna further, and though she still seethed at the information that had been withheld from her, the visceral anger she harbored abated, for the most part, once she was left to her own devices. In proper Lenna fashion, the disgusted — no longer sure if she was aspiring or not — mage had stopped by the kitchens to pinch a bottle of wine, damning guest etiquette and ignoring her fear of Mistress Juniam. After returning to her quarters and rousing up a tidy bit of magic to heal her bloodied knuckles, she poured herself a hefty glass of the velvety elixir into the red-stained vessel from last night.

"Wow," Lenna said out loud. "Not even noon yet, and I'm using a dirty glass." She sipped the wine with smirking lips before lying back on the downy bed. Thoughts and unwarranted memories were invading her mind like a Krevlum strikeforce, and Lenna recalled the steamy summer day of her mother's funeral and Thane Faircloth's talon-like grip on her adolescent shoulder. He had been so sullen, so withdrawn. Oh, how Lenna had wanted to do so much to help him, to help herself, but she had been stuck, frozen in that never-ending moment of tragedy, under her father's grasp.

Gilbert had saved her then, and saved her later that day, with his silly sparkle ponies. Long into the evening and all of the following day, they had huddled in the secret bases of their childhood, hidden crannies of Port Hollish that to adult eyes would seem ordinary and insignificant, sharing jokes and stories.

To think that while Lenna was distracted with her best friend, her father, a former Brotherhood mage, would go and just hand over an object of such immense power to a corrupt organization...

For the first time since its invention, Lenna unlocked the mechanism holding the Godjewel in place in her gauntlet, letting the blue gem fall onto the bed, its length of silver chain trailing behind it. She unstrapped the leather bindings and rubbed the skin where the gauntlet had been chafing. Rolling over and perching over the stone, Lenna swished her wine in its glass with abandon, the leggy liquid threatening to breach its confines, and studied the gem.

Had she seen it years ago, long before the night Gilbert had entrusted her with the Godjewel's safekeeping? Gilbert. It all hinged on him, and his knowledge of events. He had obviously made the connection between her father and the stone, so when he decided to come to Port Hollish and escape into the Continent via Lenna's hospitality, Gilbert had already known Thane Faircloth had once possessed the gemstone. And on his deathbed, Gilbert chose to give it to Lenna, an almost entirely untrained magic user – and a librarian of all things – instead of his lover, budding magical prodigy Luc. That decision made no sense, unless Gilbert had planned to use Lenna from the start.

The dive into Luc's memories showed Lenna that Gil had no problem achieving results for his goals. To save Luc from those bullies, permanently, Gilbert arranged it so that they became completely incapable of harming anyone, let alone his lover, ever again. He had killed them all in what Lenna, in retrospect, knew had been cold-blooded, murderous revenge. Gilbert; her father; Sebastien; the Godjewel. Matters she had for the time being considered mostly sorted were now stepping into the spotlight as front-running enigmas.

Lenna was halfway through the purloined bottle of wine and nowhere closer to organizing her conflicting thoughts when there came a confident knock at the door. After a grunt of acquiescence, the door swung open and revealed the rangy figure of Raif, laughing about "inmate Faircloth" as he strode into the room and took in the surroundings. He admired the extravagance of the Branford family's guest quarters, but when his eyes fell on Lenna, the unsheathed Godjewel, and her burgundy-stained lips, he dropped his commentary.

"While I'm not particularly surprised," Raif said matter-of-factly, "I imagine that Master Branford would frown on his pupils drinking before lunch."

"This *is* lunch." Scowling, Lenna thrust the bottle into his hand as he took a seat at the foot of her bed. Rather than look for a glass, Raif tipped back the wine bottle itself and had a mighty swig from it. He let the vintage swish about his mouth for a few moments before swallowing and letting out a contented sigh. Reaching over, he poured another few mouthfuls into Lenna's nearly empty glass.

"Good stuff, this Branford wine," Raif admitted. "Though not as good as my favorites back in Tranum." At this statement, he grimaced, the innocuous comment probably dredging up the fact that his hometown was currently occupied by the Krevlum Empire's military forces. Shaking his head, he returned his attention to Lenna, who was sipping her new pour with a gloomy expression. "What's the matter, Len? I can't imagine it's the wine that's troubling you."

Lenna replaced her glass on the nightstand and found herself, in a sudden outpouring of emotion, relaying the entire morning of events, explaining as best she could the nature of the subconscious realm and of her foray into Luc's past. Raif sat unmoving, though he did flinch at the mention of some of the details of Gilbert's lover's life. Still, he waited for Lenna to finish her explosion of a story with an indulgent patience.

"And the worst part is," Lenna concluded, finding that the wine had churned up enough feelings to bring tears to her eyes once more, "that Sebastien and Gilbert and Luc — they knew the entire time about my father. And they didn't let me know. But I can't stay mad at Luc, not after… not after what I *felt*."

Raif scratched his stubbled chin. "You have no recollection of your father having possessed the Godjewel?" He extended, rather daintily, one hand and proffered Lenna a handkerchief from the pocket of his vest.

She took the offering, removed her spectacles, and began dabbing at her moist eyes. Thankfully, most of her tears had already been shed this morning, though she imagined her eyes must be red and exhausted. "No, of course not."

"Are you certain?"

Lenna cocked her head to one side, lips pursed to utter an affirmation. She halted, though, as a stray thought skulked at the back of her mind. A memory of those final days… no, she shook her head. She didn't remember anything after all. "I can't be certain whether he had it or not, but I'm certain I didn't know."

"I can't begin to imagine what the endgame is, Len," Raif said after a moment's deliberation. "You'd have noticed something if a Godjewel was around, I imagine. As I'm sure you're aware, they have quite an imposing sense of… presence." He peered down with a look of distaste at Lenna's bed and the flawlessly smooth burden resting on its duvet. "I know what it was like for my mother."

Briet, Raif's sister, had said as much: Raif's mother, Lady Vandever, had inherited another Godjewel, the one now in Luc's possession, from her mother, who had inherited it from her mother before her. It was by family tradition meant to be passed to Briet herself, but a tragic incident, the details of which Lenna couldn't even speculate about, had resulted in their mother's death, leading Raif's father to confiscate the gem before it fell into his daughter's hands.

"You're not saying this is somehow connected to my mother, are you?"

"Not necessarily, but…"

"That's ridiculous! My mother was anything but a magician. If she had had any connection to the Godjewel, I would have noticed." Her voice had risen with her denial; she was bordering on the shrillness of Jeffer Scalla.

The trader put one hand on Lenna's knee. "Steady on there. I believe you. Okay, let's think about this. First, we should make arrangements to get you the hell out of here. For now the ship is docked in Eran Point, but it shouldn't take too much longer for them to get it into proper flying shape..."

Imperiously, Lenna leaped to the floor of the bedroom, face white and indignant. "I can't *leave,* Raif. Not yet. Not until I know more."

Raif, as hotheaded as Lenna, rose to her challenge and scrambled up from his comfortable position. "Don't be daft! We've just found out that Sebastien and your old friend Gilbert and probably that thieving little bastard have been deliberately withholding important information from you. Who knows what they have in store for you? It's foolish to stay!"

"And where would we go?" Lenna retorted. "With Khareen Valant practically camped outside, we should flee on an airship maintained by an engineer who knows about teleportation magic and designed the schematics of a previously unknown Imperial warship?" The wine filled her with fire. She might snort.

Raif threw his hands up in the air helplessly. Lenna watched with morbid fascination as she read numerous emotions on his face, intrigued by the way his expression contorted and shifted from impatience and disobedience to a dull mask of resignation. She wasn't the only obvious one around here. "What would you have me do? I'd tell you you were right about our situation, but sadly, I don't want to inflate your ego any further." He settled back down on the bed, conspicuously some distance from the Godjewel. Lenna sat at the bed's head, thinking while swirling around the wine in her glass.

"What did you find out from Lazarz?"

Raif spread his arms in frustration. "It's like talking to a child. Or a bird. Or a rock. I don't know," he said with a heavy sigh. "Apparently, he did a lot of side jobs for the family."

"And the Krevlum Empire, it would seem."

"Yes, though he was very vague in the details. He's currently being escorted back to this estate by a few local arms I had the foresight to employ. I figured it would be easier to question him all at once."

So there was information that the trader had yet to discover; if Sebastien was unaware of all of Lazarz's details, Lenna could possibly gain the upper hand if she had a chance to speak to Lazarz before he got around to it. Raif had probably given up five minutes into the questioning anyway, too distracted by his ship to be thorough. *Yes,* thought Lenna, *information is power*. She could feel her pride as a librarian welling inside her, though that was probably just the wine.

"I need to find Luc," Lenna declared suddenly.

"Is that wise? To be honest, I'm not too pleased with Sebastien for bringing Luc here. I didn't even find out until you two got into your, uh, trouble, in Eran Point." Raif's voice mirrored the concern he expressed back in Granemere Settlement.

"Luc and I, we're... a part of one another now," Lenna said slowly. "And I want to know if he saw something in my life that I missed."

"I don't want to sound redundant, but I ask again: is that wise?"

Lenna shook her head. "I don't know, Raif! But I *want* to. It's about time I made a decision for myself."

For several breathless moments, Raif looked deeply into Lenna's eyes, and whether it was wine or the attention, she could feel her cheeks begin to color. How long was he planning on staring at her? It made her downright itchy and impatient. With her decision made, Lenna was eager to set off and find the young man who had received some chunk of her life.

"May I kiss you?" Raif blurted out.

A vein in her temple bulged as Lenna's brain registered the comment, and then, holding the wine glass close to her breast, she burst into laughter. "Of course not!"

Raif visibly relaxed, the set of his frame growing less rigid. "Good, glad to see you're still somewhat rational." He sat, simpering at nothing in particular.

Harrumphing, Lenna slammed her glass to the nightstand with more force than necessary. "Come on; time waits for no librarian. Ex-librarian. Whatever I am." As she marched toward the apartment door, she caught one last glance of Raif's face and her stomach dropped at what was obviously a frown of disappointment.

Oh, what now? she thought. *He can't have been serious. Wasn't he just trying to lighten the mood?* Ignoring him, she placed one hand on the handle of the bedroom door, and then the polite cough of someone well-bred caught her attention. Spinning on her heel, Lenna regarded Raif, who, now standing, was looming dubiously over her bed. Her mind madly wondered if he was going to ask if she would sleep with him next.

"Aren't you forgetting something?" he asked, feigning innocence a little too much for Lenna's liking. He looked like her kitty friend at the library who somehow managed to look smug every time Lenna gave him a bit of her lunch.

Lenna squinted in his direction, noticing his right hand pointing downward. On the bed lay the shimmering Godjewel and its leather gauntlet. She had left the Godjewel, unguarded, on the bed behind her as she was about to storm off to find answers to her numerous questions. All dignity lost, Lenna stomped back over and began fastening the bindings of the gauntlet to her arm.

"Thoughts of the kiss distract you too much, eh?" Raif asked.

"I warn you," she chirped, "I'm feeling particularly stabby today, and I still need to get in some practice with my new sword."

Raising his hands in mock surrender, Raif pretended to give a thorough examination of his fingernails while waiting for Lenna to finish her preparations — including once again girding said sword and knife — and then escorted her out of the room despite protestations; Raif was determined that Lenna would not be caught by surprise by Sebastien, Luc, or anyone else.

The Branford Estate was disquietingly empty; the servants, trained to never be seen unless part of a meal service, had vacated the corridors. Though luncheon would be served soon, Lenna had no desire to see Sebastien, and she doubted Luc would attend, considering the morning's events. Raif kept irritatingly close to her, blabbing on about the repairs being made to the *Trilyala*. Lenna promenaded through the vast halls of Sebastien's home, shamelessly opening doors and checking its various parlors for Luc.

"This is a little brash for you," said Raif, stunned. "Throwing open doors in other people's homes."

"Raif," Lenna replied a little tipsily, "I am fairly certain my world, if not the entire world, is becoming completely unhinged." She cast open two wide paneled doors and revealed the estate's ballroom. Impressive. "Barging in on nonexistent dance parties is the least of my concerns."

"Fair enough." Raif poked his head over Lenna's shoulder and took a look at the ballroom. "Not bad. Wonder when there was last a ball here. Could you imagine that stuffed shirt waltzing around?"

Lenna shouldered Raif aside, not acknowledging his remark. Her mind still seethed at any mention of Seb and his reticence, but at the same time it recalled his arms around her, comforting her. *Romance is a stupid thing,* she thought, and imperiously continued her parade down the hall. Doors practically swung open of their own accord as Lenna drew near, fearful for their safety at the hands of the aggressive, wine-fueled woman.

One window in the long corridor overlooked a tidy courtyard, an almost secret spot enclosed by the walls of Sebastien's estate. Lenna noticed, off to the side, a glass-paned door that opened out into it, and in the center of the garden, where a small bench sat surrounded by well-tended rosebushes, perched Luc. His hands were on the knees of his trousers and he stared off into the distance, seemingly deep in thought.

"Target acquired," Lenna announced, and navigated the corner between herself and the door. Raif followed suit, but found his path forward blocked by his friend's hand placed against his chest. He blinked in disbelief.

"Am I not allowed to go with you?"

"Access denied," replied Lenna. She was feeling positively loopy. "I need to speak to Luc alone."

Frowning, Raif started to walk forward but his eyes widened at the resolve in Lenna's blockade. "You're serious."

"Yes."

"But he's crazy; he tried to kill you. Are you really ready to defend yourself with that sword and that knife?"

It was true that Lenna had brought her weapons from her room, where they had been stored safely away in the wardrobe. She hadn't expected to be on battle watch while under Sebastien's tutelage, even if a homicidal general from the Krevlum Empire could be creeping up to the estate at this very moment. It had actually restored a sense of calm to have her weaponry strapped to her body, and Lenna imagined Pim or Freewoman Dalm would be quick to praise her. And then again, she had more than just steel at her disposal.

Lenna exercised her will on the gem as she pressed against Raif's chest. It hummed with gusto as it released a pulse of raw energy outward, and the Ilyan noble, unprepared, staggered several feet back into the hallway. A look of dismay crossed his face before he regained his composure and his footing. The gem, quiet once more, reflected the light coming through the glass door; Luc would realize she had come now, but that didn't matter.

"I get it," Raif said. "You're not exactly outclassed."

"I need to speak with him alone, Raif. There are some things left unanswered, some pieces in this puzzle, and only Luc and I can put them together."

What might have been hurt marred Raif's hopeful features. Lenna felt a pang of guilt: after all, her friend was just trying to protect her. She could appreciate that and, were the situation reversed, Lenna suddenly realized she also would feel protective of Raif. She sighed. Lenna did not want to push him away – quite the opposite – but if she didn't start acting independently, instead of just letting herself be guided by the unknown plans of others, she would be nothing but a pawn until her connection to the Godjewel got her killed.

Raif must have noticed the sadness in Lenna's red-rimmed eyes. "All right," he said after a moment. "But I'm going to stick around here for a few minutes, because if he tries anything, I'm storming in with a lot of Ilyan magic at my command."

Once again, Raif's spirited demeanor lightened Lenna's mood, and she cracked a smile, albeit a weary one. "I know you would. Thank you." She put one hand on Raif's shoulder, and he started at the unexpected intimacy. "Thank you for all the risks you take to protect me and the Godjewels."

"My emphasis is not specifically on the Godjewels," he uttered. "Len..."

Lenna took a deep breath. "We barely know each other; we've only spent a collective few days together and shared some correspondence. But thank you." She looked into her friend's eyes. "Will you do me one more favor today? Well, two, actually."

"Of course," Raif replied, though his voice was a bit more monotone than normal.

"Try to keep an eye on Sebastien. I know that's difficult, as it's his estate and all, but I have a lot of faith in your... diverse skill set."

Raif very nearly giggled, his ego tickled by the compliment. "What's the other favor?"

"When Lazarz arrives, try to detain him quietly. I want to speak with him too, before Sebastien can question him."

"I think I can arrange that. The staff here doesn't seem too concerned who goes where. And," he touched a finger to his nose, "I'll keep it hush-hush from Master Branford."

"Thank you, Raif. It's good to know I have someone I can trust," Lenna said, and meant it.

Blushing, Raif nodded and retreated around the corner, allowing Lenna a wide enough berth to access the small courtyard in her own time. Making a light, reassuring connection with her Godjewel, Lenna daintily turned the brass handle and stepped out into the garden. It was sumptuous and the scent of the roses almost overpowered the small, enclosed place. There was a certain level of humidity that must have been magically maintained in order to keep roses of this quality — fully opened beauties in every shade of red and orange and yellow imaginable — in such perfect condition at this time of year. Recalling the orange trees, she concluded that Seb appeared to be fond of greenery.

Luc was still sitting, dazed, and if he noticed Lenna's entrance he showed no sign or interest. She cringed at the awkward quiet, but Lenna still had to try — for both their sakes. She took her time straggling up the narrow cobbled path, only a few feet long, before wordlessly taking a seat next to Luc. Not one muscle in his body moved. Whatever mental place the novice had found himself in, it was surrounded by walls hard to penetrate.

"Luc," she began, intending to break him out of his funk whether he desired it or not.

"You know about my time at the Brotherhood," Luc replied abruptly, cutting Lenna off.

"Yes," Lenna answered. No sense in denying the facts. "I'm sorry," she added, but the words sounded silly on her lips.

"For what?" His voice was hoarse and strained, as though it was unaccustomed to speech or had exhausted itself from screaming. "You weren't responsible for any of those events." There was a bitter turn about his lips as he continued, "As you saw, the Brotherhood's intolerance isn't exclusive to women."

Mixed emotions made it difficult for Lenna to put her thoughts into words that Luc would understand. She ran her hands through her hair and tugged at her curls in frustration. "I know. But that pain… your pain… somehow, it's now part of me too. I can't pretend that it's the same, but to realize the suffering you went through, it just breaks my heart. And I can't forgive myself for that night." For slapping the shattered boy, for destroying what little light he had left in his soul by accusing him of being unworthy of his hero's love.

After a moment of quiet, Luc broke his sullen, straightforward stare and looked Lenna in the eyes. She was, as she had been when she first met the boy, captivated by their striking clarity. "Neither Gilbert nor I was completely honest with you about the knowledge we possessed of the Godjewels, though I daresay by now you have a better understanding of how the stones work than anyone, save perhaps the Emperor of Krevlum." Luc paused, reflecting. "I'm sorry as well. I did not understand your suffering; I'm not even sure *you* quite understand the nature of your sorrows. But that's life, isn't it? I could not comprehend the impact Gilbert had on your life, and I simply could not fathom the idea that your need for him could ever be anywhere near as great as mine."

Lenna had never heard Luc make so long and elegant a statement, and she was reminded of how his voice was beautifully touched with melancholy. These were the words not of a madman but of a kindred spirit who had witnessed the grief that pierced Lenna's heart like a tiny lance, and who had, through the magic of the Godjewels, experienced that sadness the same way she had. She had seen Luc, but he too had borne witness to parts of Lenna's past, her emotions. Within Luc, now, was some part, some echo, of Lenna Faircloth.

"Luc," Lenna asked, "where do we go from here?"

Shifting position on the bench, Luc unclasped his hand to reveal a spherical green gem resting in the center of his palm: his Godjewel. It pulsed in its close proximity to Lenna's own, in unison with its blue partner. Between the two of them, Lenna mused, two young people idly sitting in the private garden, they had enough power to conquer the world. Is that what they were meant to do? Topple the Krevlum Empire's ambitions, confront Emperor Sonnet, and take his jewel for their own? Lenna shook her head. That idea was preposterous: miles upon miles and an army stood between them and the Emperor, and Lenna had no desire to take to the battlefield. Still, Pim's motto, *war comes to all Freewomen,* constantly drummed between Lenna's ears, an annoying chant interrupting her thoughts.

"I don't know, Lenna," Luc said. "I know that Master Branford intends for us to hone our skills, learn to control the Godjewels. To what end? I can only speculate. Gilbert knew more than I do, obviously, but as I'm sure you're aware..." His voice trailed off, too shy to finish the sentence himself.

"You were following him blindly, out of love?" Lenna supplied.

Red tinged Luc's cheeks, but rather than cry out in indignation as Lenna expected the youth to do, he simply nodded. "Yes. He was my world."

And Lenna had helped shatter it. "I understand. A lot of my world, too, seemed to be centered on Gilbert, one way or the other."

"Lenna," Luc began, "about your father and the Godjewel. I presume you heard what I heard, on… that day."

Lenna flushed. Despite having been such a spitfire and cavalier toward Raif a few minutes earlier, she realized that maybe she wasn't ready to hear the truth so directly, so soon. Somewhere in the more illogical sections of her mind, Lenna was frightened of the ramifications the discussion might have.

"I hadn't inquired much about you or your family," Luc admitted. "Gilbert's vehement belief in Master Branford's plan was enough for me. But it's true that Master Faircloth was a Brother and most likely is still quite the competent mage, and that at one time he possessed the Godjewel you wear on your person."

"And Sebastien, Gilbert, and yourself — everyone knew that, am I correct?" Her voice had gone queer, like she was speaking through a swaddling of cheesecloth.

"Yes. Though the extent of my knowledge isn't as great as theirs, because I simply didn't care to know." It was a wanting response, but Lenna appreciated its lack of pretense — and, after her earlier experience foraging about in Luc's brain, understood his reasons.

"So I was never a coincidence, then. Gilbert never planned to leave me behind in Port Hollish." Lenna's tongue felt slimy.

With reserve, Luc finally responded. "I'm not aware that Master Branford gave Gilbert those instructions. While I knew the connection between the jewel and Master Faircloth, I suspected we would be seeking his involvement, not yours." He looked at his feet. "Hence my displeasure at your sudden addition to our party."

So, at the very least, it was possible that Gilbert — and maybe Sebastien — had planned for me to receive the Godjewel, Lenna deduced. Could he not have just told her? She felt green and frail, the early imbibing no longer the only source of a bout of nausea. Lenna was forced to ask if Gilbert's death was intended — orchestrated, even — so that she would have no choice but to take up the burden of the Godjewel.

"Was this all… planned?" she asked.

"I just don't know, Lenna." Luc pursed his lips; he must have been thinking about the incidents surrounding Gilbert's death as well.

"Did you," Lenna said, not entirely sure how to phrase her question, "did you notice anything I might have forgotten while we were… joined? About my mother?"

Luc frowned. "That was a difficult memory to interpret. There was a certain fixation on her death, but the events leading up to it were fuzzy, muddled. There was just too much stress on your young persona for me to make any sense of them. It was a whirlwind."

Desperately, Lenna wished she had the means to reach out and contact her father. He hadn't responded to her letters, but wasn't that because of Jaice Northen's interference? Did her aunt know about Lenna's father's involvement with the Brotherhood and the Godjewel? Things were falling into place too conveniently, but all answers came up short in one regard: what was the endgame? Besides ultimate power, what was specifically achieved through the acquisition of the Godjewels that contemporary steampower and magics could not produce?

And then she realized what it was. Lenna's unique access to that strange world of the subconscious; Sebastien's recent breakthrough in "teleportation" magic. The ability of the Godjewel to get through barriers, tearing time and space. If the universe were a book in her library, then a Godjewel would be a pen to edit it, inserting chapters midway or continuing the story as the wielder saw fit.

"Luc, will you come with me? I'd like your help in questioning someone," Lenna said. A single butterfly took flight from a rose in full bloom near the young mage's shoulder.

"Together?" he asked.

"Yes, please."

"Lenna," responded Luc. "Despite what happened this morning, you shouldn't have come in here thinking that you could redeem me."

"I didn't come here for that."

"Then why are you here? I haven't offered any new information; you've gleaned enough in your invasion of my memories."

"Maybe, Luc," Lenna said, standing up and feeling the last traces of the wine-inspired courage leave her light frame. "Maybe I came here because I need you to redeem me."

The youth, mouth open but devoid of words, looked on as Lenna, crimson on her cheeks, scurried out of the petite garden with all the grace of a drunken squirrel.

CHAPTER FOURTEEN

If Luc was surprised at literally bumping into Raif, he recovered before Lenna noticed any reaction. The two of them had barely careened around the corner before the Ilyan merchant's tall figure manifested before them, his countenance clouded with consternation as he took in Luc. Perhaps Lenna should have explained to her friend that she had intended to include Luc in the questioning of Lazarz; then again, Lenna, mentally and physically exhausted — not to mention recovering from mild intoxication from indulging in a liquid lunch — hadn't really been thinking all too clearly. She smiled at Raif, trying to look innocent but failing completely, as he folded his arms and equally tried to look indignant. Luc just stared at his feet.

"You aren't seriously bringing him, are you?" Raif asked, completely disregarding Luc.

"As we all know," Lenna said grandly, "I am always serious. Where to?"

Raif puffed out his chest, an exercise in manliness Lenna found absurd at best. His eyes were suspicious as they traveled up and down Luc's body, as though they were trying to find the whereabouts of the Vandever Godjewel on the boy. Luc, though his ears glowed under the taller man's perusal, stood his ground and looked up at Raif defiantly. Lenna watched the exchange with morbid curiosity; the Godjewel, of course, originally belonged to the Vandever family and for propriety's sake should be returned to Raif, but if Luc had bonded with it, he would have to give it up willingly. Lenna wasn't certain he could, and if she were to swap boots with the well-groomed — however emotionally disturbed — young mage, Lenna imagined she probably wouldn't be able to just hand over the Godjewel either. She sighed.

"You still have it, then?" Raif asked.

"Yes." Luc's response was cursory, flat as a calm day on Bonebreaker Bay.

Raif cast a calculated look between Lenna and Luc. He had seen enough of what Lenna had experienced with the Godjewel and, no doubt, had his own reserved emotions about the misery it could bring to a family. As his lips contorted in several directions as he tried to articulate a response, Lenna was inwardly tempted to tug on them, as if Raif were a small child or a puppy. She reckoned, as she fidgeted in the long corridor of the Branford Estate, that she should strive to act more serious. The fate of the world — and perhaps something greater — was partially on her shoulders, and Lenna could barely stifle a chuckle at the sight of speechless Raif versus stoic Luc.

After an undeterminably long span of time, during which Lenna outlined the novel she would write of her adventures thus far, Raif let out a lengthy exhalation and clapped Luc on the shoulder, a motion that made both him and Lenna freeze with surprise. "It's not the easiest burden to bear," Raif said, his voice distant. "And it's partially my fault that it ended up in your hands at all. You should be as angry with me as I am with you. But I've seen the hardship it brings to people, and even though I can't stand the sight of your wretched face, I wouldn't wish it on anyone." He shrugged at Lenna, indicating to her that he was finished. "Not much I can do about it now, anyway."

Luc coughed uncomfortably. Lenna admired Raif's artful acceptance of circumstances, but she could tell that his pride — which, when she thought about it, Lenna imagined was probably more potent than his own brand of magic — had taken a grievous blow from Luc's theft of the Godjewel. Having the thief around, let alone conspiring with him, would surely weigh heavily on Raif's heart, and Lenna found herself fiercely determined to keep his spirits up, even if it meant becoming an intermediary between the two men.

"Well!" she exclaimed with more liveliness than she actually felt. The windows were curtained in velvet, making the echo of Lenna's voice undulate oddly up and down the corridor; she sounded like someone trying to speak underwater. She shook her head and wondered whether to blame it on the wine. "Where will your hired hands be taking our friend the engineer?"

"The stables," Raif replied uncommittedly. "I know I'm good, but you didn't expect me to smuggle him into the drawing room without Sebastien noticing, did you? I had all of five minutes to arrange this."

"The stables are fine," Lenna announced and swept past her friend, taking long (and hopefully self-assured) strides down the lengthy hall. With only a few hours of daylight left, the corridors were cast with heavy shadows, making crude creatures from various pieces of decorative furniture that seemed deviously positioned. Lenna realized with acute dismay that this network of passages would be a terror to navigate in the depths of the night; the shadows reminded her of the thick black clouds that had pursued her, Gilbert, and Luc when they fled the village of Brest.

It didn't take long for Raif's long legs to match Lenna's gait; he appeared at her side so stealthily that she nearly jumped when his arm brushed hers. "You seem confident," he remarked.

"Liquid courage," she said, but wasn't so sure. Lenna felt a bit queasy and anxious and wondered if she was going batty.

"Is it painful for you to work alongside him?" Raif jerked his head back, knowing that Luc was lagging only a few paces behind.

Lenna trained her spectacles on Raif and regarded him closely. "Yes," she replied. "Isn't it for you?"

"It is."

Turning back, Lenna could see Luc's vacant eyes staring ahead, through both her and Raif, no clear object of motivation in their focus. He was truly a lackluster shade of the smart — and smarmy

— boy who had arrived on the doorstep of her library. Right now, the only true sense of presence Lenna felt was the nascent pulsing of the Godjewel Luc carried.

"How about you, Luc? Is it painful for you to be coming with us?"

Raif shot Lenna a confused glance that suggested she may as well have just asked a lamppost out to tea, a gesture that didn't do much to quash her own questionable thoughts concerning her sanity. Then again, beyond the small feat of standing against the scores of people vying for the Godjewels, Luc's mental state was probably below Raif's concern: Luc was a tool to him, and an unstable one at that. Lenna still hoped she could spark Luc's pride and powerful spirit, the one that had so wholeheartedly devoted itself to Gilbert, and try to help him regain some of the peace he had lost.

He had said he didn't want to be redeemed, true, and any comments made by Lenna or Raif seemed to roll off Luc's shoulders. Lenna had hoped their talk in the garden would have dredged up some shred of the man he was before, even if it were just the caustic side of Luc that loathed Lenna, but instead he appeared to have withdrawn again, shutting her out. Luc was so convinced that he wouldn't — couldn't — be redeemed, and it gave Lenna pause to think that he might perceive her as unredeemable as well.

Delegating the role of guide to Raif to collect her thoughts, Lenna, followed by Luc, passed through the many passages of Sebastien's estate. Gallasian architecture, due to the nation's hills, tended to rely heavily on confusing corridors connecting to individual spaces. It brought to Lenna's mind some diagrams of ant colonies she had studied in the science texts in her library, with passages zigzagging, turning, and jutting out at all angles. How anyone got around some of the back areas of the estate was beyond Lenna, and she felt a pang of homesickness as she wished for the disciplined order of Granemere Settlement.

Finally the group emerged into the less luxurious network of passages used by servants. They were eerily empty and filled with an expectant hush, as though the halls themselves were awaiting the return of the bustle of the estate's earlier years. After the passing of Sebastien's parents and his commitment to the Brotherhood, most of the servants had undoubtedly been dismissed; as the new master himself had explained to Lenna, under the direct supervision of Mistress Juniam, the Branford Estate ran well enough with only a few servitors and housemaids, a cook, and a groundsman.

Raif, accustomed to large households and, more importantly, to slinking along tunnels not meant for gentry as he fraternized with servants, navigated this section with ease. In direct contrast to the Ilyan's calm demeanor, Luc's expression was sullen, frozen perhaps with horror at having taken a less dignified route. *So some of the old Luc still remains,* Lenna reflected pleasantly as she compared the two men. If you threw Sebastien into the lot, she thought, Lenna was the only member of her immediate peers who hadn't been born into nobility.

Whether it was due to his knowledge of servants' passageways or his keen sense of direction as an airship pilot, Raif soon led the three to a side door that opened out into a square courtyard. Lenna's eyes fell on the squat, open building across the well-maintained quadrangle and her nose, taking in the raw scents of horse, hay, and manure, confirmed that her guide had successfully brought the company to its goal. Peering at the barred gate that led out into the yard before the manor, Lenna wondered just exactly how Raif had managed to smuggle in Lazarz without alerting Sebastien. She squinted at him, the sun a blazing orange halo against his finespun hair, but Raif just smiled in response and extended his arm as if presenting Lenna at court or a debutante ball.

Luc, fidgeting behind Lenna, was still noticeably uncomfortable, but he had agreed to help, and Lenna would be glad of his knowledge, considering his grasp of the arcane far surpassed hers despite the little she had learned and the vague glimpses of greater magics Lenna had absorbed from Luc's memories. Once more taking the lead, she drew in a gulp of horsey air and readied her nerves for the task at hand. Each step felt more and more leaden as she walked forward. The Godjewel throbbed once, sharply, as she broached the entrance to the stables, and Lenna braced herself against the doorframe with her right hand.

"Are you all right?" Luc asked, which surprised Lenna greatly. She hadn't expected him to keep close, or to express concern for her well-being.

"Yes," she replied. "I just feel a bit queer in the head. Probably the wine."

Luc started to remark but was quickly shoved back as Raif forced his way to her side. "Everything okay?"

"Yes," repeated Lenna, unwarranted annoyance creeping into her voice. "Let's get this over with."

By this time of day, the stables were draped in shadow, though an occasional whinny and clomping of hooves confirmed that there were still several lodgers. Not bothering to search for a gas lamp or a torch, Lenna applied a bit of her will to the ether before her, conjuring into existence a globe of magelight, its rays silvery and opaline. She couldn't help feeling a bit smug; conjuring magelight wasn't really a difficult feat for any mage, even a novice, but it was hers, Lenna's own. She didn't need Raif, Luc, Sebastien, or even the Godjewel. Nerves calmed, she let her light expand and illuminate the hay-lined stalls as she stalked toward the strange, strange cohort of Raif's.

Through whatever dubious channels he employed, Raif had secured two brawny men, probably from the University, who thought their muscles made them more appealing than their intellects. Two pure white flashes in the magelight revealed winning smiles probably meant to charm the older — and obviously mysterious — female mage. She hurriedly averted her eyes and looked toward their prisoner instead.

Lazarz was sitting on a stablehand's stool, low to the ground and looking like a blissful little imp. His hair was in its perpetual state of disarray, with strands of the pale gold fleece taking to the air in all directions. Bathing in her magelight, he beamed up at Lenna with a calm, toothy smile that rattled Lenna's nerves in its serenity. *Shouldn't he be a bit more… well, jittery?* Lenna thought.

"Miss Faircloth!" he exclaimed with much unforeseen jubilation. "How lovely to see you again!" Lazarz scrambled to his feet, only to have one of the hired hands knock him back down onto the stool with a sweep of an arm. "Oof," he said, plastering the same benign grin on his face.

"Lazarz," said Lenna, secretly relieved at the return of his expected — albeit overwhelming — agitated self. The other two members of her party had drawn so close that Lenna could feel their heated breath against the flesh of her neck. It was annoying and overprotective; she wished there were some incantation or power within the Godjewel to conjure back her tragically cropped hair. Lenna brushed those feelings aside and honed in on the situation at hand. "I'm going to presume you know why Raif has had you detained here?"

"At the Branford Estate, you mean? Yes," the engineer responded, "I imagine you have some questions about my time with the Krevlum Empire, its airship, and my knowledge about certain… skills." Lazarz wrapped his small arms around his knees and rocked back and forth.

At this remark the two lads, whose knowledge of worldly matters probably extended only as far as beer and games of cards, both leaped with a synergy such that their widened eyes and frozen expressions made them appear like a pair of oafish twins. In spite of her nerves and impatience, Lenna smirked. How different she felt from those two young students; had fate gone otherwise, it could have been Lenna standing there, thinking of nothing but books, tutorials, and the next pint of ale. *Well,* she noted one difference, *I highly doubt I would have been recruited as a thug.*

"Yes," Lenna said, laconic. Why delay? Sebastien would discover their ruse sooner rather than later, so it would be best to make use of their limited time as efficiently as possible. "Raif, I don't think we need our two young escorts any longer, do we?"

The students, clearly hoping to be party to some matter of great international import, pouted in evident dismay. "No offense, gentlemen," Lenna added, "but between the three of us, we should be more than enough for one Ilyan airship engineer."

"You heard the lady, boys," Raif crooned from behind Lenna's back. "You'll find the rest of the payment with the barkeep at the public house I gave you directions to earlier."

Raif's carefree dismissal seemed to have its intended effect. Lenna even gave them a terse little wave with one hand as they sulked past the party and exited out into the courtyard. Whatever means they had used to gain access to the courtyard must have been their way out, and when she recalled that there was a psychotic killer named Khareen Valant somewhere beyond the walls, Lenna was forced to question the efficacy of Sebastien's security.

"Raif," she asked, "can you make sure we're the only ones privy to this conversation?" She looked into his eyes and hoped he understood her meaning: she wished for him to use the Ilyan detection spell that identified other living beings nearby. It was a secret from the Brotherhood, and one that Lenna, despite her new understanding of him, did not feel it was her place to share with Luc. The tall man squinted, gave a slight nod, and headed out after the two boys, his ponytail lustrous in the magelight. Luc remained at Lenna's side as a reticent witness.

"So where shall we start, Miss Faircloth?" asked an eager Lazarz. If Lenna didn't know any better — and she probably didn't — she'd have thought the diminutive man was enjoying his capture.

At least he was direct. Lenna, becoming more accustomed to the sword buckled to her waist with every moment, squatted down beside the engineer, the scabbard rising up along her like a seesaw. She looked him squarely in the eyes, which had an acute, driven quality to them; Lazarz, it appeared, witnessed marvelous manifestations in the air that no one else could see. Phrasing would be extremely important here: his brain was simply operating on a level Lenna's wasn't.

"Teleportation," Lenna stated. She willed the magelight to glide directly above the two of them, and despite the bales of hay, riding crops, and other equine paraphernalia in the background, the silvery glow that washed over Lenna and Lazarz made them, for an instant, seem like creatures made of magic itself. "I realize that we need the power the Godjewels provide to execute such a strong magical working, but since there are but three Godjewels in existence, what purpose does teleportation serve besides a means of transport for individual bearers? Can it be used to transport large masses?"

Lazarz peered at Lenna peculiarly, clearly confused at being asked so trivial a question. "Teleportation is about transferring the physical manifestation of raw ether to another place. It means that, in that instance, when the body disappears and reappears elsewhere, the subject becomes completely incorporeal, one with the energy of the universe. Then, as determined by one's will, the physical shape is pulled from that raw ether and reconstructed elsewhere. All because the will desired that location and that specific physical form. It's not transportation. It's transference. Conversion."

There was a relative stillness about the barn, so still that Lenna thought she could hear the clinking and whirring in Lazarz's brain, like the huffing of a steam engine. Raif was quick to return, a nod assuring Lenna they had their privacy and Luc shifted weight in the only demonstration that he was paying any attention to the situation at all. As for herself, Lenna had already developed a theory quite similar to Lazarz's, though perhaps she had lacked the vocabulary or courage to phrase it so concisely. And now, tucking a wayward curl behind one ear, she craved to know its significance.

"So," Lenna began with some trepidation, "with a strong will and the Godjewels' powerful magics, a magician could effectively go anywhere. There would be no limitation to distance."

"Not just anywhere," said Lazarz. "Any*when*. Time as we perceive it, L, is just an illusion, a chain we lug around to keep our physical forms from dissipating back into nothing."

Lenna heaved a hefty sigh that was both relief and astonishment. Lazarz's explanation was confirmation that through the Godjewel Lenna could manipulate time itself, though — as when it first occurred, transporting her and Luc not just physically but temporally to the outskirts of Granemere Settlement — the Godjewel seemed to choose when to exercise this privilege. Gilbert and Sebastien hadn't explained much; the majority of information Lenna had pieced together concerning the stone's powers had come from the various unwanted experiences she seemed to ungracefully fall into.

Lazarz took advantage of the silence to leap excitedly back into the conversation like he was taking his turn at a game of skipping rope. "And that's just the beginning, Len-Len! *One* Godjewel can do so much; imagine what a person with all three could do? Why, I reckon they could just... rewrite the whole universe!" He teetered on the edge of his chair, and for an instant Lenna contemplated grasping him by the shoulder, lest the jiggling engineer topple to the floor. "Well, that's a big extreme. But you know what I mean. Potential, potential, potential... even better than making airships."

No, Lenna thought crossly, *I don't know what you mean.* "What do you know about the Godjewels, Lazarz?"

"There are three."

Despite the immediate temptation, Lenna did not smack the smaller man, though she did spare a moment to glare over her shoulder at Raif, who had chortled at Lazarz's response. "If magic comes from within us," Lenna said slowly, "or rather, we, as humans, are just a sort of physical manifestation of the universe's ethereal energy based on our 'wills,' what are the Godjewels?" The conversation was tumbling down at a breakneck pace into a gorge of theology, and Lenna was not sure she currently possessed the intellectual freedom to accept the fact that her love of wine, curly hair, and bad eyesight came about because her "soul" deemed it so.

The airship expert stopped his nervous twitching, thank goodness, and cocked his head at Lenna. "Glitches. Irregularities.

Blockages in the stream of the collective pool of energy. They corrupt the system; they break the universe."

"Huh." Lenna rose. "So you don't say that the Godjewels have a will of their own, not really, but they're… they're hiccoughs in the natural order of things, and this is how they appear in physical form."

Lazarz leaped up and grasped Lenna's hands with zeal and true admiration. "Yes! I knew you were worthy, L, of Team Len-Laz! They punch holes in the design; they let strong wills, compatible wills, access far more of the universe than they should normally."

"So when did they… when did these irregularities appear?" Lenna gently pried Lazarz's grip from her hands.

Once more assuming his seat, Lazarz fluffed his epic hair and looked at the ceiling. "I don't know; I don't think I was there. I can only speculate, you see." He nodded at nothing in particular, presumably agreeing with himself.

"And what does your speculation tell you?"

"They've always been here. Because, like I said, the fabric of *stuff*, the realm where everything raw exists, it doesn't have a start or an end. So I guess they've just always been around."

Despite her desire to stay collected, Lenna scowled. Lazarz was implying, then, that the very nature of the universe itself was flawed. Or intentionally flawed. But if intentionally flawed, could one consider it a flaw? By whose design did these "irregularities" come about? Despite the scholarly training she had gained during her time in the library, Lenna's head quickly became a jumble of circular logic. She shook it wildly.

"So, truly, anything is possible with the Godjewels," Luc intoned beside her. His voice held a hint of longing, a wild despair. Lenna jumped; lost in her own musings, she had forgotten Luc and Raif were standing right behind her.

"I don't know about the any*thing*," Lazarz said cheerfully. "But any*where*, any*when*, all those sorts of things can be easily accessed if you know what you're doing. Memories can be revisited. Lost information retrieved."

To Lenna, the importance of the origin — or lack thereof — of the three Godjewels was a mallet-armed quandary pounding away with repeated strikes against her brain. How did Thane Faircloth acquire the gem Lenna currently possessed? Luc's jewel came from Raif's household and had apparently been passed down, mother to daughter, for generations. How did the leader of the Krevlum Empire acquire his? Sebastien had shown Lenna and Luc that they could revisit memories of the past; perhaps they needed to dig again.

"Lazarz," said Lenna, her voice accompanied by an uncomfortable braying from a horse and the sound of hooves thumping against a wooden door. "What is your connection to the Krevlum Empire? Why were you designing an airship for them?"

"Lenna," Raif intervened, shifting to stand parallel to her. "I do know my father had some dealings with the Empire; we're a prominent merchant family, so of course we'd engage in various negotiations with Krevlum."

"Master Vanny," Lazarz said seriously, which naturally drew everyone's attention. "Your father, of course, traded with Krevlum. But I did the work on the *Talonstrike* on my own."

"Why?" Raif asked.

"Because Aldy is an old friend of mine," he giggled. "Years and years and years ago — who can keep track, really — the whole lot of us used to take apart things, old things, new things, make things better. Dabble with some magic. It was fun! Of course I'd do an old friend a favor." He paused. "I just didn't realize the favor would result in you and Len-Len almost getting killed. Sorry about that, by the way."

Raif just sort of hung there in the funky air, mouth open wide like a great sea bream searching for dinner. Luc offered no response but regarded Lazarz with what might have been a look of interest. Lenna squinted down at the excited gnome, not liking the path that her mind was strolling along. Lazarz and Alderic Sonnet had a connection, and Sonnet had a Godjewel. Lazarz had been in the employ of the Vandever family, which also had possessed a Godjewel. That left one Godjewel — Lenna's — and here, again, was this impossible man that transcended coincidence.

"Lazarz," she said imperiously, "head back into the manor house. I'm sure Master Branford will wish to hear what you have to say as well. Raif, Luc — I want to try an experiment. I want to see if we can delve into my memory to find out more information about this." She held out her fist and, in the pale magelight, the Godjewel shone a milky blue.

Raif and Luc looked at each other. Raif had recovered his wits, but Luc's gaze remained unreadable. Raif said, "Is that wise?"

"I don't know," Lenna admitted. She tugged out her timepiece, its chain clasped to a buttonhole in her violet coat, and glanced at it with a look that would curdle a jug of milk. The crack on the faceplate by now almost entirely covered the surface of the watch. "But I think time is of the essence."

Raif nodded but continued to expound upon the dangers of any shenanigans and Luc, without comment, made his way back toward the stable entrance. With a strange sense of camaraderie, Lenna bopped Raif on the shoulder with her fist, snickering when he let out a mild grunt of protest, and pushed him along after their fellow conspirator. Figuring she had pried as much sensible information out of Lazarz as she could for the time being, Lenna was content to leave him to his own devices; Sebastien was sure to track him down before long.

"Lenny-Len-Len," the curious creature called from the back of the stable.

Lenna turned, staring down the stable corridor, where two horses had shied away from her retreating party. "What is it, Lazarz?"

"The faceplate of your watch is cracked," Lazarz said. His voice was unusually somber.

"I'm aware of that, Lazarz. I haven't had time to replace it yet."

Kicking his feet to and fro, the wide-eyed, wild-haired man locked his eyes on the hand that still held Lenna's pocket watch. "Do you want me to fix it for you? I'm quite good with timepieces too. I learned from the best." Lazarz's eyes twinkled as they caught the silver gleam of Lenna's magelight.

Unnerved, Lenna's voice was a touch shaky when she replied, "No, Lazarz. I'll manage. But thank you." She turned back and quickly regained her place next to Raif, dread welling up in her belly as she wondered whom it was that Lazarz considered "the best" when it came to clocks.

"I ask again: is this really a good idea?" said Raif. He posed like a carnival stuntman on an uneven tree stump, adding several inches to his already annoying tallness.

Dusk had set in, leaving the rows and rows of orange trees in the orchard more sinister in the retreating shreds of autumn sunlight. By now, the harebrained engineer was presumably being subjected to a very thorough questioning from Mistress Juniam and Sebastien. Lenna was banking on Lazarz keeping them occupied for some time, and pictured the unwavering wizard posing over Lazarz, demanding answers. She hardly thought Seb's striking conduct would have its desired effect on Raif's engineer.

"No," Lenna admitted. She was full of doubts about once again allowing Luc into her mind and, moreover, about what truths they might unearth by digging around in her past. Still, Sebastien would not be long behind them, and while Lenna's grievance with her instructor had been filed away into the "sort out later" section of her mind, she wanted to attempt this experiment without his interference. Who knew when they would next get a chance, unsupervised?

Luc, having arrived at the estate some days before Lenna and Raif, had suggested the fragrant Branford orchard as a site for their working; any tending to the plants would be done in the morning and early afternoon, and as night approached, the groundskeeper and Sebastien himself would be unlikely to wander among the ranks of trees speckled with their engorged, sweet gems. Being particularly fond of oranges, Lenna found it a difficult test of her willpower to not pluck one of the lower-hanging beauties with a bit of magecraft. Thank goodness bottles of wine didn't grow on trees!

She shivered. Even as far south as Gallas, the early winter that had grabbed hold of Fallowfields exerted its influence over the weather. As a child, Lenna had enjoyed the smothering white blanket of snow that seemed to stop time for the countryside in an unsullied moment; now, buttoning up her purple coat and exhaling puffs of white mist, she hankered for a fireplace and some mulled cider. As she watched stars slowly dot the vastness of the sky above, she wondered if the other two were less affected by the chill than she was, or if it was a kind of stoicism that came with being a man.

"Let's get this over with," said Luc. He had crossed his arms and was leaning against the firm trunk of a tree across the way from Lenna and Raif. In the dwindling light of day, his silhouette called forth in Lenna an immediate recollection of Luc's sullen face one month prior, and she felt a swell of unbidden images of herself and Gilbert, of Gilbert and Luc, rise to the forefront of her mind. The sensation was not unlike a dry heave the day after one too many tumblers of port; unpleasant and wrought with shame.

The ground, its tilled earth brisk in the cooling breeze, crunched under Raif's weight as he hopped down from the stump, arriving in the middle of the row between the trees. "I never thought I'd say this, but the young master and I are in agreement." The pitched tone and emphasis on *young master* told Lenna that her friend, for all his show, was still far from pleased at being in Luc's company. "What you're doing is a serious working with two Godjewels. Between the two of you, there's probably enough combined power to level half of Gallas if emotions get out of control."

Raif was right, of course. Until this morning, Lenna had only explored the unconscious realm alone out of desperation, unguided, and it had on several occasions threatened to drown her, pull her into a deep void from which no egress would be possible. If Luc or she were to succumb to intense emotional pressure while joined and using both Godjewels, who knew what the consequences would be? These perfectly sculpted orange orchards, tended by human hand and Sebastien's stabilizing magic, could be torn to shreds — and Raif as well — before anyone could even raise an alarm.

"While I don't like this idea," Lenna admitted, "Lazarz's energetic — if a bit eccentric — hints about the potential gains from our little experiment here have convinced me it's worth the try." *Yes,* her inner self spoke, *I want to know, no matter the consequences.* "Like we did this morning, Luc and I can dive back into my memories, to find out more information about the Godjewel's connection to my family. That might give us the upper hand, especially if, though I'm loath to suggest it, Sebastien is keeping his own counsel." Luc would probably also keep his own counsel if he had his way, but Lenna assured herself he lacked the intimate knowledge of the collective subconscious that Lenna possessed. It was she who would have to initiate this working.

"If you're certain." Raif's delivery didn't exactly instill confidence in Lenna, but in retrospect, lately things seldom did. The rewards outweighed the risk, though she was aware that using both Godjewels together would immediately alert any magician in the area, possibly even as far north as the other nations if they could not control the power. Sebastien and Emperor Sonnet and Valant could be counted on to take notice immediately. Lenna cracked her neck with the most satisfying of popping noises and nodded at both of her accomplices. Raif slipped back to his stump, this time taking a seat and propping up his chin with one hand.

"So how do we begin?" Luc shifted from a stance of affected aloofness to one reminiscent of Jaice's bearing as a battlemage. His shoulders were set, fingers uncurled and loose, feet firmly planted a few spans apart. The Godjewel strapped to her arm grew warm to the touch and began to pulsate; even before a hint of lily graced the air, Lenna's body tingled as she perceived Luc drawing upon his magic. Holding her breath, Lenna tiptoed out into the middle of the path.

"All right, Luc," Lenna said warily, as she was not entirely sure how to put into words the way she accessed her magic, the Godjewel, or the special realm where the stars themselves melted away. Sebastien had guided them earlier; this would be a bit more difficult, even though working with Luc was, as Lenna was always surprised (and somewhat reluctant) to admit, normally a calming, easy experience. As her boots, polished to perfection under the discerning eyes of Mistress Juniam, kicked about the dirt around her feet, Lenna let out one last breath before saying, "Give me your hand."

The resulting grimace on the young man's face was something Lenna had been prepared for, and if anything, her morning's delving into the memories of the abused boy meant she found it more touching than standoffish. As gingerly as she could, Lenna took Luc's hand with her right; her left hand, balled into a fist, was subconsciously stoking the warm kindling in the Godjewel into a steady, blue-burning flame. She let the warmth trickle up her arm and into the vessel of her soul, into that unending tome of power that held the depth of her magic in its vellum. The orchard, already laden with scent, became an intense, perfumed space.

Regardless of Lenna's mental preparation for their endeavor, she still could not help but be surprised at the gentleness of Luc's magical embrace. His presence, an astral projection of his true, inner core, was so meek and soft, like the down on a baby chick (thank you, Pim), that Lenna's own raging furnace of power threatened to consume it whole. But beside that gentleness, there was now a feral edge that hadn't existed before Gilbert's death, a creature ready to recoil from the hand of a cruel master. Lenna's strong embrace wrapped itself around the scared young man, as Gilbert had done the night Luc learned of his sister's death, and pushed through any harshness, any fear. The very contained, well-structured layers of the young man named Luc Tural peeled away and succumbed to Lenna's guidance.

And so down she brought them, a burning torch leading a moth on a spiraling course into the depths of reality, their perception shifting from the physical world to the psychic. Delicate tendrils that connected all of life wafted between the blurring orange trees and Raif, a burning, pulsating star in his own right, and Luc and Lenna, or at least the combined entity they had become, reeled with vertigo as before them spread out the vast network of the makings of all life. It was a stupefying sensation, and the intertwined might of the Godjewels gave Lenna-Luc a palpable, intrinsic knowledge that the power to pluck the stars from the heavens or uproot all of Gallas was only a whim away.

Lenna-Luc tried to recall Sebastien's delicate leading, a kind of affectionate prodding that guided the being's thoughts in the right direction. Lenna-Luc remembered its purpose: to delve into the portion of the entity that was Lenna, and to find some poignant moment, something, anything, in the past that might illumine the mystery surrounding Thane Faircloth's connection to the blue Godjewel. Something that Lenna might have witnessed but ignored, or blocked out, in her past. The entity bored into its Lenna aspect, searching and digging, uprooting images of Gilbert, scenes of Port Hollish. The Lenna aspect saw itself, sitting alone, knees tucked up on a single bed before an open window, reading a worn leather-bound volume.

And then a deluge of images began manifesting before the entity's unconscious eye. Thane Faircloth, taking great care to adjust the springs of a clock-in-progress with miniaturized tweezers. Alanna Faircloth, sliding the mother-of-pearl knife back and forth across a whetstone, her hair plaited and wound around her head. A young Lenna kicking leaves in the garden and Alanna, arms folded, looking put-upon as she watched her daughter. A dying woman, fair hair turned to grey, cheeks hollow. Even the calluses on the once-proud warrior's hand seemed to sag and shrivel as she lay in bed, a questioning Lenna and a frowning Thane standing over her.

No, thought the part of the unity that was still Lenna. It rejected the image and pulled away from Luc's mind, a surge of power from both gemstones giving her the strength to tear away from her connection to the other mage. She could feel Luc being pushed away, rushed to the surface, to the realm of the conscious. That momentum propelled Lenna downward, toward infinity and nothing, where she became one with the fabric of the universe.

All of Lenna's being felt both Godjewels vibrating; their movements tumultuous, tremors of an impending divine earthquake. A trouncing bouquet of lavender streamed into the copse of orange trees, and the physical manifestation of Lenna could hear faint cries of her name — muted, as though she were submerged back in the baths — coming from Luc and Raif as a helix of blinding azure and verdant energy from the Godjewels spiraled up around her body. Subconsciously, Lenna kept pushing, mentally kicking away from that image, far away, to a place where that image didn't exist.

The Godjewels roared and Lenna embraced the magic surrounding her before giving one final hoist away from the pallid husk of Alanna Faircloth. Away away away. Voices in the nothingness seemed to sing in counterpart to Lenna's cry: Sebastien; Valant; a chorus of protests, some familiar, some new. *Away,* Lenna strongly willed, and the lightning of the Godjewels streaked through the air in a blinding whiteness.

CHAPTER FIFTEEN

Lenna's ego was shattered. She felt as though someone had beaten her brain against a washing board and then hung it out to dry on one of the clotheslines in her neighborhood. She tried opening her eyes, but all that was before her were rapidly flaring flecks of light. Did she still have limbs? Lenna couldn't be entirely certain; but everything was tingling, and after deep thought she concluded that the pins and needles in her extremities probably meant she was whole. Mostly.

Slowly, the pulses of light began to recede into something bluish with whorls of white. The sky. *Oh good,* Lenna thought. *Ouch.* Soon her fingers and toes began to twitch, and she felt something crunchy beneath her hands, pliable but sharp. Grass. *I am lying in a field.* The jabs of pain Lenna experienced whenever she processed a thought were gradually becoming less prickling and frequent. *Thank goodness for that. Ouch.*

After a moment or so a new kind of pain assaulted Lenna, something digging right into her back. A stick? She attempted, with great effort, to heave her arm and feel around the proximity of the prodding. Her hand coiled around a long, cylindrical, and rather hard object. *Of course,* she thought, *I'm lying on my sword.* Sucking in a massive gulp of pleasantly warm air — warm? — Lenna, pins and needles and all, threw her weight and rolled off the Freewoman blade, thankful it hadn't slipped out of its scabbard and eviscerated her in the process.

Process of what? Lenna hauled her muddleheaded self to an upright, sitting position. She gave herself a brief once-over; all limbs and clothing accounted for, even the knife. The only thing that had changed was, well, her location — that was fairly obvious — and she had fallen on her blade. So she must have teleported. This wasn't part of any memory; that experience had been pointedly different. When she relived Luc's past, while she felt what he felt, there was still a sense of detachment, a unique "Lenna" quality present. If she was revisiting her own memories, as she had intended, this was no scene she remembered, and she was still the same Lenna she was moments earlier; there was no psychic attachment or sensation of Luc either.

So, pressing questions: where was she, and why was she there? Pain receded to the point that standing up seemed a task she could accomplish, so Lenna hoisted herself to her feet, smoothing out the creases in her jacket and adjusting the sheath buckled to her belt. Looking around, Lenna appeared to be standing in a field on the outskirts of a forest; the grass was green and spiky, not a well-tended estate's lawn. The scent on the air, woody from the forest and herbaceous from the grass she had been rolling around in, reminded Lenna of something. On the wind as it blew across the plain was a trace of brine, the salty air of the sea.

"Oh, hell," Lenna swore. "I'm in Fallowfields." Port Hollish was probably only a few miles from her. But when she left Granemere Settlement and Fallowfields behind, hitching a ride on Raif's airship, the nation was already in the throes of an early winter. The heat, the breeze, the mossy-green tint of the knoll beneath her — everything indicated to Lenna that this version of Fallowfields was currently in early summer. Lenna hadn't just teleported, accessed the "anywhere" as Lazarz had so eloquently put it — she had shot through time to a completely different anywhen, and she hadn't the slightest idea of when that "when" was.

"Or how to get back." She looked dourly at the Godjewel, which had thankfully stayed locked into her gauntlet. It had an unearthly calm about it; there were no subtle vibrations or strange patterns of blue swirling beneath its glassy surface. That brought another unpleasant thought to mind: even if she knew the proper method by which to return to her time and to Gallas, Lenna wasn't entirely convinced the power of her cerulean dynamo alone would be enough to propel her back: Lenna had been pulling on the power of two Godjewels, not one.

Determined not to wallow or even allow herself the luxury of yet another exasperated sigh, Lenna trod forward a few paces, her hand resting idly on the pommel of her blade. Without any frame of reference other than the weather, the lost apprentice had no idea how to determine "when" exactly she had landed. The best course of action, however trite, would be to follow her nose; if Port Hollish was within walking distance, and the breeze told her it was, Lenna should be able to find her way back and ascertain — delicately — some sort of helpful information. Eyeing her garb, she hoped she hadn't traveled to some period when her clothing would be severely out of place.

"I am being remarkably level-headed," Lenna announced to herself. Telling herself so seemed to reinforce this new feeling of calm. Why, there was nothing more she desired than a visit back to her hometown, her city on the sea! At least, as long as she kept thinking that, that there was some pillar of normalcy not an hour's trek from her current location, Lenna could tell herself she was safe. Lenna could believe she wasn't a terribly stranded, doomed young woman who had no idea what was happening or how to get back home.

A few yards from her current position on the grassy hillock was a path, the natural kind that assumes a happy home in the crook of nature's arm, created by constant travel rather than any engineer's scheme. Though over the past few years Lenna hadn't left the confines of her walled city very often (an exception, of course, was her recent departure in the company of strange magicians, childhood friends, and magical artifacts of questionable origin), once she set foot on the well-worn trail she realized she recognized the route. She was north of Port Hollish;

in fact, this was the very path she, Gilbert, and Luc had used to flee the city with the Godjewel.

Reassured, Lenna began her journey down the lane, the warm weather, oddly enough, leaving her inclined to whistle. The plains of Fallowfields were rich and thriving, a sharp contrast to the dusty emptiness and sparse growth Lenna had journeyed across last month. It smelled pleasantly of her youth, and the breeze made her think of picnics, good books, and sparkling cider. Daydreams of such comforts gradually replaced the more pressing thoughts in Lenna's mind, and her feet, remembering the way home, took her solidly forward.

The minutes seemed to tick away slowly, though Lenna didn't bother to consult her pocket watch; she dreaded what impact the landing might have had on it and besides, however gifted Thane Faircloth might be, she doubted his watches automatically adjusted for time travel. Shading her eyes with her hand to check the sun's place in the sky, Lenna estimated that it was just past midday. She had a few more hours of growing warmth left, and not unpleasant warmth at that, especially considering the trouble her proper year's winter seemed to bring with each passing day.

After about forty-five minutes of continuous progress (or as best as Lenna's internal clock could judge), her stomach began to growl. It had been nearly dinner back in Lenna's time, and she hadn't brought along any rations or supplies. While she was somewhat versed in what-berries-are-delicious and which-berries-will-kill-you, this area of Fallowfields didn't have much in the way of places to forage. *Next time,* she deliberated furtively, *I will remember to pack a kit well-stocked with food when I decide to go exploring the inner workings of the universe.*

Still, she continued contemplating, Seaways Tavern (assuming it existed whenever Lenna was) would be less than a mile down the path, and she'd be able to grab something to eat and perhaps gather some more information as to the anywhen to which she had come. In the warm summer weather, some fried fish and a pint of light ale sounded a right cure to her ailments. Suddenly her footfalls felt lighter and more determined; perhaps time travel, if one managed to get to the right when, was not without its benefits.

It wasn't long before Lenna heard the steady clickety-clack of well-shod horses. Despite being unpaved, the rustic path was smooth and the earth packed from its frequent use by travelers coming to and from Port Hollish; the uniform rhythm of fine steeds traveling at equal speed echoed through the countryside. Curious, Lenna skirted off and stood on a mound of grass to the side, looking down the road, if one could call it that, expectantly. Fallowfields was, as the name suggested, an expanse bestowing upon most travelers a decent view of others wandering the roads.

Rising from the horizon about a half mile south of Lenna, a pair of horses and their riders were cantering up the path. Even at their casual pace, they would be upon Lenna within moments, so, rather than get caught in the upturned dust of the steeds' strides, she took another step back into the grass and polished and adjusted her spectacles, attempting to affect the look of someone comfortable and perhaps moderately bored. She hoped that no one mistook her, however improbably, for some sort of bandit.

As the horses drew nearer, Lenna replaced her glasses and properly discerned the shapes of the riders. Both sat solidly in their saddles, accustomed to riding horseback, but as they were outlined by the rays of the strengthening summer sun, it was an easy feat to realize that the horses were carrying women, not men. Lenna smiled in spite of her unique circumstances. Two women riding comfortably through the countryside meant that either she had traveled to a time of relative peace, when highway robbery was not a great concern for travelers, or, and Lenna secretly hoped the latter was true, the two riders were Freewomen of Laur.

It was several moments before the riders halted their horses in the dusty road by Lenna. They were both dressed sensibly for riding: simple leather trousers rubbed tan with constant wear and scuffed riding boots. The taller of the two women, who wore her hair in a long, heavy brown braid over one shoulder and down her blouse, which to Lenna's eyes probably needed to be buttoned up a few more spaces, sat back in her saddle with a confidence

Lenna admired. The eyes assessing her were clear and knowing, drinking in every detail of Lenna's attire, position, and gear. For her own part, Lenna's focus was stuck on the long, gnarled staff, wrapped in straps of leather, fastened to the side of the woman's mahogany horse.

"Hail," said the woman. "Where are you headed, Sister?"

This served as confirmation enough to Lenna that the riders were indeed Freewomen; the familiar usage of "Sister" indicated an acknowledgement of equal standing and age. The other woman, with honey blonde hair in two braids woven together into a kind of lattice, eyed Lenna but said nothing. Her mouth was impassive and peaceful and she reminded Lenna of someone, probably Pim, who looked too young to be any sort of warrior.

"To Port Hollish," Lenna answered. There was no point in deception, since travel on the road made one's destination fairly obvious.

"You're heavily armed," the first woman noted, her eyes on Lenna's longsword and knife, "to head to such a peaceful place. You must be planning on heading farther out. What settlement do you hail from?"

Inwardly Lenna cursed herself. She knew very little about any of the Freewoman villages except for Granemere and, considering its proximity to Port Hollish, if these Freewomen were locals, they'd more than likely be familiar with it and its residents. Lenna's garb — weapons aside — was of high-enough quality to show that she was no low-ranking trainee. The darker-haired woman's eyes had narrowed, as if she were expecting a lie. The diligence of her stare was stark and disarming; anyone caught under its questioning would be hard-pressed to escape unscathed. This woman was leadership material.

And then familiarity asserted itself with a ferocity that might as well have been a slap across Lenna's cheek. She barely managed not to lose her footing and slide down the small incline, tumbling out into the road. Lenna took it all in: the woman's perfect posture and skinny but muscular frame; her authoritative command of tone and judging eyes. A staff as a weapon of choice. There were no lines of stress creasing the young woman's forehead, but Lenna blanched at her realization.

"I'm afraid I can't divulge that," Lenna lied. She hoped that her intuition would be obligingly accurate. "I'm on special dispatch at the moment and am forced to avoid stopping at many of our settlements on the way, though I've been in recent contact with the mayor of Granemere." Lenna tried not to fidget as she prepared her delivery. "You must be the promising young battlemage she mentioned. Jaice Northen, am I correct?"

In a display of red like a winter sunset, the dark-haired woman's cheeks provided affirmation. Lenna was privy to a rare sight in witnessing this woman, so strong of character, faltering for words: the only sound falling on her ears was the gentle call of birdsong. As best she could, Lenna kept her expression impassive; she knew she had to remain firm in her guise or the astute Freewoman would call her bluff.

Luckily, youth and pride still had some sway on the woman on horseback, and after she regained her composure, she bowed her head. "I have to say I'm deeply embarrassed, Sister," the woman said. "Mayor Hannahl gives me too much praise."

So Lenna had been right. Before her, on that mahogany horse, sat a younger version of Jaice Northen, the future mayor of Granemere Settlement and Lenna's future aunt. If Jaice was only slightly younger than Lenna's current age, then Lenna had, via the power of the Godjewels, been transported not only back to Fallowfields but well over twenty years into the past.

"Well," Jaice said, "I'm honored that you've heard of me, Sister, though if anyone is the competent battlemage, it's my partner. She doesn't even care to carry a weapon, despite Freewoman Dalm's insistence."

The blonde woman let out a single, pruned laugh, the laugh of one who had been through this discussion so many times that its repetition made it the dullest of topics. It reminded Lenna of Luc, who, in his aristocratic prattishness, hated associating with what he deemed boorish company. Lenna squinted at the blonde woman and realized that, much as Jaice said, the woman carried no visible weapon, yet she sat as cocksure in the saddle as any honed warrior.

"Don't be silly, Jaice." The woman's voice was harder, more stern, than Lenna would have expected from her almost soporific demeanor. "You know you're just as good as I am; I'm just lazy about keeping a blade sharp enough."

Jaice shrugged helplessly at Lenna. "Allow me to introduce my battle-sister, who, despite her fudging of the facts, just very recently happened to save my life when we were traveling in Gallas. Er...?"

Lenna swallowed hard. "Oh. My name is Lenna," she said, her voice hoarse. "Forgive the lack of more information, but, as I've mentioned, this mission requires some delicacy."

"Lenna," commented the blonde woman. "That's a lovely name; you don't hear it much in these parts anymore."

"In any case," Jaice said loudly, "Sister Lenna, allow me to introduce my battle-sister, returning with me to Granemere Settlement, Freewoman Alanna Ameary."

Much to her own surprise, Lenna let that revelation roll off her back. *Just another of those days, it seems.* No doubt sometime in the future — when? — her mind would start screaming in sentiments Lenna probably didn't have words for, but for now, it merely accepted the fantastic truth of the person before her. She nodded a greeting at the diffident young woman, though some rebellious part of her brain was eager to have her tongue rattle off the phrase, "Hello, Mother."

Lenna, reunited (or rather, meeting) with her future aunt and the woman who would in some years' time give birth to her, found herself at something of an impasse. As she stood on the dusty road, Lenna cranked her mind up to an impressive speed, all its wheels and cogs a rival for any streamtrain. To make her lie plausible and maintain secrecy, Lenna by her words should be continuing her journey south, parting ways with Jaice and Alanna. However, a tugging sensation in her balled fist — a "Hello!" from the Godjewel — and the very fact that whatever power had been unleashed had sent Lenna here convinced her that she was at this spot for a purpose, to see these people.

"I'm glad to see such confidence in our ranks." Lenna's tongue was misbehaving, damaging any sense of command the pretend Freewoman spy was attempting to display. "You're both returning to Granemere, then?"

"Yes," said Jaice, as ever a paragon of brevity. "We were more than lucky in Gallas and are eager to return home."

Alanna snorted, the first uncouth action Lenna had seen from her, and for a moment Lenna noticed a resemblance to the stern, forceful woman she would grow into. Lenna could do naught but shake her head, pushing aside strange feelings in search of an excuse to dawdle around the pair of Freewoman mercenaries a bit longer. She parted her lips to speak — though what phrase she was planning on uttering was still a mystery to her — when Jaice spoke up again, apparently having chosen to ignore Alanna's rude interruption.

"How were the roads, Sister? Bandit-free, I hope? With the new plans for the steamtrain everyone's talking about, I imagine sometime in the near future we'll not need to rely on horses as much." Jaice patted the flank of her steed affectionately.

Yes, and the damn thing will interrupt your sleep on a regular basis, Lenna inwardly grumbled.

"I imagine we're still some years away from that," Alanna said, her voice distant. "Implementing such a large-scale infrastructure throughout one nation, let alone connecting all the nations of the Continent, will take over a decade, maybe even two."

Jaice cast a telling glance at her partner. "That's rather knowledgeable for someone who shows little interest in mechanical engineering."

If Alanna was bothered by Jaice's remark, she showed no sign. Her expression remained flat and serene as she replied, "My point is, we'll probably have our horses a bit longer."

"Speaking of horses," Jaice segued and corrected her posture into one ready to spur her horse into action. "We are about to be overtaken by some company from the north."

Lenna swiveled and peered up the section of the road she had just recently been traversing. Kicking up great clouds of dust at a gallop was a rider on a dappled horse; by his build Lenna confirmed that the rider was a man, and trailing behind him in the wake of upturned dirt flecked with white froth from his mount were short robes with billowing sleeves in a deep blue color. Robes of an apprentice from the Blue Crescent Brotherhood. Surprising herself, Lenna found that her right hand was already wrapped around the hilt of her sword.

"A Brotherhood apprentice," Jaice said unnecessarily. Lenna cast a glance at her two companions and noticed that Jaice, too, had lowered one arm to rest on the long staff strapped to her steed's side. Despite being years younger than the woman Lenna knew in her present time, this woman clearly already harbored very particular misgivings about the order. Alanna stared forward, neither alarmed nor excited.

Intuition was an aspect of her being that Lenna was not prone to calling an attribute, but with recent events and the Godjewel's predilection for placing her — ever to her growing frustration — in "convenient" locations and times, she didn't need to wait for the sun to catch the ginger hair of the male rider to identify him as a young Thane Faircloth. He was working the horse hard, kicking it with a determined thrashing that he, if he were the man Lenna knew as an adult, would only give a steed if flight was of great importance.

"What could he be running from?" Jaice addressed the group.

"I can't imagine any trouble with any of the homesteads or outlying villages to the north," said Lenna.

"He couldn't be coming from as far north as the Empire at that pace. He'd kill his horse."

Frowning, Lenna replayed some of her more recent dealings with the Krevlum Empire in her mind and shuddered. She liked horses, in theory. Still. "There are some things in the Empire worth getting away from, even at the expense of a horse."

"Interesting," Alanna commented. "It's certainly more advanced technologically than the other nations on the Continent, but we've nothing to fear from the Empire."

"Alanna's first settlement was in Krevlum," Jaice explained.

Lenna winced. This bit of information was something that had never been disclosed, not by her mother herself, by her father, or by Jaice. Lenna had been led to believe that her mother was a native of Granemere, not an undisclosed settlement located in what Lenna believed to be the most perilous of places on the Continent. And if her guess was correct, that her eventual father — an apprentice from the Blue Crescent Brotherhood, no less — was fleeing from the Krevlum Empire, exactly what in the universe was happening? Had Lenna the freedom, she might have snarled at her balled fist for its impudence.

From behind Thane, amidst the bits of earth and dust, a sudden darkness, a thick veil of oily fog, sprang, roiling, into being. It lagged only meters behind the mage and, as though he noticed Lenna's eyes widening in fear and recognition, Thane cast a look over his shoulder. Though he was still too distant for Lenna to clearly discern his expression, the way he returned to an even tighter, hunched riding position and kicked his horse harder yet told Lenna that the young Thane realized what the cloud was.

"A sending," said Alanna. Her matter-of-fact delivery irked Lenna.

"After a Brotherhood mage? Who in the four nations would attempt such folly?" Jaice asked.

"We need to get moving," Lenna said, trying to keep her voice calm. The last time she had seen a conjuring such as this was the day she lost her best friend. "The apprentice has the right idea."

"Lenna," Alanna said, "ride with me." It was the voice of command, and it reminded Lenna so poignantly of her mother — in the future — giving calm but stern instruction to the young girl. *Lenna, sharpen your knife. Lenna, run to the greengrocer.* Lenna wordlessly took Alanna's grasping hand and heaved herself up into the saddle behind the Freewoman. In her stupor, Lenna realized, she had actually managed to mount a horse without falling over her sword. Freewoman Dalm would be proud.

"Right," said Jaice. "Lenna, where shall we go?" The future mayor clicked her tongue and brought her horse back to attention.

She held the reins with a loose but capable grip that Lenna had yet to master; her own grip tended to be of the white-knuckled variety.

Of course, Lenna thought. *I went out of my way in my subterfuge to convince them that I outrank them, or at least possess some sort of knowledge they don't, so they're deferring to me. Well, shit.* After going through her mental checklist of swear words, Lenna kick-started her brain into working order. "I'd hate for a sending like that to fall on any of the innocents in Port Hollish." If Lenna's assumption was correct, this far back in the past North Gate would be wholly undefended and unprepared. "Take us out into the fields; we want to stretch the sending out, expending its energy in the chase, rather than let it concentrate."

"Agreed," said Alanna.

"We ride, then." Jaice nodded and launched her steed into a gallop; a few seconds later Alanna followed suit and Lenna found herself, for preservation's sake, with her right arm around the young woman's waist. The sensation overwhelmed her; it forced Lenna to recall her youth and came with a heavy sadness. Though similar in appearance, this version of Alanna was drastically different from and full of more secrets than Lenna's version had been.

As the Freewomen galloped off the road and into the vast, flat lands of Fallowfields, Lenna, her curls tangling in her spectacles, glanced over her shoulder. Her future father, Thane Faircloth, had altered his course and was in a dead-heat run toward her group, the ominous cloud of death nipping at the pounding hooves of his horse.

Jaice and Alanna spurred their horses onward at a steady pace, attempting to increase the distance between themselves and the deadly sending, though Alanna's steed, unaccustomed to carrying two riders, faltered in its steps as they pressed on. Lenna was more inclined to attribute some of the horse's clumsiness to her own lack of skill in the saddle. Jaice had reined her horse in to match the other mount's pace, and it quickly became evident that Thane and the black fog would be upon them soon.

"Ahead," Lenna called out. "There is an apple farm not a mile off. We can take advantage of some of its outlying fields; hopefully no one will be working so far out this time of day." The strange recurrence of her own flight chilled Lenna to the core, despite the warm weather; she was leading the Freewomen — and by extension, her father — to the Meekses' orchard. A thought niggled at the back of her mind: could Lenna's directions toward the Meekses' farmstead be the reason for her mother's and Mistress Meeks's original acquaintance? She shook her head; time, she fathomed, could be made sense of later.

Voicing acknowledgement, Jaice and Alanna urged their horses toward the orchard, the robust trees visible and growing larger as they neared. Lenna did not want to bring trouble to the Meekses, but if her gut was correct, the sending would soon be upon Thane, and he would need some assistance to survive. Lenna tightened her grip around Alanna's waist: she did not want to think about the consequences for her personal future should Thane die in the past.

Glancing back, the apprentice's horse, frothing furiously, looked on the verge of collapse. Be it by his decision or not, Thane Faircloth would be dismounting very soon. The air was rank and fetid as the sending swelled, slowing in its assault as the four riders forced it to expend more of its energy in the prolonged pursuit of its target. Lenna silently thanked Gilbert for this tactic.

The scent of apple quickly hit Lenna, a different kind of tartness compared to the overwhelming scent of the orange groves of the Branford Estate. The horses whined and grunted and Jaice and Alanna brought them to a halt on the edge of the orchard. The group was still some distance from the manor home; there were no signs of any Meekses or workers about the trees, whose strong branches had yet to become fully fecund with the crisp apples for which the farm had made its name throughout Fallowfields.

Fumbling with her damnably long sword, Lenna dismounted with less grace than she'd have liked in front of the others. She hastened up beside Jaice, who had freed her staff from its bindings to the horse's side, and Alanna, who stood with folded arms and regarded the approaching Thane Faircloth like a particularly difficult mathematical puzzle. His horse was visibly struggling, its canter almost comical, as though someone had soaked its oats in brandy. Foam, flecked with bits of red, dripped from the poor beast's mouth and landed with a disgusting plop on the ground. A slick sheen of sweat coated Thane's face and after the mage pulled his steed to a halt he leaned against its neck; the rider, it seemed, was as weary as his mount.

"Freewomen of Laur," Lenna's future father croaked. His voice was still softened, like that of the Thane Lenna knew, but less confident and more desperate in cadence than she had ever heard. His lanky body and flushed, freckly face made him appear far younger than the three Freewomen. Lenna watched on, her heart beating at a peculiar pace, as her father panted before them, pleading. "I beseech you. Help."

The murky menace had slowed its pursuit, sweeping across the fields soundlessly from about a quarter mile back. At its current speed, Lenna calculated, they would have a few moments to gather their wits and hopefully mount a defense against the vile magics of the sending. As if it could sense the lurking fog, the Godjewel quivered ever so faintly with an almost human trepidation; she hoped against hope than none of the three magicians — all quite powerful, as she had gathered — would not detect its (for the moment) subtle presence.

"An apprentice from the Blue Crescent Brotherhood," chimed Alanna. "Asking Freewomen for help? That's new."

Jaice smirked, leaning on her staff. "Since when have you lot been keen on cooperating with the weaker sex?"

Lenna was about to interrupt when, much to her surprise, her future father slid from his saddle with exhaustion and fell quickly to his knees. Both of his hands were raised in the Freewoman sign of supplication. "Please. That sending will kill me."

Alanna and Jaice regarded each other with deep but unreadable gazes; if they were communicating, Lenna thought, it must be through telepathy. Suddenly everyone had turned to her, Lenna, the leader. *This is a curious shift in paradigm,* she thought.

These were the "grown-ups" who were supposed to be giving her the orders, not the other way around. Yet Lenna's weaponry, garb, and knowledge had proved her rank to Jaice and Alanna, and they now deferred to her judgment, and Thane, it would seem, recognized her as being in command.

All right, then. Much like the sending that had relentlessly pursued her, Gilbert, and Luc a month ago, this conjuration would be upon them before long, and ironically Lenna probably had the most experience with this sort of magic out of the whole group. After all, despite how promising a mage Sebastien had admitted her father Thane had been, he was weary and, as Lenna probed his magical aura, not very powerful at the moment.

"The apprentice is right," she said in what she hoped was an authoritative tone. "I've heard of sendings of this magnitude before. And," Lenna added, "be he from the Brotherhood or not, Freewomen of Laur don't just let people die."

Her eyes were locked on Thane's; his shoulders sank with relief and his hands fell to his sides. Jaice and Alanna were out of her line of sight, but some tension in the air had diffused and been replaced with resignation that left her oddly levelheaded. Lenna's choice of words must have been good. She stepped forward and extended her right hand toward the road-weary apprentice at her feet. Thane, wiping his grubby hands on his robes, accepted Lenna's arm and allowed her to help him to his feet.

"Thank you," he spoke quietly. "I'm Apprentice Thane Faircloth."

"My name is Lenna." She turned and nodded at the Freewomen, naming them as she did so. "We haven't much time. First, Alanna — give Thane some water."

For the first time, Alanna let surprise conquer her tightly controlled face; her brow arched in curiosity, but she obeyed the order, grabbing a water skin from the saddlebag of her mount and tossing it to Thane, who fumbled a bit but managed to avoid letting it fall to the earth. He began to drink eagerly, and Lenna took the opportunity to slide up to Jaice. The stony woman looked at Lenna expectedly.

"Jaice," Lenna began. "This sending will be violent." As if on cue, a burst of yellow-bright lightning lashed out from the edges of the approaching cloud. "How rested are you and Alanna? How are your magical reserves?"

"We're more than capable, but that apprentice won't have much to offer in terms of magic."

Lenna nodded. "I agree. If you, Alanna, and I feed him enough power, and leave the shaping of the shielding to Thane, I think we might be able to survive its onslaught."

A familiar line of worry creased the young Jaice's forehead as she considered Lenna's plan. "I'm not completely unaware of the kind of magic we're about to face," she said. "And I can sense strength within you too. Alanna and I aren't weak, but even so — are we strong enough to stand against *that*?" She pointed her staff in the direction of the encroaching darkness.

Thane and Alanna were silent. The apprentice had returned the water skin to the intrigued Freewoman, and both now looked toward Lenna and awaited the answer to Jaice's question. Lenna quickly recalled the events surrounding Gilbert's death with bared teeth. That night, she, Gilbert, and Luc had been exhausted and at the time Lenna had barely had any concept of her own strength or how to use her magic. They relied on stealth, flight, and then simple shielding when they could. Their wards had held for the most part, and Gilbert had dispatched the sending's various manifestations with ease.

"Brotherhood shielding is very efficient," Lenna pronounced. She wasn't surprised to hear Jaice and Alanna gasp in dismay as a fellow Freewoman praised Brotherhood magic. "So yes, we'll let the young apprentice handle the shaping of the shield. Thane, do you think you can hold the pattern in your mind? Will you accept our magic?"

Thane's lips puckered up in thought and, after a second's deliberation, he replied. "Yes," he breathed. "I can do it."

"And Alanna and Jaice," Lenna continued, "are you aware of how to bolster the apprentice's magic and, moreover, do you agree to work with him?"

"Yes," Jaice said. Her reply came out reserved, her hesitation obvious. Lenna imagined she must be violating any number of Freewoman tenets.

"Alanna?" Lenna asked again.

"Oh," said Alanna, coming out of some kind of daze. "Yes, I agree."

"Then that's the plan. We'll weather this storm, together."

"Lenna?" Thane asked. "It's not that I doubt the strength of the Freewomen of Laur. But do we simply have enough magic?"

"If it's power you're worried about, Apprentice Faircloth," Lenna said tartly, "I wouldn't worry. We've got that in spades."

CHAPTER SIXTEEN

The malevolent black shroud rose fifteen meters high, but the four mages — though Lenna grimaced at the very notion of thinking herself a mage — stood defiant. Jaice, quick on the uptake, led the horses into the rows of apple trees, where they would be protected from any sort of magical backlash the ensuing conflict might cause. Thane knelt on the ground and in the most surreal of fashions, Lenna and Alanna, his future daughter and wife, took their places behind him, Lenna with her right hand on Thane's left shoulder, and Alanna the reverse. It reminded Lenna of her youth, and she found herself deep in thought.

"Lenna," began Alanna, "is something the matter?"

Coughing, Lenna forced herself to confront the situation at hand. She shook her head and smiled at the young woman, whose eyes had yet to become so lined with worry, whose body had yet to become so frail, and… "It's nothing for you to worry about. As soon as Jaice is back, we'll begin."

Alanna nodded, but there was something playing about her eyes that betrayed her lack of belief in Lenna's words. *Nothing to do about that now,* Lenna thought. She swallowed her nerves, hoping she wasn't changing her history too much. Task complete, Jaice trotted up and stood behind the trio. Placing one hand on Lenna's shoulder and one hand on Alanna's, Jaice completed the formation of a tight diamond, a shield against a magical barrage.

Now that they were in physical contact, the transference — Lenna smirked, wondering what Luc would think of her terminology — should be a simple task.

"Is everyone ready?" Lenna asked.

Both Freewomen nodded and Thane politely said, "Yes, Lenna," which Lenna found to be very timid and frustrating. Her father was never overly verbose, and being a member of the Brotherhood, secluded on an island without any females, must have had its effects on a young man interested in the opposite sex. Especially when faced with such formidable members of the opposite sex...

Thane was exhausted, so it was up to the Freewomen to provide the power behind the warding. Lenna knew Jaice and herself to both be naturally strong, but had no idea as to the level of her mother's power. If Jaice wasn't bragging, and the Jaice Lenna knew seldom did, perhaps they would have enough strength between the four of them for Lenna not to worry about relying on the power of the Godjewel. Hopefully.

"All right, everyone, I want you to reach into yourselves, finding the source of your magic. Let down the barriers between your hearts; Thane, you should begin to feel our presences." So natural had the act become to Lenna that she didn't even think to lean on the power of the gem in her left hand; instead, she delved down into her psyche, accessing the vault of energy that she visualized as her magic. She fed her power to Thane, who at first was shy and reserved: the wall surrounding his core, protecting his ego, was still erect and covered in briars. As Gilbert and Sebastien had demonstrated, Lenna nudged her consciousness up against Thane's, prompting him to open up, to let go of his reservations.

The fields around them were saturated with rich magic as Thane bared himself to the three women, and the scent of each person's magic fancifully commingled, creating a heady potpourri. Lavender from Lenna, and a subtle, herbaceous scent of chamomile from Jaice; the scents from her future parents, however, dumbfounded Lenna. She was a little girl again; a honeyed astringency emitted from Alanna, rekindling memories of reading books by the hearth, its crackling fire warming the chillier months, and Thane's magic was as tangy and sweet as his homemade cider. *I've come home,* Lenna thought, and let her power flow freely.

Thane, his defenses down and sense of self unguarded, was swept up in the magic of the three Freewomen standing behind him. He was hesitant at first, but as their power grew, like an intense pour from a growler of ale, Thane steadied himself against the torrent of arcane energy. The eagerness with which he absorbed and shaped it proved to Lenna that Thane Faircloth was used to such power; though he was exhausted and burned-out, every skin cell on Lenna's arms tingled as the apprentice nimbly shaped an intricate web of protection. He cast the net around the four of them and held the pattern in his mind — so focused that in its potency it was almost visible to the naked eye — as the harrowing black tide broke upon them.

Spikes of topaz energy whipped against the group's shield whenever the dark fog came into contact with the globe of force encasing Lenna and her companions, the discord and lights making Lenna jerk with each explosion. Before long the all too familiar odor of ozone from the residual strikes filled the atmosphere around them, and Lenna struggled not to let her mind wander back to Gilbert's death; rather, she tried to keep her thoughts on home, her times as a young girl spent with older versions of Alanna and Thane, and the more she dwelled on those happy times, the more her soul relinquished its power to herself and subsequently the young apprentice.

In moments the entirety of the sending had surrounded them and clashed madly against Thane's glimmering shield. As they struck the barrier, bursts of energy were channeled downward to the ground, causing explosions of soil and rock to clatter up against their ward. Lenna squeezed her eyes shut so tightly tears began to well up in the corners, but she fixated on supplying Thane with the magic he'd need to keep this shield going against the darkness. Her plan was different than Gilbert's — his objective had been flight — but then again, the Brotherhood did not teach cooperation with Freewomen, and Lenna was resolute in her belief that fleeing wouldn't fix this problem.

Whinnies of fright cut through the thunderous convulsion of the sending, though Lenna could spare no thought for the horses now. One lapse in concentration on any party member's part could result in the shield dropping, at which point all would fall. She felt Alanna's calm and concentrated presence and Jaice's firm determination. Thinking back to her first encounter with Jaice, when her (although unbeknownst to Lenna at the time) aunt had silenced Lenna and the Godjewel with a slight exertion of will, Lenna appreciated the arcane gifts bestowed upon her Freewoman family.

"Good," Lenna said with more authority than she actually felt. "The shield is holding. The sending can't keep up this level of attack much longer."

"I have an idea," said Thane abruptly. "You're strong — all of you. Give me more. I'm going to fight back, push it off with the shield."

Was such a thing possible? Lenna's magical education was lacking compared to the three people whose destinies were currently very much under her direct influence, but it might work. In her anger she'd learned to emit waves of pure force, and what was a shield but force that had been harnessed and shaped to a purpose? If Thane could visualize and rework the pattern of the shield as the Freewomen channeled even more of their magic toward him, Lenna thought that, logically, there was no reason why he could not expand the range of the shield and push away the darkness, putting the sending on the defensive. All it required was loads of power and loads of skill.

Thane Faircloth is one of the most precise mechanists throughout the four nations. And, Lenna thought, *he's your father, you silly sausage. Have faith.* "Let's try it," she said. "Alanna, Jaice, give Thane as much as you can."

Alanna and Jaice were quick to voice their surprise at a Freewoman so swiftly agreeing to a mere apprentice's suggestion, but there was no dissent. All three women breathed in unison and reached inward, bringing forth all the magic they could without pushing themselves into madness. Thane took their power masterfully and Lenna watched, curious, as the enormity of it filled Thane's body. His entire frame had begun to shudder until in one catastrophic heave he released all the magic into the pattern of his shielding. The sending exploded into sparks and crackling rays of energy as it was repelled from the shield, pushed back nearly ten meters. Gaps in the fog began to reveal the daylight once more, and the writhing mass of darkness coalesced more slowly than it had before. Their shield, however, was no more.

"Again!" shouted Thane. "Give me more, quickly!"

"Do it!" Lenna commanded.

Panting now, the Freewomen strained to offer whatever energy they could muster. Quickly, they supplied Thane the necessary magic, and Lenna was amazed at Thane's composure despite the energy building within him. The pale man, with his ruffled red hair, had begun to glister as he took in more and more of their magic. How much would be too much? Lenna wondered if it was possible for someone to take in too much power and rupture like an overfilled balloon, to be overcome as she had been on numerous occasions with the Godjewel.

Thane hollered something between a grunt and an obscenity, and heaved again, this time throwing out his arms. The cloud, hurling itself toward the group, was suddenly confronted with an impeccably patterned arc of concentrated magical force. A screech in the air and a horrific popping rang strongly across the wide fields, and in one terrific collision of fiery magics the entire shroud of darkness burned out into the warm summer air. The sending's power was depleted.

A moment later all three women and Thane found themselves collapsed on the grassy field outside the apple orchard. The air was an offensive brew of cheap perfume and stinging ozone, and, around the group, a crop circle had been cut. Within the dome of their shield, the ground remained pristine, but outside of it, for nearly five meters, the soil was overturned and bits of rock and earth crumpled what little grass remained standing.

Chest heaving up and down, Alanna turned her head to Thane, a pace or so away from her on the grass, and said, "That was impressive work, Apprentice."

Thane grinned, an awkward, lopsided and completely uncomfortable gesture that Lenna had rarely witnessed in his older years. "Thank you for the strength, ladies," he said.

"Freewomen," Jaice's voice rebuked.

"Freewomen."

Lenna kept her mouth shut – another rarity – and concentrated on slow, deep breaths. Her mind was racing, not only at the implications regarding the magical working the group had just performed (had they invented a new method of magecraft?) but at the amalgamation of emotions at having done so intimate a working with people that would, in the years to come, raise Lenna and become her family. They didn't know it now, but Lenna had already bonded so strongly with each of the other three in her proper time that she was certain the ease of the magical transference had been her doing. Had she, then, served as the spark that spawned the intimate bonds between these people that lay in the grass beside her? Did she just unwittingly organize the construction of her own family?

"And so the strange day gets stranger," she wheezed.

"Pardon?" asked Jaice.

Damn. Lenna hadn't realized she had spoken aloud, though certain dalliances or lapses in judgment, she considered, must be allowed considering the sheer overflow of information she had processed in what was proving to be the longest twenty-four–hour period of her entire existence. *If life keeps going at this rate,* she fancied, *I'll have at least three books to write by the time my story is done.* "Never mind," Lenna said airily. "That was just some unique magecraft. I'm a bit light-headed."

The group performed a perfunctory check of their gear and persons as they scrambled to their feet. Despite the magical expenditure, the unique bonding of the group had not drained the three women nearly as much as Lenna supposed it should have; much to their unified surprise, after they regained their breath, all four felt conversely energized. Thane, or so he claimed, felt better than he had before his hasty flight from the north. This, of course, was a statement that immediately segued into a questioning as to what the mage — an apprentice, no less — was doing tearing through Fallowfields at headlong speed.

"I'm not allowed to comment on that, I'm afraid," Thane said in response to Jaice's fervid questioning.

"The Freewomen of Laur just saved your life, *Apprentice,*" Jaice said.

"I was under the impression we saved each other."

"We wouldn't have been in danger if not for your Brotherhood machinations..." The future mayor's normally checked temper began to peak.

Lenna derailed the argument as quickly as she'd derail a steamtrain. "While both parties deserve praise for that magical achievement, I sincerely doubt that whatever motivated an individual to actively pursue young Apprentice Faircloth with so powerful a working will stop there."

Thane looked down at the earth as Jaice and Alanna, the former leaning on her staff, loomed expectantly over him. Lenna's experiences with the Brotherhood thus far had demonstrated there would be a large amount of information that Thane would keep to himself, but Jaice — brusqueness aside — was correct in pressing him for some enlightenment. As the three Freewomen were now involved, their lives were possibly in danger as well.

"I really can't talk about it," Thane said again.

"Thane," said Lenna, "I understand that the Brotherhood demands its brethren guard its secrets with unparalleled ferocity, but you've just put three Freewomen of Laur in harm's way, and whatever clandestine mission you were on, no matter what its purpose, you've just gotten yourself tangled in a whole mess of diplomatic nets. Would it be safe to presume the sending was from someone in the Krevlum Empire?"

The apprentice bit his lip, the uncertainty on his face clear, but eventually Thane, however reluctant, nodded in affirmation to Lenna's question. "Yes, I'm fleeing from the Empire."

Frowning, Alanna inquired, "Fleeing from the Krevlum Empire? Whatever for?"

"I'm not allowed to comment on that, I'm afraid," Thane repeated.

Lenna sighed. This line of questioning was getting them nowhere, and she was more than eager to resume her own line of research: how to return to her own time period. "A sending that powerful is localized, and you couldn't have outrun it for very long. I'd wager you're being pursued by more than just magical clouds of death?"

Thane looked between the women before framing a response. "The Empire has been uncovering some… things," he said, clearly choosing his words with great caution. "Old texts. Certain items of interest to the Blue Crescent Brotherhood."

"And you were sent to gather information?" Jaice nearly growled. "Not surprising. The Brotherhood is always up to something."

"It isn't like the Freewomen of Laur don't have their own information network," Thane retorted. He shot Lenna an intent look, and she was momentarily aghast at the depth and understanding in his eyes. They were the same as her father's; penetrating and knowing. "I imagine Lenna might have some information concerning that as well. I know Freewomen are trained in magic, but she knew a great deal more about that sending than the average battlemage."

All eyes on me again, Lenna thought, irritated. "It's not the first time I've been trapped by such a working, obviously." How much information should she give?

"So you were fleeing from Krevlum as well," Alanna said. Her voice was guarded again and weighted with a reserve that made Lenna begin to question whether Alanna's loyalty to her home nation of Krevlum colored her perception of its actions. *Then again,* thought Lenna, *it wasn't until recent times — my time — that the Krevlum Empire became so outwardly aggressive.* "Why, Lenna? Or, like Apprentice Faircloth, are you not permitted to comment on that?"

It was a challenge; Alanna's tone reminded Lenna of being chastised as a child for telling a fib. Behind that veil of calm, Lenna knew her mother would stand firm until she received a satisfactory answer. "I was seeking information, similar to the apprentice," she lied. *How far was Alanna Ameary planning on taking this,* Lenna brooded, *and more importantly — how much lying am I prepared to do?*

"Then Lenna will understand reinforcements are on their way," Thane added hastily. His grey eyes darted toward the line of the orchard, to where Jaice had herded the horses. The apprentice must be eager to get on his way. If he made it to Port Hollish, Lenna reckoned, he'd be safe with the emissaries from his enclave at the Embassy.

Jaice was quick to her feet and coaxed the steeds out of the tempting trees — no doubt against the horses' wills, judging by the disappointed neighs — and led them to the group. The Freewomen's horses appeared refreshed despite the harsh gallop and the magical battle; their eyes were bright and they eagerly knocked their heads against their riders. Thane's horse, however, seemed the worse for wear: the muscles in its flanks were twitching with overexertion, and though it had ceased its panicked frothing, its head sagged low to the ground. Lenna stroked its forelock.

"Thane," she said, "I don't think your mount is up for any more hard riding."

"And you somehow fled the borders of Krevlum without a horse of your own," Thane said.

"I set mine loose a few miles back," Lenna fibbed again, probably unconvincingly. "My exit must have been a little less hurried than yours."

"I can lend you my horse," Alanna offered. "I'll ride double with Jaice back to Granemere."

The other Freewoman, her thoughts even now focused on her settlement, thumped her staff against the ground. "Alanna, I'm not sure we'd be rewarded for giving up a good horse."

Time for more creative lying. If Jaice and Alanna returned to

Granemere Settlement and reported Lenna's actions before she managed to get away, suspicion and alarm would no doubt be raised, and her charade over. She couldn't be certain what sort of effect it would have on her own timeline if the Freewomen of Laur started sniffing around for an unknown agent operating under her name and, more importantly, found her. Lenna closed her eyes and allowed herself one last sweet whiff of the blooming apple trees before making up her mind. This would probably in the long run make things worse, not better, but for the time being keeping her father safe and the Freewomen delayed in returning to Granemere felt like Lenna's safest bet.

"Alanna, Jaice, rather than rob you of a horse, I'd like to recruit your assistance in escorting Apprentice Faircloth and myself to Port Hollish. I understand it's out of your way — backtracking, even — but my mission is of great importance to the Freewomen of Laur, and the apprentice needs our help."

All parties held their tongues as Lenna hoped she had phrased her plea in a manner that would encourage her Freewoman compatriots to comply willingly. Fostering cooperation between political entities who were quite frank about their mutual dislike was never something Lenna considered a skill of hers, though thus far the smooth transitions — and her dealings with Ilyan merchant families and Gallasian landlords/former Brotherhood members — might be enough to warrant her a future in diplomacy. If she lived. *Three books,* she repeated to herself.

Jaice leaned on her staff and gave a stiff nod in Lenna's direction. The warrior was plainly displeased, but thanks to Lenna's lucky (though in her present day they were currently disappearing one by one) stars, she still seemed happy to defer to Lenna's leadership. Alanna, arms folded, had been studying Thane and Lenna equally, her eyes calculating the benefits and deterrents to accepting Lenna's proposal. Ultimately, Alanna slid her hands to her hips and shook her head in defeat.

"You two are mysterious. Lenna." She addressed her with such authority that Lenna was half-tempted to say, "Are we, Mother?" in response. "Lenna," Alanna repeated. "Your magic is strong, but

I sense something strange about it. Out of place. That makes me curious. And Thane." The cool-headed woman shifted her eyes to the scruffy man fidgeting off to the side. "Your flight from Krevlum intrigues me even more. I'll go."

Lenna sighed in relief; one more problem temporarily sorted. "Right, let's mount up, then."

"Alanna, with me," Jaice said.

"No," her friend replied. Lenna thought she detected a faint trace of whimsy in the woman's voice. "I'll ride with our young Brotherhood charge."

"Strange days indeed," Jaice echoed Lenna's earlier words. "I never thought Alanna Ameary would choose to ride with a man."

Alanna shot her friend a sword-sharp stare that could smite even the mightiest of future mayors. Jaice cleared her throat and swung herself into the saddle of her mare before offering a hand to Lenna. Grateful, Lenna let Jaice yank her up behind her onto the horse and was pleased she wouldn't be in charge of guiding the steed. Both riders watched Alanna and Thane with interest.

Thane looked between the horse and his riding partner, unsure of how to mount. After another moment of hesitation, Alanna made an exasperated noise and swung up, mounting quickly. She looked down at the gangly mage. "Well?" she said and extended her hand.

The apprentice took it, embarrassment evident in his red ears, and scrambled up behind the smaller-framed woman. He shifted about in the saddle, adjusting his position, as though to stay as far away from Alanna as possible yet still remain seated on the horse. Jaice and Lenna couldn't help but snicker like a pair of juveniles at the precious scene; to Lenna, it bordered on endearing. She knew her father was reclusive, but never so shy. Then again, the only woman Lenna recalled Thane Faircloth interacting with outside of business-related matters was her mother, Alanna, and he had known her for years by then.

"Off we go, then," Jaice said, and urged her horse forward.

Alanna followed immediately, her horse a meter or so to their rear. Over the clattering of hooves, Lenna trained her ears on the unusual couple's conversation as they made their way to Port Hollish.

"Faircloth, is it?" Lenna heard Alanna's questioning. "I've heard that name before. Is your family a well-known line of tailors?"

"We used to be," Thane replied. "Long ago, just after the God War. We weren't tailors as such; we were just some of the few remaining people with the ability to sew quickly. Good hands, or so I'm told."

"And now?"

"Clocks," said Thane. "My father makes clocks."

"Ah," Alanna said. "So that's where I've heard the name before. Your timepieces are popular, even in Krevlum."

"Yes," he answered after a moment, "they are indeed."

Alanna asked him a few more questions, but Thane seemed steadfast in maintaining his silence, much to Lenna's disappointment.

With Thane's overworked mount left behind to forage about the Meekses' apple orchards, the company was free to head on to Port Hollish, though, other than ensuring her future father's safety, Lenna remained puzzled as to what she hoped to accomplish once they arrived. Peculiar facts and questions bounced about her brain, demanding to be addressed, but the steady clopping of the horse confounded any chance at sorting out matters. Jaice's horse, snorting in displeasure at having to bear a rider as inexperienced as Lenna, nevertheless diligently drew them closer to their immediate goal.

"Lenna," asked Jaice, her voice barely above a whisper. The clomping of the horses' hooves helped further mask her words. "Is whatever is pursuing that boy involved with your mission from the Freewomen?"

"I don't know," Lenna replied honestly. It was nice to be able to be truthful about something. Whatever Thane Faircloth was fleeing from, Lenna had too little knowledge of the matter to speculate: in her time, the Krevlum Empire was capable of procuring any number of nasty devices to solve its problems. Some twenty-five years earlier, before any noticeable signs of aggression had yet to be seen in the Continent, the extent of the nation's power was unclear to Lenna. Arm around Jaice's waist as her bum thumped achingly against the saddle, Lenna flipped through the indices in her memory to recall the name of the man who would be the current Emperor. For some reason, her thoughts stayed fuzzy.

"Everything all right?" Jaice asked.

"Yes, just a bit tired," Lenna lied. As they loped closer to her hometown, Lenna was becoming increasingly frustrated that she was having difficulty recalling certain details of her own past. Was time changing, muddling certain facts, eliminating truths she had always believed? Was her interference erasing pieces of her past?

"Jaice," called Alanna. "Hold up, please."

Jaice jerked on the reins, skirting her horse around to face Alanna and Thane as their steed came to a halt. As Lenna's mind once more focused on present matters, her attention was drawn to a pale, wide-eyed Thane gesturing manically in the direction from which they had come. She scratched the tip of her nose and waited for either of her future parents to speak.

"She's coming," said Thane. "The woman who's been chasing me, a soldier — I can feel her magic from here. With our horses bearing two riders each, she'll be upon us before we make Port Hollish."

Letting out a snort worthy of her horse, Jaice leaned forward and patted the beast's crest. "One soldier, against four trained mages? Let her come; she'd be no match for us. Look how we handled the Empire's working." What a rash attitude for Jaice! Lenna felt a pang in her breast as she wondered just how much this Jaice Northen had been involved in the upbringing of Pim.

"You haven't met this soldier," Thane said, guarded. "She's different, and strong."

Alanna cocked her head to one side, like she was gauging the direction of the wind. She sniffed once and then scrunched up her forehead as a young Lenna had seen her older self do whenever Lenna's actions were not befitting a proper Freewoman of Laur. Something had unsettled her. Reaching out with a nebulous psychic touch, Lenna attempted to discern the magic Thane had mentioned. Off in the distance, on the very border of her mind, there was a smear of grease on all things magical, drawing nearer. Thane was correct; someone was coming for them.

Jaice shifted in her saddle, obviously coming to the same realization the other three had, though Lenna wasn't privy to the expression on her face. "That is some decidedly foul magic. It's… slimy."

"It's tainted," said Alanna, looking upward to the sky and addressing no one in particular. "Like when someone of exceptional talent is never trained, and the power is pushed to the point of driving them mad."

"But surely the mages in Krevlum would never allow that; their soldiers are so tightly strung and trained to be brutally cool," Lenna said.

Alanna looked at Lenna with eyes far too perceptive for Lenna's liking. "You have much experience with the military operations of the Krevlum Empire, then, Lenna?"

"There's no time to delay," Thane inserted hurriedly. "We have to do something. Prepare a defense. Or hide. I don't know; there's something wrong with her." His breath, labored, wheezed against the otherwise quiet summer day. Somewhere nearby a gull cried and Thane flinched in the saddle.

Gliding ever closer was the viscous draping of corrupt magic. The Brotherhood apprentice was panicking, and Lenna was beginning to piece together why, but she chose not to voice her concerns. Since the group had deferred to her leadership once before and she had proved herself effective, Lenna — however unwillingly — was prepared to assume command again. *Besides,* she thought, unconsciously reaching up to fuss with her cropped, wavy hair, *if this is what I think it is…*

"All right," Lenna said, and with a dexterity she didn't know she possessed, she slid away from Jaice's side and landed on the dusty road with a soft thunk. She didn't even bash Jaice or the horse in the side with her sword as she dismounted.

"What are you doing?" asked Thane, bewildered.

"Jaice, I'll reimburse Granemere with a new horse from Port Hollish. I've the coin and the authorization. Give your steed to Apprentice Faircloth."

The Freewoman's jaw dropped for a second, Lenna's assumed authority jolting her composure, but she nodded with pursed lips and hopped down beside Lenna. "You're rather bossy, Lenna. You'd make a good mayor someday."

Ha, thought Lenna. "I'll leave that job to those more politically inclined. Thane, take Jaice's horse and go with Alanna toward Port Hollish. Jaice and I will hold off our pursuer."

Thane obligingly dismounted, looking at Lenna with genuine fear in his marbly eyes. "Are you sure you know what you're doing? This woman that's following me… she's unique."

Lenna, having somehow found her courage or at least compensated for the lack thereof with sufficient recklessness, put her right hand on Thane's shoulder and squeezed it, the roles of father and daughter oddly reversed. "I have a good idea of what you're running from." She inched closer, her lips close to Thane's ear. He smelled of apples and sweat and horse. She whispered, "Whatever you have taken from the Empire, despite my thoughts regarding the Brotherhood, was probably worth relieving them of."

It took a moment, but Thane finally nodded and trailed back to Jaice's horse. The warrior, eyeing Thane with aversion, vocalized with emphasis as he slipped one foot through the stirrup that the young initiate was not to let any harm come to her horse, or the wrath of Granemere Settlement would be on his head. Alanna, all the while, dressed down Lenna from her mount with her disarming stare.

"And what am I to do?" she asked. "By Jaice's own admission, I'm the stronger battlemage. And I'm still uncertain about the nature of your magic…"

"It's precisely because of your strength that I want you to

accompany Apprentice Faircloth, Alanna," Lenna replied. "Make sure no harm comes to him; he's under Freewoman protection."

The entity was advancing at speed, and Lenna's ears, though far from having perfect hearing or the training the others would have, distinguished the sound of galloping hooves over the ambient environment noise. She felt the dread register on her face and something, some grousing voice of intuition in her mind, told her things were not about to end peacefully. Whether she survived what was to occur here, in the past, was irrelevant: if Lenna Faircloth as a person ever wanted to exist at all, if she wanted her consciousness as it was now to be part of the wills in the realm beyond, she needed to guarantee her parents' survival.

"All right," Alanna complied. Her complacence was welcome, though her voice carried an undercurrent of the mildly displeased. "Off we go then… Thane."

Thane had, under the thorough surveillance of Jaice, finally settled astride the docile horse and, though still suffering from a case of the jitters and visibly fatigued, appeared to be at ease in the saddle. "Thank you, Freewoman…?" his voice trailed off, no doubt searching for her surname.

"Just Lenna is fine, thank you," Lenna replied hurriedly. After a moment's thought, she addressed Alanna again. "Freewoman Ameary, take this. No matter what you say, extra protection is never a bad idea." Lenna squatted down, unbuckling the straps that bound the knife strapped at her thigh. Standing up and refusing to acknowledge the paradox she was creating, Lenna casually tossed her future mother's knife to Alanna. "May this be a shield to protect rather than oppress."

Alanna deftly snatched the knife from the air and slid it from its sheath. "This is a beautiful piece of craftsmanship, Lenna; I've never seen its like. Where did you get it?"

Lenna smiled. "Someone very important wanted me to have it, in case I ever needed to protect myself or someone I loved. Magic might not always be enough. Take it, please."

Despite previous assertions that Alanna Ameary needed no weapon but magecraft, she strapped the knife to her side with the quick fingers that Lenna remembered from her childhood. "I'll see it's returned to you once this is sorted out," she said.

Nodding, Lenna exhaled and turned to Jaice. "Will you stand with me? Sword and staff?"

"Of course."

"Good, because we don't have much time." Lenna smacked the flank of Jaice's horse, startling Thane and steed alike into a spritely gallop. He quickly pulled on the reins and, in clouds of dust and pebbles, veered his way south toward Port Hollish. Without a word, Alanna kicked her horse forward and followed him in speedy pursuit. Jaice and Lenna were alone, and Lenna took out the long, curved blade she had won in battle one month ago — and several decades in the future.

"Do you know who is coming, Lenna?" Jaice asked.

"Mmm," she said.

The taint in the ether was quickly upon them, like a rising scent of garbage and refuse from a city slum. A rider came into view along the road, galloping effortlessly, as though the horse hadn't suffered the same long ride Thane's miserable creature had endured. The beast was jet black, and on its back sat a woman dressed in the crisp white uniform of a soldier of the Krevlum Empire, her long silvery hair cascading behind her. It struck the light of the summer sun and dazzled wildly as the rider brought her mount to a halt before Lenna and Jaice.

"Freewomen of Laur," said a voice, so cut and precise in clarity that it sounded as if it might slice Lenna's ear off. "I am pursuing a thief from the Blue Crescent Brotherhood on behalf of the Krevlum Empire. It is no secret that he is fleeing to Port Hollish. I am going to presume he came this way." The woman was young, in her early twenties, and her face glowed with a shining constitution. She carried herself with the righteousness of a thoroughly trained soldier, and strapped to her belt was what appeared to be a standard-issue longsword from the Empire.

Jaice quirked her head in Lenna's direction. Lenna was thankful for the deferral. "He did pass this way, but I don't believe we're going to allow you to pursue him."

"The Krevlum Empire does not have any quarrel with the Freewomen of Laur, and this is a matter between the Empire and the Brotherhood. I would suggest you not interfere.

Lenna's immediate reply was to let the sunlight enhance the luster of her long, curved blade. "The Brotherhood apprentice has been placed under Freewoman protection. Though," Lenna added, "I doubt this will ever be made known, because I don't believe you're acting under official Imperial orders."

The stiff woman slid from the saddle and drew her own blade, lackluster compared to the gorgeous smithery of Lenna's own, and took a step forward. "You presume much, Freewoman. I'm afraid I must continue my mission, however."

Jaice slid her grip along her heavy staff, feet finding firm root in the dusty path of the road. "You'll find continuing difficult with us in the way."

The woman shook out her silvery hair and pinched a smile. "Very well. You're right: this task — and your subsequent dispatching — will be off the official records as far as the Empire is concerned."

"Whom do you really serve?" Jaice asked.

"My lord, the Baron Alderic Sonnet, one of the foremost scholars, mages, and archaeologists of the Krevlum Empire. And I am Captain…"

"Khareen Valant," Lenna stated.

Both Jaice and Valant stared at Lenna with heated accusations in their eyes. How did Lenna know this woman's name? Suspicion was so palpable Lenna thought she could taste it in the air, and to her it had the flavor of a stinky cheese that would need a particularly strong red wine to stand up to it. It was highly intoxicating for Lenna to allow herself the privilege of being the person with secret knowledge. She even ventured a cheeky sneer at the Krevlum officer.

"How do you know who I am?" asked Valant.

"Oh, worry not, *Captain*," Lenna said, "your reputation precedes you." She tightened her curled fingers around the hilt of the blade in her hand and was instantly reassured by an encouraging hum from the Godjewel in her left palm.

CHAPTER SEVENTEEN

The summer Fallowfields air was heavy with the putrescence of Khareen Valant's magic. The young woman, near Lenna's age, was collected and calm in appearance, but there was something beneath the pearly jacket, beneath the surface of her skin, that sullied the atmosphere like cog oil spreading across a mechanist's apron. This young version of Valant lacked control; her body was nothing more than a stopgap holding back the corruption within, a power that threatened to shred its shell and smother all around it.

"It seems we have a predicament on our hands," said Valant. "I always follow orders, and you appear unwavering in your desire to prevent me from completing my mission." With a satisfying metallic slickness, Valant's blade danced about her hand before Lenna had the opportunity to utter a response. She swung it about in a circular motion, her wrist rotating it swiftly and making it appear as if the sword itself were itching to fight.

Lenna assumed a two-handed grip on her silvery weapon, the length of the light blade and her own nerves leaving her too shaky to wield it confidently with only one hand. *This is madness*, she thought. Freewoman by birth or not, Lenna had barely had enough experience with a knife, let alone a longsword; Valant would have years of proper military training behind her. Eyes wide, Lenna gaped as Valant uncoiled and swept her sword in a swift overhead strike in line with the crown of Lenna's head. Time slowed as Lenna fleetingly cursed her reckless gallantry.

One solid shove from Jaice and Lenna tumbled to the ground, her maladroit grasp faltering and launching the blade off along the dirt path. Its landfall scattered some of the roosting gulls and with the heavy thwack of elm, Jaice Northen's staff was there, blocking the strike Captain Valant had directed at Lenna. Both women, weapons locked, peered down at the fallen Freewoman with similarly shocked expressions.

"Lenna, your sword!" barked Jaice.

"It appears the Freewoman's weapon was more for show than war." Valant leaped back and fixed her gaze solely on Jaice. "I'll have to worry about you first." She flicked her free hand in Lenna's general direction, and the air around her grew misty, forming thick coils of force that weighed down on her. It felt as if gravity had been increased severalfold, and the taint of Valant's magic made Lenna sick to her stomach.

Swearing, Jaice swung her staff toward Valant, who danced backward once more, out of the weapon's reach. The sunlight reflecting in the deep tunnels of her eyes set them ablaze and though Lenna strained to tear herself away, she found herself captivated by the raw power emanating from them. Even Jaice appeared uneasy near the Krevlum officer.

"What are you?" she asked, easing her choke on the staff as a bar against further assault. "Your magic is corrupted. You shouldn't... be."

Valant flashed a winning grin. "My training is beyond what you pathetic Freewomen learn. I have borne witness to the very threshold of magic; I have ridden along the borders of what lies beneath."

"You're insane," Jaice said succinctly.

If she could have nodded or hurrah with agreement, Lenna would have, but whatever rank enchantment Valant had placed over her was stifling her motor functions. "The borders of what lies beneath," Lenna realized, must refer to the subconscious realm she visited more often than she cared to, where all matter and magic were one. Lenna, too, had once strayed too far, gone too close to the source, and she had almost lost herself in darkness. If Valant had been forcefully pushed to the brink, it could easily explain such derangement.

Little grey tufts of fog began circling Valant's free hand and, one by one, the clouds began to crackle with ripe lightning. "I have access to magic far greater than yours, Freewoman." Lenna sensed no gathering of power from Jaice; why wasn't she even bothering to shield herself?

The captain took a step forward, but Jaice held her ground and replied with the decisive, brusque tone that would make her an effectual mayor in the years to come. "That doesn't matter. You're sick. And you know what? Whatever Imperial dog made you his bitch is a hell of a lot sicker."

Valant snarled, her angular, tight features turned beastly in disgust. Losing her control for that moment, she inadvertently released the mass of fog surrounding her hand and it burned out into the atmosphere in a quick whoosh and gout of flame. Once more she shifted to carnal, physical attacks, her wrath driving angry strikes at Jaice, who blocked blow after blow without giving ground. Valant was incensed, almost rabid, and she switched back to the husky language of the Krevlum Empire, barking coarse, cutoff sentences. The only word Lenna picked out was "Sonnet."

Lenna blinked with a sudden realization that her extremities didn't feel as cumbersome as they had a moment ago, and her breathing came with less of an effort. Jaice hadn't needed a shield because she played a card much more cunning: she manipulated the captain into losing her cool. This wasn't Valant twenty-some-odd years in the future with decades of experience at her command; whatever Sonnet had done to her, it was recent, and her self-control was imperfect. A trigger word — and in this instance, apparently Emperor, or rather Baron, Sonnet sufficed — was all that was needed to shatter Valant's loose grasp on her sanity. The phantom shackles binding Lenna were gone. This was her chance.

"Do it, Lenna," she whispered to herself. "Choose to live again." With Jaice keeping the raging Valant distracted, Lenna focused on calming her frayed nerves before dipping her consciousness into her pool of magic, careful to avoid the alluring call of the Godjewel. Recalling her improvised working against Sebastien, she coiled power around an etheric loom fashioned from her will and, net woven, threw the mystical bundle like an arcane bola.

And Valant faltered. Lenna's shaping was crude and lacked the backing her Godjewel could afford, but it was enough: blinded by her own fury, the captain tripped over Lenna's blunt magic and, from the momentum behind her furious assault against Jaice, Valant stumbled forward. Jaice slid her hands about her staff with the familiarity of a lover and batted the Krevlum sword from Valant's hand. The blade shot into the distance and disappeared into a patch of heather.

"To think," Valant said with labored breath, "I let the rage come back so quickly…"

Jaice leveled her staff at the disarmed captain's jugular. "Though it was your intention to kill us, we Freewomen do not kill when we can take prisoners. Surrender."

As the two women stared each other down, Lenna scrambled to collect her dropped sword, which had mercifully landed only a few yards away. She assumed a position a few paces from Jaice and Valant. What option would Captain Khareen Valant choose? And how would it impact Lenna's original timeline? If Lenna's past — future — experiences with Valant were anything to go by, she didn't believe the Krevlum soldier would consider turning herself over to Freewoman authorities a viable option.

"Surrender? And you think *me* insane? You know the sword is not my only weapon. No, surrender I will not. You fooled me once, but not again."

The stench of rot filled the air, and Lenna gagged. She could feel an iron-solid shield spring to life around Valant, and this time Jaice was quick to follow suit in erecting her own. Lenna, though the pattern was crude in comparison, managed to bring up a ward as well, hoping against hope it would be strong enough without the Godjewel. The gem vibrated so strongly against her fist that her hand began to spasm; it was as if the Godjewel was reminding Lenna of its presence, telling her to pay attention to it.

The extra power was tempting, but the ramifications of using it could be disastrous; Lenna didn't know the location of the stone in this time period, and the possibility of using it while an identical version of it was somewhere out in the Continent seemed far too risky. What if the two reacted together somehow? If Valant insisted on a magical battle, Lenna grimly acknowledged as she dug her feet into the ground, it would be one fought with Lenna's magic alone.

Valant coursed with power and on that magic seemingly floated on the tips of her toes. The air around her rippled like a pond in a rainstorm, and Jaice and Lenna fell back when the captain's ichorous aura slimed its way along the edges of their shielding. Any sign of Valant's fury had vanished: her next move would be calculated but direct, and now all they had to do was wait for her to strike.

"Since you are so determined to protect the Brotherhood and its stolen magics, I have no choice but to destroy you," Valant delivered in one line, smooth as her hair. "And then..." Her eyes flitted to Lenna's sword. "Once you are dead, I will have a new toy to play with."

Lenna looked down at the sword in her hands and recalled how Valant had asserted she had acquired the blade. Before she died in Lenna's future, the general recounted that she took the intricately wrought piece from a Freewoman — at the cost of the Freewoman's life and Valant's own ear. Was this the moment when Valant claimed her treasure? Had Lenna somehow orchestrated her own death? She swallowed, hard, wishing for Pim, Sebastien, Gilbert... someone to provide her with the strength and courage to keep up her barrier against the Krevlum captain's ozone-laden blows that sullied the fresh sea breeze.

Valant's magic was resilient and pungent, and with each successive strike Lenna bit her lip in frustration, her mind furiously trying to hold together the shape of her unraveling wards. She resisted the ever-growing urge to siphon some of the

Godjewel's power as a bulwark against the attack, despite its sweet invitations. Jaice had crept closer to Lenna, and the two women let their individual workings buffer each other's.

"She could not have summoned that sending and still have much power left in her," Jaice panted. Beads of sweat were carving canyons in the dirt on her brow.

"You don't know Khareen Valant very well," Lenna muttered. She knew her response was abrupt, but it was imperative that she devote all her concentration to maintaining the mental image of her shielding lest Valant find any gap in her armor.

Odd distortions in the air bubbled about Valant's person, as though the magic she flung at the Freewomen was being leached from the environment around her, not from within. Lenna squinted and in a burst of clarity fathomed the meaning behind Valant's words: the vast amount of energy the officer was channeling must be coming from her link to what she had described as "what lies beneath." That would explain the distortions; Valant was, in effect, pulling magic from the very air and grass around her. Done well, it could probably give a trained mage power levels similar to an inadequate user of a Godjewel…

"Jaice," Lenna breathed, "Valant is using more than just her own magic."

Grunting, Jaice cushioned Lenna's own diminishing power with a fresh surge of vigor. "What do you mean?"

"No time to explain." *No time to think, either; I have to act.* Lenna had to somehow quickly sever the mysterious link between the environment and the captain and then dispatch Valant before she could reestablish a connection. But how? Should Lenna herself venture into the psychic realm and engage her target there? Without the power of the Godjewel behind her, Lenna's strength alone might not suffice, but it was the only option that sprang to mind. "More power to your shield." Lenna slid closer to Jaice, letting the bulk of the beating fall upon the Freewoman's defenses. It was a gamble, but at least it was a creative one.

Lenna let go of her wards and felt the insubstantial screen melt away into the atmosphere. The pattern of Jaice's shield would mask the lack of Lenna's for a few precious moments, giving Lenna only one chance to get things right. She took slow, measured breaths, grasping for calm amid the furious chaos bombarding their barrier. With a feather-light touch, Lenna used her magic like a rope, tugging her consciousness down, turning herself inward. The transition was more sluggish than before; thanks to the Godjewel, Lenna was used to being loaded with bucketfuls of magic, not just her own strength, to anchor herself in the realm of the arcane.

Instantly her perception of time slowed. Lenna was still vaguely aware of the clean skies of Fallowfields, the ground at her feet, and the pounding of strikes like thunderbolts falling upon Jaice's shielding, but those things felt so distant, miles away. She had become accustomed to the peculiar sense of detachment by now, the disconnection of her mind from her physical self.

In the depths of this unconscious realm, Lenna existed by force of will alone, a point of light among myriad others spiraling across an endless expanse of deep, bluish black. Keeping her consciousness from unraveling would require more magic and focus than Lenna could keep up for long without aid, so her actions would have to be decisive, no second-guessing. Nearby she could perceive an oscillating stream of magic swirling around a burning torch that represented Jaice and her subconscious connection to the ether.

More conspicuous, though, was a blotting whorl of darkness pervading Lenna's psychic senses. It was siphoning multiple currents of pure energy from all directions, even from other points of light in the great spiral, and beaming it toward the shadow that was a manifestation of Valant's psyche. Lenna's mind's eye visualized a faint chain connecting these two blots of darkness, as if it were a hose pumping power from a node directly to Valant's psychic self. Somehow, Lenna realized with revulsion, the captain had gained access to magic beyond that of her own; she was a psychic leech, bleeding dry the stars themselves.

Lenna imagined the slight curve of her glimmering Freewoman blade, and a glowing representation of it appeared in the right hand of what she had become. In this lawless dimension beneath the mind, she had conjured an astral projection, a picture as she saw herself; she drifted, naked, in a great pool of stars, long hair curling into the darkness and girded with an ethereal sword. The sensation was overwhelming – Lenna had drawn on creation itself and harnessed it into a weapon of light, hers alone to wield. *I do not need the Godjewel,* Lenna's mental voice trumpeted.

Strike, a voice called out across the chasm. From where or when it came Lenna couldn't ascertain, but it felt ancient, weary with constant fatigue, and it strained against some great distance.

Who's there? Where have I felt you before? The presence was both familiar and alien, at once daunting and comforting Lenna. In her uncertainty, her resolve wavered.

Strike! The quick command felt like a rush of wind against her back, similar to when Sebastien used his magic to propel Lenna and himself across the gullies of Gallas, and her emanation was thrown forward. Lenna rode the momentum like a ship might the crest of a wave, her sword becoming a lance of psychic energy. There was no time for hesitation; the voice, whomever it belonged to, pressed Lenna straight toward the link that connected Valant and the great star-fueled darkness. Her spirit blade struck the chain between Valant and her arcane conduit at its direct center, and a satisfying roar of cosmic wind jarred Lenna back to the physical realm.

Sweat blanketed Lenna's face as though she had just run twelve laps around Port Hollish's market in the midsummer heat. Valant lurched back, her face one of unadulterated anger; the strange ripples in the air around her had dispersed and, with them, the fury of blows against Jaice's shielding had ebbed. Lenna shook a little on her knees — that trip had expended far too much of her natural magic — but soon found support in Jaice's sturdy frame.

"I have no idea what you just did, Lenna," panted Jaice, "but it worked."

Valant bared her teeth and, with eyes wide, leaped toward Jaice and Lenna despite being unarmed. Uttering one final cry of desperation, Valant swept her arm through the air in one swift raking from her dwindling magical reserves. The ferocity behind it took Jaice by surprise, and as Lenna had severed Valant's link, so did Valant's last torrent of energy shred the shielding Jaice had been so steadfastly maintaining.

The silver-haired woman collided with Lenna as Jaice, who had been supporting Lenna, slipped and fell backward, twisting on her ankle and rolling down the hillock and into the road. Buckling under Valant's sudden weight, Lenna found herself knocked prone, all air rushing out of her lungs. Both women grappled with the curved sword that lay flat between their bodies. Lenna attempted to roll, but Valant's weight grounded her; with a crazed light haunting her eyes, Valant one by one began to pry Lenna's fingers from the hilt as Lenna squirmed, helpless.

"Jaice!" she called, and jerked her head to look back over the crest, but Valant was quick to yank Lenna's body back.

"The Freewoman's head seems to have made an untimely acquaintance with a rock," Valant growled in Lenna's ear.

Lenna stared upward into the mad eyes of Khareen Valant, the woman who had been taken to the edge of chaos and had brought it back with her. The Godjewel began to leak sharp spikes of light between Lenna's clamped fingers. *Not now,* Lenna pleaded, but the Godjewel seemed unwilling to heed her command. Lenna could feel it responding to her own growing panic: if Jaice had been rendered unconscious, Lenna could never best Valant in a physical confrontation.

"What is that light?" Valant asked, unable to shroud the eagerness in her voice.

"Not... now." Lenna tugged twice — once mentally, once physically — on stone and sword, urging them both to fall back into her control. The light from the Godjewel painted Valant's leering face with an unholy glow, her cheeks gaunt and wraithlike. Her eyes drank up the stone's brilliance and Lenna, paralyzed with revulsion, let the despair consume her and all control slip.

The Godjewel sang an unnatural chorus of strange syllables

and Lenna and Valant cried out in unison as a cataract of unwanted memories assailed them both.

"This isn't part of the training," said Khareen. Her blonde hair was pulled back, taut, and her uniform freshly pressed. To be summoned before nobility at her age was an event so out of the ordinary that she surprised herself by speaking out of turn.

The tight smile of the clean-cut man dressed in a white suit was neither happy nor approving; it was cursory. He pushed up the gold frames of his spectacles with one finger, showing off several rings encrusted with precious gemstones that caught the gaslights of the spacious commander's hall.

"Just open your mind to me, and I will guide you downward," the man said.

"Yes, my lord," said Khareen, careful not to let any hint of wariness creep into her voice. She noticed that Baron Sonnet had extended his hand; was it within protocol for her to take it? This situation was so remarkable the young officer wasn't aware if such protocol even existed. She put her cold hand in his smaller one.

Baron Sonnet smiled again and looked off to the side. Khareen let her eyes follow his. Leaning against a marble pilaster was an older woman with thinning, straw-colored hair and hollow cheekbones, clutching a thick, leather-bound tome in her arms. Her eyes were shockingly clear, and when they locked onto Khareen's for a moment their deep blue seemed to pull her into a spiraling tunnel of light. Khareen feared where those eyes would take her; she tore her gaze away, looking down at her feet.

With one hand, Baron Sonnet gently cupped Khareen's cheek and drew her face back toward his. "Do not be frightened, Sergeant Valant. Just follow me."

Summer in the garden was a happy time for Lenna. She liked the way the reedy bunches of lavender waved in the breeze, attracting honeybees. Mama kept the flowers pretty in the garden, and Lenna was content when she was allowed to just poke about the plants and kick at the grass. Lenna didn't like training, though. Mama was very particular about that. She always became so strict.

Lenna sat in a corner of the yard watching a bee bounce from blossom to blossom, enjoying the break from Freewoman lessons. Mama had hurried down the back path. Someone had come calling and Mama would be out front for a few minutes. They didn't often get callers during the day, and Lenna, curious, wondered just who it could be. She tiptoed over, her curly locks getting caught and tangled around her spectacles. Mama would insist she cut it soon, but Lenna hated haircuts almost as much as training.

Mama was at the end of the path, talking to a woman Lenna had never seen before. Lenna couldn't make out much of her other than that she seemed very excited. Mama stood with her back to Lenna, back straight and hands resting on her hips, standing like she did whenever she caught Lenna not paying attention to her lessons.

Lenna wondered what they were talking about. The only other lady Mama talked to was Mistress Meeks, and that wasn't her. The hair was different and she didn't look as grown-up. Mama sounded angry, though. Lenna wasn't very good at sneaking; being quiet in the grass was something Mama constantly tried to teach her, so Lenna wasn't too surprised when she stepped on a stick and Mama turned back around, glaring.

"Whoops," Lenna giggled.

"Lenna," Mama called, "go back and play."

Once Mama's head had turned in her direction, Lenna saw the stranger's glassy eyes flash bright blue in the sunlight. She didn't like it.

"Lenna, at once."

She nodded and went back and sat in the grass. The sun had gone behind a cloud and Lenna shivered.

The marble floor was cold, so very cold, against Khareen's clammy skin. She came to, curled up with her knees to her chest. Her teeth chattered, and it felt as though her soul itself was shivering from exposure to the frosty expanse of what lay below. There had been so many minds, so many stars in the dark expanse, that Khareen worried she might get lost. It was not the first time Baron Sonnet had shown her this place. She hated it.

A warm, moist cloth pressed against her cheek. Kneeling next to her, Sonnet cooed, "It's getting easier every time, isn't it?"

"No," said Khareen. "Sir." She looked up at him, her eyes wide with a paralyzing fear and an unspoken plea never to return to that place again. The place where Sonnet's mind invaded hers so thoroughly.

"You can move her faster, Sonnet," said a female voice off to the side.

Alderic Sonnet smiled at Khareen, that same, emotionless smile. He stood up and tugged down on the jacket of his suit before heading off into the shadows and engaging the voice in low tones that Khareen couldn't make out. She wasn't sure she cared to; for now, she shut her eyes, hoping to find reprieve, only to see the stars again and scream.

"You look like a big red apple," Lenna pronounced. "Can't you eat your strawberries more neatly?"

Gilbert grinned, a gap-filled smile that was missing a few teeth. His lips, cheeks, and fingers were covered in the syrupy remnants of the basket of strawberries the two had gobbled up under the tree in their secret hideout. "Sorry," he said, and stuck out his tongue. He threw a clod of dirt at Lenna, who scrambled away around the side of the tree, her braids — already loose — following her like cat tails.

"Hey!" she said.

"Lenna," said Gil in a hushed voice. "Look! There's some weird lady up there."

Lenna's eyes leaped to where Gil's chubby finger was pointing, to the top corner of the walled courtyard that had fallen into disarray on the outskirts of Hollish Commons. The sun was behind the woman, cloaking her in shadow, and Lenna squinted to see her better. She looked very peculiar; her hair was chopped short and she was wearing trousers. No lady around here wore trousers. Maybe she was from Ilya?

The woman reminded Lenna of something in the way she stood, sort of like how Mama used to stand poised, ready for action. But this felt weird, wrong, and Lenna didn't want to think about her mother right now. She shrank back from the tree, and Gilbert, in his short trousers and untucked, seed-flecked shirt, stood protectively in front of her.

"Hey, lady!" he called up. "This is *our* hideout!"

"I know," said the woman and hopped back, out of sight.

Gilbert turned to Lenna. "It's all right, Len," he said. "She's gone. Did you see how creepy her eyes were? What a weirdo!"

Lenna shook her head, braids irritatingly flopping back and forth. "Let's go home."

"Can I come to your place for dinner?" Gilbert asked. There was a pleading look in his eyes.

Papa would be cooking tonight, or rather, attempting to cook, so it was a good thing Gilbert had had a fair share of strawberries. His remaining appetite probably would be wasted on her father's cooking, but lately Gil seemed to want to spend more and more time at her house.

"Of course," Lenna said.

"Wahoo!" Gilbert grabbed her hand and pulled her from the courtyard.

Blinded by blue light, Lenna tried to rip her mind away from Valant's. They rolled about on the grassy mound, swearing at their magical entanglement. Sword and gem were both locked in battle and memories from both women tore at their minds.

"Get out of my head," Lenna spat.

"Release your grip!"

"No," hissed Lenna, and the Godjewel flared again.

Dark, oily flames consumed the wood around her, and smoke billowed listlessly into the dusky air. The screams had long since been silenced, and this outlying Krevlum village would be, by dawn, nothing but ashes. A bulky machine rumbled by her side, a shoddy contraption of wires, metal, and magic. Against it leaned the honorable Baron Sonnet, regarding the scene with the calm of someone watching a game of polite sport. Tucked under his arm was a leather tome.

"Between this new technology," he said, voice barely discernible over the splintering of wood, "and your magic, Captain Valant, we have single-handedly obliterated this rebellious village."

"Yes, my lord," Valant responded. She was proud of pleasing Baron Sonnet, and she closed her eyes, not fearing the stars she saw but embracing the power they gave her.

"Are you not bothered by this destruction?" he asked.

"Of course not, my lord."

"This was the village of your birth."

"My parents are already long dead, and my sister abandoned our nation for some worthless Fallowfieldian." Valant paused. "I am contented to serve you and your cause."

"That is delightful news indeed, Captain." Sonnet approached and put one manicured hand on her shoulder. She shivered.

"I am glad to have proven myself," Valant said. Off in the distance, shrouded in smoke, the mysterious woman with the glowing eyes and wispy hair stood, looking like a creature of fire.

Sonnet must have sensed her dismay. "Worry not, my vassal. Now that you've come this far, I don't believe she will be required any longer."

Valant nodded, and the figure shrank into the gathering smoke.

Papa nudged Lenna closer, up to her mother's bedside. The room smelled sick; it stank of tonics, of sweat, of vases full of water and dead flowers. It repulsed Lenna and she had avoided the room as much as she could; avoided the truth as much as she could. She tiptoed across the creaky wooden floorboards, beginning to sweat at the roaring fire her father kept blazing in the hearth. Her mother insisted the room was freezing.

The bedroom was rosy from the glow of the fire, but even the warm light couldn't bring color to Mama's face. Lenna thought of the lessons she had ignored, and how they stopped altogether once Mama couldn't walk anymore. For the past six weeks, Lenna's mother had done nothing but writhe in bed, shifting between moments of lucidity, eerie silences, and fits of quick-tongued gibberish. *She is present today,* her father had said.

Lenna gulped as she broached the woman. Where her mother was once bursting with youth like the overgrown lavender in the garden, now she was the withered, grey remains at the end of summer. Her cheeks sagged and her once warm, honeyed hair was ashy and white. The skin had retreated and slackened around her eyes, giving Lenna's mother a look of constant surprise.

"Lenna," Mama said. Those two syllables alone seemed an effort. "You came."

"How are you feeling, Mama?" asked Lenna. Her mother was bundled in blankets and duvets up to her neck, so Lenna had no hand to hold or arm to squeeze.

Her mother made no attempt to smile; instead, she tried to maintain the same calm, if a bit stern, expression that Lenna had come to learn was a hallmark of her mother's people, the Freewomen of Laur. Lenna wondered if her mother would rather be back there, in some forest somewhere, instead of trapped in her bedroom. Maybe a touch of nature would do her good; after all, Mama always seemed to glow after she finished her training exercises in their garden.

"I want you to have something, Lenna," her mother said.

Lenna's father coughed loudly, a noise of interruption, and Lenna wondered if he was angry. He stormed up next to Lenna and loomed over her bedridden mother. "No, Alanna. She cannot have that. We agreed. And if that woman comes around again, I'll..."

Rolling her eyes, a habit Lenna had picked up and been scolded for at school, Mama's voice took on the same tone she used when Lenna stuffed up a Freewoman exercise. "Not *that,* dear." She wheezed for a moment, her entire blanketed form rocking from the fit. It took her some seconds to regain her breath.

"Lenna, are you sure you won't take my knife?" she asked feebly.

Now it was Lenna's turn to be exasperated. She didn't want a *knife,* she didn't want to be a Freewoman, she wanted her mother to just *be well* again. "I don't need it, Mama. It's not like I'll ever become a Freewoman."

"Lenna," said her father, "you should respect your mother's wishes."

"No, Thane," Mama said. "It's fine." Her voice had become the faintest of whispers, and in the glowing firelight Lenna noticed a single tear slide down her cheek. Had she said the wrong thing? She didn't mean to make her mother cry…

"Lenna, wait outside." Seldom did her father give an order, so Lenna, awestruck, did as commanded without question.

"Thane…" she heard her mother begin.

Lenna peeked around the doorframe to see her father untuck the blankets and pry a curious, shiny object from her mother's clasped hand. The light struck it and the bauble flashed blue, a deeper, prettier blue than Lenna had ever seen.

"No!" Lenna cried. "I don't want to remember that; I *can't* remember that!" Her mind began to rampage and spin, and she could feel her consciousness sinking into incredible darkness.

"What is that delightfully painful memory? Is that where you got this power, this stone?" As Valant's loaded words sank into Lenna's ears, shame and grief reverberated in the infinite crystalline reaches of the Godjewel, showering both women in sparks and brilliant luminosity. "You are no Freewoman! You are filled with lies, with deceit; you rejected your own mother's dying wishes and then stole her power!"

"No!" It was the only word Lenna could produce, the only sound that escaped her throat other than screams as Valant clawed at her hands, trying to pry away the Godjewel and the sword. Their psychic bond was broken, thankfully, but the Godjewel had awoken and its fury — Lenna's fury — rose up from its core faster than any airship could take to the skies. Lenna let it, because any place but this place and any time but this time, where her memories were being exposed, would be better.

Blue-white lightning began to arc between the two flailing bodies as Valant's magic returned and she unleashed concentrated bursts of power to shake Lenna's grasp without concern about any damage to her own body. Blisters and burns began to spread along the arms of both of them, each little jolt like the tiny prick of a knife. The knife Lenna refused as her mother died. Died holding the Godjewel.

The Godjewel. Its power was released, exposed into this world. She didn't have Luc behind her, but now was her chance. The past be damned. Lenna shut her eyes against the world, the searing pain, and sent her thoughts into the very core of the gem, where a ferocious tornado of energy bellowed. *Please,* she pleaded. *I want to forget.*

Push, came back that strange voice.

Push?

Push away. Flee.

The burns on her arms were tortuous and Lenna was uncertain whose screams were louder: her screams of agony or Valant's howls of rage. Lenna invested her being, believing the words echoing from the center of the Godjewel, and released her grip on her sword, raising her nails to fiercely claw at Valant's face. She tore into the woman's flesh with her fingers, pushed her away. Trails of blood lined Valant's cheeks as Lenna's hands latched onto the sides of her head. Valant drew on more magic, showering them in sparks, and the drive to disappear in Lenna was so fierce she barely registered Valant reaching for the hilt of the abandoned sword. *Away.*

A cooling sensation, like a shower of forgetfulness, dulled Lenna's senses and her incensed mind. She could feel those terrible memories slip aside into some deep recess of her mind and, buffered by the power of her Godjewel, Lenna heaved all of her weight — physical, mental, magical — away from the woman tussling with her. Whether Captain Valant was atop Lenna or below, it did not matter. A searing bolt of energy erupted into the sky, piercing Lenna, her darkest recollections, and the wails of pain of her tormentor.

CHAPTER EIGHTEEN

Lenna crashed mightily into faded pink wallpaper, the kind of textile that would have been in fashion among the affluent crowds of any major city or estate when she was a child. Cheek pressed against the pattern, she instantly recognized it: she was back in the magical gymnasium Sebastien had fashioned from his late mother's sitting room. Considering her normal means of entrance after any form of magical transport, this sudden appearance – spinning on a crooked axis into a wall – was downright graceful. Lenna was, after all, still standing.

From all around her came shouts of surprise in multiple tones. Lenna's vision was spotted with angry disks, remnants of the burning blue Godjewel magic that had sundered the summer sky and brought her, apparently, back through time. Arms wrapped around her waist from behind and swept the befuddled woman up into the air, and despite Lenna's predisposition to loathe such random displays of sentiment, the clean linen scent of Raif instantly calmed her shaken nerves, and the last traces of azure light from the Godjewel trickled away, leaving nothing but a gentle droning behind.

"I thought we'd lost you," Raif stuttered. He primly placed Lenna on the floor as she struggled to regain her wits.

Casting her eyes from side to side, Lenna took a quick survey of her situation. Several people gawked openly at Lenna, their individual expressions demonstrating wide-eyed shock and relaxed relief, with perhaps a dash of annoyance thrown in for good measure. Sebastien stood by the open door that led to his study, biting one lip, while Luc leaned into the corner, his short-cropped hair and clothing both unrumpled, but his face boasting a blackened eye. Lenna nearly gasped when she witnessed Lazarz cheekily wave in her direction, and standing beside him stood Gallas's own queen of good conduct, the commanding Mistress Juniam.

"What the hell is everyone doing in here?" Lenna asked.

Mistress Juniam clucked at language obviously inappropriate for a young woman and asked, "Lenna Faircloth, what happened to your hand?" Her voice was as unyielding as her posture.

All eyes fell to Lenna's right hand, currently clutched in a tight fist, red with congealed blood and dripping unsavory juices onto the floor of Seb's training room. Curiously separated from reality, Lenna unballed her fist and revealed the severed, pristine ear of a young Khareen Valant. *What the Krevlum warrior had lost to gain a Freewoman blade.* An urge to vomit welling up in her belly, Lenna quickly dropped her unwanted trophy of war. Mistress Juniam swept in grandly and produced a handkerchief worth far more than any general's — or rather, captain's — ear, with which she scooped up the organ and removed it from sight.

"Lenna!" exclaimed Raif.

"Lenna?" asked Sebastien, sprinting from his position at the door toward the bloodied mage. Off to the side, Lenna could hear Lazarz whispering in a voice far too loudly, "I bet we're in for an earful!"

Lenna hadn't yet bothered to fully assess her current situation. After the conflict with Valant in the past, during which Lenna had released the power of the Godjewel in one tremendous magical eruption, she had been flung forward in time again in a jolt of searing pain. She hadn't noticed any aftereffects from the transit itself, but now, glancing down with some alarm at her arms, Lenna realized her sleeves had disintegrated and harsh, crimson welts were beginning to surface along her burnt limbs.

"Ouch," she said needlessly. Lenna buckled under her own weight and fatigue, and mercifully Raif was still there to scoop her up before she collapsed into a useless heap of librarian on the floor. All of the exhaustion Lenna had hoarded into various compartments of her body was in one mighty instance released. It was different from normal Lenna exhaustion, the kind she could just wish away with a daydream of a bath and a glass of wine. Her heart fluttered unevenly.

Sebastien hastened to a crouch as Raif cradled Lenna in his arms. "Lenna, where have you been?"

Lenna's voice came out weaker than she had intended; apparently all her authority had been expended a few decades ago. "The past. Not memories; not just witnessing. I was in the past." She scanned the members of this makeshift council, not sure how much she dared expose. "I was with my parents, when they first met, and Jaice, and…" Lenna let her voice trail off, her eyes unconsciously traveling to Mistress Juniam, who held her hands behind her back.

A cough from Raif made Lenna cry out in agony, and Seb's hand flew to her forehead, spreading a blanket of light, pure relief across her body. She felt like she was floating; the pain and exhaustion were still part of Lenna, but miles below her consciousness. As Sebastien removed his hand from her brow, Lenna's awareness grounded itself once more and she wondered why neither Raif nor Sebastien questioned the ear; they must have recognized it and derived its meaning.

"Lenna," said her mentor in a controlled pitch, "you've been gone for a week. You vanished; we thought you dead."

"A week?" Lenna was amazed her tongue could even shape the words.

"Six days, but who's counting?" Raif interjected with more force than necessary in Lenna's opinion. She squirmed as the muscles in his arms tensed protectively around her.

"Six days," she repeated. Her own voice was beginning to grate on Lenna's nerves, but she couldn't seem to quell its frailty.

"For you to attempt that kind of working without my

supervision…" Sebastien began, and Lenna sensed a raising of power between Raif and her tutor, the immediate atmosphere leaden with magic and aggression.

"That was not what we planned," Raif started.

"Quiet." Mistress Juniam's voice rang across the gymnasium, pure in its finality. Ignoring her elegant garments, the head of house knelt beside the trio and caressed Lenna's cheek with one hand. Her touch was not frigid or talon-like, as Lenna had feared, but delicate: the hand of a mother.

"Mistress Juniam?" asked Lenna.

Juniam drew herself up to her full height and lorded over both Raif and Sebastien. "You foolish boys," she stated. "This woman's magical reserves are nearly drained, and her arms are severely wounded. Are you going to let her slip into unconsciousness while you pacify your egos, or give her the aid she needs?"

Sebastien placed one hand behind his head, a childlike gesture Lenna doubted he used except when receiving a reprimand from Mistress Juniam. Raif, equally rebuked, relaxed his grip and slowly slid Lenna to the floor, which, although not quite a fluffy carpet or a feather bed, felt like her own personal portion of paradise. She sighed and let the stiffness of the floor prop up her aching muscles, trying to ignore the returning sting from the hot rakes along her arms.

Her pains quickly dulled as Sebastien and Raif worked in tandem, healing and soothing at the same time. The room became a web of peculiar angles and smudged lines, as though Lenna was witnessing events through an opium-fueled fugue. As the curative magics danced about her injuries like tiny swarms of fireflies, all Lenna clearly discerned was one pair of eyes, Luc's, trained on her and the gauntleted hand that stowed the Godjewel. *Does he still yearn for its power, after seeing this?* The lids of Lenna's eyes grew heavy as cool relief swam up her arms.

"Six days," she said quietly.

"Yes, damn you," swore Sebastien. "You came here for training to control this power, a power that can change the universe, and you…"

"Funny," Lenna musingly interrupted, "I seem to be able to change the universe without much training at all."

"Hush, Lenna," said Raif. "It's been a long six days."

A sudden rumble resonated through the manor's walls and a tremor visibly shook the pair of mages perched over Lenna. Worry lined their faces, and though Lenna's thoughts were muddled, they weren't muddled enough to prevent her from noticing that Raif and Sebastien were disturbed. It was no thunderstorm brewing outside: something was occurring, something that forced this mismatched group of characters to hide out in what was, Lenna's brain proposed, probably the most well-defended area of the Branford Estate.

"What's going on?" she asked.

"Six days with only one Godjewel here," said Sebastien. Had Lenna more energy, she would likely smack Seb for being so cryptic.

Frustration must have registered on her bruised face. Raif straightaway began to explain, words quick. "You vanished, physically. The presence of your Godjewel was gone, but there was... a sort of taint, a smell. Any magician worth his salt could tell that something unnatural happened, and that it..." Raif nodded down at Lenna's gauntlet before continuing. "That the Godjewel was gone. So the only gem left would be the one that our little prodigy has." The blonde man shot a decidedly unpleasant glance into the murky corner of the room.

"Only one Godjewel," repeated Lenna.

"Yes," Sebastien said. "Only one here and one out there. One untrained, one trained — and with a great amount of control and military force behind it."

Lenna pressed her eyes shut, bemoaning an impending headache for what was already a thoroughly throttled brain. "One out there? There's only one person besides Luc or me that has a Godjewel."

"That's right."

A moment or two passed and though her field of view — considering she was on the floor — was limited, Lenna felt everyone's gazes shy away from her. They didn't want to put into words the truth Lenna's foggy mind had pieced together. Lenna eventually said, "Emperor Sonnet — he's here?"

Another shock struck the manor, and Seb frowned, the gem in his ear swaying back and forth in the aftermath of the blast. "Yes. Alderic Sonnet perceived the magic from two Godjewels during your experiment, but only one Godjewel remained in the aftermath. He is here to claim it. And," he added, "until you arrived, he was getting perilously close to doing so."

Raif's long fingers worked their way into the crook between Lenna's neck and right shoulder, applying both magic and pressure, and instantly a numbing sensation slid down her arm and blocked all pain. Lenna realized with fascination that some of the welts had ruptured, closed back in on themselves, and begun to heal with only the faintest of white scarring. *Alderic Sonnet,* she thought, *here to claim Luc's — or Raif's — Godjewel. And now I'm back.*

"I don't want to fight," Lenna said.

Such a hush had descended that she could hear the plaintive disappointment in the drawn-out exhalations of everyone in the room. The group — Seb, Raif, Luc, Mistress Juniam, and the eclectic Lazarz — had been holed up in the Branford Estate for almost a week while Lenna had been manipulating the events surrounding her own creation. Whether she desired the Godjewel or not, it was bonded to her, and she owed it to these people to take responsibility for her part in these matters.

"I don't want to fight," she repeated, "but I will." Lenna groaned as she attempted to rise to a sitting position against the tidal wave of protests from Mistress Juniam, Seb, and Raif.

"Lenna," said Raif, "you don't have to."

Sebastien thankfully held his tongue, so Lenna just continued on. "I don't want to fight; it's ugly, it's not what I'm made for." She paused. "At least, I don't think it's what I'm made for, though I seem to find myself in the awkward position of doing it fairly frequently, and I come out relatively unscathed." The redness of her arms was beginning to look more like a bad sunburn than the backlash from a magical firefight. "I don't relish it. I don't relish it at all." Lenna was alarmed to find her voice so shaky. "But Gilbert died for this jewel, and Raif's mother died for the one Luc... holds," she said tactfully. "Too much is attached to each one." *Far too much,* Lenna thought, thinking of her father and mother and Jaice and Valant. "I won't let Sonnet take another so easily."

There was another heavy pause before — in the most gloriously comedic of moments — Raif and Sebastien attempted to throw their arms around Lenna at the same time, clonking their heads together. Lazarz burst into fits of high-pitched giggles and even Luc, the sullen lout, smirked. Lenna witnessed, as Raif and Seb disentangled themselves, a sparkle of amusement in Mistress Juniam's almond-shaped eyes and a small upturning of her lips.

"Are you sure, Lenna?" asked Raif, rubbing his forehead.

"No, Raif," Lenna replied. "I'm never sure, unless I'm in a library and have a nice catalogue with which to look up whatever obscure detail I need at the moment. But." All eyes looked at Lenna again, but she turned and addressed Sebastien alone. "Apprentice Faircloth is ready to try."

Seb smiled and stood up, dusting off the knees of his trousers. "Damn the formalities, Lenna," he said. "It's just good to see you again."

With only a bit of flailing, Lenna struggled to her feet under the careful guidance of Raif. He squeezed her biceps encouragingly. "That's the Lenna I know," he whispered into her ear.

"First things first," Lenna said. "What are you lot using for a toilet? It's been twenty-five years or so since I've popped to the ladies'."

After Lenna had vanished, surfing the currents of time, the scent of her Godjewel remained concentrated around the Branford Estate, but in a corrupt way, like the stench of a decaying corpse. Raif and Seb described it as "entirely unpleasant" and, moreover, "horrifically permeating." It loitered in the air, and within hours reports from border patrols between Fallowfields and Gallas confirmed that those magically inclined had noticed the putrid essence. It came as no surprise, as Lenna was told, that the present-day Khareen Valant became aware of Lenna's sudden disappearance; of course Valant would then in due course assess and notify her master, Emperor Alderic Sonnet of the Krevlum Empire, of Branford's defenses.

Lenna watched the final wounds on her arms close, leaving behind a smattering of measly pink scars up her limbs. *This adventure is not boding well for my physique,* she thought as Mistress Juniam delicately shielded her with the great mass of her skirt while Lenna relieved herself into a chamber pot in the corner of Sebastien's training room. *How are they disposing of this?* Though Lenna was not one to prefer fashion over practicality, she was ironically thankful for the ample amount of cloth spent in the creation of Mistress Juniam's ensemble: Lenna might as well have been in a tent.

After finishing and forcefully shaking her brains into reality, Lenna strode back into the center of the training room, drawing with her the gazes of all save Mistress Juniam, who merely stood, stoic as a statue. *If I ever wanted someone to watch my back,* Lenna amused herself by thinking, *she'd definitely be high on the list*. Lenna coughed deliberately, trying not to buckle under the heavy weight of everyone's attention.

"All right," she said. "What are the Imperial forces up to? Specifically. I've gathered the manor is under siege."

Sebastien's sparkling earring caught the faint gaslights of the room as he skirted inward to meet Lenna in the center. "About eight hours after the strange disappearance of you and the Godjewel..." Sebastien paused to grimace in the general direction of Raif, who now stood off in one corner, arms crossed. "...Magical assaults began striking the perimeter of the estate. I had cursory wards in place..."

"A lot of good they've done," inserted Raif.

"Raif, hush," said Lenna, and dismissed him with a wave of her hand. "Let Sebastien finish."

"You've become quite the commander," Sebastien said, though if he was impressed or shocked by Lenna's demeanor, his delivery didn't show it. "To continue: those wards were to protect the estate from petty thieves and simple novices attempting to try their luck at a proper mage's residence." Luc and Raif both very audibly scoffed at this, and Lenna could tell by the throbbing vein in Sebastien's right temple that it was taking all of his composure as a well-bred gentleman to prevent him from lashing out at either of the two.

"Keep going, Seb." Lenna could feel her magic returning, and she was encouraging its reassuring dominance. The Godjewel, too, was humming happily and, her arms healed, Lenna enjoyed the feeling of her fatigue and sense of dread lessening, achieving an almost pleasurable high from the arcane adrenaline coursing through her veins.

Sebastien nodded, this time without comment or condescension. He waved his hand in a nimble, economical manner – though Seb had a propensity, in Lenna's mind, for showing off and being a bit of a dandy, he was centered and had no desire for grandstanding right now – and before them particles of light gathered, forming a somewhat fuzzy but well-rounded interpretation of the topography of the Branford Estate. Lenna, studying the new magecraft, could distinguish without effort the manor, its grounds (including the stables where Lazarz had been interrogated and the orange groves from which Lenna had plunged herself into her own time stream), and even some of the outlying environs.

"The Empire fell on us quickly, as I said," Sebastien continued. With one finger, he drew an arch of light across his illusionary map. "The preliminary wards were torn through without any great effort on the Empire's part. But the barriers around the manor took longer, as I had arranged for specific designs some months ago to make certain that this place was guarded against attack." Seb's words were chosen carefully, Lenna was convinced, as he looked her straight in the eye. Of course he had planned for Gilbert to be here, with the Godjewel, and— if the traitorous thoughts in Lenna's mind held any truth – he had more than likely planned for her to be here too.

"But those wards surely couldn't hold against the Empire and a Godjewel for nigh on a week," Lenna said, not shirking at the incredulity in her voice.

Seb let his guard down and cracked a wry smile. "While it wasn't the Godjewel I was expecting to be sheltering here, we weren't without one." He jerked his head back toward the shadowy corner of the room, where Luc brooded with the subtlety of a first-year dramatics student.

"Luc has been using the Vandever Godjewel?" Lenna asked.

Shuffling into the space between Lenna and Sebastien, his hair catching the eerie light of the conjured map and distorting its proportions, Raif spared no time in voicing his discontent. "If it were up to me, it would be back in my charge, not left to some young, damaged boy. But the damned thing has bonded with him, and we needed its power."

From the corner, Luc spoke. "Don't worry, Lenna. I'm not doing anything drastic. Gilbert trusted you to protect what Emperor Sonnet seeks so strongly; who am I to deny his wishes?" His eyes were manic as they fell on Lenna, almost asking for a challenge.

They're pushing him too hard, too far, Lenna thought. Although he had perhaps spoken unkindly, Raif was right: Luc was damaged, and the pressure of the Godjewel would have him on edge, unsteady. The last thing any of them needed was for Luc to snap, and Lenna realized it was time for her to assert her position. She didn't care about a warm bed or cider or wine or a good book — she cared about making sure this nonsense *stopped,* and if she had to stop it herself, the steady beat in her palm told her, she would.

"But the warding is failing, even with Luc's assistance and the Vandever Godjewel," Lenna said with emphasis.

"Yes," both Raif and Seb said together.

"But I am back."

"Yes, you are," said Raif, and he drew a tiny bit closer.

"Yes," Seb said more or less at the same time, though unlike Raif he remained still. Luc, in the shadowed distance, made a disgruntled sound but otherwise resisted commenting.

"Luc is a trained mage." Lenna was stating the obvious: Luc, especially under the tutelage of Sebastien, should be wielding the power of a bonded Godjewel much more effectively than any librarian ever could. "You should be able to stand against Sonnet, at least magically. He can't even have that much of a military force here in Gallas, except for Valant and the remnants of her crew…"

"Lenna Faircloth." Two voices rang out in the cramped room, speaking Lenna's name at precisely the same moment. Mistress Juniam and Lazarz sauntered into the center of the room, toward Sebastien's illusion. Lazarz, skipped eagerly toward the curly-haired de facto commander, but the graceful curve of Mistress Juniam's arm barred his way. Her regal deportment seemed to push back everyone, including Raif and Seb, so that it was just Lenna and Juniam.

"Do you think," Juniam began, "that you are not worthy of the weight you bear?"

Lenna looked into the eyes of the matron before her. They were eyes that had seen pain, had seen love. Mistress Juniam might now be a woman of immaculate conduct and command, but there was a sense of heroic desperation that reminded Lenna of a champion of days gone by, the kind that Lenna would read about in her library.

"Mistress Juniam," Lenna asked, "what do you know?"

"You're missing a scabbard, I believe."

Lenna cast her eyes downward; her overcoat had been very tidily singed into rags, and her sword had become the possession of a deranged Imperial patriot twenty-five years or so in the past. She fiercely recalled her memory of the separation, the pulling that had propelled Lenna back into her current time, and she realized with great remorse that the beautiful sheath for the Freewoman sword that Chait had made Lenna had either been left behind or vanished into nothingness. She raised her head and regarded Mistress Juniam once more.

Those eyes. "Mistress Juniam, do you have a daughter?"

Mistress Juniam smiled, a flawless visage that Lenna knew was the pride of a mother. Juniam drew back her hand and said, "Yes, her name is Chait, and you know her from Granemere Settlement."

Face warming, Lenna couldn't help but feel foolish. Was this common knowledge? Were all of Lenna's personal interactions and entanglements so utterly visible to those around her? "Chait has been very kind to me," Lenna said, pushing a stray lock back behind her ear. Her shredded garments and lack of weapons, save the Godjewel and its gauntlet, left Lenna feeling overly exposed. The scabbard was a labor of love and friendship: to lose it, Lenna thought, was as painful as losing the blade itself.

"She has written of you over the past month," said Mistress Juniam. "I cannot think of another person who could do as well as you have in possession of a Godjewel." With that statement, Mistress Juniam cupped the fist carrying Lenna's troubles with her hands. Sebastien, Raif, and Luc choked in either relief or even misogynistic frustration — Lenna couldn't tell — while Lazarz shouted, "Team L!" in the background.

"I don't want to be in charge," Lenna said, her voice quiet.

Mistress Juniam leaned forward until her lips were a breath's gap away from Lenna's ear. "No one person is perfect, or capable of bearing such a hefty burden alone," she whispered. "But I think you're much stronger than these namby-pamby louts who insist on sheltering you." Juniam placed a kiss on Lenna's cheek with the gentleness of a spring breeze and pulled away before assuming her matronly role. "Now," she said. "With two Godjewels, let us prepare to diffuse this breaking storm."

Lenna clenched her fist and the Godjewel chirped merrily in reply. *I am in control, you,* she said. *You will not get the better of me. For I am Lenna Faircloth, librarian, apprentice — and one day, I will be free from you and your curse. Until then, you do my bidding, and not the other way around.*

According to Sebastien, shortly after Lenna's sudden disappearance, he had dismissed the few remaining servants and groundsmen, save Mistress Juniam, who, according to Seb, "probably wouldn't allow herself to be dismissed anyway." With constant instruction and reinforcing from Master Branford, Luc had — to the point of exhaustion — been consistently maintaining a large-scale ward around the mansion. As the strength of the attacks increased, a fact that Sebastien could only attribute to the appearance of more powerful magics, such as those of a Godjewel, the small group retreated inward to Sebastien's study and, ultimately, the makeshift arcane gymnasium. Here, at least, they would be able to hold out against any foot soldiers should the final wardings around the house fall.

Seb pointed out key areas in the infrastructure of the room, noting particular corners and specific woodwork that were credible spaces to hold one's position during a siege. He led Lenna around the chamber's perimeter with military gruffness, like a proud general showing a rookie commanding officer the layout of a base. It was all obscure and useless information for Lenna, who, despite the quick healing from Seb and Raif and the emotional bastion of Mistress Juniam, still felt a bit discombobulated from her journey in time. Though she tried to tabulate the number of hours she'd been awake, Lenna found herself constantly confused.

They stopped at the doorframe against which Luc was leaning. Lenna noted, however briefly, that his cheeks were cadaverous and his eyes, in addition to sporting quite the shiner, were sunken, lined with dark circles. "Lenna," Sebastien said. "Are you paying attention?"

Lenna pulled her eyes away from Luc, who didn't appear to be concerned at her inspection. "No, Seb, I haven't been paying attention at all. Have you been keeping Luc awake this entire time?"

Luc regarded her like an interesting painting, one that wasn't quite in his style or worth his money but that he appreciated nonetheless, and Sebastien drummed his fingers against the wooden frame, not bothering to contain his impatience. "Yes, I have. I've taught him how to draw on the power of the Godjewel to bolster his stamina; additionally, Master Vandever and I have been bolstering his magical reserves at the expense of our own. I am not," he said, "as completely useless as you might think,

Lenna Faircloth. Before I betrayed the Brotherhood, I was quite highly regarded."

Don't I know it. Lenna's thoughts were getting as caustic as Luc's speech, but she had neither patience nor time to stroke Sebastien's ego. "So what's the plan?"

"The outer wards are still holding; I invested considerable energy in them over the past few years." Lenna eyed Sebastien shrewdly at this comment; she already knew his machinations had been in the works for some time, but this was the first time he had openly commented on the subject. "So, with some minor reinforcing, they've stood up to all but the most brutal of assaults. From what Brotherhood information I possess, I know that Sonnet uses his Godjewel with considerable restraint and finesse. I believe he's testing us. We've been careful not to be too aggressive so as to not give away too much knowledge about the kind of power we have at our disposal."

It made sense, Lenna pondered, for the Emperor to be conservative in his tactics. Luc's control of the filched Godjewel was even less than Lenna's, and while she had no doubt that Emperor Alderic Sonnet's information network would confirm this information, an economical use of magic from Luc would make it far more difficult for him to assess the group's innate strength. Now that Lenna had returned — in what was no doubt a noticeable pop of power — Sonnet would be forced to make a decision: strike quickly, or potentially face two Godjewels working in harmony.

Lenna cracked her knuckles, pleased that all the soreness had subsided. The transport back had left the Godjewel calmer, or at least it appeared that way; its normally stormy interior glowed only faintly, lacking any of the lightning-like flickers it usually displayed. She wondered if its quiet meant it had retreated into a state of dormancy that would complicate any attempts to harness its power. When she broached this topic, Seb shook his head.

"The Godjewel is so uniquely attuned to you by now that it's more likely its current state is a reflection of your mood. You are calm and slightly aloof; distracted. It is reflecting that." Sebastien puffed out his chest like a teacher about to expound. "The amount of power a Godjewel possesses is still…"

"…A matter of some debate," quipped Lenna, cutting off her mentor. "Right. So now that Sonnet knows I'm back, it's only a matter of time before he comes at the final shields, full strength. How powerful do you reckon he is?"

Even Luc smirked at the dejection plastered on Sebastien's face, and Lenna might have detected the very faintest of sighs escaping Master Branford's lips. *So much for that unshakable confidence,* Lenna thought, waiting for Seb to recover his wits and respond. He tugged at his collar and coughed as though all the starch from years of laundering was threatening to suffocate him. Resisting the urge to laugh, Lenna had counted to nine by the time her tutor regained himself.

"His magical talents were often discussed among the Brothers," Seb spoke with deliberation. "But compared to many of us and even some of the Freewoman mages, he was pretty much of average talent. However." Sebastien lowered his voice as if divulging a great Brotherhood secret. "It's his intellect that has always been our biggest fear. The man is cunning beyond words, and an unmatched tactician. Through training and diligence his magical prowess could probably overwhelm more powerful magicians, and then once you add a Godjewel into the mix…"

"Bottled chaos," uttered Luc. There was a sweet, almost self-deprecating smile tilting at the corner of his mouth. "I can feel him, like a storm in a cage. Or a hysterical woman bound by ropes." Lenna did not bother to conceal the annoyance flashing in her eyes at Luc's jab. "He has complete control."

"So, up until now, sheer force wasn't an option, was it?" asked Lenna.

Raif, at some point during Seb's lengthy exposition, had slipped up to Lenna with his usual quiet grace and now hovered close to her body protectively. Their elbows were a hairbreadth away from brushing against each other, and Lenna's ears grew warm with an irritating predictability. "Ultimately, he could starve us out. Even with two Godjewels and supportive magic from Sebastien and myself, we don't have the raw resources to outlast a proper military conquest," he told her.

"Can we contact the Freewomen of Laur? There must be settlements here in Gallas."

"There are indeed three settlements in Gallas, Apprentice Faircloth," said Sebastien, "but at the moment, magical interference from the wards and the Empire's attacks render magical communication all but impossible. And, physically, I have no means to get a messenger out."

"It's safe to assume, with the fall of Tranum and the attack on Granemere Settlement," offered Raif, "that the Freewomen of Laur are already mobilizing."

And Jaice is an excellent strategist, aware of the potential behind the Godjewels and the connection between them and my family. Lenna shook her head. "Sebastien, I find it positively inconceivable that you did not account for the Krevlum Empire — or rather, Alderic Sonnet — coming to seek the Godjewel once it was brought here."

Off in the corner, over the chittering of a hyperactive Lazarz, who was currently engaged in sketching schematics of some sort on the floor with pink chalk, Mistress Juniam raised her deliciously resounding voice. "Master Branford has been making arrangements for some time indeed." Lenna thought she could detect something — a challenge? — in Mistress Juniam's tone, buried under layers of complex emotion and rigid aristocratic rules she couldn't follow.

Sebastien cleared his throat, casting frustrated looks at all parties in the room. He held out his hands, either in supplication or in exhaustion at having his methodology questioned, before speaking. "Of course I knew a force from the Krevlum Empire would come here. Of course I planned for that." The skilled mage gesticulated widely around the room. "Hence the wards. Hence why we've survived this long. But, Lenna," Seb said, his voice rising and falling into something almost pitiable, "I never planned for two Godjewels to be here. And especially not in the hands of the grossly untrained." He made no secret of whom he was talking about by nodding directly at Lenna and Luc.

"You didn't intend for me to receive this stone?" Lenna asked, and every noise — even Lazarz's indecipherable babbling — stopped.

"No," said Sebastien without hesitation. "Certainly not. And I strongly doubt anyone foresaw the Vandever Godjewel falling into the hands of Apprentice Tural. Our stalwart defense and use of Godjewel magic after your departure was probably what led General Valant, and subsequently Emperor Sonnet, to surmise that Luc is here with it. "

"You're talking about a fair amount of coincidence," Raif said, not bothering to hide the derision in his voice.

"Master Vandever is right," Luc said suddenly.

"Luc?" Lenna asked; she couldn't recall the boy ever using Raif's name.

"It's too much coincidence. But only one person could have known the two bearers well enough — and known Master Branford's plans — in order to arrange for this kind of situation."

Lenna felt her stomach fall like the bridge of Raif's airship as it plunged toward the *Talonstrike*. She knew to whom Luc was alluding: the one person uniquely attached to Lenna, Luc, and Sebastien.

"Gilbert?" Sebastien asked, his cheeks so pale Lenna was half-tempted to cast a glamour on him herself. He clearly believed his pupil would never have engaged in subterfuge — well, at least not subterfuge that Sebastien hadn't organized himself.

"Gilbert," Lenna contemplated aloud. He was the only one with such connections. But why would he manipulate Lenna and Luc here? What was the end goal? Right now, they were trapped, under siege. Were they just supposed to wait for their deaths? That certainly served no purpose, and while she had various doubts and some legitimate concerns, she still could not help but trust her childhood friend and Luc's savior. "Assuming Gilbert somehow manipulated things so that we would be in this situation, I refuse to believe he'd expect us to sit down and starve to death."

"So what do you propose?" asked Raif.

Lenna let a rare, wry laugh escape her lips. "Let's change our strategy and lay our cards on the table. The next time Emperor Sonnet comes knocking, I say we let him in to parley."

CHAPTER NINETEEN

Luc's black eye was a source of fascination for Lenna; she wondered who had bestowed the shiner and what the biting young man had said to deserve it. Why hadn't they healed it away? Several hours later, as the troop of them — a questionable mishmash with the addition of Lazarz — tramped along the extensive corridors, Lenna mustered up the courage to ask, much to the loud protestations of Sebastien, who apparently found the attention of a time-traveling, catty apprentice difficult to monopolize. Raif, having reined in his long-legged stride to match Lenna's pace, was reluctant to yield to her questioning.

"It happened a few days ago," he said, scrutinizing the ceiling as a carpenter might survey for cracks.

"But it wouldn't happen to have been inflicted by one Ilyan airship captain?" Lenna asked.

Raif shrugged and tugged on his ponytail. "I suppose something might have come up when he questioned my people's magical aptitude," he finally admitted. "And yours."

The recent barricade meant that many gas lamps went unlit and the shadows of the complex Branford Estate disguised Lenna's stumble. Not that she and Luc had become bosom friends after sharing each other's past, but she found herself nettled that he still doubted her ability. True, he had years of training at his disposal, whereas Lenna had barely a few weeks, but surely she had proven herself as of late. Or so she thought.

"I don't think he really meant anything bad by that," Raif added hastily. Perhaps he had noticed the misstep after all. "The situation was intense; he was very drained, and in close quarters, tempers can get heated..." His voice began to trail off.

"And?"

"Well, I might have said something like, 'if Lenna were here...'"

"Oh, great."

"He got very frustrated..."

"And you've never been particularly fond of him."

"Would you hate me very much if I just explained away the black eye by saying, 'It's just been one of those weeks'?"

"You might end up in a similar state to a certain apprentice," Lenna retorted. She was starting to feel some haunting effects of the magical effort she had exerted to rip her out of the past and fling her back to the Branford Estate, and those effects were making her irritable. "You know he's sensitive and under incredible pressure, Raif." Lenna couldn't believe she was standing up for her former nemesis, but she needed to make sure, especially now, as they were advancing into very new, very dicey territory in actively engaging the Empire, that Luc trusted them. "The bond with the Godjewel... it's not easy to bear. And Luc himself hasn't received much kindness of late. You could have at least offered to heal it."

Raif uttered a strangled noise. "He'd probably prefer the black eye to your heavy-handed defense of him, Len. Still, you're probably right." Lenna thought she detected a detestable hint of sniveling but let it go, chalking it up to, as Raif had said, it just being "one of those weeks."

Sebastien's grievances eventually dulled to nothing more than a grunt every now and then, and he guided the party out of one of the lesser-used servants' passages and into the grand lobby of the manor. Lenna hadn't spent much time in this part of the house, as most of her travels took her through side entrances. The floors were once an unblemished marvel; now, as she stared out across the foyer, she noticed with dismay chipped tiles, the black smudging of scorch marks, and bits of debris littering a tattered rug that, in its original condition, would probably be worth the property value of Lenna's neighborhood in Port Hollish.

The entrance doors, formerly elaborately carved and polished to a sheen, were reduced to splinters hanging on hinges; shards of wood and the metal hardware sat in heaps around the open entrance. Sebastien grimaced and Lenna placed one hand on his shoulder, squeezing lightly. He recoiled at the gesture and looked back at her in surprise.

For all his family history and reluctance to accept his role as a Gallasian noble, Lenna could only guess how greatly his heart ached at the wanton destruction of his childhood home. Even Raif bowed his head in sympathy. "No one would take this lightly," she said.

Whatever wards Sebastien had erected around the main parts of the house had long since fallen to destructive magics; no wonder the group had willingly sequestered itself in a more sheltered section of the manor. Beyond the open portal lay the spruce blades of grass of the main lawn and the paved path that led beyond the trees out into the curving highways that had given Lenna's stomach such a turn. The sun, a magnificent orange globe, hung just above the trees and cast a mellow ochre glow over the greenery.

In the center of the lawn, seemingly in expectation the group's imminent arrival, stood a demure man with white-blonde hair that gleamed fiery in the light of the setting sun. His three-piece suit, also white, sharply contrasted with the grass on which he stood, and its stark fabric struck Lenna as incongruous with the destruction abounding within the Branford Estate. Like Lenna, he wore spectacles — gold-framed — and bound by a chain to his waistcoat was a fob watch of the same metal. She sensed the power in him right away.

"Emperor Alderic Sonnet," she gulped.

Lazarz began to wave, but Raif, jaw snapped shut, swiftly kicked the kooky engineer. He yelped and scurried off to the side.

"Well, Apprentice Faircloth," said Sebastien, off to Lenna's left. He stood inflexibly, shoulders set and prepared for any situation, even a delicate diplomatic one with the leader of the Krevlum Empire. "You've found the right person to parley with." Lenna wasn't sure if the deadpan delivery was meant to be comical or not, but she wanted to kick him, as Raif had kicked Lazarz, either way.

"Three Godjewels, together," murmured Luc from the shadows behind Lenna.

There was a noticeable tingling creeping up Lenna's arm, like an oncoming chill. She peered down into her open palm and noticed that the blue stone's squally center pulsed in a steady beat. *A second heart,* Lenna thought. She turned, wondering if the jewel now hanging from Luc's neck was in sync with her own. Their eyes met, and together both Lenna's and Luc's necks jerked toward the Emperor.

A sudden longing overcame Lenna, and her feet, as if drawn by a magnet, stepped past the doorframe and onto the path, matching Luc's stride for stride. Sebastien and Raif raised no outcry but hastened forward to thwart their marionette-like progress toward Sonnet. Lenna smacked into Raif's back and heard Luc grunt when he collided with Sebastien. Although rough, the impact seemed to have blocked whatever force had enticed their feet forward.

"Stay focused, my apprentices," Sebastien warned. "We don't know what will happen with all three Godjewels in one location."

"Come now, Brother Branford!" called the Emperor from across the lawn. "No need for such whisperings!" He opened his arms broadly, a welcoming gesture sickly juxtaposed considering the situation. "It's a pity your poor manor has taken such a beating. Once I sensed the return of Miss Faircloth, I took the liberty of dismissing my remaining forces and ceasing the siege."

Sebastien stepped forward a few feet, clearing his throat as he approached the grass. "Emperor Sonnet, there are proper political channels…"

"I think we all know that there isn't much protocol for this." Emperor Sonnet smiled warmly.

Lenna watched the passive expression on Sebastien's face with ardent interest and wondered if she would ever be in such control of her faculties. Her left hand, bearing the Godjewel, felt heavy, threatening to drag her to the ground. The stone had begun to seep motes of energy, and they caught the breeze like the seeds of a dandelion. The Godjewel in Luc's possession was also sparking, but with a more desperate fervor — perhaps, Lenna thought, she had gained some control over the last month after all.

Even the clouds seemed to pull back as the tendrils of light — blue from Lenna, viridian from Luc, and a glassy pale gold from Emperor Sonnet — rose to the sky, intertwining in something like a fireworks spectacle moving backward through time. All heads raised to watch the three-hued helix spinning in a strange, serpentine courtship. The more Lenna squinted, the more she could make out extraordinary images in the tiny gaps between the spiraling arcs of light. A barren lawn, similar to the Branford Estate but ravaged by war; a short-haired woman, her back turned, fighting with a long knife; Luc, covered in blood and holding the hand of a pale girl; Emperor Sonnet, a scar creasing his face, garbed in dented armor.

"Interesting phenomenon, isn't it?" Sonnet said. "The three Godjewels in close physical proximity often twist the folds of what we humans perceive as reality."

"Fascinating," Lazarz chimed in.

"...But an unnecessary side effect, one that I'm sure is being encouraged," said Sebastien wryly. He extended one arm skyward, without showmanship, and the images blurred and gradually dissipated, allowing patches of sky to once more peek through the twirling arcs of light. "Emperor Sonnet, for nigh on a week a unit of your troops has assaulted my home. What is your reasoning in standing here now, alone?"

The Emperor cleaned his fancy lenses with a silk handkerchief and replaced them upon his slight nose. "With the arrival of Miss Faircloth, my ability to match your magical potential has changed greatly, even with General Valant's considerable talent and my own abilities. I'd find myself at quite a stalemate if there were suddenly two Godjewels working against me."

"Don't you think that leaves you rather vulnerable now?" Raif interjected. Lenna nodded. It made no sense to her — if the Krevlum Emperor realized that he no longer held the upper hand, wouldn't he want all the backing he could gather? Alone, the man was preposterously overpowered. Then again, Lenna recollected, Emperor Sonnet had chosen the word "stalemate," heavily implying that all was not as it seemed.

"We're all vulnerable, Master Vandever." Emperor Sonnet smiled again. "But I prefer to work as efficiently as possible in all matters. I'm sure reason and logic will prevail where Brother Branford and Miss Faircloth are concerned. And I come bearing proof of my sincerity."

"Proof?"

Emperor Sonnet held out his hand and narrowed his gaze to his open palm. There was a quick golden flash of light and a cloth bag shaped like a misshapen watermelon gradually materialized in the air before him. Lazarz squealed in exhilaration at the display, resulting in not a kick from Raif but in Mistress Juniam grabbing him by the ear and tweaking mightily. Sebastien must have had quite a colorful upbringing.

"What's in the bag?" Raif asked. Something about the shape of it and a metallic scent wafting toward Lenna made her decidedly wary of its contents. The way the Emperor held the sack away from his tailored suit set Lenna's stomach reeling once more.

"It's a peace offering," he stated. "I thought I would bring a gift to show my good intentions, as such." With the gleaming sheen of his teeth and hair, the Emperor was like a miniature nova that had alighted on the ground. His very presence in the sunlit lawn compelled Lenna to shade her eyes.

"A peace offering?" Raif stroked his chin. "What in all of the four nations would the Krevlum Emperor freely give to us?"

Sonnet slung the satchel, letting it arc in mathematical perfection over the vacant space between himself and Lenna's party. It landed with a liquidy thud at Raif's feet. At some point mid-flight the bag's mouth had opened and the lip of the cloth drooped down, revealing a red and sticky-looking mass. Lenna stifled a gasp at the sight and turned, burying her head in Sebastien's shoulder. His body grew rigid as he drew his arms up around her. The muffled sound of someone shuffling about told Lenna that Raif had knelt down to investigate.

"Is this a sick joke, Sonnet?" demanded Raif. He had apparently lost any desire to adhere to formalities and address the Emperor by his title.

"Not at all. Miss Faircloth didn't care for my general very much, so as a sign of good faith, I've terminated her."

Despite every rational instinct telling Lenna not to look, she had to know. She tore her face away from the warm comfort of Sebastien's body and stared down at Raif. He was holding, albeit very determinedly away from his person, a severed head, letting it dangle from his hand by a span of straight, silvery hair. Khareen Valant's eyes remained open wide, as though she had been taken by surprise.

"Is that really her?" Luc's voice shook like a teaspoon balanced precariously on the edge of a saucer. *Of course,* Lenna thought. Though they had probably mentioned her in some capacity around Luc, he had yet to confront the cruel reality that the general with whom he had briefly conspired was back among the living.

But now Valant was dead again. Her first death was at the hands of Lenna and Pim — the Valant that Lenna had relieved of an ear — but somehow she had been brought back to an even more tainted life, filled with hatred for Lenna and a desire to please Emperor Sonnet. Would her master, whom she so zealously followed, summon her forth once more, once his point here was proved?

"I see that your teacher and Miss Faircloth haven't shown you how to achieve what you've known to be true from the moment you bonded with the Godjewel." Alderic Sonnet paused, either for dramatic effect or out of genuine contemplation. "But, Luc Tural, I suspect you have long known the potential of the Godjewels. What they're capable of."

"Then it's true. The dead can be brought back." Lenna heard the trembling in Luc's voice. Was it… hope?

"Yes," Sonnet answered simply.

"Apprentice… Luc, listen to me," Sebastien said hurriedly. "He's not telling the whole truth. You'd never be able to bring back the person exactly as they were. They'd never be the same. It's a perverse power; you'd never get Gilbert or your sister back!" The elder mage's voice was breaking; Lenna had never witnessed Sebastien so unhinged, though she understood his desperation. She thought she had come to accept the possibilities and pitfalls presented to her by wielding a Godjewel, but even if the person were different, the chance to have a loved one back…

"It's true there are limits to the number of times one can be brought back before the data becomes corrupted," said Sonnet. "With each subsequent resurrection, the essence of the person changes, however subtly. I had already pushed Valant hard to become the soldier I wanted; any further revivals and she'd probably be far too unstable to be any use to me." He paused. "Though it would certainly be interesting to see."

With this, Emperor Sonnet gestured with one hand, and Lenna felt the taut strings of relativity tighten around Valant's severed head and tear it from Raif's grasp like the pitching of a kickball. As it barreled toward Sonnet, he leaned forward into an elegant lunge. His left foot connected with the eviscerated remains and launched them off into the air in what in any sports match would have been an excellent strike. A meaty thump accompanied Khareen Valant's final send-off; her head spun on an axis, sailing to the northwest and out into the dusky sky.

Lenna wrapped both arms around her stomach, trying with all her might not to gag. Raif swore in Ilyan and punched Lazarz in the shoulder when he exclaimed, "Goal!" To the side, Mistress Juniam had the grace to divert her attention to the destroyed remnants of the entranceway, but Sebastien, quiet and pale, regarded an expressionless Luc. There was no reaction from the boy: his eyes remained locked on Alderic Sonnet as the bespectacled man straightened his thin necktie.

"As you can see, Apprentice Tural," Sonnet said with a honeyed tongue, "the power of a Godjewel is the power to control life and death." The Emperor held out his hand yet again and there appeared above the grass a vague shimmering riding on a shift in the airstream, a blurry rendition of a messy-haired youth Lenna immediately recognized as Gilbert. It wasn't a perfect likeness; it was an ethereal charcoal sketch colored by a grey wind. Lenna was the first to gasp.

Luc stiffened visibly. Then he began to walk: his steps, one after the other, fell slowly and determinedly in a slow trek toward Gilbert, toward Sonnet. Why did no one stop him? All around her, her peers held themselves strained, ready to launch, yet only Apprentice Tural marched unimpeded toward the blurry image of his dead lover. Was there some magic of Sonnet that was binding their legs, or were all simply too stunned to follow Luc?

Do it, Lenna, she willed herself. She opened her heart to her Godjewel, finding in it a determination that transcended the lethargy restraining her, and somehow she strode forward. Each footfall felt to Lenna like she was walking across an uneven sand dune in a windstorm and her progress toward the ghostly visage of Gilbert slackened the closer she came.

"Luc," she called out. "It's just an illusion; Gilbert isn't really there." Lenna willed the gem snug in her palm to banish the specter, to drive the cheap imitation of her best friend away. Subtle orbs of faint blue light, like will-o'-the-wisps, appeared in the air around Gil, and his features shifted with the refraction of the globes' spectral illumination. Within a second the sketch of her best friend changed form and became, as Lenna cried out in dismay, a vision of her mother, not as she had seen her in the past, but the mother of Lenna's youth. The face was one of strictly controlled emotion, patience, and what Lenna perceived as grim resignation.

Craning his neck over his shoulder and snarling, Luc lashed out wildly with one arm and an arc of green light walloped Lenna directly in the stomach. Already unbalanced, she fell to the ground: it wasn't a strong blow, but enough to knock her down and break her concentration. The influence she had exerted over Sonnet's manifestation was lost: Alanna Faircloth drifted away into particles and this time, in her stead, the wind took the form of a young girl on the threshold of womanhood. Her delicate features were set with two deep, sad eyes and her hair hung down in a straight jet curtain to her shoulders.

Lenna heard Luc call, "Clarie," and at once she knew any influence the group had garnered over the young mage during the course of the past week was lost. Luc broke into a run, barreling straight for the conjuration, and Lenna, glancing at the smug, self-righteous expression on Sonnet's face, brimmed over with abject loathing. Who was this man to pick apart the memories of a fragile youth, manipulating them for the sake of some stupid stone?

The stone. It was the key with which Lenna and Sonnet — and Luc, should he learn — could so easily tap into a font of such memories, could unlock the door to the past. As Luc broached the apparition of his sister, one hand outstretched to caress her cheek, Lenna hoisted herself to her feet and, despite the shouts of protest from her friends, launched herself, in one epic attempt to stifle the Krevlum Emperor, across the lawn. *The stone is the key.* Pulling on the power of the Godjewel, she summoned a massive orb of flickering light to her hand and, as she flew forward, its haunting blueness highlighted the stupefaction on Alderic Sonnet's face.

There was no time for him to shield, not as she approached so quickly, but a wave of molten gold confronted Lenna's own conjuration and the two workings erupted in a cacophony of sparks and queer sounds as they collided, like the squealing metal of an airship's bulkhead buckling and breaking apart. Pure energy tore through the straps of Lenna's gauntlet and the sheer force from the recoil shot her back toward the lawn. Just as she was about to break away, something iron-strong gripped her arm and yanked her around. She yelped, waiting for the residual spots of light on the lenses of her eyes to dissipate so that she could once again see freely, but she found instead that her vision was obscured by tears of pain and anger. In the blast, her gauntlet had been torn from her arm, and she was trapped, arm and body contorted by the clawlike grasp of Emperor Sonnet.

"So what do you think, Apprentice Tural?" asked Sonnet. His hold on Lenna's wrist forced her arm to bend in ways the universe did not intend. Resisting the urge to cry, she looked outward across the courtyard of the Branford Estate at the ashen faces of the others. A few paces before Lenna stood Luc Tural, his wanting eyes looking straight through her and honing in on the Emperor. "You know what I am offering you," Sonnet said further.

And between the groups, nestled tidily in the grass, were the gauntlet, its torn leather bindings, and its ward, the Godjewel. The gem vomited great sprays of magic, spilling out pale blue miasma across the lawn. Any shards of grass that had survived the concussive wave of magics released from Lenna's attack on Sonnet blackened and sank into pools of muck as the Godjewel corrupted its surrounding environs. Save her own natural magic, Lenna was defenseless, and though she was gifted, she certainly could not match Sonnet's years of mastering his sun-bright Godjewel.

Luc rocked back and forth on the balls of his feet, like a bereft man dancing a partnerless waltz. The fading summer breeze, still acrid with the scent of char, ruffled his hair, raising it up in shaggy chunks. Waning behind the surrounding trees, the red sun struck Luc's gleaming eyes and the emerald jewel he now dangled haphazardly before him. What choice would he make? What choice would Lenna make, given the same situation?

The deceivingly frail frame of Alderic Sonnet shuddered in what Lenna could only guess was impatience as the green Godjewel drew closer. She squirmed involuntarily and immediately regretted such foolishness: with extreme economy of movement, the Emperor jerked upward and Lenna yowled as the ball of her shoulder rotated in its socket. "Apprentice Tural," Sonnet's voice tinkled with the insistency of an offended piano. "I am offering you a partnership that can restore all you're missing. I know the secrets of the deep darkness; I know how to bring back those you have lost."

Bathed in the auburn sunset, Sebastien and Raif gazed intently at the young man who stood before, in an almost catatonic calm, the most important decision of his universe. Sonnet was offering him on a velvet pillow everything that Luc's damaged soul yearned for; in fact, the impetus for his theft of the Vandever Godjewel originated in the boy's desperate desire to mend his broken world. And the promise of reincarnation wasn't without its temptation for Lenna either. Gilbert, her mother…

The grass crunched, suddenly brittle with winter's chill, as Luc took a tenuous step forward toward Sonnet and his prisoner. Lenna felt the bitter cold creep up over the yard, and white puffs of condensation from Luc's heavy exhalations swirled in frosty clouds as he drew near. What should have been the waning heat of a warm autumn day had in a moment become a deep-rooted cold — a cold as gripping as it was on the night of Gilbert's death. In her mind's eye, as clearly as a lithograph sliding over the topography of the Branford Estate, Lenna saw the whirling flakes of snow blowing in the breeze and a shroud of darkness inching across the warm dusk of the Gallas sky. It mirrored the blanketed winter landscape of Fallowfields.

"Will you really bring them back?" Luc's hushed words one by one fell on Lenna's ears like damnations.

"You know I can," said Sonnet. "We can."

"I will work with you," Luc said, though Lenna noticed the caution in his voice. The promise of dreams fulfilled was seductive, and Luc's mental state was highly questionable, yet even through his pain his intellect and wariness of other humans — his inability to trust — still remained. "But I will not relinquish the Godjewel to you."

Lenna bit down on her lip. Unless the bearer of the Godjewel willingly severed the bond, consciously bequeathing the psychic link, another person wishing to acquire the stone would not be able to use it to its full potential, not until all traces of the previous owner's psyche were erased in a lengthy, exhausting process. This fact and this fact alone, Lenna realized through the pain jutting through her upper arm, was the reason she had managed to stay alive so long. As if to further solidify this theory, the rock on the ground mere paces away from her person illuminated each and every phantom snowflake in a cerulean light show, calling to her.

Sonnet was unmoved by Luc's response, and if he, too, was experiencing the unnerving mirage shrouding the natural landscape, his committed stance — and grip on Lenna's arm — did not betray any surprise. He let a smile grace the porcelain plate of his face. "Cooperation is enough for me," Sonnet said. "General Valant's methodology was effective more often than not, but costly on many levels, as you witnessed firsthand. I daresay that if we do need to bring back the psychopath, she'd be terrifically exciting this time around. The head football was an entertaining diversion too."

"No," Luc said. "I don't want to bring her back." His arms were folded and the air was rich with the smell of lilies in full bloom, intensified by the power of the Godjewel. A warding sprang into existence, a mystical net similar to the one Lenna had used to confine Sebastien in the corner of his training room the other day. It was a slapdash but firm wall between the group standing at the estate's grand front entrance and the three Godjewel bearers. Luc, it appeared, would have no interference from the other mages, and Lenna bet that if Seb or Raif tried to push through or dismantle his working, Sonnet would be ready to reinforce the magic.

"Very well," agreed Sonnet. "How shall we proceed, then?"

"I just want to make the world better." There was no trace of his usual anger or disdain, or the desperate grief that had tormented him since Gilbert's death. Lenna searched Luc's eyes for some kind of answer or hidden truth, and she learned that he was simply just trying to find a place where who he was, what he wanted, what he could be, was acceptable. It was what everyone wanted. A place where it didn't hurt to love someone.

"As for this one," Sonnet said, gesticulating with Lenna's body grandly, her limbs having no choice but to dance in his thrall, "this vessel will not likely relinquish her hold on the stone; the Godjewel's bond with her — and her own inflated sense of self-worth — would never allow her to give it up willingly." Sonnet twisted Lenna's arm and she spun once more until their eyes locked, and this time he curled the cold, delicate fingers of his free hand around her face, cupping her chin. "Or am I mistaken?"

Lenna's thoughts had slowed, frozen in the moment and the strange landscape. There was no sound; there was nothing, not even the cool whisper of the phantom winter wind. They were alone: just her, Alderic Sonnet, and Luc Tural, each a host to a Godjewel. Lenna had been told a month earlier in a conference with Khareen Valant and Raif's father that if she gave up the magical artifact of her own accord, severing the bond, all her troubles would disappear. Was it really that easy?

Two arousing offers were placed on the table. Lenna's mind soared as the mental landscape transformed in a panoply of shifting rainbows, as though multihued lenses had slid over her pupils. What had been an empty, snow-laden winter's night was now a study of languorous richness with a bright fire crackling in its hearth. The room's walls appeared to be comprised almost entirely of bookshelves, each housing a complement of rare texts that, had Lenna's library been capable of envy, would have had it drooling in desire. Lenna, and Luc beside her, suddenly found themselves seated in the miserably fashionable chairs reserved for Master Vandever's guests, and behind the large desk, this time completely empty of any paper, sat Alderic Sonnet. They were back in Tranum, in Raif's home.

Two offers, thought Lenna.

"That's right," said Sonnet. "Like Master Tural, you can work with me and we can tease back the mysteries of the stars into the forms we desire, or you can entrust me with the safekeeping of the *cexer-sur*."

"*Cexer-sur*? Is that what the Godjewels are really called?" Lenna asked. The name meant nothing to her in the Continental tongue, and it certainly wasn't a word she recalled coming across in her perusal of texts in other languages. Yet she felt she had heard it spoken once, in the ephemeral twilight between dreams and waking.

The Emperor sighed, a smile creeping into the corner of his mouth. "There's so much I can teach you, Miss Faircloth. Lenna." Sonnet played with the word, letting the syllables trickle along his tongue. "The infinity of our unconscious…" His pacing hurried, he began to expound into a diatribe Lenna wasn't interested in.

Lenna knew when a man was sweet-talking her, and especially in this case, the Emperor's saccharine words had already been proved false by Lenna's own experiences. She witnessed the stars fading from existence and their lost, potent vitality leaking out into the physical world as uncontrolled magic. Sonnet himself had said that Valant's multiple resurrections had altered her, corrupted her very essence. Even if there was such abundant energy, it was not infinitely capable of being manipulated, even with the power of the Godjewels.

"You're lying," she said flatly. Lenna pretended — insisted, even — that the cracking she felt was not the tightening of Sonnet's grip on her jaw; she concentrated her thoughts on the prickly, propping points of Klem Vandever's uncomfortable chairs.

The astral projection of Alderic Sonnet smiled the tight, restrained grin of someone thoroughly displeased but too polite to say as much. "You are as infuriating to deal with as your father," he stated.

Off to the side, a fuzzy voice — that of Luc, who was probably still unaccustomed to such potent psychic manifestations — warbled. "Emperor, what is the truth?"

Sonnet, ensconced at Vandever's desk, glowered at the projection of Luc. "Now is not the time to question me, Apprentice Tural. You've already made your decision."

"But if Gilbert or Clarie were to come back…" he began, searching for the word, "…different, then it would all be for naught."

Yes, thought Lenna fiercely, flinging her will toward Luc. *Even this timeline that I created by manipulating reality with the Godjewel — however similar it feels to me, nothing is entirely the same as it was. Your world would never have your Gilbert again.*

Sonnet rose from the desk angrily, and Lenna presumed her mental plea had been heard by more than just Luc. "The world is how I shall make it," he said, though to whom he directed this statement, Lenna hadn't the faintest notion.

"Lenna," said a quiet Luc. "Gilbert wanted to change the world. To make it better than it was. He always talked about the cyclical nature of our universe, how everything spirals back around... can't I bring him back as he was?"

A stench like charred onions, the smell of anger, distracted Lenna. Sonnet was on the verge of physically fuming, his wrath was so strong. "You can have any 'Gilbert' you desire, Master Tural," he said.

"No," uttered Lenna. "You can't. He would never be completely the same. And if Gilbert wanted to change the world, he wouldn't want to be brought back like this."

The psychic emanation of the Vandever study dissipated in one jarring disconnect as Lenna felt her body crash heavily into the grass of Sebastien's lawn. All parties were back, alert, probably distracted only for seconds during their psychic meeting. Sonnet loomed menacingly over the prone woman, and Lenna, annoyed, hoisted herself into a sitting position and glared at him in defiance. Traces of gold flickered in the Emperor's irises.

"Will you join me?" Sonnet asked.

"No," Lenna said.

"Will you give up the Godjewel?"

"That's another 'no.'"

"Then two Godjewels will have to do, until the traces of your existence are wiped clean from the gem." Sonnet raised his hand as if to strike, and Lenna held her breath when she saw a vivid golden glow sparking in the core of the jewel hanging from the Emperor's neck. Without her own gem at her side, Lenna's magic wouldn't be strong enough to safeguard her from the blast she knew was coming. It would end here, and despite all of her anger, Lenna sank slowly into reconciliation; a weight had been lifted, and if death was what granted that relief, it felt deliciously welcome.

A dulled ringing fell on Lenna's ears; somewhere in that instant she had closed her eyes, wondering if death's peaceful embrace had finally crept upon her. She heard no cries – and somewhere in the not-dead recess of her mind, Lenna was annoyed that she heard no shouts of dismay regarding her impending doom from Raif and Sebastien – and felt no charring blast of magic, only the weight of stagnant, dry air around her. And then she realized that, up until now, the lawn had been breezy. Now something was blocking that breeze.

Opening her eyes, Lenna peered up, awestruck, as Luc Tural stood before her, a shimmering arcane shield blocking the whiplike bolts of energy outpouring from Sonnet's hands, magic from the Godjewel in its most primal form.

"Luc," she gasped.

"Apprentice Tural," Sonnet spoke, his voice muffled from Luc's shielding. No wonder Lenna heard no outcry from her friends. "Even with that stone in your hand, you are not strong enough."

The Godjewel, Lenna thought, her brain awash with panic and confusion. *If I can get to my Godjewel, I can help Luc…* But the blue stone, still emanating its magic in regular waves, was yards away; to attempt to reach it, to rise to her feet and sprint, would mean leaving the protection of Luc's ward and exposing herself to assault from the Emperor. She hesitated.

"I don't want to join you, Sonnet," Luc said, his voice loaded with a calculated vitriol that Lenna happened to loathe, though it was not, this time, aimed at her. It was chock-full of condescension and arrogance, with a grating undercurrent of superiority. To Emperor Alderic Sonnet, no one would dare speak that way. No one, that is, save Luc Tural.

Lenna wasn't aware that people's skin could literally turn purple unless they were decomposing. Certainly, she had seen various shades of pink (particularly that of Jeffer Scalla), but the violet tint to Sonnet's pale skin was freakish. His concentration completely shifted: his target was no longer the antagonistic librarian; it was the haughty apprentice from the Blue Crescent Brotherhood who dared to refuse him.

She seized her chance, knowing that Luc's mastery of the Vandever Godjewel had no chance of outclassing Emperor Sonnet. It would be a matter of seconds before the apprentice's shield fell to the Emperor, so Lenna, as though sprinting to Freewoman Dalm's to avoid another scolding, shattered the fear-spawned paralysis and sprang on obliging legs toward the shredded leather gauntlet in the middle of the yard.

Run, she commanded herself. Lenna closed in on the Godjewel, on the *cexer-sur,* as Sebastien and Raif ran toward her from the direction of the estate, Luc's barrier having fallen. She could feel them drawing on their magic, ready to provide support, but, doing quick calculations of the distance between herself and Luc and her allies, Lenna knew that Seb and Raif would not make it in time. This was her moment to save Luc, to undo some of the wrong that had been done to him, to protect Gilbert's love.

Not bothering to halt, Lenna dug her heels into the grassy expanse before her and spun around, swooping down with one hand to snatch the tattered gauntlet. The Godjewel's omnipresence was so penetrating and domineering she would have been able to grab it in the darkest of nights. Kicking up bits of dirt and pivoting, Lenna let her momentum propel her around to face Sonnet and Luc. Her consciousness immediately pulled on the magic of her Godjewel and the stone greeted her with an overwhelming embrace of power.

And then, in a crash of light, a beautiful, sky-shattering release of gold blinded Lenna and, judging from the aggravated grunts, those behind her as well. It took a moment for her eyes, tearing from the sheer brightness, to adjust to natural lighting. The sun, just as it dipped beneath the tree line, had set the foreground ablaze in a pool of red, masking any trace of the lawn's remaining greenery.

But it wasn't the sunlight, Lenna realized, that painted the ground. Her eyes fixated on a singular point in her immediate vicinity — a young man, prone, clutching a gaping wound in his chest from whence poured ruby blood, staining the lawn around him. Standing proud, almost beatific, and glowing with an ethereal pale yellow light was a composed Alderic Sonnet, who in addition to wearing the softly pulsing golden Godjewel now clutched a new item in his blood-coated right hand: a green, glowing orb that dripped little streams of moss-colored magic.

Lenna had been too slow. "Luc," she breathed.

She ran to his side, as she had done for Gilbert, and fell to her knees, not caring about the gore sullying her trousers. Instinctively, she shaped the power of the *cexer-sur* around the two of them, forming armor fueled not only by the pure magic of a Godjewel but by her fury and disappointment in herself. Taking both of Luc's hands in her own, Lenna pressed the youth's palms to the wound in his chest, trying to stop the hemorrhaging.

"I will heal you," she said insistently, ignoring the ashy coloring of Luc's cheeks. "Please, let me heal you."

"Gilbert told me to trust you," Luc wheezed. A trail of blood trickled down his cheek, out of the corner of his mouth. "This is the best way."

"Please don't try to talk!" Lenna shrilled. She focused her magic, her strength, everything she had, into a huge working that sought out the individual bits of life in Luc's bloodstream, telling his veins to stop leaking, his heart to repair, to be well, to pump. Magic strikes casually echoed off in the distance, but nothing penetrated her shielding — no attacks, no wind, no sound. The dome was so complete it blotted out the entire world, leaving only Lenna and Luc surrounded by a small bubble of blue.

"Will you fix the world?" His teeth were chattering, and the scholar in Lenna said acutely, "He's going into shock. Work faster." Delirium was setting in and Lenna didn't know how to answer his questions. Sweat dropped from her brow and mixed with the gushing of Luc's blood, which for her own life Lenna could not seem to halt. Where was Gilbert now, to guide her?

"I will fix you first," Lenna said, distracted.

Luc coughed, a frothy, pink substance spewing from his mouth. Lenna's healing wasn't taking. "Favor," he muttered.

"Name it." Lenna channeled more of her power into relaxing the boy, making him feel comfort.

"Friends?" he asked. "Need more friends."

Lenna blinked hard; salty tears were blurring her vision and leaving streaks on the lenses of her spectacles. "Of course, friends. Now let me help you *live,* damn you!" With some psychic nudging, Lenna pumped at the mage's heart, trying to keep its slowed beating from stopping completely.

"Thank you," Luc said. His voice was quiet and calm, thanks to Lenna's soothing charms. "Thank you for defending me, at the pub. Gilbert was right... choosing you. I choose you too."

"Choose me for what?" Lenna grew frustrated; damn his cryptic talking! She lurched forward, as if some soused ruffian had punched her in the gut. She didn't need more *babbling,* she needed Luc's cunning barbs. Where was the caustic little prat to scold her and infuriate her? To make her strive to work harder, just so she could prove him wrong?

"Sparkle ponies," Luc gasped, invoking the password of her childhood promise. "Gil..."

And he coughed once more, weakly, before Lenna felt the energy — the life, the soul that was Luc Tural — slip away from the empty vessel of a broken young man, hopefully to reunite with the one person who had made him feel completely safe.

"Luc," Lenna said again, and her shoulders sank as she dropped the magical shielding that kept her protected.

CHAPTER TWENTY

Alderic Sonnet stood before Lenna, oozing raw power from the golden gem looped around his neck. Lenna's hands and knees and clothing were sopping with Luc's blood, and she turned her head to look into his butcher's eyes. Through the golden glimmer masking his irises, Lenna saw no trace of remorse or even surprise at the massacre. How many had fallen before him? A tingling memory of Sonnet and Valant standing over the ashes of a village…

Lenna shook her head. "How could you? He was just a boy."

"A boy with a tremendously powerful magical artifact I require, Miss Faircloth."

"And now you'll murder me too?"

"Unless this demonstration has persuaded you to yield, yes."

"I won't yield to you, you soulless bastard."

The Emperor shook his head, almost regretfully, as he looked down at Lenna. "Very well, then. I…"

And his mouth clicked shut, puzzlement crinkling the smooth skin of his face. He looked down at the bloody stone in his hand as though he had just, for the first time, noticed its existence. For seconds, in comic disbelief, Alderic Sonnet looked between the Godjewel and Lenna. The built-up power emitting from his thin body wavered. Sebastien and Raif were at Lenna's side, jerking her to her feet.

"Well?" Lenna said. "Do it! Or is one Godjewel and two mages too much for the great Alderic Sonnet? Go on! You have two of what you want!"

Sonnet hissed like an adder, all the color draining from his face. He gathered the green Godjewel into a tightly clenched fist and backed a few paces away. "Welcome to the God War, Lenna Faircloth."

It happened in an instant, more easily than Lenna had ever done it: the Emperor shut his eyes and there was a brilliant flash of golden light. When the dancing stars in her eyes dissipated, Lenna noticed that the place where Sonnet had stood was now devoid of his Imperial presence. Teleportation, simple, without effort, executed as expertly as a fully trained Brother would create magelight. Lenna heard Lazarz, yards away, squeal with excitement.

"He's... gone," she stated. Her voice had gone funny with detachment.

"Just like that?" Raif fumed. "When the third Godjewel was within his reach?"

"I can't believe Emperor Sonnet would flee when he clearly had the upper hand," Sebastien commented.

Lenna stared thoughtfully at the space Sonnet had occupied. It didn't make much sense for the Emperor to leave the scene when his strength would be incomprehensibly more powerful than Lenna and her Godjewel, even with the assistance of Sebastien and Raif. He had won; why would he choose to flee? Unless...

"It's still all over," Raif uttered in one drawn-out, mournful exhalation. "Sonnet got away, and now two of the Godjewels are at his disposal. It will be Tranum all over again, but this time... the entire Continent will fall under Krevlum control." A gentle breeze blew across the manor's courtyard, ruffling his ponytail, and Raif's expression was distant. Lenna placed her hand on his arm and gave it a light squeeze.

"Not quite," Lenna said, unable to hide the resignation in her voice. "Only one of the Godjewels is at Sonnet's disposal."

"What do you mean?" asked Raif. Seb had slipped up behind him and regarded Lenna, ponderous.

"He hasn't bonded with it," Seb offered.

"That's just a matter of time. I know that the former bearer's trace stays behind on the stone, which is why he'd prefer to have it relinquished freely, but eventually Luc's signature will be gone. The jewel will be free again."

"No, Raif," Lenna interjected. "The stone was relinquished willingly."

Lenna had adapted over the past months to being the center of attention, but she was still nervy under the inspection of all those eyes, including the heavy inspections and manic staring of Mistress Juniam and Lazarz respectively. Still, she didn't allow herself the opportunity to blush. "Luc bequeathed the Godjewel to me. I felt it take."

"That snide little snot gave it up? To *you*?" Raif gaped.

"He said he wanted to be friends." She crossed her arms and rubbed at them; the advancing evening carried a little bit of a chill. Lenna avoided looking behind her, where the boy lay still in the wavering grass.

"That's why Sonnet withdrew," Sebastien added thoughtfully. "Not because he had only one Godjewel at his full command, but because staying meant Lenna would have two. He would have felt the bond take. Even though it was in his possession, with the gem's close proximity to Lenna and Lenna's solid connection to her own stone…"

"I could have potentially overpowered him," Lenna affirmed.

Raif tugged on his ponytail. "So what now?"

"The Vandever Godjewel will leave traces, burn brightly with its magic, as a signal for Lenna to find it. The Emperor won't be able to hide it. We could go after him," Sebastien said.

"Enough." Lenna couldn't care a lick about Emperor Sonnet or the Godjewels at the moment. The memories of Luc's childhood, his pain, and her own loss of Gilbert — all those feelings battled for precedence, drowning any other quandaries that might attempt to surface in the quagmire of her thoughts. "We see to Luc first. Let's respect his sacrifice." There was no room for disagreement in Lenna's tone.

Custom in the Blue Crescent Brotherhood, Sebastien said, would have any member, even an apprentice, burned in a traditional funeral pyre, though the Tural family's Krevlum lineage dictated a burial. Raif, humbled and strangely wary of Lenna's current mood, said he would defer to her judgment, though Seb was in favor of cremation. "After all," he said, "the Blue Crescent Brotherhood was far more of a family to Luc than the Tural family had been."

Replaying some of the more visceral scenes of Luc's youth, Lenna couldn't help but frown: the Brotherhood wasn't entirely a sanctuary for the boy, who suffered regular verbal and physical abuse, all because of his aptitude, his social status, and, worse, his sexuality. Still, through all the beatings, the bruises… Lenna clasped her right hand, still holding the Godjewel, to her heart and relived his smiles at Gilbert, the warmth of their embraces, and the little kindnesses that each day caused Luc to swell with pride at being in the Blue Crescent Brotherhood. For it was there — among hatred and cruelty — that Luc Tural had truly known love.

Lenna agreed to the funeral pyre, though she begged Sebastien and Mistress Juniam to take care of the arrangements. The grief was so near and so close to overcoming her fragile composure that the idea of preparing Luc's body, nothing more than a vacant remnant of the complex young magician, made her want to double over and wail. Sebastien nodded, or rather gulped and nodded as Mistress Juniam swept up behind him and bowed her head. Lenna sighed in relief.

"It will take a few hours," Sebastien said tersely, as if he were chewing on a mouthful of gravel. He paused, his composure seemingly faltering, and placed his hand on Lenna's shoulder. "Go rest for a bit. We'll see him off at midnight."

Nodding automatically, not really listening, Lenna allowed Raif to take her by the hand and lead her away from the Branford Estate's courtyard, down the path and back toward the orange grove. It didn't seem as lovely as it had earlier in the day. Days. Or years, by Lenna's reckoning. As she and Raif passed under the first few branches and into the tailored rows between trees, Lenna slowed her pace.

"Was it very wrong of me," she whispered, "to have told him I was his friend?"

Raif turned around and tilted his head. In the rising moonlight, his Ilyan features were pronounced, his skin so strikingly pale it was almost opalescent. "Weren't you his friend?"

"No," Lenna answered. "At least, I don't think I was. I didn't treat him like one." She shuddered, recalling with gut-wrenching clarity her palm striking Luc's cheek. "I was horrid to him."

Letting go of her hand, Raif tilted Lenna's chin up to meet his gaze. "He wasn't exactly nice to you, as I recall." He smiled ruefully. "Or me either. Can't say there was much love lost, Lenna. He robbed my family." His shoulders had sunk in forbearance and his breaths were measured. "Still. He was troubled, but I don't think he was bad. And I don't think you're bad either. That magical barrier you invoked shouldn't have been able to hold up against the kind of power Sonnet was throwing at you; it was an incredibly strong ward. And you were healing on top of that, too."

"So you're saying the Godjewel didn't give me that power?"

"I think," Raif said, "that it came from love."

Lenna choked on the sweet-scented air. "Don't be so soppy."

"Sometimes, Len, soppy is good." Raif pulled her close and pressed his lips against hers and, for once, the desire to deck him didn't arise.

Luc was dressed in the regalia of a full-fledged member of the Brotherhood, not the simple robes of an apprentice. Brocaded sleeves in deep blue fanned out to his sides, and Sebastien had arranged for his hands to be clasped as he rested atop the makeshift casket. Heaps of dried branches, bundled and tied, were neatly placed around his body with bunches of orange tree leaves and white flowers Lenna didn't recognize. Luc looked at peace for the first time. There was no scowl or grimace, no condescending smirk. The serenity on his face stung Lenna; it emphasized how appallingly young, how terrifically innocent, Luc had been.

Off to one corner of the pyre, Sebastien stood, not in his robes, but in a long cream coat that fell just above his ankles, over a white shirt and pale blue silk cravat. He completed the ensemble with a periwinkle vest and tan trousers. It was a fitting suit for the aristocracy, and he wore it with grace. Still, Lenna found it highly curious — and in slightly poor taste — that he had bothered to dandy himself up, considering the circumstances.

"I only had one set of Brotherhood robes here in Gallas," Sebastien explained, a forlorn smile creasing his lips. "And in Gallas, it's only appropriate that I wear my finest to honor a comrade, particularly one from a noble family such as the Turals. This is how we show respect."

Lenna nodded with newfound insight, recalling snippets from her books and her memories of the Gallasian silk merchants in Tranum; finery such as this was an art for these people, so naturally the greatest way to show respect was to celebrate with the best one had to wear. It was true respect, though Lenna found herself dumbstruck that proud Sebastien Branford had given up his only set of robes, proof of his mastery of magic in the Brotherhood, for the death of an apprentice.

"You really cannot hide your emotions, you know," said Sebastien. "I'd avoid playing trumps with an Ilyan if I were you." He rubbed the piercing in his ear, as though his thin stab at humor had somehow irritated the jewel. "While he was not ordained via normal means, in the end I believe Luc demonstrated the qualities of a proper Brother. And my rank permits me to ordain those I see fit in circumstances such as these, even posthumously. Though," he added quietly, "I imagine the Brotherhood would very likely refute any claims I make toward such a privilege."

Squatting beside the pyre, having had no time to change, Lenna felt grubby beside Luc. Her battle with Khareen Valant and her attempt at saving Luc had left her coat in shambles and dyed deep scarlet with blood. Raif had, thankfully, encouraged her to wash her face and hands before coming back to the center of the courtyard where Luc's body had been settled. Again, Lenna was stunned — she hadn't expected Seb to host a funeral in the middle of the lawn. This too, she discovered, was Gallasian custom.

Raif, Lazarz, and Mistress Juniam — who had changed into a silk gown that blanketed the grass and reminded Lenna more of a wedding dress than funeral attire — gathered and stood off to the side, their eyes trained on Lenna and Sebastien. Lenna, only vaguely aware of Brotherhood customs from her dip into Luc's memories, glanced at Sebastien and hoped for some guidance as to how to proceed. He shifted a step closer to Lenna.

"Usually, a high-ranking Brother would speak at a death, or a former master if he was still alive. But in this case, I think it might be more appropriate if you spoke. I think you understood him better."

"Me?" An understanding of Luc Tural was not something Lenna had ever claimed or even really desired. Still, between Gilbert, their shared memories... perhaps Sebastien was correct. Perhaps Lenna would be the best person to speak on behalf of Luc. "I've never been very good about speaking in public."

Raif said, "This isn't public, Len. It's just us. Come on."

Lenna stood, poised over the young man, recalling the pain of Taryn's taunts, the beatings, and the love from Gilbert that made all of those tortures bearable. Tolerable. But why should he have had to endure such pain? Why was the world full of terrible loss and people who sought to encourage such suffering? It seemed to Lenna that everyone around her was forced to cope with such anguish: Luc and his sister, and Gilbert; Raif and his mother and the fall of his city; even Sebastien and his estrangement from his father and destruction of his childhood home. Lenna and her mother. Was love, then, worth the cost?

She placed one hand atop Luc's folded ones. They were cold and taut, lacking the warm softness Lenna's plundered memories held. Images of similar situations, the tactile recollection of saying farewell to Gilbert and her mother, all threatened to devour her, but she could not succumb to her own grief. Not yet. Lenna pulled her eyes away from the sight of Luc and turned to address the group; Sebastien had already backed off and stood rigidly near the others.

Where to begin? "Luc Tural made it very clear that he didn't want to have anything to do with me from the moment he saw my face at the back door of my library. Why did he dislike me so, I wondered. At first, I thought it was simply because I was a woman, and because I knew that the Blue Crescent Brotherhood, the order to which both Gilbert and Luc had dedicated themselves, treated women as inferiors.

"And so I let that color my perception of him. I let it blind me to the fact that Luc was much more than some stuck-up kid with a misguided view of my sex. Hell, it was easier that way. It gave me an excuse to dislike him. An excuse to make backhanded comments, little shots here and there — all unjustifiable, looking back, but I told myself at the time that he was beneath me and deserved it. The truth is that I was just jealous of his attachment to my best friend and I didn't want to give him a chance."

The sharp gazes of her friends were locked on her, transfixed by the syllables she uttered. Lenna wrung her hands, feeling naked in her tattered garments and lacking her gauntlet; the Godjewel was once more a weight around her neck, not a shield strapped to her arm. She had to continue. "Gilbert, my friend, and Master Sebastien Branford — those men told me of his potential, hinted at his troubled past. I didn't bother to consider any of that in my assessment of Luc's character. After all," Lenna said as she held out her arms in suppliance, "I had my share of tragedy in my life. I, too, felt isolated. So what gave him the right to treat me so harshly?

"He had no right, of course. But I don't think I acted much better. I just assumed my own personal sadnesses — the loss of my mother, for one…" Lenna's voice trailed off, a knot of emotion clogging up her windpipe. She was not accustomed to speaking about this in front of anyone. "I believed that my personal sadnesses outweighed his. And after this past month, after seeing what people have done out of love, or for power, for even this stupid stone, I think I realize now that maybe, just maybe, no one's personal sadness is any more poignant, more special, than another's. The circumstances may be different, but the pain felt may be very, very similar."

Lenna turned and glanced down at the stiff, almost doll-like Luc. Sebastien's glamour hid any trace of the miserable end he had met; in comparison, Lenna's appearance was much direr. It felt perverse that in his death Luc seemed clean, unfettered, and in life — in surviving — Lenna, caked in grime and gore, was ever chained, bound now by two Godjewels. Even now, from wherever Alderic Sonnet had fled to, the Vandever gem pulsed and diffused a constant stream of power, connected directly to her. Lenna could feel its pull. She was almost envious of Luc's freedom.

Mistress Juniam's earlier words echoed, still sounding fresh and uplifting. *No one person is perfect, or capable of bearing such a hefty burden alone.* Luc had known kindness from his sister, Clarie, from Gilbert, and hopefully, at the end, from Lenna herself. She could never take back any of the barbs that had hurt him, but maybe, at least Lenna hoped, both she and Luc had realized the pain of the other. Gilbert, too, had known of pain — and it was through him that both Lenna and Luc had been saved. Now, Lenna felt, it was her chance to repay the favor.

She spun about and raised her voice so that it carried across the lawn. "There is not a soul in this universe that does not experience pain. Even Khareen Valant was not without her sorrows, despite all the damage she caused. We can't make excuses for our own or another's behavior, but we can try to move forward and do well by those around us. And I think, in his final act, Luc Tural acted out of love. And so I accept that gift and all its complications — not because I want the power of the Godjewels but because I respect, and love, my friend Luc."

All parties bowed their heads and Sebastien skirted around Lenna, muttering something esoteric and making gestures that were part of the traditional funeral rites of the Brotherhood. Lenna let herself fall into the enfolding embraces of Mistress Juniam and Raif, where stinging tears, hot as the fire that began to play about the wood surrounding the pyre, finally began to flow freely: tears not just for the loss of Luc, but for the loss of a love that she had denied for so long, for the loss of Gilbert and her mother, and for all the suffering people might have felt at her actions.

Brotherhood tradition dictated, much to Lenna's surprise, a sharing of wine — in the case of this party, several bottles' worth — and a recounting of stories about the deceased Brother. Though Lenna had, thanks to her delving into Luc's past, a fair share of intimate details about his life, she chose to keep those private. Sebastien spoke a bit of Luc's advances in magecraft, of his quick thinking and ability to work complex magics with a subtle hand. It was a removed, scholastic review of his abilities and promising features, and though it praised Luc's talents, Sebastien's recounting lacked anything that touched upon Luc himself.

Raif had little to say, but he did have the class to salute his fallen comrade and laud him for his ultimate trust in Lenna, at which she blushed. When all was spoken and the funeral pyre slowly settling to embers, Lenna's cheeks matched the glow of the dwindling fire. She hadn't eaten nearly enough in the past twenty years or so to stand up to the number of glasses she had already consumed, and if she weren't careful her brain and balance would resemble little more than a sorry collection of wobbles before long. She peered down at her timepiece, the face of which was thoroughly cracked, so much so that it resembled a spiderweb of glass.

"Time's up," she said to the smoldering heap before her. Dawn would be coming soon.

"Lenna?" asked Raif. Involuntarily, Lenna had come to lean on Raif, who looked weary himself. His ponytail had come undone so that his ashy blonde hair blew in the breeze, wispy, and his chin was lined with golden stubble. Even his eyes were bloodshot. "Come," he said, hoisting Lenna to her feet. "You need some sleep."

A little ways off, Sebastien eyed the pair with a vacant expression in his eyes and sipped at his wine in steady intervals. Lenna idly wondered how Seb was coping with the deaths of Gilbert and Luc, both by all rights players primed to be molded into leading members of the Brotherhood, matters further complicated by the fact that a wildcard by the name of Lenna Faircloth was now psychically bonded to two of the three Godjewels.

She broke away from Raif and crept toward the well-groomed magician. Upon closer inspection, there was a dolefulness in Sebastien's eyes, a few deep lines around the corners that Lenna had never noticed before. His head, though, he still held high with dignity, and his suit remained tidy as ever, as if he would not permit even the predawn mist to rumple his composure.

"Apprentice Faircloth," he said as Lenna approached. "Your speech was very kind. Not that I'm surprised, but I imagine Gilbert and Luc would have been pleased."

"Are you all right?" she asked. There was such a great distance between them, one she hadn't sensed since their first encounter on the streamtrain to Tranum one month ago. Since that time, Seb and Lenna's unique mental connection — not dissimilar to her bond with the Godjewel — had stripped away his coifed outer shell for the most part, and Lenna was usually able to perceive his warmth and sense of self more easily. But tonight, Sebastien Branford was guarded, protected by a wall of psychic brambles that Lenna couldn't negotiate.

"No." The mage's sudden candor made Lenna almost drop her wineglass; blatant admittance of weakness was one thing she had not thought possible of her friend and mentor. "How do you handle the burdens so well, Lenna?"

Despite the grim reality of her situation, Lenna guffawed, guiltily clipping her laughter off as soon as it began. "I don't handle it well at *all*, Seb!" She was shocked that Sebastien could even imagine Lenna was handling everything happening in her life well, let alone admit to it. "Until now, I've just been... resigned, really. Resigned that life is kind of against me and that somehow my circumstances made me more important. Self-important? I don't know. I also get drunk. A lot." At this point Lenna mimed toasting grandly with her glass of wine; thankfully, it was empty enough to prevent any spillage onto Seb's suit.

Sebastien smiled and ruffled the tangle of curls that was Lenna's hair. She frowned up at him, wondering how to respond.

"You do drink more than an average librarian." His mouth quirked. "And certainly more than I would suggest an apprentice should, though I imagine a fair number of our novices at the Brotherhood could hold their own against you."

Lenna recalled her evening spent beside the fire of the Tawny Apple Inn with painful accuracy, but she found herself smiling at the thought of the silly hangover she suffered the next morning. Gilbert, though he had matched Lenna goblet for goblet, seemed unaffected as he ate breakfast like a voracious bear freshly awake from hibernation. Maybe Sebastien was right: the Blue Crescent Brotherhood might have its merits, after all. Still, Lenna was curious about Sebastien's sudden self-doubt.

"What is it, Seb?"

He ran his fingers through his hair, ruining his perfect part. As Lenna glanced up, the stars began to slowly fade away into the brightening dawn and trailing wisps of smoke, and automatically she frowned. *The stars are disappearing*. Seb seemed to echo her thoughts. "I orchestrated the plan to steal the azure Godjewel from my Brotherhood because I knew of my order's desire to use its power to achieve political and military superiority."

Sebastien turned to face Lenna. "I knew that some of this was in response to the Brotherhood's knowledge that Alderic Sonnet had come into his own Godjewel in addition to other artifacts and writings that predated the God War. Our council had vague knowledge that one of the other Godjewels had been passed down through a prominent Ilyan family, but the nation's complicated spy networks are very hard to infiltrate, and Ilyans don't join the Brotherhood. It wasn't until Thane Faircloth traded the Godjewel currently in your possession to the Brotherhood that we began to formulate plans.

"Gilbert was a brilliant student, diligent and insightful. His kindness toward Apprentice Tural convinced me of his moral convictions and character."

"And now you're not so certain."

"I don't believe it's a coincidence that it's you, Lenna, who is now bonded to two Godjewels."

"How could anyone have so much... foreknowledge?" Lenna asked.

"You've seen it, experienced it, firsthand, Lenna." Sebastien pulled her body close to his once more, like they were back on the hills of the Gallasian countryside. "These Godjewels can propel you through time and space, allow you to perceive past events. It's not unheard of that forces could have been long guiding you to this moment."

Sebastien was right; Lenna herself was responsible for altering timelines, however inadvertently. Could there be someone else traipsing about time, trying to shape everyone's actions? Many of the memories of her struggle with Valant were foggy, and some of them she had begged the Godjewel to purposely stifle. Fleetingly, she plucked out from her jumbled recollections a peculiar figure with deep, deep blue eyes, eyes the color of the sky-bright stone Lenna wore around her neck. Just how long had Thane Faircloth been in possession of the *cexer-sur*, and how, pray, did he happen to come across it? What had he stolen from the Krevlum Empire that day, decades in the past?

"Guiding me to what moment?" Lenna asked.

"The moment where you're forced to choose," said Sebastien.

"I wasn't aware I had many options."

"You could continue your tutelage with me, though with each passing moment Alderic Sonnet will be one step closer to total military conquest of the Continent, and no doubt the Brotherhood would see the ensuing war as an opportunity to pry the Vandever Godjewel from him, since he hasn't bonded with it. You could drop your stone into the sea." Sebastien smiled sadly. "You could hide with the Freewomen, or seek shelter in Port Hollish. How long any of these places will be safe is debatable. Someone is operating with information inaccessible to me."

"So I'm no longer safe here, with you," Lenna summarized. "Or anywhere."

Sebastien sighed and abruptly hugged her close. "You would make a promising pupil, if you gave up the wine and lost the cheeky attitude."

Despite the gravity of her situation, Lenna laughed. Her voice sounded mad as it scampered across the dewy lawn, and Raif, Juniam, and Lazarz eyed her as though she were deranged. Maybe she was, a bit. "So my choice, then, is to curl up in a corner with a bottle of wine and wait for the armies of the world to come after me," she said slowly, "or to go greet them myself."

Raif and Juniam crunched their way across the increasingly chilled morning ground and joined the two. Slipping out of the embrace, Sebastien gathered up a neatly folded length of deep blue silk and spread it over the remains of the funeral pyre. "You've seen older texts and artifacts than Port Hollish's library ever will; I'd say you've surpassed your role as junior librarian."

Mistress Juniam put her steady hand on Lenna's shoulder. "And you've demonstrated the ability to control the magic within that stone far better than any Brotherhood apprentice."

"It sounds like a graduation is in order," Raif said, and grinned. Lenna noticed with some frustration that he had sidestepped his way into the space between herself and Sebastien.

"No longer librarian, no longer an apprentice," Lenna mused.

Having finished tucking the funeral sheet over the remains of the pyre, Sebastien wiped his hands with a clean handkerchief. "Despite the thousands of soldiers and magicians pursuing your head, Lenna Faircloth, it would seem that, for the moment, you're a free woman."

"A free woman, huh?" Lenna smiled. Her mother would probably approve of the wording. She inhaled the sweet autumn air deeply and skipped forward, turning to face the ragtag group that had gathered to rally behind her and her decision: a dashing Ilyan air captain and aristocrat, an excommunicated member of the order of wizards she had effectively robbed, the stern matron who mothered a friend in Granemere Settlement, and a madcap engineer with even madder hair and questionable ties to an Empire seeking domination of the entire Continent.

And here Lenna was, standing tall in the country where, in another time, she should have probably been anyway, attending University and learning what knowledge its thick tomes and professors had to offer. "If I have any trouble," she started, looking at each of her allies in turn, "you'll come help me, right?"

"I'll come flying," Raif breathed, and returned Lenna's smile.

"Team L, forever!" exclaimed Lazarz.

"You will always have friends in my daughter and me," Mistress Juniam added.

"I can't teleport without you," Sebastien said seriously, "but I'll be there as fast as the winds can get me."

Giddy from her tipsiness, Lenna held up her battered pocket watch and stared, fascinated, as the rays of the breaking dawn refracted off the shattered glass of the faceplate. Multiple reflections of her face stared back; some appeared cheeky and jolly; other faces were distorted, and some grotesque, covered in battle scars. Her hair was longer or shorter depending on the rendering. Everything was disjointed, and the real Lenna shook her head to rid herself of the images.

She no longer had her sword or knife, Gilbert or Luc, but she had herself, Lenna Faircloth, and all the magic within her. The Godjewel might be bonded to her and might exercise its persnickety will whenever it chose, but she would prove to herself she could force her own resolve right back on it. Perhaps time itself was running out. Or, Lenna wondered, perhaps time was just changing; either way, she had no desire to be bound by the hands of its clock any longer. She dropped the fob watch to the lawn and stamped mightily with her booted foot, smashing its delicate handiwork.

Time waits for no one, especially not a free woman, she thought.

"You'll all hear from me soon," Lenna said, smiling warmly, a smile probably provided by a bit of wine-induced swagger. With a subtle pop and a whoosh as air replaced the space the woman had occupied, Lenna Faircloth blinked out of sight. She wasn't there to see the stunned expression of Sebastien or hear the appreciative whistle from Raif, let alone detect the delicate combination of lavender and lily clinging to the early morning breeze.

Lenna's adventures conclude (or do they?) in book three, *Freewoman*.

www.ingramcontent.com/pod-product-compliance
Lightning Source LLC
Chambersburg PA
CBHW030422310726
48979CB00009B/1576/J